THE ENCHANTED TOWER

Liz Michaels

ISBN-13:978-1492293217
ISBN-10:1492293210
eISBN:978-1-927878-00-2

Cover Photo and Art: Elizabeth Wrobel

Acknowledgements

A big thank you to Connie Weaver, Maureen Molnar, Dolores McKenna, Fay Rothlander, Christine Brooks, Terri Werbeski, and Susanna Somogyi for your generous advice and encouragement; to Dawn Renaud, without whom this book would have never had seen the light of the day; to my long-suffering husband and son, who see my back more often than my face; and to the readers who are willing to take a chance on this book.

Dedicated to my family, and friends, and to the readers

Part 1

Outside Time

Chapter 1

I'm lost.

Lost and alone on a soggy trail in the middle of nowhere in a late summer downpour.

If that wasn't enough, I'm soaked to the skin despite my jacket.

Worse still, I don't have the slightest idea how I ended up here. One second I was hiking with the other camp counselors; the next second they had vanished as if the ground had swallowed them up.

The trail we've hiked so often looks unfamiliar. More wild. I've never seen those rotting stumps, this gnarled tree, or that moss-covered boulder. No footsteps have disturbed the dark soil and wet leaves at my feet. Obviously, no one has hiked this way for a long time. Turning, I retrace the tread marks of my boots. They are clearly visible for about twenty paces then, abruptly, nothing. No more footprints. No sign of a fork in the trail.

My stomach tightens. What's going on?

I must find my companions.

I shout and whistle, but the only reply is a deep silence.

With growing despair, I look around. All I see is an empty trail, the forest, and the rain.

Chest heaving, I lean against a tree. Rain is streaming down my face and a shiver starts at the base of my spine, runs upward, and shakes my shoulders.

What am I to do?

Follow the trail. It must lead somewhere, to a house, a shelter, something. But which way should I go?

Does it matter? Just go.

I slog through the rain mile after sopping mile until an elaborate, perfectly maintained wrought iron gate blocks the path. I should feel relieved. I don't. The contrast between the elegant gate and the wild abandoned forest is so eerie, if I weren't drenched and desperate for shelter I would think twice about going through it. But my need to get away from the rain outweighs any trepidation.

The gate opens easily.

I step through it and feel as if entering another world, an enchanted place. I find myself on an avenue lined on both sides by solemn beech trees, giant sentinels silently guarding some ancient secret. Their branches touch each other, forming a green roof over the road. Thick moss and fallen leaves cover the ground and swallow the sound of my footsteps.

I tread gingerly between the trees. Though other roads intersect the avenue I am on, I follow it faithfully for what feels like an eternity. And then … I heave a sigh of relief. Through an opening between the trees, I notice the outline of battlements against the darkening sky.

Invigorated, I race up a small incline toward the building until, out of breath and dripping wet, I arrive at a tower house.

The tower sits in the middle of an open meadow. It's one of those ancient buildings, most of them in ruin, which dot the countryside. This one is not in ruin. A tall, fortress-like structure made from rough stones, it stands dark and forbidding, except for the inviting yellow light that beckons from some of the windows.

I hurriedly find the entrance, an artfully hammered bronze door, and with all my might pound on it with the heavy knocking ring. A very old, very proper butler opens the door.

"Good evening," he says, unperturbed by my disheveled appearance. "What can I do for you?"

"I'm lost," I pant, still out of breath. "May I use your phone, please?"

He hesitates for a moment before saying. "I am sorry. We have no phone here."

No phone. Great.

"Could you please give me a ride to the Mosquito Creek Camp?"

"I am afraid that would be impossible," he answers without showing the slightest concern for my plight.

Rats. What am I to do? I am tired, cold, have no idea where the camp is, or what place this is. And it is still raining. "Could you tell me where I am?"

"This is Bancloch Tower," he says with dignified calm.

Although I've spent the entire summer in this area, I have never heard of the place. "How far is Mosquito Creek?"

"I do not know."

This guy's sure no help. Okay. Think. I have two options: stay outside in the rain, or ask to spend the night in the tower. Neither is enticing. "May I please come in and stay for the night?"

"You may come in," he says steadily. "However, I must warn you, if you enter you must remain here until you pass three tests, and if you fail them you will perish."

What? "Excuse me, let me get this straight. If I come in I will have to pass three tests or die?"

He nods.

"You're kidding me, right?" His face remains solemn, and my stomach sinks. "You—you are serious."

"Yes, I am."

"What kind of tests would I have to pass?"

"I may not say."

That's helpful. What should I do? I would definitely die from hyperthermia if I spent the night alone in that creepy forest in my soaking wet clothes. If I must die I'd much rather do it in a dry, warm place.

"I will take the challenge and try to pass the tests," I announce.

He bows and shows me into the tower. "This way, please."

~ ~ ~

He escorts me into a tall, spacious hall furnished with colorful Persian carpets and heavy carved furniture. A piano nestles in one corner. Coats of arms and hunting scenes are painted directly on the walls above bookshelves. Two comfortable-looking armchairs are in front of a merrily burning fire, and books are scattered everywhere. It is a welcoming and very masculine place.

I would love to stay to browse through the books and curl up to read next to the warm fire in those inviting armchairs—well, if I was dry. But there's no time for daydreaming. The butler hurries me on through the hall and up a flight of turnpike stairs.

"This is your chamber." He opens a door and ushers me into a smaller room dominated by a large canopied bed and a wardrobe, which barely leave space for a small writing desk by one of the recessed windows, and pillowed seats by the other two. "You have plenty of time before supper. Have a hot bath, change into some dry clothes—you will find them in that wardrobe—and as soon as you hear the bell ring, go downstairs to meet the master. Be prompt," he adds in an almost fatherly manner and leaves.

Exhausted from the hike and apprehensive of my situation, I sink into the chair by the desk.

What kind of pickle did I get myself into?

Better not to think about it.

In an alcove off the main room, I find a deep copper tub. Next to it on a ledge is a collection of metal-tagged decanters containing all sorts of mysterious elixirs: pimpernel water, butterbur powder, cowslip tincture, lavender oil … At least I know what lavender oil is. I fill the tub with hot water, add some oil to it, strip off my wet clothes, and sink up to my chin in the hot, fragrant water, thoroughly enjoying it.

Who knows, this might be my last bath.

I soak until the chill leaves my body. Wrapped in a large luxurious towel I open the closet. It is filled with extravagantly frilly, seemingly new dresses in a style women wore hundreds of years ago.

Strange. This entire place is strange.

As I am the jeans and t-shirt type, none of the elaborate, low-cut dresses appeals to me. I choose a light blue one because it has the least number of bows, laces, and frills.

It takes a while to figure out how to tie everything. I just finish dressing when the ringing of a bell calls me to meet the master.

~ ~ ~

The master is standing by the bookshelves, reading, and turns toward me when I arrive.

Omigod. He's drop-dead gorgeous. He is in his late twenties, about six feet tall, athletic, with long wavy dark-blond hair, and even though he's dressed in black trousers and shirt somehow a medieval knight comes to mind. Luckily, he has a smug, arrogant expression. Good. I've never liked smug and arrogant.

"Good evening." I curtsy lightly. Curtsy? It's not how I normally greet people.

He puts the book down, takes a few steps forward, scanning me from head to toe. "You must address me as your highness," he drawls in a stern, authoritative voice, in a dialect I cannot place.

Your highness?

I greet him again, heavily emphasizing "your highness."

He bows his head condescendingly.

"You have a lovely place here," I say, attempting to start a friendly conversation.

He shrugs it off.

I try again for a pleasant response. "Thank you for letting me stay."

He closes the distance between us. "You do not need to be thankful. I trust you are aware of the risk to your life."

"Yes, but it's not much of a risk. I probably would have died from fear and hypothermia in the forest." I realize I am trying to convince myself.

His expression softens a bit.

Encouraged by his friendlier demeanor, I ask, "Please tell me about the tests."

He frowns. "My lady, I am forbidden to disclose anything about the tests. However, if you are unsuccessful, I will inform you which one you failed and why."

"Before or after I die?"

He studies me for a few seconds, then says in a more amiable manner, "I am His Royal Highness Prince Christian John Rupert, the ruler of Bancloch."

"Nice to meet you." I extend my hand. "I'm Ann-Marie Burke, but you may call me Ann."

He takes my hand and lifts it toward his mouth but before planting a kiss he asks, "Which princely family are you from, my lady?"

"As far as I know, I am not from any princely family."

Disgusted as if he had touched something foul, he drops my hand. "You are not a princess! How did you enter this domain?"

"That's something I would like to know." His face shows such disapproval and scorn I am afraid he will throw me out. To distract him, I quickly change the subject to the first thing that comes to mind. "Would you tell me why you have such old fashioned clothes in the guest room? This kind of dress," I point to my gown, "went out of style hundreds of years ago. Or is this some kind of dress-up party?"

He wrinkles his brows. "Hundreds of years ago. What century is this?"

What kind of question is that? "It's the twenty-first century. Why are you asking?"

He gives a little shrug. "Why indeed; after all, it is hardly relevant."

"What do you mean?" I feel more mystified and concerned by the second.

He regards me with piercing hazel eyes. "Time moves differently—or, I suppose I should say, it does not move—in this tower. I have been here since the twelfth century. I know this sounds an incredibly long period but in actuality it is not."

Okay. This man must be crazy. Is he dangerous? "Are you sure you've been here that long?" I ask politely. "It would make you rather old."

"Yes, I am certain. If this is the twenty-first century, I am over 900 years old."

"You look good for your age."

He answers with a tiny bit less haughtiness, "You think I am mad—"

"To be honest, it did cross my mind."

"I am not mad. This is an enchanted place—"

"Is it?" I burst out. "I sensed it as soon as I entered the grounds." Did I just say that? Maybe I'm going nuts, too.

His lips narrow. "I would much appreciate if you refrained from interrupting me."

"I will try," I say, knowing that I'm unlikely to keep my promise.

Scowling, he studies me. "It still puzzles me how you could enter this domain if you are not a princess."

"I definitely would not know." I shrug my shoulders. "Maybe there is a shortage of princesses nowadays. Or maybe it was a mistake."

"That is impossible. You must have royal blood in you."

"Okay. Let's pretend that I do, and stop fretting about my pedigree." Why is he so concerned with my ancestors? I have far more important things to worry about, such as how to stay alive. "Are you positive you must keep the tests secret? Could you at least give a hint?"

"No, my lady, I cannot give you a hint," he answers firmly. "But before we continue our parley, I recommend we fortify ourselves with an evening repast." He gestures toward the table and I realize I am ravenous. "May I have your hand?" He offers his arm ceremoniously.

With a theatrical gesture I place my hand on his. He leads me to the long table in the middle of the room and "helps" me into my chair.

The table is loaded with exotic looking food: many kinds of soups, fish, meat dishes, vegetables, sauces, cheeses, pastries, fruits, and different beverages—a veritable smorgasbord.

"Are you expecting company?" I ask when he takes his seat on the far end of the table.

"You are the only visitor, my lady."

"Oh. Do we have to eat everything?"

"Eat as much as you please," he answers curtly, then says grace, and with a wave of his hand invites me to select something.

What should I choose? I have no idea what is on each platter or in each tureen, and in the low light provided by the dimmed chandelier it is impossible to tell.

I randomly point to a tureen. "Your highness, please tell me what's in that dish?"

The butler, who is standing by the table ready to serve us, answers, "Stewed peacock with fennel, my lady."

"May I know what's in that bowl?" I point at some greens.

Again, the butler answers. I ask the names of most dishes, ignoring the prince's disapproving glances. In the end I have stewed peacock, jellied forest greens, a slice of roasted boar with wild mushroom sauce, and mead. Though the flavors are unusual, everything is delicious.

During supper I try to strike up a conversation with my host. One-syllable answers and frustrating silences reward my efforts.

"Thank you. This was a most enjoyable meal," I say as I line up my knife and fork on my plate. "You must have an excellent cook. Is he or she also nine hundred years old?"

"I suggest we discuss this by the fire after supper," he says between two bites.

I wait politely in an uncomfortable silence—at least it's uncomfortable to me. While he eats, I study the painted coats of arms, then my eyes drift to the bookshelves. What kind of books are in them?

Finally, he finishes his dinner, says another grace, offers his arm, and leads me to one of the armchairs by the fireplace.

~ ~ ~

The chairs, separated by a small table, face each other at an angle that makes it as easy to watch the fire as the person sitting opposite.

Two teenage boys in medieval clothes clear the table in silence. When they leave my host turns to me. "My lady, let me elaborate on the situation. I am a prince—an enchanted prince."

What?

"To be more exact, I am a prince under a curse, unable to return to my previous life until the curse is broken. Since life is lonesome in this isolated place, the wizard, who cursed me, provides a companion from time to time. You, my lady, are my companion. This means you will spend a year—"

"I can't stay a year," I interrupt. "My family will miss me. Also, school will start in a couple of weeks."

He scowls. "I have told you, this is an enchanted place. No one will notice your absence."

"Would they notice if I died?"

Ignoring my interruption, he continues, "You are more than a companion. You are here to break the curse, and if unsuccessful, you will perish at the end of the year."

My stomach tightens. Is this guy playing some kind of morbid game? "Did other girls try to break the curse?"

"Yes, many," he says calmly.

"Many!" I swallow. "How many?"

He shrugs. "I did not keep count."

"What happened to them?" I try to sound nonchalant, but my voice has a slight quiver.

"They passed away."

"They died? How did they die?"

"I cannot tell you," he answers, unconcerned.

"Did you kill them?" The question bursts out.

"I would never lower myself to killing a woman."

Good to know. "So you mean that I am safe until next summer?"

He nods. "I assure you, my lady, no harm will befall you as long as you obey the rules."

Rules. "What kind of rules?"

He pulls himself up imperiously. "The rules are as follows. Do not try to escape. The instant you step outside the gate, you will perish. Stay away from the top floors. They are my domain, and you will die the moment you enter them. Every so often, I have company. You must refrain from leaving your room while my visitors are here. Do not attempt to join us, and do not spy on us because—"

"I know: I will die. Are there any activities which wouldn't kill me?"

"Yes, plenty," he answers in the same imperial manner. "However, please bear in mind you are here to be my companion. You shall join me for meals, and spend the mornings and evenings with me. You shall pass your afternoons alone with any occupation that pleases you."

I don't know what to say.

Is this place really enchanted? Is this guy really a cursed prince? "Why are you under a curse?" I ask.

He frowns, stands up, steps to the fireplace, adds a few logs, then turning his back to the flames, says, "It is a lengthy, byzantine tale."

"That's fine." I smile encouragingly. "We have lots of time."

He returns to his chair, crosses his arms, and watches the fire. "I was a tyrant. Offensive, ruthless, and profligate." He casts a glance at me. "People's lives were of little worth in my eyes, killing someone was nothing to me. Taking the serfs' daughters for my pleasure was a diversion, an agreeable pastime. Until I seduced a damsel whose uncle was a wizard. He cursed me and I became a prisoner of this tower."

"And you don't know how to break the curse." Hardly a brilliant observation.

He makes an impatient move. "My lady, I have already told you."

"Have you tried apologizing?"

"I apologized at least a thousand times. It was fruitless."

"I guess if you're still here. Did you actually feel sorry?"

"Of course I did," he snarls.

"I don't mean sorry because you ended up in this place, but genuinely sorry." Leaning forward, I elucidate. "Like putting yourself into the victims' shoes and feeling—profoundly feeling—their pain and suffering."

He frowns. "How could I?"

"By using your imagination," I say eagerly. "Imagine how much grief and sorrow you'd experience if you had lost someone you loved."

He draws his hand through his hair, and says in a low, angry voice, "I do not have to imagine it. I lost someone I loved. I lost my mother."

Oh. "I am sorry to hear ... my condolences ..." My voice trails off under his hostile gaze. I look down and straighten a bow on my skirt.

Is he an enchanted prince or a madman? He seems forlorn, frustrated, and scornful, but sane.

"My lady," he says in a friendlier voice, "pray tell whence you came and how you happened upon this place?"

I can't repress a smile. "I have no idea how I found this place. I was on a farewell hike with five other counselors—we worked at a summer camp. The storm came up in the afternoon and the others disappeared. My only choice was to follow the trail and it led me here."

"Are you able to read?"

"Of course."

He hands me a small recently published book about Zen Buddhism. "Please read the next chapter aloud."

"You're reading a book about Zen Buddhism?" I ask, somewhat surprised.

"I study religions," he explains haughtily. "Do you know anything about Zen Buddhism?"

"A bit. Like it originated in Japan; you have to meditate a lot and solve some mental puzzles called 'koan,' which can only be solved by the intuitive mind; stuff like that."

"Correct. Here is a koan for you." He peers at me. "How could a twelfth century prince and a twenty-first century maiden read together about Zen Buddhism?"

"I have a question, too. How can I tell you are from the twelfth century?"

He frowns. "You must take my word for it. What is your answer to my question?"

"As we are reading together now," I blurt out the first thing that comes to my mind. As I look at him for his reaction, our eyes meet and something exchanges between us.

"I think we must work together to break the curse," I say. "Neither of us can succeed alone."

He is aghast. "You mean you … and I … collaborate … doing what?"

I shrug. "We have to discover it together."

He points to the book. "Would you kindly read now?"

I do. But my eyes soon become heavy and no willpower or concentration will keep them open. I skip and stumble over words and sentences.

"My lady," he sneers, "your reading skills are in definite need of improvement."

That's it. "Listen, my reading skills are excellent, except when my eyes are closing because I am dead tired after a day of hiking, getting lost in a deluge, finding an enchanted place with a cursed prince, and not knowing which century I am in. All those activities make a person rather sleepy by the end of the day."

"Fine," he says icily. "You may retire." He stands up and politely offers his arm. "May I escort you to your room?"

I lay my hand on his, and he leads me upstairs. When we arrive at my door he says goodnight with a graceful bow.

"Good night," I curtsy then add with more bite than reverence, "your highness."

Chapter 2

I wake to bright sunshine and stare into the light without having the slightest idea of where I am. Then all the memories of the previous day spring at me. With a surge of nervous energy, I fly to the closest window to orient myself.

I open the window to the fresh damp breath of sea and forest, the sound of waves, the twittering, chirping, cooing, and warbling of hundreds of birds and the shrill cries of seagulls.

I love mornings. And this morning is exceptionally beautiful. I long to go outside but in the end stay in my room for two reasons: it is still very early, and I don't know if it is safe to roam the grounds. Moseying from window to window, I study the view.

The tower sits on a rocky cliff that sharply drops toward the sea and continues along the coast. Three small, windswept islands are close to the shore. On the opposite side, to the south is forest as far as the eye can see, except for one large building a fair distance away, only its roof visible between the trees.

After studying the view, I put on my clothes, which have dried overnight, then settle in one of the window seats to ponder my perplexing predicament while watching the gulls reel with the wind.

Have I really wandered into an enchanted tower, or some lunatic rich boy's abode? Whoever heard of an enchanted place with running water and electricity?

Did this man kill people, as he claims? Am I going to be his next victim? He doesn't look like a murderer. But how many murderers do I know? He acts like royalty. Well, he should. He's a prince from the twelfth century. Yeah, and my grandmother is the Queen of Sheba.

If he were from the twelfth century, wouldn't we have

trouble understanding each other? I read somewhere that the language was so different a thousand years ago, it was practically a foreign tongue.

And what about his rules? *Do not enter my room.* Why would I snoop around his room? Bluebeard comes to mind. I will definitely avoid his floor. Do I want to find the dead bodies of my predecessors?

Do not spy on my visitors. Who cares about his visitors?

Do not step through the gate. That's a tricky one. If anything goes wrong, the gate would be my only escape route.

I should have said "no" and stayed in the forest yesterday.

I laugh.

In the bright sunshine, in my dry clothes, staying in the forest seems an easy option. It sure felt different in that downpour last night.

What if the impossible happened, and this is an enchanted place, and I have to pass some sort of tests. What kind of tests do protagonists face in fairy tales? Dragon slaying. No. Dragons belong to the boy's department. Solving riddles? I hope not. I hate riddles. What else?

The bell calls me to join the prince for breakfast.

~ ~ ~

When I arrive downstairs, the prince eyes my jeans and t-shirt. "My lady, where did you find those peculiar clothes?" he sneers.

I ignore his rudeness and smile sweetly. "Do you mean my jeans and t-shirt? People dress this way in our century."

"You look plebeian."

"Because I am plebeian," I answer sans the sweetness. "Those fancy dresses you are providing are not exactly my style."

He frowns. "You certainly looked more becoming in that blue dress than in this getup."

Is this a compliment? "I prefer pants to skirts."

He frowns again. "That is most unladylike, but if you insist, you can wear trousers during our training. Not these. You will find more suitable ones in your room."

"Training? What kind of training?" I have not given any thought to what we'll do every morning and evening for a year.

"In the morning we shall practice fencing, archery, and horseback riding."

My stomach flips. "I've never tried any of those activities."

"I will instruct you, but first we shall break our fast."

Breakfast, like supper the previous night, is a feast. With copious amounts of cereals, bread, fresh milk, butter, cheeses, cold meat, sausages, egg dishes, jam and fresh fruit, I overeat. We are silent during the meal except for me saying, "It's a lovely morning," and the prince muttering, "Indeed." The long table definitely impedes any kind of intimate discussion.

We finish breakfast, and the prince escorts me upstairs. "In your room you will find suitable clothes for our morning exercises," he says, "kindly change into them. I shall return soon."

Laid out on the bed are comfortable trousers, a linen shirt, a short leather tunic, and soft leather boots. By the time I change, the prince is at my door. His tunic accentuates his broad shoulders, and his tight trousers and buskins make him look …

Never mind.

He ushers me outside where a groom waits with two horses: a tall, magnificent golden stallion for the prince, a black mare with a white spot on its forehead for me.

"This is Star." The prince takes the horse's reins from the groom and leads her closer. "She is a friendly, intelligent and responsive animal; perfect for a beginner." He pats her muzzle.

"I've never realized horses are this big," I blurt out, taking a step backward.

Oh, don't be a chicken. If other people could learn to ride, I should be able too. I step closer to the animal and cautiously stroke her side. She moves her head, looks at me with large brown eyes and my fear evaporates. I realize the prince is talking to me. "I'm sorry." I turn to him.

"Kindly pay attention while I demonstrate how to mount and dismount," he says with disapproval in his voice. "You always mount from the left side of the horse. Place your left foot in the stirrup, hold the saddle and the reins—do not pull on them—then swing your right leg over." He demonstrates, then shows how to dismount. "Pray, my lady, you try."

He holds the horse's reins and pats her neck while I mount. I am in the saddle in an instant. Wow.

"Excellent," the prince says surprised.

"Thank you." I grin, pleased, although I am much higher than feels comfortable.

When I am on the ground again, he says, "Well done, my lady. Kindly mount again." He has me mount and dismount many times before he approves. "This seems proficient. Now, we shall ride."

He swings onto his horse (when will I mount like that?) and from the saddle explains how to stay balanced, move with the horse, handle the reins, and more. Even with my best intent, I cannot follow his instructions because I don't have the slightest idea what he's talking about.

To my surprise—and satisfaction—I do well. After a few rounds of slow walk, turns, stops and starts, we trot, and since I am still on the horse, we canter. I easily adjust to the horse's movement.

Shouting something, the prince trots off into the forest, and Star, without any command from me, follows.

I love the ride. I love the rhythmic thumping of the horse's hoofs; the green, shaded lanes where shafts of sunlight cast bright patches on the ground; the bittersweet scent of the forest floor; the constant racket of the birds, but most of all I love the soft breeze created by the speed of the horses—in its gentle caress is freedom and exhilaration.

We travel many trails until we arrive at the large building I saw earlier from my window. The groom, who is waiting for us, takes the horses.

"If this is the first time you rode on a horse, my lady," the prince says as we dismount, "you are a born equestrian."

"Thanks." I beam at him. "I was always good at sports."

We enter the bright, spacious building. It's a cross between a conservatory and a ballroom, with high vaulted ceiling, tiled floor, full-length mirrors, and large French doors, which open to a riding and shooting range. The prince calls it "the pavilion."

We exit to the riding field and jog around until, out of breath and with a stitch in my side, I have to stop. So much for bragging about being a good athlete. The prince keeps loping along easily. I watch him while catching my breath. Damn. He's attractive.

We do stretching and strengthening exercises, then start to fence. The prince demonstrates the basic positions and moves, and makes me repeat them, constantly correcting and explaining what to pay attention to. He is a very exacting teacher.

"Well done, my lady," he says after drilling me for a long time. "Now we shall have a bout."

"A bout. Honest. I don't even know how to hold a sword properly. How could I have a match with you?"

"We have a bout so you can become skilled at facing an opponent, reading his moves, discovering his strengths and weaknesses—"

"I can't even recognize my own moves never mind an opponent's," I protest.

His mouth twitches.

"Okay, I'll try."

He shows how to don the chainmail vest, gloves, and helmet.

As we face each other with wooden rapiers in hand, the prince explains, "Facing a foe, it is advantageous to watch his eyes—"

"Wouldn't it be better to watch his sword?"

"No, his eyes reveal his intentions."

I look into his eyes. They have a friendly glint in them—or maybe I've only imagined it. I find it sexy to face the prince with a sword in hand. However, the match is anything but. If we fenced for real, I would have died many times this morning.

"I must commend you, my lady." He shakes my hand. "You performed very well."

"You just beat me one hundred to nothing and you tell me that I did well. Now, that's what I call chivalry."

"You fought admirably," he answers seriously. He does everything seriously.

If fencing is difficult, archery is worse. The prince shows how to stand, hold the bow, set the arrow, aim, and then ... better not to mention the result. Shooting with a bow is a very humbling experience, especially considering that my father was an outstanding target shooter with pistols. The arrows land everywhere except on the target.

On my next try, the prince watches me carefully. "Kindly shoot from your other side."

I do. Do I do better? If you can call hitting the board once "better," then yes.

"I have a brilliant idea," I say brightly. "We should call whatever I hit, the target."

He scowls.

I realized a long time ago that physical activity creates

intimacy and connects people faster than anything else. As we ride side-by-side back to the tower, I feel as if some invisible wall that separated us has disappeared. In spite of my total lack of aptitude for fencing and shooting, I enjoyed the morning training—and the prince's company. I've always relished the challenge of learning something new. Even the prince seems happier, not as bored and standoffish.

At the tower the prince is at my horse's side the instant we stop. How did he do that? He offers his hand to help, then presents his arm, and escorts me to the tower.

"We will have dinner shortly," he says as we enter the main hall.

"Dinner? In the middle of the day?"

"Yes, my lady, and kindly change into a more suitable attire."

I assume by "suitable attire," he means one of those fancy dresses. I open the wardrobe, and a big surprise awaits me. Gone are the frilly gowns; in their place are modern skirts, blouses, dresses, sweaters, even a few pairs of elegant trousers, all of excellent quality. Whoever picked these garments definitely has good taste. The colors are pleasant, the fabrics luxuriously soft silks, cottons, linens, and wool. The drawer holds a selection of tasteful under-garments, and the footwear lining the wardrobe floor includes a variety of classic styles in neutral tones. My friends would be envious if they saw them. Still. It would be nice if I had a say in what I wear.

"Oh, stop carping," I scold myself. "The guy is obviously trying to please you. Maybe he's not so bad."

I choose a blue heavy-silk skirt and a medium-blue silk blouse, and, though I seldom use make-up, I put on mascara and lipstick. The cosmetics are new, too.

When I arrive in the hall, the prince studies me as if appraising a horse. "Very becoming. Do you find your new garments more appealing?"

"Yes, I do." I smile at him. "How did you change everything in such short time?"

He shakes his head. "I cannot divulge it."

Dinner is a feast with enough food for a wedding reception. I try different dishes: beef marrow fritters, fruit-venison pie, carrot-parsnip-celery sauce, and spiced pears for dessert. I plan to sample every dish eventually. Everything tastes good. Our ancestors, or whoever these people are, sure know how to cook.

At the end of the dinner, I ask, "Is it okay for me to explore the grounds alone?"

"Yes, as long as you stay away from the gate," the prince answers.

In the end, I don't go anywhere. I lie down for a few minutes and doze off. By the time I wake up, it's too late for a walk. Also, the weather has turned cloudy and windy, so instead of exploring outside I descend to the main hall to check the books.

Thousands of books are on the shelves in total disarray. I am amazed to find some ancient tomes next to the latest bestsellers; volumes of philosophy, history, religion, science, and poetry; classics mixed with trashy novels and how-to books.

My eyes fall on a book about archery. I settle by the window and study it until the prince arrives.

~ ~ ~

After supper, from the chair by the fireplace I watch the servants clear the table. "How many servants do you have?" I turn to the prince and notice that he is watching me.

"I would estimate forty." He's definitely friendlier than last night.

"You have forty people taking care of you?"

He raises an eyebrow. "They look after the buildings,

grounds, food, animals, clothes, and everything else that needs attention."

"Are they also nine hundred years old?"

"Nothing here is nine hundred years old," he answers. "We are outside time; you do not age here."

"Wow. This would make an excellent beauty spa location."

He frowns. "My lady, the people who enter this place cannot return to their time."

"That's not a problem." I wave away his objection. "We just send them to some other time."

"They would perish in any other time but their own."

"That might be a problem." I nod. "We'd have to make sure they pay before leaving."

He scowls. This guy has no sense of humor. Then an idea occurs to me. "You said people who enter this place cannot return to their time. Is that why I would die if I stepped outside the gate?"

He hesitates for a moment then agrees.

"By entering this tower, am I under the same curse as you?"

He slowly shakes his head. "I think not. You are able to open the gate but I am not. I would have done it if I could."

"You said that stepping outside the gate would kill ... do you mean ..." I gasp, "you would have committed suicide if you could?"

"You may say it that way," he answers calmly.

"Come on," I cry. "It's not that bad here. You have everything. You live in a beautiful location, you don't need to worry about where your next meal is coming from, you can organize your days any way you want, and even your reading material is up to date. I know many people who would call this place heaven."

He leans forward. "Would you call this place heaven?"

I have to think for a few moments. "It depends on your

attitude. If you were satisfied this could be heaven, but the instant you longed for something else it would cease to be heaven." With a giggle I add, "This was the most philosophical thing I've said in a long time."

He ignores my mirth. "My lady, do you know what a zoo is?"

"Of course. It's our bathroom when my mom, my sister and I try to use it the same time."

"I am talking about a place with wild animals in cages," he says testily. "Do you think the animals are contented in a zoo?"

Gosh, this guy asks weird questions. "They are probably miserable in tiny cement cages where they cannot do anything, but large enclosures might be all right." Tigers and bears, which always look bored or restless, come to my mind. "I guess some of them are just as miserable in large enclosures. Not consciously unhappy, but they probably have an instinctive longing for the free life in the wild."

"Sometimes I feel akin to a tiger in a cage," he says.

Does he really feel like a captive animal? Am I a captive too? Obviously, if I cannot leave without dying. "How come no one could break the curse for such a long time?"

He impatiently moves his hand. "You have already asked that question."

"I know, but I haven't got an answer yet."

He peers at me, then asks, "May I have the pleasure of learning more about you and your life?"

"About me?" I smile at him. "I am twenty-one years old, five-four, 114 pounds, and my acne has finally cleared up. I attend university taking library arts, or—if you prefer fancy words—information science, to become an information professional. Before I became lost in the witchy woods, I worked at a summer camp as a counselor, which is a glorified name for someone who runs after kids. I like children and hope to be a school librarian. I took ballet and gymnastic lessons for many years and enjoy reading." I pause. What else can I say? "My father is an architect, my mom an economist. It's a shame neither of them came from a royal family. On top of not being of blue blood, they divorced. My father remarried ... I'd rather not talk about that ... I have a younger sister, and we are good friends ..." This should be enough. "This is it; the brief and concise summary of my unglamorous life." I smile again. "Now you tell me about your life and family."

"At your pleasure." Leaning back, he crosses his arms. "As you have already learned, I am the Prince of Bancloch, which is a small principality on the north shore. I was born at the end of the eleventh century, in the year of 1080 to be exact. My sire was the lord of Bancloch, my mother a princess of Norbury, which is a nearby principality. I have an older sister and a younger brother. My mother passed away in my tenth year and my father in my nineteenth, at which time I became the sole ruler. I must confess I was an unworthy prince. I preferred hunting, jousting, and revelry to ruling." He swallows. "I was also cruel, unfair, and uncharitable. Everyone feared and loathed me for good reason; I was a despicable tyrant. I have paid dearly for my transgressions by becoming a prisoner of this tower. I have been here for nine hundred years—nine hundred long years." He sighs. "According to the wizard I ought to have a complete change of heart before I can be free.

"Over the years, many worthy maidens have edified me, and I have reformed. I repented, asked for forgiveness, learned about fairness, compassion, how to be a good ruler. I am ready to compensate the families I have harmed, but I am still here ... and I do not know what else to do." With a big sigh, he leans forward and drops his head into his palms.

His honest distress touches my heart. "So you must have

a complete change of heart. Let's see what you've tried, to discover what remains to be done."

"I have tried everything," he growls.

I have an idea. "Have you heard about brainstorming?"

He straightens up and looks at me questioningly. "Brainstorming?"

"Yes." I smile at him. "In brainstorming you come up with all sorts of harebrained—I mean creative—solutions to a problem, evaluate them, and try the ones you deem useful. Maybe we could do some brainstorming to figure out how to break the curse."

He frowns. "That is a good notion, my lady. What kind of ideas do you have in mind?"

I shrug. "We'd have to think about them."

"In that case, I recommend we do your brainstorming tomorrow."

What?

"Do you enjoy music and singing?" he asks.

His sudden change of the subject annoys me. "Do you think music and singing could break the curse?"

"No, my lady. It would keep us entertained."

"Entertained?" I huff. "I don't want to be entertained. I want to help you to break the curse and return to my life. I'm not here to sing until I drop dead."

"It is rather late for serious work," he says in a pacifying voice. "We will do the brainstorming tomorrow." He rises from his chair, strides to the piano, and picks up a lute. "I shall commence with an old ballad," he says as he returns to his chair. I cross my arms sulkily.

He sings a long ballad about bards who would rather die than praise their country's conqueror. After the massacre, the conquering king goes mad.

The prince's singing is superb. He has a good voice. Even better is the way he conveys emotions: the silent recalcitrance of the bards and the loud madness of the king. Carried away, I stop sulking and listen attentively.

"You gave me the shivers." I applaud. "Would you sing something else?"

He smiles. "Allow me to sing something happy for you."

He sings a love song in which a knight praises the beauty and graciousness of his beloved asking her to return his love. An interesting choice and he sings it very convincingly. In between glancing down at his lute, closing his eyes, or staring into the distance, he dreamily gazes into my eyes.

Omigod. He's flirting with me. No, he is not. He's just singing some silly old love song. He does not mean it for me.

While he sings, I study his face. Okay, I ogle. He has intelligent hazel eyes, high forehead, straight nose, plump, sensuous lips, square jaw, and the sweetest round chin. Damn, he's sexy.

He finishes the song.

"I love your singing," I applaud. "It really touches the heart."

He frowns. "I probably would have made a more satisfactory minstrel than prince."

"You seem a good prince."

He glances at me, unconvinced. "You have known me only a day; how could you tell?"

I shrug. "I just know."

"Could you sing something to me, my lady?"

"I could, but I am not very good." I sing the first song that comes to my mind. It happens to be *Con te partiro,* better known as *Time to Say Good-Bye* sung by Andrea Bocelli and Sarah Brightman.

I finish and the prince sings again then asks me to recite another song. Luckily, my sister used to take piano and singing lessons and practiced her songs so many times, I've learned them all. This knowledge sure comes in handy now.

The prince and I exchange songs late into the night. I enjoy the singing.

Actually, I've enjoyed the entire day.

Chapter 3

Next morning my first challenge is to get up. Every muscle in my body is stiff. My ballet teacher said that the best remedy for sore muscles is movement. I crawl out of bed and do a few half-hearted bends and stretches. Instead of taking away the pain, moving makes me more aware of it.

My next challenge is to decide what to wear. I've never thought I would ever worry about how to dress for breakfast. I pick a soft light-gray cashmere top, charcoal-gray silk-lined trousers, low-heeled slippers, and put on some mascara. This should please the prince.

In the hall the prince greets me with a light bow. "Good morning, my lady. Do you suffer from any sore muscles?"

"They are all sore," I groan.

"I advise you," he grins, "to keep up with the training. It will strengthen you."

With the prince, I have no choice but to keep up with the training. Though the day is foggy and drizzly, it does not bother him. We are off to ride the horses, exercise, and practice fencing and archery.

The forest looks mysterious with mist swirling between the trees—a different beauty from yesterday's cheeriness. But I love it. And I love horseback riding.

Fencing and shooting are another matter. If possible, I fare worse than the previous day. My sore muscles don't help. The prince keeps reassuring me I'm doing fine for a beginner.

Of course, "doing fine for a beginner" is a euphemism for "awful." Anyway, I know he is only being polite.

After another change of clothes—how many times a day

we change around here!—and dinner, I explore the grounds. I follow a trail along the cliffs. It's a very enjoyable stroll. The fog has lifted; it is sunny and warm with a pleasant breeze off the sea.

I saunter for about an hour, until I come upon a quaint, moss-covered stone building. No one answers my knocking, so I open the door and find myself in a bright chapel. It smells faintly of incense and candles. Light from the jewel-like stained glass windows falls softly on pale blue and yellow walls. It is empty except for two stiff armchairs and an altar, which is covered by a floor-length burgundy velvet cloth embroidered with an elaborate cross in gold thread. Behind the altar is a glass wall; through it, I can see the rocky shore, the restless, gray sea, and the waves breaking on the rocks. The view and the chapel perfectly complement each other. It's a very peaceful and soulful place.

I stay for a long time watching the mesmerizing sea and the waves, but eventually pull myself away to explore further. About an hour later, I arrive at a wide shallow creek that runs into the sea. A stone bench looking down on the creek and the sea offers a wonderful lookout point. The trail continues along the stream, but I don't follow it; instead I stay and watch the shorebirds for a while, then return to the tower.

~ ~ ~

"I came upon a lovely chapel this afternoon," I tell the prince as we settle in the armchairs in front of the fire. "Do you ever use it?"

"Yes, we celebrate Mass there every day."

"You celebrate Mass every day? Why didn't you tell me? Could I join you?" I have to admit I want to join more to meet people than out of devotion. Other than the prince, the butler is the only person I've spoken to, and he only talks to me—with as few words as possible—when I ask something.

"If you wish, my lady. Mass is before breakfast." Probably

to exonerate himself, he adds, "I did not realize you would be interested in attending Mass. I heard people in your century are too enlightened to believe in God and religion."

"Yes, many people think God does not exist," I agree. "My mother's family is in that camp. Others are absolutely fanatic about religion and since both the atheists and fanatics are very loud, the ordinary believers simply disappear among them."

"What kind of believer are you?" he asks with a friendly glint in his eyes.

"I'd say the ordinary kind, but I'm not a churchgoer." He frowns, so I explain, "I believe in a supernatural something—I call it God. Unfortunately, when you say God most people think of a Big Someone in the Sky, who only loves you if you are good, which is really no love, and will either punish or reward you depending on how well you keep the petty rules of the church you belong to. I would like to know the real God, but the churches I've visited seemed more concerned with dogmas, rules and morals, money, and condemning others than with God."

"My lady," he says, amused, "you want to know God, not an idea of God. Are you some kind of a mystic?"

I laugh. "I am definitely not a mystic. You said you study religions. What do you think of the different religions? Is any one of them better than the others?"

For the rest of the evening he talks about religions, mystical traditions, religious ideas, philosophies, and philosophers and their teachings. While listening to him, I realize he is far more knowledgeable than I supposed. He becomes excited, and I enjoy watching his animated expressions, frowns, evening stubble, and deep, intelligent hazel eyes, as much as I enjoy hearing about how certain teachings of Aquinas lead to Kierkegaard's conclusions.

Later in bed, it strikes me: we did not brainstorm.

~ ~ ~

The next morning is foggy again with a light drizzle. We ride in a comfortable coach to the chapel. About twenty people are present. They all bow as we enter. The people are dressed in medieval clothes: tight trousers on the men, long skirts on the women, and both men and women wear colorful tunics. They smell fresh, like the forest and the earth.

I feel as if visiting another century. I also feel an outsider.

The prince makes no effort at introductions, and since we sit in the two armchairs (an extra chair has been brought in) facing the altar, while everyone else stands behind us, I can't even have a good look at the people.

The priest—a slightly balding, short, round man in his early forties, dressed in colorful garb—chants everything in (I assume) Latin and talks (luckily, not in Latin) about how only forgiveness and love can free us from our sufferings.

At the end of the mass everyone, with a bow to the prince and me, disperses.

"How come you didn't introduce me to anyone?" I ask in the coach on the way back to the tower.

"My lady, I beg your pardon, why would I introduce you?"

What a question. So I could talk with someone other than him. Because we are social beings. Because it is rude not to introduce people. Many more reasons race through my mind, but I only say, "So the people would know who I am."

"They know who you are."

"But I don't know who they are."

"They are the servants."

No kidding. I leave it at that.

Breakfast is the usual sumptuous affair. With so much food in front of me, I have two options: gain weight or use all my willpower not to overeat. I decide to try the latter.

We are off to horseback riding, exercising, fencing, and shooting. The riding part I love, the exercises are okay, fencing is not bad, at least not until we bout, but archery … I feel ridiculous while sending arrows to the ground, the side of the building, the moon, everywhere except the target. If there were people around, the place would have to be evacuated.

I lower my bow and grin at the prince. "Did you know that I am under a curse too?"

He looks at me questioningly.

"I have a wicked neighbor, who made archery my nemesis. It happened on a Saturday afternoon, as I was leaving home. He accosted me, reached out a hand, and said, 'You, my girl, because you were born with two left hands, will never ever hit a target—not even if your life depends upon it. My curse shall prevail until you collect the wisdom teeth of seven dragons, learn to spell words longer than eight letters, and bring me the silver flower from the top of the universe. Until then, even His Royal Highness Prince Christian John Rupert of Bancloch will not succeed in teaching you.'"

The prince laughs.

This delights me so much I keep joking and saying silly things. I want him to laugh again. Maybe laughter can break the curse.

Unfortunately, our merriment does not improve my archery. I hit my nose and keep sending arrows in every which direction. The prince constantly corrects everything I do: how I stand, hold the bow, use my wrists, and on and on. He even stands beside me (my heart makes a little flip), guiding my hands to show the right angle. I still don't get it.

"My lady," he grins. "I am afraid you would starve if you would have to hunt for your food."

"I am afraid if *I* had to kill the animals I eat, I'd be a vegetarian." We ride back to the tower in good spirits.

~ ~ ~

In the afternoon, I visit the chapel again. While sitting cross-legged close to the window watching the swelling and retreating sea and the raindrops dancing on the rocks, I decide to use my free afternoons to practice meditation. I've been to a few meditation classes, but never had the time to practice. With four hours every afternoon and nothing to do, I definitely have the time now.

First I concentrate on my breath. As soon as I pay attention to it, I stop breathing, then yawn. Minding my breath has never worked for me; better repeat a mantra. What word should I use? I cannot remember the Sanskrit phrase. I could repeat "ohm." No, "ohm" puts me to sleep; so does counting. I could repeat "in and out" or "god," or "love" or "peace" or … for heaven's sake, pick a word, something, anything. Okay. I'll try all of them. I settle into the lotus position in front of the window, keeping my back straight, close my eyes, and repeat the words.

In no time at all, my mind wanders off to think about the prince and my situation—mostly about the prince. Sporadically I remember to concentrate on the mantra, but after a few repetitions, my mind strays again.

~ ~ ~

"I tried meditating today," I tell the prince in front of the fire. "Do you ever meditate?"

"Occasionally." He is politely uninterested.

He looks handsome in the firelight, and suddenly, I have a vision of us meditating together. "Would you meditate with me?"

"No." His curt manner leaves no room for bargaining.

"Could you at least show me how you meditate?"

He frowns, but before he could refuse me, I put my hands together pleadingly. "Please, please, pretty please."

He gazes at me, bemused. "What do you desire to know?"

I hide my triumph. "I'd like to know how to sit, what words to use, and if there are any shortcuts."

"There are no shortcuts in meditation," he says, then

gives a lengthy lecture comparing Eastern and Western meditation practices and traditions, finishing with "I have a book on the subject." He searches for it, and I wonder how he can find anything on those disorganized shelves.

With meditation out of the way, I move to the next item on my agenda. "Do you remember we talked about brainstorming? Let's do it now."

He frowns. "Brainstorming … ah, I remember. It is to come up with harebrained solutions."

I laugh. "Hopefully we can come up with something useful. I will write down our ideas." I look around. "Do you have any paper and a pen?"

He summons the butler, who soon returns with a stunningly decorated diary and a fountain pen.

"A fountain pen. A twelfth century prince with a fountain pen."

"Would you rather use a quill?"

"No, no. Let's begin." I open the diary. "You said you must have a complete change of heart. Let's see what you've done and what remains to do."

"I appreciate your enthusiasm," he says coolly. "I have tried everything possible in the past few hundred years. I apologized; no result. I prayed; no success. I learned to respect women, but I am still cursed. I learned to be a good ruler—"

"What you're doing is not brainstorming," I interrupt. "In brainstorming you throw around ideas without negating them, such as apologize, pray, love, respect women, ask for forgiveness, for God's help, angels' help, fairies' help, find a counter curse, fight a dragon, go on a quest." I write them on the first page of the diary. "Can you think of anything else?"

"No," he answers sharply. "Neither can I see how your brainstorming could help."

"First, we make a list," I explain patiently. "Evaluate each idea, and follow through with the ones we deem useful."

"Let us talk about something else," he commands.

"No." Why is he so off-putting? "I want to break the curse and return to my life. I don't want to die here."

"Have you ever asked yourself why you are so afraid of dying? Everyone dies. Death is not the worst tragedy in life. Every one of the princesses who dwelled here before you would be dead by now even if they broke the curse."

"Yes, you are right, everyone dies. But I'd much rather die after a long, happy life than a short, happy one. It's easy for you not to worry; you won't die at the end of the year—I will."

"It is good to die young," he mutters. "Especially if you are burdened with too many memories you would rather forget. People who seek immortality are insane. They do not realize how many sorrows and disappointments they would have to carry with them." He looks at me. "My lady, do not desire a long life."

I roll my eyes. "Thanks for the advice. But I want to tell my grandchildren about meeting an enchanted prince, and how he was so eager to brainstorm with me."

He grimaces.

I glance at the page. "Let me read the list to you." Before he can object, I begin.

When I finish, he takes the diary from my hands. "I do not want to offend you, my lady, but your ideas make no sense." He points to one of the entries. "'Find a counter curse.' Could you explain how to find a counter curse? I know nothing about curses." He points again. "'Go on a quest.' We cannot leave this place; how could we embark on a quest? 'Fight a dragon.'" He looks at me. "If you locate one, I will gladly fight it for you. 'Ask for fairies' help.'" He frowns. "How do you come up with these ideas? Have you met a single fairy? If I need help, I pray to God." He makes a disparaging face. "What else is there?"

My eyes smart and an angry lump forms in my throat. I snatch the book back. "The list is to help us to think outside the box, to come up with fresh ideas. Here is what else I've written: apologize, pray, love, respect women, ask for forgiveness. Can you add anything else?"

"I have already tried all those to no avail."

I feel frustrated by his refusal and ready to fight. "If you've done everything on the list, why are you still here? You must be missing something important."

"Maybe I am," he says haughtily. "However, I refuse to discuss this subject any further."

Damn. I glower at him, he stares back, and our eyes lock. Since my sister and I used to lock eyes when angry, I am good at staring contests. Apparently, so is the prince. We glare into each other's eyes, then ... omigod ... sweet arousal makes my body tingle. I quickly break the stare and ask with pretend calm, "What should we do?"

"We could talk about history." There's feigned casualness in his voice. "I have studied history to learn how to be a good ruler."

"Have you learned to be a good ruler?" I ask with forced nonchalance.

"I have." He smiles. "Do you wish to hear about it?"

Avoiding his eyes, I nod.

"A good ruler," he begins, "cares about and loves his people. He allows them to prosper, and refrains from lording over them. He ensures good defense, yet strives for peace. He is honorable, chivalrous, scholarly, skillful in fight, yet avoids confrontation. He is strong, yet humble and restrained; just, yet merciful. It is a high calling and only a few great men have attained such perfection. For example—" he mentions names of kings I've never heard about, then goes on talking about good rulers and history.

History was never my favorite subject. With all those strange names, dates, and wars to memorize I couldn't become excited about it. The prince makes history come alive. He points out the connection between ideas and events, explains how art, philosophy, religion, economics, and science are interrelated and shape the future.

I enjoy listening to him and watching him. I especially love his intelligent, soulful, and—surprisingly—warm eyes.

He also has a very kissable mouth.

~ ~ ~

I've been at the tower for over a month and have two problems. The major one is how to break the curse. The minor one is how to address the prince. "Your highness" sounds stupid; "my lord" too uncomfortable (also, he is not my lord); "Prince Christian" feels too awkward, while "Christian" is too intimate. In the end, I don't call him anything; that also feels wrong. My sole consolation is he only calls me "my lady."

If you enjoy peaceful and predictable (okay, monotonous), life is good in the tower. In the morning, we exercise. I learn fencing moves—en guard, lunge, parry, riposte, and many others. Unfortunately, as soon as we start a match I forget every move we practiced.

I improve in archery too, at least my vocabulary does. I learn the meaning of anchor point, nock, nocking point, clicker, and many more terms. Too bad terminology does not make me a better archer, although I hit the target more often.

During the afternoons, I practice meditation in the chapel, and explore the grounds. I soon realize it is impossible to cover the entire place on foot, so I ask the prince if I may ride Star alone in the afternoon.

He regards me for a few seconds. "Yes, Just do not try anything fancy. Though, I suppose, if you hurt yourself we should be able to find you."

In the evenings, we play games, sing, or talk about different subjects such as life in the twelfth and twenty-first centuries, books, history, and religion.

One evening the prince asks if I know how to play chess. When I say "not really," which means "no," he offers to teach me. Actually, I know the basic moves, but was never fond of the game, and while playing with the prince I understand why. In card games or dominos, luck plays a part in who wins. In chess only knowledge counts; there's no room for luck.

So besides beating me in horseback riding, fencing, and archery, the prince beats me in chess too. I wonder in what activity I could outshine him, but realize he has an advantage: he had nine hundred years to learn whatever interested him.

The only thing he does not seem successful in is curse breaking. Unfortunately, I have no expertise in that either. But I can always try.

"Please tell me about the girls who stayed here before me," I ask one evening.

He crosses his arms. "Why would you desire to discuss such a subject, my lady?"

I cross my arms too. "To know what they tried and why they failed."

"I have already explained this; they failed the tests."

I uncross my arms. "We talk about passing the tests and breaking the curse; are we talking about the same thing? If I pass the tests would I automatically break the curse, too?"

He cuts his eyes to me. "Sometimes you amaze me." Is that a compliment? "They are two different challenges."

"Surprise, surprise. If I pass the tests am I free to leave, even if I don't break the curse?" I ask eagerly.

"You also have to break the curse."

"In this case there are *four* challenges; three tests *and* breaking the curse? Did anyone pass the tests?"

He frowns. "Yes, a few princesses did."

"But no one could break the curse." A brilliant conclusion. "How come you never mentioned this 'small' detail about the tests and the curse before?"

"I am not to discuss this subject with you."

"So you know what the tests are," I say, determined to find out more. "But not how to break the curse, am I right?"

He agrees reluctantly.

"Do I have to pass the tests first, and then break the curse?"

He grimaces. "If you break the curse, you are free; you would not have to face any more tests. But if you fail any of the tests, you will die. You will also perish if you cannot break the curse by the end of the year. And kindly refrain from asking any more questions."

"Only one more," I say quickly. "If I die here, would I die in my other life too?"

"You have only this life. When you die here, you die. This is not a dream."

Chapter 4

"Hold your shoulders back. Don't lean into your attack." The prince corrects me for the umpteenth time while I'm practicing the lunge. When I still lean forward, he places his strong, warm hands on my shoulders, holding them back. Since I took gymnastics and ballet for many years, I am used to hands-on correction, but the prince's touch has a different effect—instead of helping, it distracts me.

"Are you an impatient person?" he asks, his hand still on my shoulder.

"Yes, I am." I turn my head toward him. "How can you tell?"

He lets go of me. "From the way you fence."

Interesting. "What else can you tell from my fencing?" I straighten up and lower my sword.

"You are a perfectionist, competitive, and nervous."

This sounds anything but flattering. Unfortunately, it is also true. "Can you see any good qualities in me?"

"My lady, there are no good or bad qualities. Every quality is bad if you let it control you, and good if you control it. As to some of your other characteristics, you are smart, persistent, eager to learn, and good company."

"Thanks," I say, feeling happy. "You're good company too."

In spite of being "good company" to each other, I am lonely at the tower. I miss the hustle-bustle of the people around me, and especially miss my sister and friends.

As I explore on Star deeper into the forest, I come across the picturesque hamlet where the servants and, to my surprise, their families live. I also find the walled-in vegetable gardens, orchards, stables, barns, and pastures. During my wanderings I hardly meet anyone and when I do, the people quickly bow and slip away while children stare at me as if I'm something peculiar. When I smile at them and say "hello," they flee shrieking. I often have the feeling the other residents are avoiding me. One evening I mention this to the prince.

"That is good," he says. "They should be as invisible as possible."

"Did it ever occur to you that you would be less lonely if you were friends with the servants?"

He looks shocked. "You cannot make friends with the servants."

"Why not?" I raise my eyebrow. "They are people too."

"They strongly believe in social segregation and would never be your friends."

I don't buy it. "You should tell them we are all equal

regardless of the work we do."

"These servants are from the twelfth century," he says condescendingly, then shrugs his shoulders. "You may attempt making friends with them if you wish."

~ ~ ~

Next time I hear chatter and laughter from the kitchen, I go downstairs to join the conversation. The kitchen, a high-ceilinged, spacious room, is in the basement, and smells of roasted garlic. Seven women are working at a large wooden table.

As soon as I enter they stiffen, stop talking, bow deeply, and one asks, "What can we do fer yeh, yer highness?"

"I've come to have a good chat," I say.

They stare at me as if I said I've come to meet Martians.

"My name is Ann-Marie." I smile at them and turn to a young woman sitting on a stool plucking a chicken. "What's your name?"

"Martha," she mumbles.

"And yours?" I ask the woman next to her; she's chopping a large chunk of meat.

She gapes at me. I give an encouraging smile, and she slowly forces the word "Joan."

I turn to my next victim. Wait a second. Why do I think they are my victims? I guess because they look so uncomfortable. The woman next to Joan is keeping her eyes down as students do when they don't want their teacher to notice them. One of the older women gawks at me as if I have lost my marbles. I give her a warm smile. "May I know your name?"

"Why are yeh here?" she asks fearfully. "Anythin' wrong?"

"Nothing is wrong. I just—"

"What's goin' on?" thunders a deep voice. The chef, a large round man who looks more like a warrior monk than a cook, waddles in. "Why aren't yeh—" He notices me and stops. "Yer Highness," he says in a smarmy voice and bows deeply. "What can yer humble servant do fer yeh?"

I can feel a communal sigh of relief coming from the women. Let the chef deal with this lunatic.

"I came to see who prepares those wonderful meals," I say. I am not going to tell him I came to make friends.

"What an honor, yer highness, what an honor." He rubs his hands and glowers at the women who quickly resume their chores. He turns to me with a forced grin. "I'm pleased yer highness is happy with our simple and humble cookin'."

"Simple and humble. It is the best food I've ever tasted."

"Thank yeh, yer highness, thank yeh." He bows again.

I feel uncomfortable but not ready to retreat yet. "Could you please show me around?"

The chef conducts a tour of the kitchen. One wall is dominated by a large fireplace with hooks for caldrons, stands for turning spits, a brick "stove" with openings for pots on the top, and a tall bread oven. By another wall is a cupboard with pewter plates, pitchers, crock-pots, skillets, and other mysterious items. The prince's modernization, obviously, has bypassed the kitchen except for a few light fixtures, and a large stone sink with a tap.

Animal carcasses and all sorts of dried herbs hang in the storage room, and large earthenware pots with wooden lids stand on the floor. Next, the chef shows the buttery, which houses barrels of ale and mead—no butter. He answers my many questions, constantly kowtowing. The women keep bowing and grinning every time we pass by them.

Maybe I should be more persistent, but I no longer want to make friends with the kitchen staff. We finish the tour, and I thank the chef for his time while he keeps thanking me and telling me how grateful he is.

As soon as I leave, the women start to chat and giggle.

The prince was right. The servants would never see me as one of them.

In the evening I tell the prince what happened, and he bursts into a raucous laughter. I roll my eyes. "Thanks for not saying 'I told you so.'"

Since the servants strictly enforce the caste system, the only person I can talk to or call any kind of companion is the prince. He is an okay companion. He is intelligent, well informed, but moody. Some days he's warm and friendly, some days distant and arrogant. I cannot fathom what affects his mood. Regardless of his disposition, he is always—The Prince.

~ ~ ~

One question has been puzzling me since day one: how a prince from the twelfth century can have the latest books and clothes, not to mention comforts such as hot and cold running water and electricity—they aren't exactly twelfth century conveniences. How has he learned about history, science, technology, and the many other subjects of which he has such thorough knowledge?

Finally I ask him, and, to my surprise, he answers.

"The wizard installed a device in my room; through it I can visit the past or present in any part of the world in any century—"

"Is it like a computer?"

"It is more like a wardrobe. I step into it, and it transports me to the place and era where I want to be. I can also material-ize through it anything I want."

Wow. "Could I visit my family through your device?" I ask eagerly.

"You would be like a ghost to them; they could not see you or talk with you."

I had a different kind of visit in mind. "Could they come here through your device?" I ask, still hoping.

He frowns. "I have never tried to bring anyone here. Even if I could, they would have to agree."

"I didn't agree to come here," I object.

He leans back with a smile. "Yes, you did, my lady. When the butler asked, you took the challenge."

"What would have happened if I said 'no'?"

His smile turns impish. "You would have returned to your companions."

"What? Do you mean instead of spending the night in your creepy forest, I could have been back with the others?"

He nods.

I glower at him. "This is cheating. This is entrapment. Why didn't your butler tell me this before I said 'yes'?"

"You did not ask," he answers calmly.

"I assumed—"

"You assumed. You should have asked."

I want to say a few nasty words, but since it would not change anything, I resist and return to the original subject. "If you can travel to anywhere, anytime through your device, why don't you return to your life?"

"That is impossible. You cannot escape from this place, not even through that device."

"How do you know?"

"I have tried."

I repress a smile. "So you think I could visit my family?"

"Probably, except the device is in my room, and entering it would kill you."

Humph.

~ ~ ~

The days turn cooler. The forest becomes a patchwork of flaming colors, and I more and more miss my family and friends. One afternoon while riding on Star, such strong yearning overcomes me I decide to find the gate. I don't want to leave; I just need to see it.

I locate the beech-lined avenue. It is as eerie as when I arrived. I slide off Star and amble toward the gate, holding her reins. A soft female voice whispers, "Don't go there."

I stop, look around, but see no one. I take another step. The voice, which seems to come from the trees, whispers for the second time, "Stay away from the gate."

I pause. The longing for my family and friends becomes almost unbearable. I am aching with it. I step forward, and the voice whispers once more, "Don't go any closer to the gate."

I stop. While contemplating whether to follow the voice or my heart, I have a vision. I am outside the gate with my mother and sister.

"Where have you been?" Mom asks. "We were worried about you."

"I was in an enchanted place and met an enchanted prince."

"What is he like?" my sister asks.

"He's okay. He can be arrogant and standoffish but I like him. He is smart and I have learned a lot from him."

"Are you two friends?" My sister wants to know.

"Sort of."

"Don't you feel sorry leaving him?" Mom asks.

A deep sorrow floods my heart. "Mom, I have to go back. I feel badly about leaving him; we still have work to do."

My mom and sister seem concerned.

"Don't worry about me." I smile at them. "I'll be fine. Take care, and say hello to everyone for me."

The vision disappears, and I am back on the avenue holding Star's reins. I have a last look at the gate and turn back to the tower.

In the evening, the prince is friendlier and happier than ever. Deciding to keep mum about visiting the gate, I ask, "What would happen if we managed to break the curse?"

"Probably we would live happily ever after," he says light-heartedly, then adds more seriously. "We could return to our lives."

Return to our lives. Could I return to my life as if nothing happened? No, I could not. "I will never be the same after this adventure."

"Neither will I. However, if we manage to break the curse, I intend to return to my people and recompense the families for all the misery I have caused."

The thought of us parting saddens me.

The prince asks if I would like to play chess. I agree and lose six games in a row, some of them in only a few moves.

"My lady," the prince says, "your problem with chess is you do not think ahead. Chess is a game of strategy. It is essential to consider how your move will affect everything else on the board."

My problem is that I loathe this game—and I mean more than chess.

~ ~ ~

Growing up in a big city, I've never noticed the subtle changes and small wonders nature presents every day. The infinite shades of gray in the heavy, low clouds; the odd beauty of a few colorful leaves still clinging to the branches; the variety of tunes the "wuthering" wind hums almost non-stop; the ever changing sea. They revitalize mind, heart, and body.

I enjoy my stay at the tower except for the inconveniences of not knowing how to break the curse and finding the prince too damn attractive. He can be downright charming if he wants to—and flirty too. Even if my mind has ruled out any kind of romantic involvement, and brings up all sorts of rational arguments why it would be a terrible mistake, my heart is unconvinced.

As far as the curse and the tests are concerned, I am as ignorant as I was on the first day. Actually, I know a bit more. I know the prince must have a complete change of heart. What can change a person's heart? Love.

"We should talk about love," I say as we settle in front of the fire. The prince stiffens and gives such a contemptuous glance I quickly add, "You can't break the curse without it."

"What kind of love do you have in mind?"

"I'd like to discuss how loving you are."

He guffaws. "How loving I am. Would I be here if I were a loving person?"

"You loved your mother," I say, mustering all my patience. "Who else did you love? Did you love any of the girls who stayed here?"

"I loved them all."

I roll my eyes. "You loved them all. How could you love them all?"

He draws his hand through his hair. "If I have learned anything in these 900 years, it is that love is always present. When people's lives intertwine, they affect each other. I disliked some of the princesses and some disliked me, but regardless of our dispositions, we had something between us I can only call love. Therefore, I concluded love is a given. You can embrace it, or reject it, but you cannot escape it."

His words touch my heart. Yes, love is a given. What we do with it is entirely up to us. What have I done with love? Have I embraced it? Have I encouraged it? I sigh, then notice that the prince is watching me.

"Did you fall in love with any of the princesses?" I ask.

He grimaces. "That is irrelevant."

"Maybe falling in love would break the curse."

After a short silence he answers in a low voice, "It did not."

"Oh." I feel a prickle of jealousy and quickly change the subject. "How are the girls who come here chosen?"

He shrugs his shoulders. "The wizard sends them."

"You said only princesses could come here."

"Yes, I insisted on princesses."

"So you also have a say."

"Not really—are you a princess?"

I roll my eyes. Why is he so obsessed with my ancestry? Another question pops into my mind. "What would happen if the wizard died? Would it break the curse, or would you be trapped here forever?"

"He will not die," the prince answers.

"How do you know?"

"I know."

"Could you explain?"

"No."

Damn.

~ ~ ~

Time marches on. On many mornings, hoarfrost covers the trees, shrubs, and grasses. Then Christmas arrives.

On Christmas Eve Day, the butler brings in a small yew and, to everyone's amusement, I insist on decorating it. The butler provides the decorations, which, I assume, have come through the prince's device. In the evening, instead of the usual feast we have only fish and bread. We reminisce about past Christmases, then attend Midnight Mass.

At breakfast on Christmas Day the prince tells me, "We will have dinner in the pavilion; kindly dress befitting a princess."

Spread out on my bed are three gorgeous evening dresses. I choose a maroon velvet gown richly embroidered with gold and silver threads and precious stones. I also put on make-up and cover my long hair with gold netting. Sheer silk stockings, ankle-height soft leather boots, and a maroon cape complete the outfit. I look at myself in the mirror and hope the prince will be satisfied.

In the main hall, the prince peruses me for a few seconds then says matter-of-factly, "My lady, you look beautiful."

"You do, too." I smile at him.

It's true. Dressed in midnight blue trousers and shirt with gold embroidery along the neck and cuffs, a velvet tunic with long, split sleeves, a gold belt, dark leather boots, and a fur-lined cape, he looks very handsome.

"Your hand, please." He offers his arm with a light bow and leads me to the carriage that takes us to the pavilion.

The pavilion is decorated with evergreen boughs. A shorter table with chairs and tablecloth is at one end, while two long tables and benches are set up along the sidewalls. The cooks and kitchen helpers are busy preparing the food outside. Mouth-watering aromas waft into the building.

I think everyone who dwells at this enchanted place is present: both the folks who work in the tower and their families, from little babies to old matrons. I never suspected so many people live around us.

We sit at the table with linen cloth, silver plates, cutlery, and chalices. The priest's wife (I am surprised to discover that in the twelfth century Catholic priests could marry) sits beside me and I seize the opportunity to make friends with her. She is pleasant and shy. Talking to her is a challenge because her children, who sit at another table, keep skittering up to us, constantly interrupting our conversation.

Next to her sits the steward's wife (I did not even know the place had a steward), a fairy-godmother-like woman with warm, twinkling eyes. I like her the most.

The festivities open with breaking of the bread and a blessing, followed by a feast, which goes on for hours. As the pages carry in each course, the people cheer, clap, and whistle. The prince is the first one served. I am next, then everyone else. Two fiddlers and two flute players entertain us with some lively jigs, though it's hard to hear them with all the noise. Servants top up our mugs with mead or ale. With each round of food and drink, the noise level increases.

By mid-afternoon we finish dinner, and the festivities continue with a court dance. The prince asks me to be his partner. I agree, realizing too late that I am unfamiliar with the steps, which are rather complicated. I have to keep looking at the other dancers to see what to do. The fact that only four couples participate while everyone else is watching does not make me feel any better.

We finish, and other people begin to dance. The priest's wife is teaching the steps to a few children while other kids horse around. Older folks play games, or sing, or sit at the tables talking and drinking. Later everyone participates in a chain dance in which the only rule is that one must invite a member of the opposite sex. The prince asks me, and I ask the butler—the only person I know. As the line grows longer, the music speeds up until the chain falls apart with tremendous laughter.

When I'm not dancing or talking with someone, I watch the people—I love watching people—and conclude that if you ignore the difference in manner, hairstyle, and clothes, twelfth century and twenty-first century folks look much the same, although twelfth century people are generally shorter.

Later, it is time for each couple to kiss under the mistletoe. This is supposed to keep them together for another year. The people insist that the prince and I start the kissing. We glance at each other and shake our heads "no."

"We sure aren't too eager to stay together for another year," I laugh.

"If you wish, my lady, we could kiss."

How romantic. "Fine, let's do it—just for safety's sake."

Amid loud hooting and clapping, with my heart thumping in my throat, we march to the mistletoe. The prince takes my hands, brushes my lips with his … the next second his mouth is devouring mine. His kiss electrifies my entire body. As our tongues touch, the surroundings cease to exist. All I sense is the pleasure of the prince's mouth on mine and his strong arms around me. When my attention returns to the room, everyone is cheering. Omigod. I've just kissed the prince. Although it takes a while before my wildly pounding heart calms down, I act as if nothing extraordinary has happened.

With lots of off-color jokes, laughter, and some playful licentious grabbing, the couples take their turns. The kissing and joking continues for a long time.

As evening approaches, two young men bring in a large red bag, and every child receives a toy from it. The chaos intensifies as excited, shouting children show one another their new treasures.

The celebration winds down late at night. Children stop running and quietly play with their new toys; the younger ones fall asleep on their parents' laps. Some of the older folks fall asleep too; others just sit around watching the few remaining dancers. A group of drunks sings funny songs, which have more to do with women and drinking than Christmas.

Back at the tower, I tell the prince, "This party was the best Christmas present. We should have one every month."

"You seemed happy, my lady." He warmly smiles at me. "Christmas is the only time when lords and subjects mingle."

"Why haven't I met the priest's or the steward's wives at Mass?" I slide off my cape and hand it to the butler.

"The lord's household celebrates a separate Mass."

I should have known. "Would you teach me the court dance with which we began the celebration?"

"It would be my pleasure."

I lie awake for a long time reliving our kiss and convincing myself it meant nothing. It was just a freak moment. Maybe we had too much mead. The prince does not care about me, at least not that way.

But he is a good kisser.

Chapter 5

A few days later the prince announces, "My lady, I will have visitors for the next few days. You must stay in your room. Do not open your door except to the butler who will bring your food."

I'm taken aback. "You mean I will spend New Year's Eve alone, locked in my room?"

"Alas." He smiles, apologetic.

"How long will your visitors stay?"

He frowns. "A few days, perhaps a week."

I gasp. "I will be a prisoner in my room for a week? What am I going to do? May I take a few books with me?"

"Certainly," he answers with unusual kindness.

"May I sit by the windows in my room?" I might see his visitors from there.

"Yes. You may do anything; but under no circumstances open your door, or leave your room. Not until I tell you it is safe."

I collect books while the prince stands close by, watching. As I add yet another volume to my pile, he asks, "My lady, are you certain you will read all of them in a few days?"

I laugh, spin around, and almost collide with him. "You have too many books I like. Also, what else besides reading can I do while being locked in a small room?" Perhaps practice fencing; I should take my sword, too.

In spite of my protests, the prince orders the butler to carry the books, about twenty of them, to my room, and, in spite of the butler's protests, I help.

"May I know who is coming to visit?" I ask the prince when I return to the hall.

"I cannot tell you."

During the evening the prince is friendlier than usual, also more tense and distracted. He jumps from one subject to another, unable to concentrate on any of them.

As he escorts me to my room, I feel closeness between us. We stop at my door and I turn to him. "Christian, everything will be fine."

"Thank you, Ann-Marie." His intense hazel eyes bore into me. "I beseech you to stay in your room." He kisses my knuckles, turns, and descends the stairs.

I sit on my bed, apprehensive, then notice I am holding the fingers he kissed to my lips.

~ ~ ~

At midnight the visitors arrive with so much noise they wake me from my sleep. I hear male and female voices, and loud laughter. However, I cannot hear them well enough to understand what they are saying. An unfamiliar male voice talks for a while, followed by an explosion of laughter. More visitors arrive. Musicians begin to play.

How can anyone sleep with all this noise? I toss for a long time, then turn the light on to read. I can't concentrate on the book; the sounds from below hold my attention. Close to dawn I doze off and have all sorts of bad dreams until the butler wakes me. He has brought breakfast on a large silver platter.

"I shall leave this with you." He places the tray on the desk. "I will come back for it at dinner time."

I thank him, wondering if I should ask about the visitors. I shower and put on my jeans and t-shirt. The jeans are a bit tight—no surprise, with so much food tempting me.

By this time the noise level in the hall has subsided; the sounds coming up are very pleasant. I can hear soft music, chatter, and laughter. A lilting female voice talks about something, people laugh.

I want to know who the visitors are and what they are talking about, but regardless of how much I strain my ears, I can't understand a word they say.

Maybe if I open the door a bit …

No. The prince warned me to keep the door closed. To distract my mind, I occupy myself with different activities. I sing. I read. I dance. I watch the rain. Nothing holds my attention.

I want to join the party.

I take a long, hot bath. By the time I finish, the butler arrives with my dinner, but I'm not hungry.

I ask the butler who the people are; he says he is not allowed to tell me. In the afternoon I practice fencing moves, sing some more, dance around the bed, read. I cannot find my place. The sounds from below intrigue me. Would I really die if I spied on the prince and his visitors?

More than once I put my hand on the door handle. Finally, I lock the door, throw the key to the back of the wardrobe, and try to entertain myself while the day drags on.

The butler brings supper, and I scramble to find the key. I have no appetite and sleep poorly. As soon as I turn the light off, the sounds intensify. Do these people ever sleep? Who are they? Are they the prince's family or friends?

The next day is just as bad. It takes all my willpower to stay in my room. During the following night, the party changes from soft and gentle to wild and loud. As soon as I doze off, thunderous drumming and shouting wake me.

It is midnight, the beginning of a new year.

I congratulate myself for still being alive, wish myself a happy New Year, have a glass of mead, and feel very, very lonely.

The party becomes boisterous with loud music, guffawing, and shouting. It's impossible to ignore it. I cover my ears, read, take a bath, practice fencing, and sing. Nothing helps. How much longer will this revelry last? I am tired of the noise and the effort it takes to stay in my room.

A couple has a long and loud make-out session in front

of my door. Worse, the man sounds like the prince. I'm not a prude, but damn. Couldn't they find a better place? I resist the urge to open the door and tell them where to go.

The party continues. I hardly eat or sleep and wonder if the prince has had any sleep at all. Finally, on the fifth night, a merciful silence descends. In the morning, a knock at my door wakes me from a deep sleep.

It is the prince. Relieved, I open the door. The prince looks as if he has not had any sleep at all in the last few days. He is pale with black circles around his eyes. My heart fills with compassion. "You look awful."

He smiles faintly. "You are free, my lady, but I will not join you today. I need some rest. Have a good day." He bows slightly and plods up the stairs.

I'd like to comfort him. How? I watch his back until he disappears around the curve. I dress and descend to the main hall. It looks the same as always.

I spend the day alone. I ride Star, exercise half-heartedly, and practice target shooting. It is strange to be alone. The prince's absence makes me aware of how much I relish his company. He skips supper and our evening talk.

Next morning he looks as fresh and healthy as always. Neither of us mentions the visitors.

~ ~ ~

Another month passes. The days are getting longer; the earth is awakening. Thousands of snowdrops and starry yellow winter aconites bloom in the forest, heralding the warmer days ahead.

"You are ready for a moving target," the prince announces one morning during archery.

I groan.

It's true I can hit the board quite regularly. Once in a while I even hit the bull's eye, but that doesn't mean I'm ready to hit some stupid ball flying through the air, not even if the prince thinks so. Or maybe he just needs more entertainment.

We also practice bareback riding and galloping. I love galloping. At low tide, the prince and I descend to the beach below the cliffs and race freely along the shore. It is thrilling.

He can't beat me so easily in sword fights. Sometimes I even manage to score. The first time I strike him, I apologize, "Sorry, I didn't mean it."

Laughing, the prince lowers his sword. "I hope you are aware, my lady, the objective of fencing is to strike your opponent."

More than anything else, except maybe galloping, I enjoy our evenings. We sing, or dance; the musicians who played at the Christmas party provide the music. The prince has taught me the court dance, and I have taught him (for a change I have taught him!) a few modern dances. I am memorizing some of the ballads, too. Occasionally, he plays hauntingly beautiful melodies on his lute. We also play games, read stories or poems, or talk about his favorite subjects: religion and history.

In my free time I work diligently on meditation. With practice, the moments I spend concentrating on my mantra become longer and more frequent. It might be the effect of the meditation or the surroundings, I feel calmer and more focused than ever.

My only problem: I still have no idea how to break the curse or what the tests are.

~ ~ ~

One evening the prince tells me he is going away for a few days.

"You said you cannot leave this place."

"I must go with the wizard."

I know it's pointless to ask why or where. "You mean I will be here all by myself?"

"The servants are staying."

"A blessing. Maybe I'll make friends with them."

"If you desire, my lady." He grins.

Once the prince has left, the butler is much friendlier. He talks in the same fatherly manner he did on the first night. Normally, he shows as much friendliness as a statue. I ask what he knows about the curse and the previous occupants, but he tells me he's forbidden to talk about them.

I should have known.

I keep to the same routine we usually follow. The days are empty without the prince.

I also have to deal with an unexpected temptation: an irresistible desire to visit his room. Maybe I could check out his magic device to see my family.

No. And no. And no. I won't do it.

The temptation hounds me.

I should. This might be the last chance to visit my family if I die here.

According to the prince, I will drop dead as soon as I enter his room. That would pretty much guarantee I'll never see my family again.

How do I know I will die?

How do I know I won't die?

Anyway, I will not snoop. I've never wanted to poke around other people's private spaces. Why the strong urge this time?

For three days I struggle with the temptation. Every time I arrive at my door, the prince's room entices me. On the third evening, as if sleepwalking, I start up the stairs. The same voice I heard at the gate shouts "no." I ignore it. I hear "no" again, and again, but keep going. The prince's door is slightly ajar.

Oh no. What am I doing here?

As if waking from a trance, I sprint down the stairs into my room and slam the door. Slumping against it, I gasp for breath.

An understanding dawns on me.

I know what the three tests are.

I laugh.

I've passed them. Thank God. I have passed the tests.

~ ~ ~

In the next second, a short, round man is standing in my room. "Good evening, Ann-Marie," he greets me in a deep, kind voice.

"Good evening." I straighten up. "You must be the wizard." He even looks the part with long white hair and beard, and a long purple star-dusted cloak.

His face crinkles into thousands of laugh lines. "I have come because you have passed the tests, and as a reward I am granting you three magical wishes."

"Were the tests the 'rules' the prince told me on the first night?"

"Yes, my daughter." There is kindness and warmth in his deep-seated grey eyes. "Those restrictions still apply. It is still unsafe to pass through the gate, enter Christian's room, or meet his visitors."

Oh. "Are the magical wishes for real?" I ask. What a stupid question.

"Yes, my child," he answers. "You can ask for anything at any time"—I immediately know what I want—"but only the requests which come from deep in your heart will be granted."

"That's good. I'd hate to waste my magical wishes on something trivial." I push away from the door. "Could I use one wish right now?"

He nods.

"Could you tell me how to break the curse so both the prince and I could be free?"

Damn. I should have asked him to set us free.

"Even if you had asked, I could not set you free." Can he read my mind? "Only you two can break the curse, but I can tell you what to do. Both Christian *and* you must learn to forgive the unforgivable, love the unlovable, and be grateful for misfortune. This will set you free."

This sounds like a riddle. Forgive the unforgivable, love the unlovable … does he think we are God? "It's a high order, sir. Can anyone do it?"

He smiles. "Yes, anyone can do it."

Okay. Maybe anyone can. Can *we* do it? And how? "Would you please explain more precisely what you mean?"

He strokes his long beard. "Begin with your own selves. You can only forgive and love others when you have learned to forgive and love yourself."

This makes sense, but he hasn't answered my question "*How* can we do that? I mean, what method should we use?"

"You will have to discover that on your own."

"We have only half a year left. Can we do this in such short time?"

"Yes, if you apply yourselves diligently."

Diligence is not the problem. "I still don't know what exactly we are supposed to do."

"This is all I can reveal." He smiles kindly. "The rest you must discover on your own."

"How?"

His face tightens. "Ann-Marie, what method you use is irrelevant. Any method will work if you really want to change, and nothing will if you do not. Anything else you wish to know?"

I'd like to ask more questions about what to do, but I'm afraid of trying his patience; best not to annoy a wizard. "What voice has tried to stop me at the gate and on the stairs?"

"It came from your heart."

"Oh." I feel disappointed. "I thought it was something supernatural, like my guardian angel, or God, or whatever."

"In some way it is supernatural. It reflects the deepest desires of your heart."

The deepest desires of my heart. What are they? Staying alive? Helping Christian? Doing what is right?

The wizard's voice breaks into my thoughts. "It is time for me to go. I wish you and Christian good luck." With a wave of his hand, he vanishes.

"Wait, wait," I shout, but the room is empty. And I realize I have not even thanked him.

~ ~ ~

The prince is back in the morning, waiting for me in the hall. "I've passed the tests, met the wizard, and know how to break the curse," I say in one excited breath as soon as I see him.

"Good morning, my lady." He bows calmly.

"Good morning." I force a smile. "And welcome back. Now would you listen?"

"I know what has happened. We will discuss it in the evening."

In the evening! Is this guy for real? "I know how to break the curse," I exclaim.

"Yes, and I ask you to kindly defer our discussion until the evening."

Damn. How can he be so indifferent?

The day is a total loss. I am too excited to concentrate on anything. I can't eat. I can't shoot or fence. I can't even ride properly.

"My lady, use some self-discipline," the prince admonishes me during fencing. "Kindly focus on what you are doing."

I take off my mask. "If you'd let me talk about what happened, I could concentrate much better."

"We will discuss it in the evening. There is no need to upset our schedule." He raises his sword, ready for the next bout. "Now, kindly concentrate."

I glower at him. "You sound like old folks. Nothing is allowed to upset their schedule."

"I am over 900 years old."

I roll my eyes.

In the afternoon, instead of meditating I think about what we should do and, slowly, plans form in my head.

Finally evening arrives, and as soon as we settle in front of the fire the prince says, "My lady, kindly relate what happened."

"Here's the scoop," I begin. "I've passed the tests. Even better, the wizard granted me three wishes. Since my first wish was to learn how to break the curse, he told me we must work on forgiveness, love, and gratitude."

"I've been working on those for many years." There's disappointment in his voice.

I swallow hard. "Here is exactly what the wizard said: 'You must learn to forgive the unforgivable, love the unlovable, and be grateful for misfortune.'" Since the prince still looks skeptical, I add, "He said we should start by forgiving ourselves."

His eyes narrow. "How can I forgive myself? Only God can forgive sins."

From somewhere the phrase, "whatever you forgive on earth will be forgiven in heaven," pops into my mind. This makes sense. "Nothing in this universe can absolve your sins if you are unwilling to forgive yourself."

"Perhaps, but—"

"No 'but.' We have very little time to accomplish this. At least I do. Let's share what we want to forgive ourselves for."

"Right now?" He sounds supercilious.

"Yes, right now. Do you want to be first?" He's eying me as if I've gone mad. "Okay, I will start. Let's see, what I want to forgive myself for." My mind goes blank. Great. "Erm ... I should forgive myself for being so nasty to my sister when we were kids. ... I felt she was always intruding into my life and upstaging me, so to bring her down a notch or two, I kept bugging her until I made her cry. I also want to forgive my spitefulness ... and envy too." This is easier than I expected. "And I should forgive myself for being so rebellious with my mother ... And for being so ordinary. I never had any special talents, never stood out in any way ..." My mind goes blank again. This should be enough for starters. "How about you?"

"Could you explain to me how we forgive ourselves?"

"You didn't tell what you want to forgive yourself for."

"My lady, I've already told you about my offenses. Why should I repeat them?"

Right. "When I asked the wizard how to forgive ourselves, he said we have to discover it on our own."

He gives me a disparaging glance.

"Don't despair," I add quickly. "I have an idea. I read in a book that in order to forgive ourselves,"—or was it to change our lives?—"first we must be scrupulously honest, acknowledge what we are doing wrong—without this step you cannot succeed—then discover our reasons for it, then change ... I mean forgive."

This sure sounds lame. Could this actually work?

He stares at me incredulously, making me feel defensive. "If you have a better idea, feel free to share it."

"I will think about this."

Later, at the prince's suggestion, we play chess, my least favorite activity. During the game the prince says, "Do you realize, my lady, you are the only maiden who has discerned what the tests are?"

"Am I?" I brighten. Maybe my cognitive ability is okay, even if I will never learn to play chess

Chapter 6

Next afternoon, I want to work on forgiving myself. How? Why wouldn't the wizard tell me?

I meditate first. During meditation I stumble on an idea: I will use the words "I forgive myself" as a mantra. Good. Now where should I start? I'll begin with my sister, Sarah.

Although Sarah and I get along well now, I used to be very nasty to her. She is only fifteen months younger than I am, and that year and a quarter made a big difference while growing up. I was always taller and smarter, and this gave me the upper hand. At fifteen, she caught up in every way. Now she is a bit taller and much smarter than I am. She is also an excellent singer and pianist.

But she used to be such a pest. She bugged me by repeating everything I said, and always wanting what I had. If I used a red pencil she wanted the red pencil, if I used a black one she wanted the black one. It drove me nuts. Adults weren't much help; they kept telling me *I* must learn to share.

Our mother also bought identical clothes for us, thinking it was cute. I hated it.

And she insisted I take my sister with me—everywhere. Come on, Mom. How could I look cool and independent with my little sister in tow?

I will never forget when in middle school the hottest boy in our class, Dan, invited me to go skating. Mom would not let me go unless I took Sarah along. I gave Sarah a tenner to stay home. As soon as I closed the door, she started to scream like a siren, and wouldn't stop until I caved in and agreed to take her with us. She and Dan had a good time while I fumed. On top of that, she never gave back my ten.

How annoying she was …

Suddenly, I remember I'm supposed to work on forgiving myself.

The first memory that pops into my mind is locking Sarah, who was terrified of darkness, into our windowless bathroom and letting her scream until the neighbors came over to see if someone was being murdered. It will be a good offense to start with.

I repeat, "I forgive myself for locking my sister into the bathroom, I forgive myself ..." It feels dumb. What else can I do? Maybe I should apologize first. How? I apologize in my mind, then repeat, "I forgive myself, I forgive myself, I forgive myself." The words sound silly and empty. Who cares? Just do it. I keep repeating the phrase regardless of how false it sounds.

Soon other memories emerge. One of them is when we had only a spoonful of ice cream left in the bottom of an ice cream pail and had the biggest screaming match and tug-o-war over it. Suddenly we looked at each other and laughed. How stupid could we get? Fighting over a useless spoonful of ice cream.

It was the turning point in our relationship.

We went to the corner store, bought a tub of ice cream, and ate it in the park while talking about how foolish we were. By the time we finished both the ice cream and the reminiscing, our tears were flowing—not because we were so emotional but because we could not stop laughing at our own stupidity. We became the best of friends.

It turned out my sister is good at keeping secrets, so soon she was one of my confidantes. We discussed boys, parents, friends, and other relevant topics. As a plus, we could share each other's clothes. By that time we bought our own, and they were not identical.

We had already forgiven years ago over that tub of shared ice cream. Why should I work on it again? To break the curse.

I keep repeating the words "I forgive myself" for many afternoons. Nothing happens, except more memories emerge and I feel worse than before. One afternoon, the words change to "forgive me." I easily repeat them hundreds of times. They switch to "I forgive." For the next hour or so, the mantra alternates between "forgive me," and "I forgive." The words are coming from somewhere deep within. They carry me away. For the first time my meditation flows effortlessly. I finally open my eyes. I am different. Something has shifted inside me. I feel peaceful and light, and I know that, somehow, all my trespasses against my sister are forgiven.

I turn to my less than stellar relationship with my mother. We always had tension between us. She has no sense of humor and wants to run my life according to her ideas. She is not pleased with me majoring in library arts. "You should study something challenging," she often grumbles. "Something you could earn a decent living with." And regardless of how good my marks are, she tells me that I could do better. Does she think I was born an Einstein?

My biggest beef with her is that she kicked our father out. I mean our father left, but Mom … never mind.

I remember an embarrassing incident. Some bank president invited our mother and her family to a formal dinner at his home. Mom is vice-president at one of the largest banks. At the dinner, I deliberately behaved like a bum, slurping my soup, asking stupid questions, and spilling my drink. I made a total fool of myself and probably ruined a promotion for Mom. I was an angry and rebellious thirteen-year-old—a lame excuse.

I begin with the dinner episode by repeating the words, "I'm sorry," "forgive me," and "I forgive." As other bad memories emerge, I smother them with my mantras.

Maybe because I am in good training, I soon reach that peaceful state where I know I'm forgiven.

I turn my attention to my father. I always had a good

relationship with him, except for being jealous of my sister. I should work on that.

So why was I so jealous? No one enjoys being the second fiddle, but there was more. It all becomes clear as I contemplate our relationship. I believed that since our father liked Sarah more, he loved me less.

I laugh.

Love is not a piece of bread—if you give it to one person, you won't have anything left for another. As I meditate, I realize with absolute certainty my father loves me just as much as he loves my sister.

After many, many days of meditation, I reach the now-familiar peacefulness.

I start to work on forgiving myself for hurting other people. I recall so many wrongdoings I wonder how anyone could ever like me.

As I meditate and repeat "forgive me" and "I forgive," I know I am changing deep inside, shedding my old self in some mysterious way.

~ ~ ~

I often wonder if the prince is working on forgiveness. He never mentions it and (call me a coward) I'm reluctant to ask. As long as I don't know, I can hope he is. What could I do if he refused? How could I persuade him? And—the most important question—could I escape death?

One evening the prince announces, "Forgiving myself has brought remarkable results."

"You've tried!" I cry with sudden excitement and relief. "Fantastic. What did you do? How do you know it has worked?"

He gives me a warm, slightly self-conscious smile.

This is a first. His humble smile makes him look extremely endearing. "I discussed your suggestion with the priest, confessed my offences, and he absolved me."

"Okay. The priest absolved you, but have you forgiven yourself?"

"Yes, my lady. Once I knew I have been forgiven I easily forgave myself."

"And it worked."

He nods.

"How do you know it has worked?"

"I am different." He smiles. "My soul is at peace."

"It has never occurred to me to ask for someone's help. Maybe I should have worked with the priest too. I struggled days and days and I am sure I had a lot less to forgive than you did."

He frowns. "I struggled too, my lady. It is not easy to confess to someone your worst iniquities."

"I guess. So, have you finished forgiving yourself?"

"I have." He nods lightly. "And you, my lady?"

"I think I have." I hope I have. "Should we start to work on forgiving others?"

"Yes, my lady." He sounds almost enthusiastic. Wow.

"So what do you want to forgive?"

His face darkens.

"If you're not ready, we can talk about it another time," I say, feeling oh-so-considerate.

He frowns. "We might as well tackle it now."

"Do you want to go first?"

He bites his lower lip. Clearly, he does not.

"Okay, I'll go first." I've been reflecting so much on my life and family these last few weeks, it is easy to talk about them. "I need to forgive my parents that instead of learning to live together peacefully, learning to compromise and accept their differences, they divorced. I should also forgive them that they cared more about their jobs than us, their daughters. Often, we only saw them on weekends when they spent most of their time fighting … I need to forgive my dad that he left us for another woman, and he likes my sister more than me." I swallow. "I need to forgive Mom that I am never good enough for her … and my sister that she is more talented, more outgoing, and prettier than I am …" What else? That's enough for starters. "How about you?"

He peers at me with penetrating eyes. "I have to forgive worse ills than you do. I have to forgive my father for our mother's death—"

"He killed your mother?" I ask, incredulous.

"He did not directly kill Mother … I do not …" He draws his hand through his hair. "I suppose I should talk about it."

"It's up to you."

The prince gazes into the fire. "My parents had an arranged marriage." He turns his gaze to me. "Father never cared about Mother. She was gentle, intelligent, and much younger than him. Father was loud and brutal. He spent his evenings in drunken revelry and merrymaking with his lovers, while our mother spent her evenings with us. Father both neglected and abused her."

What does the prince mean by abuse?

"Mother spent many days in tears because of his cruelty." The prince picks up a chess piece, turns it in his hand. "I think she had tender feelings for our tutor, although I do not know if any indiscretion happened between them. One afternoon, while we were having lessons and Mother sat by the window listening to us, Father burst into our room, called our mother a whore and the tutor a traitor, and stabbed him to death right in front of us."

A shudder runs through me.

"A few days later Mother became ill; she passed away in less than a month. I think she died of a broken heart." The prince is squeezing the chess piece so hard his knuckles turn white. "You would think after the murder and her death I would have hated Father; the opposite happened. I started to adore him. I yearned to be like him: strong, loud, and brash—what a real man was in my eyes. At first I found my actions repulsive, but I forced myself to behave as he did. He was proud of me, which in turn made me feel proud.

"My younger brother, Ryan, was different. He was afraid of Father, turned pale whenever he saw him. Ryan has our mother's looks and temperament. He is gentle, thoughtful, never given to drinking, fighting, and womanizing. Father despised him, but I stood by Ryan as much as I could, protecting him from Father's ire." He stops for a second as if gathering his thoughts.

"When I was nineteen, Father, while drunk, fell down the stairs. By the time he landed at the bottom, he was dead. I continued his legacy. For many years I ruled like the devil. Then the wizard cursed me and I became a prisoner of this tower." He pauses. "This might sound foolish, but I am thankful to the wizard. He saved my soul." He glances down at his hands and releases the chess piece.

Evidently, being a prince is no guarantee of a happy childhood. "This will be hard to forgive," I say.

He squares his jaw. "After forgiving myself, I shall have no problem with this."

~ ~ ~

I start on forgiving others. After the hell the prince revealed, I am thankful for my life. The most traumatic event was my parents' divorce. I decide to begin with that one.

My parents' marriage started very promising—at least, that is what everyone says. They met when Mom was a loan officer and Dad and his friend applied for a loan to open a construction company. Mom went out of her way to secure a loan for them, and Dad went out of his way to secure her for himself. It seemed a match made in heaven. They were both bright, ambitious, and deeply in love. According to my aunt, there was so much physical attraction between them they could barely keep their hands off each other. Soon Mom was both a partner in Dad's business and his wife.

Family gossip says trouble began with our arrival. Dad wanted Mom to quit her job and stay at home, but she refused.

They had other problems too. Our dad is easy-going and fun loving, while Mom is serious and cautious. She disapproved of our father's act-now-worry-later attitude. Dad has always been the life of the party, while Mom is the more introverted type. I guess opposites attract.

The way they fought was different too. When angry, our father would blow up then quickly forgive and forget. Mom has a problem with forgiving and never forgets. She sulks. And sulks, and sulks, and sulks some more, and becomes irritating. As time went on and their differences became more and more prominent, the atmosphere in our family turned poisonous. Dad stayed away, and Mom sulked even more. It was only a matter of time before their marriage reached the breaking point.

The first memory that pops into my mind is something I'd almost forgotten. Late one evening, I woke up and heard my dad and mom arguing in the living room. We lived in an apartment built at the end of the nineteenth century, with doors between every room. I hid behind the dining room door.

"Meg," my father said, "I am sorry for what happened. I promise it won't happen ever again. Please forgive me. I want to come back. I love you and the girls. I—I don't want to lose you."

"Never, James." Mom's voice was like a sharp knife. "You bastard. How could I ever trust you again?"

Dad kept begging and Mom kept refusing him. I stood behind the door shivering with cold, disappointment, and anger. Finally, Dad left, Mom burst into a feverish cry, and I crept back to the bedroom.

I did not know at that time what our father's offence was. I just knew he was not coming home regularly, and if he was there, my parents either fought or avoided each other. A short time later, our father moved out for good.

It took two years before the divorce was finalized—two years of bitter fighting over everything. I hated it. If they had to divorce, why couldn't they do it more amiably as some other kids' parents did?

I repeat the words "I forgive" while holding the scene in my mind. Tears are running down my cheeks; I let them. As I continue with "I forgive," slowly the tears dry up and the pain diminishes. It still takes several days and repetitions before the pain completely disappears.

~ ~ ~

April rolls around. Hundreds of daffodils bloom in the meadow around the tower, while sweet violets perfume the air along the pathways.

Our daily routine stays the same. I'm getting good at everything, even archery.

One morning as I face the prince with sword in hand, a voice in my head says, "Why don't you just play today instead of trying to prove yourself?"

I become relaxed and enjoy our fencing match.

"What has happened to you?" The prince lowers his sword, and pushes up his mask. "Where is your usual tense aggression?"

I push up my mask, too. "I've decided to have fun fencing."

"That is the spirit." He grins.

One crisp sunny morning, the prince tells me, "You wanted to travel all the trails. Let us do it today."

As soon as we mount, he gallops off toward the forest.

"Come on, Star." I spur the horse. "Time to catch up with him."

We soon gallop side-by-side, then slow down to let the horses cool.

It's a delightful day. Nature is bursting with the renewed energy of life. The spring wind is dancing between the tree-branches, which are still bare, although some shrubs show delicate green leaves. Overhead, an invisible little singer trills the most cheerful tune.

On the whim of the moment I take off, and Christian races after me. In no time he catches up, and we thunder side by side, only slowing down as we turn onto the trail that leads to the creek delta. At the bench, the prince hops off before his horse even stops and is by my side, taking me by the waist as I dismount. He lowers me to the ground. I glance up at his radiant face, windblown hair … and cannot deny any longer that I am in love with him.

We gaze into one another's eyes for a long time. Christian lets go of my waist, takes my hand, and leads me to the bench. With his handkerchief, he wipes away the raindrops from last night's downpour, and we sit, legs stretched out.

He wraps his arm around my shoulder. I smell his leather tunic and his enticing masculine scent.

"This was a good ride," he says.

"Yes, it was," I agree.

"Life is good," he announces cheerfully, pulling me closer.

It is good. So why do I want to cry?

I lean my head on his shoulder, and we watch the sea in complete harmony. Not for long. Our pants soak up the moisture from the bench.

Chapter 7

I want to forgive Tom, the first boy I fell in love with, for dumping me for my best friend, Nicole—and Nicole for betraying our friendship.

I was a high school junior; Tom was a senior and new at the school. He was cute. More than cute, he was hot. Tall, handsome, with thick brown hair, brown eyes, and the kind of athletic body I find very attractive; the kind the prince has. I wasn't the only girl who had a crush on him.

Our lockers were close—the only advantage I had. We started to talk when I accidently (I swear it was an accident) knocked over my soda, splashing his jeans. I was surprised (and thrilled) when he interrupted my profuse apology to invite me for pizza. We hit it off on our first date and from then on had an easy, fun relationship. He was everything I ever wanted in a guy: smart, funny, good-looking. I was in love.

Nicole wanted him too. She flirted with him every time the three of us were together, which happened more and more often. The more fun they had, the more I sulked, until a few months later Tom dumped me to date Nicole. A short time later he dumped her and dated a girl from the senior class, then another, then … My only consolation was that I was the first and longest-lasting of his girlfriends in our school.

It took a long time to get over the hurt and disappointment. Eventually Nicole and I mended our friendship, though she has not given up her bad habit of wanting my boyfriends.

I repeat the mantra "I forgive" and "forgive me" until it sweeps all the remaining anger and sadness away.

I want to clear out what I would call secondary hurts. I want to release and absolve everyone.

I forgive my aunt for accusing and punishing me for breaking the barn door. I did not even know it was broken. When I insisted I was innocent, she also punished me for lying. Years later my cousin, Joe, confessed that he broke the door by backing the tractor into it. He told his mother I did the damage because he knew I would get off much lighter than he would. I forgive him too.

I absolve the most obnoxious person I've ever known, a neighbor girl, Veronica. She would make a derogatory remark about me every time she passed by, which was every day since we lived in the same apartment building, went to the same school, and shared many classes.

My grandma kept advising me never to pay attention to people like her. "You should feel sorry for her. She has no confidence, and must put others down to feel better about herself." I tried my best to follow Grandma's advice and ignore the hurt of Veronica's nasty remarks. It was hard. It was also good training in self-discipline.

More bad memories emerge. What happens to our memories? Are they just sitting innocently in our minds, or are they silently influencing everything we do? Does it make any difference whether we forgive them or just bury them?

I know the more I forgive, the happier and freer I feel.

Finally, after many weeks, I run out of bad memories. I search my mind, but cannot recall anything still bothering me.

"I have forgiven everything," I announce to Christian in the evening.

"You mean you have forgiven everyone every trespass?" he asks, doubtful.

"Yes. At least, everything I can remember," I answer confidently. "I did not have much to forgive. I had a pretty good life so far."

"So you have forgiven your parents." He sounds like a prosecutor cross-examining a witness.

I nod.

"And your sister," he adds.

I nod again.

"And your father's second wife."

I am about to nod. "No, I did not even think about her." At once, I recognize the seriousness of my omission and sigh.

"I guess I am back to the drawing board." I look at him. "How about you? Have you forgiven everyone?"

"I've definitely forgiven the most important offences," he answers.

"Have you forgiven your father?"

"Yes, my lady, I have."

"And your mother?"

"My mother? My mother had never done anything wrong to me. She was the gentlest, kindest woman. You would have liked her very much."

"Have you forgiven her that she died and left you three orphans with a monster of a father?"

"What?" He stares at me angrily. "My mother died because—" He suddenly stops. "Because she … loved …" His voice trails off. "No …" He looks into the fire and shakes his head. "I have never thought of it this way." With a sigh he looks up. "I suppose I still have some forgiving to do."

~ ~ ~

Next afternoon I begin to work on absolving Dad's second wife, Martina. I have only one problem: I don't want to forgive her.

She has never been good to me. She took away our father, and she is even more critical of me than my mother is.

She is the spoiled daughter of some super rich developer who owns loads of shopping malls. Martina has never worked an hour in her life. All she cares about is her looks and her socialite friends. She is snotty, and not very bright. Our mom is a hundred times better than Martina is. It puzzles me what Dad finds attractive about her.

What can I forgive her for? For dating a married man? Wouldn't forgiving mean I condone what she has done?

I hear the wizard's words: "You must forgive the unforgivable." Was her offence unforgivable? There are lot worse transgressions than breaking up an already crumbling marriage.

I must forgive her. This is my challenge.

But I want to hate her. I want to despise her. It's the only way I can pay her back for what she's done to our family.

Could I absolve her and still hate her?

I must forgive if I want to break the curse and leave this tower alive.

I think about reasons to vindicate her. At least she did not kill anyone, and she and our dad seem to get along pretty well. Grudgingly, I repeat, "I forgive, I forgive, I forgive." The words pain me, but I force myself to say them.

All of a sudden, so much hatred and anger surface from somewhere deep inside it scares me. Omigod. I never thought I had this much rancor in my heart, or mind, or wherever. I don't want this hostility. I don't have to like her, but this strong animosity is horrible.

As if my life depends on it, I repeat, "I forgive, I forgive, I forgive." I recall Martina's face and keep saying, "I forgive you, I forgive you, I forgive you." It takes many, many days before I can think of her without cringing with anger and helplessness.

My anger wanes, and I understand something else. In forgiving her, I'm taking control away from her. While I hated Martina, she had a hold over me. I gave my power to her. By overcoming my negative feelings, I take my power back. I am becoming free.

~ ~ ~

"This time I am certain I have forgiven everyone," the prince announces one evening. "How are you progressing, my lady?"

"Ditto," I answer, although I am not sure. "Do you want to move on to the next step: learn to love the unlovable?"

"Yes." He smiles at me. His eyes are so alive. Have my eyes changed too?

"Shall we begin with what we find unlovable in ourselves?"

"Yes, my lady, if you are ready to tackle it."

"Do you want to go first?" I ask.

He glances at me, and I am sure he will refuse, but to my surprise he says, "I am a coward."

"You're not a coward," I protest.

"I am, or at least I was." He draws his hand through his hair. "I was afraid of my father; therefore, to please him, I became like him. If I were brave, I would have resisted. Deep down I knew what he and I did was evil, but I was too weak and scared to stand up."

I want to reassure him he was not a coward. Why? Why do I want him to deny what he feels is true? Isn't denial a form of lie? If he believes he is a coward, he probably is, or was. Suddenly, I see clearly what the wizard wants us to do. Instead of denying what we don't like about ourselves, instead of self-loathing, we must accept our vices as part of who we are—and still love. "I guess you must learn to love yourself, with your cowardice," I say.

"I will." He chuckles. "What do you dislike the most about yourself, my lady?"

"Being so ordinary," I answer without hesitation. "I want to prove myself. I want to excel. I want to be liked by every-one, admired …" I crack a small rueful smile. "I think the name for all these desires is vanity."

"Fear and vanity." He laughs. "Two of the worst vices."

"That makes us the perfect couple." I laugh too. "Between the two of us, we have all the bases covered." He laughs again, and peers at me in such an unsettling way, I quickly add, "Maybe we don't have all the vices covered. Pride and greed are still missing."

He gazes into the fire, lost in his thoughts, then with a half-smile turns to me. "Have you ever realized that all vices spring from fear? Greed is the fear of deprivation. Pride is the fear of losing our flattering self-image. Jealousy is the fear of losing love. Fear is behind our every action. It moves the world."

I balk at his conclusion. "I thought it was love. Even the song says love is all we need. And since the wizard advised us to learn to love, it cannot be fear."

"My lady, enlighten me: why have you undertaken this spiritual work?" Before I can even think of an answer, he says, "You are afraid to die."

"Maybe you're right," I concede. "But I want to live in a world propelled by love." I have another idea. "Maybe fear and love are the same thing—I mean, the opposite sides of the same coin."

He's quiet for a moment. "You are talking like a mystic."

I feel proud. The prince thinks I am like a mystic. Damn, why am I such a sucker for praise? I sigh. "I guess all we have to do now is learn to love ourselves with our fears, vanity, and other shortcomings."

Piece of cake.

~ ~ ~

Next afternoon I start to work on loving myself. I decide to use the same method I've used for forgiveness. I repeat the mantra "I love myself." As I say the words they feel phony, laughable. All kinds of objections pop into my mind telling me why I should not love myself. I persist. Many days pass, but my resistance is as strong as ever. It seems an impenetrable wall is surrounding my heart, keeping self-love out.

One evening as I glance into the mirror, I remember reading about a therapy in which people have to tell to their image "I love you." I try it, but it feels so ridiculous I can't do it. I cannot tell myself "I love you."

~ ~ ~

The weather turns warm and pleasant. To enjoy it, I ride on Star almost every afternoon.

The day is delightful. The soft green forest echoes with

bird song, unknown sweet fragrances waft in the air, and every now and then I see some small animals scamper under the bushes.

Suddenly a huge snake slithers out in front of Star. With a loud neigh, she rears up then, in total panic, bolts into the forest. She wildly zigzags between the trees.

I cannot calm her.

I cannot do anything.

I am hanging on for my life.

I see a branch in front of me and duck—

Chapter 8

When I open my eyes, I am lying on soft, mossy ground. Christian is kneeling beside me, his pale face only a few inches from mine.

"Stay put." He places his hand on my shoulder.

Christian this close. I must have died and gone to heaven— or maybe I'm dreaming. My forehead is throbbing, and I feel a dull ache all over my body. Since there's supposedly no pain in heaven, I must be dreaming. I close my eyes again.

Slowly my brain begins to work. I remember the snake, the wild race, and the branch.

"Is Star all right?" I ask, opening my eyes.

"She is." Christian is leaning so close I can feel the warmth of his breath. He gently touches my face. "How are you doing?"

How am I doing? I've felt better. However, his closeness and concern makes me glad—too glad. "With you so close I feel great." Oops, I didn't mean to say that aloud.

He smiles, takes my hand, and makes little circles on it with his thumb, sending pleasant shivers up my body. "Can you remember what happened?"

I ignore the tingling. "A huge snake frightened Star. She

took off in blind terror and I think a branch hit my head."

"That explains the bruise on your forehead."

I touch my forehead and feel a wet cloth. I take my hand away; it's red. I try to sit up, but Christian holds me down. "Lady Ann-Marie, I need to feel your limbs to ensure none of them are broken," he says uneasily. "Do you feel any sharp pain in any part of your body?"

"Not really. I just feel a dull pain all over."

He examines my eyes closely, asking many questions, then carefully feels my legs, arms, spine, and neck. I know he's only checking me as a doctor would, but his every touch scintillates my senses, and the way his hazel eyes study my body with total concentration makes my heart cavort wildly.

He finishes, and gives me a smile. "You are fortunate; nothing is broken. Your bruises will hurt for a few days. The injury on your forehead is shallow enough to heal perfectly."

I want to say something profound to thank him for his care, but only sappy stuff comes to my mind so I just mumble a "thank you."

"You're welcome." He takes my hand again. "I have sent for a stretcher to carry you back to the tower."

"If nothing is broken, I could walk back."

"You should not."

Lying on my back makes me feel ... exposed ... vulnerable. "May I sit up?" I ask.

"Yes, just move slowly, and lie down if you feel any dizziness or sharp pain." He helps me to sit up. "Do you wish to lean against a tree?"

When I say "yes," he scoops me up, gently leans me against a trunk, sits down in front of me, and gazes at my mouth. My tongue involuntary touches my lips. Oh, rats. To avert his attention, I ask, "How did you find me?"

"Through the device," he answers, moving his gaze to my eyes. "When Star came back without you, I knew something must have happened."

"Did you think I'd left through the gate?"

He shakes his head. "I would have known if you were close to the gate."

I am surprised. "You would have known? How?"

"An alarm goes off if someone approaches the gate."

Great. "Did you know that I went to the gate last fall?"

"I did." He lets go of my hand and gently traces his finger over my cheek. His eyes are holding mine captive. "I watched you. When you returned I was so relieved, I could not deny that I cared about you."

"You cared about me? You could have fooled me."

He reaches for my hands. "I have liked you since the first night and it upset me. I did not want to fall in love and be hurt again. Entering this place is a death sentence. No one has left alive yet ..." He smiles sadly. "I might still lose you."

His words make me feel pensive. "Sooner or later we lose everyone we love. Still, we never lose them. The person might depart but the love remains." I touch his face. "Christian, if I die at the end of this year I will leave my love with you. Eventually, it will help you to break the curse."

I hardly finish the sentence when Christian pulls me into his embrace. He softly kisses my hair and eyes; his mouth finds mine and we melt into each other.

I have never had a kiss like this. There is fulfillment in it, and delight for love offered and accepted, and the promise of more love to come. Our kissing intensifies, until Christian pulls away. "We should stop."

I lean back against the tree trunk, take his hand in mine, and smile at him. "I'm glad I fell off the horse. If I hadn't, I wouldn't be here with you, feeling utterly happy."

He squeezes my hand. "If I remember correctly, being grateful for misfortune is one of the requirements for breaking the curse."

"Yes, it is. And I think you've passed it, too. I recall you telling me you were thankful for the wizard's curse."

After a short pause, Christian says, "This may sound crazy— I am even thankful for my family, including my father."

"I am too." I laugh and so much gladness floods my heart I am bursting with it. "I am grateful for everything in my life: for getting lost and meeting you, for my parents, my sister, my grandparents, even for Martina."

His eyes shine with warmth. "I feel the same way. I am grateful for everything: you, my family, this world, life. They are such precious, undeserved gifts."

I wholeheartedly agree. We hold hands and let gladness and gratitude wash over us.

The butler arrives with four young men and a stretcher.

They carry me back to the tower while Christian keeps pace with us. I've never been transported on a stretcher. I watch the tree branches as they glide by overhead. The swaying motion makes me so drowsy my eyes close.

~ ~ ~

I awake to Christian's lips on mine. "This is a nice way to wake up." I smile at him. I am in my room and Christian is sitting on the edge of the bed.

"I will wake you every few hours to ensure you are fine."

His closeness and the way he looks at me with warm, loving eyes makes my body tingle.

He asks, "Do you know what brought you back to your senses?" He answers his own question. "I kissed you."

"Just like Sleeping Beauty," I giggle. "At least I did not have to wait a hundred years for my kiss."

"I waited nine hundred years for mine."

I laugh and kiss him.

Christian keeps his vigil, waking me every few hours with a kiss. I awake at dawn to find him asleep on the chair.

"Christian." I gently shake his shoulder until he opens

his eyes. "Come, lie down on the bed. It's more comfortable than the chair."

"Lady Ann-Marie, I would not want to besmirch your good name."

"Don't worry about my good name. I won't put this on my resume. Anyway, you've already ruined my reputation by spending the night in my room."

He gazes at me intently then swallows. "I better keep my distance. I must stay celibate while in this tower."

"I won't attack you."

"I might attack you."

I wish. "I am sure you won't. You're too much of a gentleman."

He sighs, takes off his boots and lies down on the edge of the bed, keeping a safe distance between us. I doubt I'll be able to sleep with him so close.

When I awake, Christian is sleeping beside me. I watch his peaceful breathing, study his noble profile, his day-old stubble, and smile joyfully at his closeness.

I love him. If only we could break the curse and stay together. We might even do more than lie side by side like two sticks.

~ ~ ~

To my delight, Christian spends the week with me. We go on long strolls, talk about ourselves, and share childhood memories.

He tells me about crawling into a bear den, on a dare, when he was eight years old.

I tell him about parachuting out of a second story window with an umbrella at age six after watching an air show.

A week later Christian pronounces me healed, and we return to our daily routine.

The first morning I meet Star again, she nuzzles me as if saying "I'm sorry."

I hug her neck and pat her nose. "I know you didn't mean it."

Although Christian advises me to take it easy, we train as hard as any other morning. In the afternoon, I return to the chapel to continue to learn to love myself. I try to meditate but all I can think about is Christian, our week together, and details of his life he shared with me. For the first time it sinks in what different worlds we came from.

A few days later during our evening chat, I ask Christian, "How do you work on loving yourself?"

"I do not work on it."

What? "Christian, you must!" I cry out.

"I cannot love myself."

"That's why you must work on it."

He smiles at me. "Let me explain this. Do you remember I told you about the love that was always present in every relationship I had?"

"Yes?"

"I have realized the same love is present all the time, and loves me in spite of all my detestable deeds. I just need to connect to this love." I must look confused because he asks, "Am I clear?"

"I'm not sure."

"Let me explain this better." He leans forward in his chair. "Ann-Marie, have you noticed you are more than one person inside?"

I nod.

"Those different personalities make up your ego, or earthly self. Beyond them is a deeper self; some call it the god-self, your immortal essence, your soul, or spirit. It does not matter what you call it. This deeper self—that is beyond likes, dislikes, love, and hate—loves you, not in a superficial egoistical way, but with a love that surpasses all understanding. Do I make sense?"

"I think so," I say, uncertain. "But how can I find and connect to this love?"

"Try repetitious prayer."

"Would meditation work?"

"Repetitious prayer and meditation are the same thing. They are both designed to quiet the ego—which is constantly chattering in your mind—so you may connect to the love beyond."

"This might take years," I moan. "We have only a couple months left."

He reaches for my hand and squeezes it encouragingly. "Ann-Marie, you will do it."

I sigh.

Next afternoon I'm meditating again with the words "I love myself." But I don't love myself. Maybe I should find a mantra I feel more comfortable with; maybe I should just repeat the word "love." Love, love, love, love.

I struggle on for weeks; nothing changes. The wall around my heart seems as impenetrable as ever. I must break through. I must. I must. I must.

One day, while I'm looking for something to read, a bookmark falls out from a book. It reads, "I have loved you with an everlasting love."

The words jolt me.

I have loved you with an everlasting love.

I've read a story about a Zen monk who struggled for years to reach nirvana. It happened when a bamboo stick snapped. The quote is my bamboo stick. As I look at it again, I can clearly see the love Christian talked about: the Love, which is always present; the Love, which loves us with an everlasting love; the Love, which surpasses all understanding. I feel a tremendous joy. Heaviness I have never realized I had, lifts from me.

Next afternoon I repeat, "I have loved you with an everlasting love." Eventually, it shortens to "I love you." The words come easily without any resistance.

A few days later I glance at my image in the mirror, and remember how I was unable to tell myself, "I love you."

I smile at my reflection and say aloud, "I love you with an everlasting love."

I answer myself, "I love you too," and begin to cry.

~ ~ ~

Once I've learned to love myself—connected to the love that's always present—loving others is easy. I simply cannot hate. I cannot be angry with anyone, not even Martina.

Yes, we hurt each other; yes, we do selfish things; we grasp for acceptance and love, failing to realize we can only find it inside. No one can give it to us.

I am so overflowing with love I must send it to others. I hold the person in my mind and surround him or her with love—first Christian, then my parents, sister, grandparents, relatives and friends. Tom. Nicole. Even Martina.

This is fun.

~ ~ ~

The meadow around the tower is bursting with wildflowers. Thousands of bees are collecting sweet nectar; their constant humming fills the air. In the morning, dew sparkles like jewels on the flowers and spider webs. Swallows dart in and out from their nests under the roof. The days are long and pleasantly warm.

Even the evenings are balmy. We often spend them outside on the bench by the creek or by the entrance. I have never seen as much night sky as here. It is breathtaking, fascinating, a dark velvety indigo with myriads of little gems. I find being a part—even if only a tiny part—of such vast grandeur both uplifting and overwhelming, empowering and humbling. I explain this to Christian, and he tells me he often feels the same.

He is familiar with all the constellations and points them out. They are confusing, and I hope I'll never have to find my way by the stars.

In fencing, I can see what Christian meant by reading the opponent. Although his fencing is way superior to mine, I can read his moves; now and then I even anticipate them. In shooting, I can hit a moving target—sometimes. I have memorized the ballads I wanted to learn. Even my chess playing has improved in spite of my loathing of the game.

This is the best summer of my life. We are in love, we are happy—we spend one wonderful day after another horseback riding, fencing, shooting, wading in the sea, talking about everything, or sitting silently watching the stars.

For some unexplainable reason, we've stopped worrying about breaking the curse. The curse and being stuck in the tower have become irrelevant, although, occasionally, I feel some concern. My year will be over soon. What will happen then?

Chapter 9

One evening, while we watch the sunset from the stone bench by the creek, I ask Christian, "What else do you think we should do to break the curse?"

"You do not need to do anything else," answers a voice. We jump up and wheel around. The wizard is behind us. "You broke the curse."

"We have?" we ask simultaneously.

The wizard smiles at us. "Yes. Congratulations. You are both free."

"Ann-Marie, I am free!" Christian exclaims jubilantly.

"Wow." I kiss him, bursting with joy, then turn to the wizard who is watching us with a smile that is both pleased and sad. "How did we break the curse?"

"By your willingness to forgive and to love," he says.

"That's all?"

"Forgiveness and love are far more powerful forces than you realize." He strokes his beard. "Actually, you two broke the curse some time ago. You could not be this happy while under it. Seeing your happiness, I decided to let you enjoy it, but now it is time to choose your future."

Our future. I thought we would live happily ever after once we broke the curse.

The wizard steps closer. "You still have a lot to learn before you could live happily ever after," he answers my thought.

Christian wraps his arm around my shoulder. "Sir, we would like to stay together."

"I gave you plenty of time to ask Ann-Marie to marry you. You did not. Everything would be much simpler if you had."

"Would you—" Christian turns to me.

"Yes," I interrupt eagerly.

Before either of us can finish, the wizard lifts his arm. "Too late now, but you have other options. Listen carefully, so you can choose the best one. You can stay together in this enchanted tower, which is outside time, and live here happily forever but you could not return to your own times. This means you would be dead to the people you left behind."

Christian and I glance at each other.

"Or, you could live together in the twelfth century. In which case, you, Ann-Marie, would be dead to your people. I also have to warn you, Christian. If you choose to return to your castle, within two years enemies will attack it and you along with everyone else within its walls, will perish. However, you could save many lives."

Christian starts to say something, but the wizard stops him with a wave of his hand. "If you two choose to live in the twenty-first century, you could rebuild this tower, which will be a ruin once you leave. But you, Christian, would be dead to your folks."

We glance at each other again.

"Or you can part, return to your own times separately; however, in that case your hearts will be longing for the other as long as you live." He peers solemnly at us. "You have a day to choose. I shall be back tomorrow evening for the answer." He vanishes.

~ ~ ~

We are flabbergasted.

"We sure have lots of choices," I say after a long silence. "Too bad none of them are any good."

Christian is still staring at the spot where the wizard stood. I doubt he even heard me. Finally, he turns to me with a sigh. "I guess we must make a decision. Which option would you choose?"

"They all suck. Why can't we just live happily ever after?"

"Let's sit down and think this over."

We return to the bench.

"What would you choose?" he asks again.

"What would you choose?" I ask back. "Should we stay and live in this tower as two ghosts? What kind of happiness could we find? Is our happiness the most important thing?" I heave a sigh. "My family would be devastated if I died. Should they pay the price with their sorrow for my happiness?"

"No one would be too devastated if I died, but what good is a change of heart unless I make up for all the sufferings I have caused?" Christian stares at the ground, then looks up at me. "I am sorry, Ann-Marie, I could not live happily, knowing I let my people down when they needed me the most. I am their prince. I must be with them in time of danger, especially since the wizard said I could save many lives."

"I could come with you," I say in a low voice.

"I would love to have you with me, but it would be unfair to your family."

"None of the choices are fair," I burst out angrily. "I hate this lose-lose situation. I wish we could stay together both in your time and mine."

"Do you want to pray for some guidance?" he asks.

I nod. He takes my hands and for the first time we pray together. We begin with words, but soon the words give way to silence, and we both know what we will do.

We will part.

It's over.

My fling at the tower and with Christian is over. Now I can pine for him for the rest of my life.

Hey, look at the bright side. I am still alive, and we broke the curse.

Christian draws me to him and tenderly kisses my forehead. "Ann-Marie, I will love you forever."

"I will love you forever, too."

We hold onto each other for a long time. My sorrow is beyond tears. Memories of our year together flood my mind. "Christian, would you tell me who your visitors were at that party?"

"They were demons."

"Demons?" I sit up surprised.

"Yes, the demons I let run my life—"

"But—"

"They are banished. The wizard told me a long time ago they will be when I break the curse."

"What would have happened if I left my room to join the party?"

"They would have torn you apart."

I shudder. "How do you know?"

"I saw it happen."

I shudder again. "What would have happened if I visited your room?"

"The same as if you went through the gate. You would have disintegrated."

"Disintegrated?" I wrinkle my nose. "Have you seen anyone disintegrate?"

"Yes, I have."

"That must have been awful—"

He puts his finger on my lips. "Stop talking about what could have happened. The past is past; better enjoy our last few hours together."

I lean on Christian's shoulder, and we silently watch the sky as it changes from luminous yellow to orange, red, purple to dark ink.

I try not to think. I want to enjoy the sound of the waves, the breeze, the evening chorus of the birds, crickets, and Christian's closeness. I want to take this evening with me. I ask Christian if we could stay together for the night. His presence numbs the ache inside me.

We hold hands while sauntering back to the tower by the dim, silver light of the moon, then sit on the bench outside the entrance and talk all night about our plans.

The predawn chill creeps up from the water. We go to my room, lie down fully clothed. While following the lines in the canopy with my eyes, I say, "I wonder where we will find ourselves upon returning to our lives."

"According to the wizard, in the same place and moment we left."

"Will we remember all that happened here?"

"We will ask the wizard."

We talk some more until our talk slows down and we drift into sleep.

I awake in Christian's embrace, his face only a few inches from mine. I study his tousled hair, straight nose, closed eyes. I notice how long his eyelashes are. His full lips are slightly apart, and stubble darkens his chin. I love his even breathing, his scent, the weight of his arm on my side. I feel content in his arms. I want to stay in his embrace all day.

I kiss his sandpaper cheek. He opens his eyes, smiles, pulls me close, and kisses me on the lips, first gently then with more and more passion, then pulls away. "We should visit our favorite places and engage in our favorite activities."

"Okay," I sigh. "Then no chess today."

~ ~ ~

The day feels melancholy, like the last day at camp, except we cannot exchange phone numbers and promise to keep in touch on the internet. Even the weather is sad. The morning is misty, the first sign of the approaching fall.

We attend Mass. I say a silent good-bye to the people. Although I've never become acquainted with them, I saw them every day for a year.

"Will the people return with you?" I ask Christian on the way back to the tower. "And would they remember the nine hundred years they spent here?"

We eat our last breakfast in silence, then ride most of the trails. This cheers me up a bit. "I will definitely take up horseback riding at home," I tell Christian.

We have our last fencing match.

"You are good at fencing," Christian praises me, lowering his sword and taking his mask off. "You could beat some of our soldiers at home."

"How come I can't beat you?" I ask, taking off my mask.

He smiles. "I am one of the best in the country."

"Oh, I am glad I got lessons from one of the best. Are you one of the best in archery too?"

"Yes." He nods.

"Are you one of the best in horseback riding?"

"Yes." He pulls off his gloves. "Lady Ann-Marie, I am

one of the best knights in my country."

"Are you one of the best at being humble?"

He laughs. "Yes, I am."

We have dinner, and visit the bench by the creek.

"It was here I realized I am in love with you," I tell Christian.

He peers at me, surprised. "I did, too."

We sit on the bench for a long time, Christian's arm around my shoulder. We don't talk. There is nothing left to say.

We visit the chapel again. As we stand in front of the window-wall watching the waves, my throat tightens. I will miss this chapel, the view, the waves, the murmur of the sea, the meditating. "If you ever marry," I tell Christian, "you should meditate with your wife."

"I will not get married. I shall die in less than two years."

The thought that Christian will be dead in two years upsets me more than anything else has. "You mean you will remember me only for two more years?" I start to weep uncontrollably. Christian presses a handkerchief into my hand, and I wipe my nose. He is gently caressing my hair, repeating, "I am sorry."

When I finally calm down and glance at him, I notice his eyes are wet too. He pulls me to his chest, and we hold each other for a long time.

Silently, like a beaten army, we trudge back to the tower.

We eat our last supper, and drift toward the cliff. We don't know where to go or what to do.

Suddenly the wizard is in front of us. We exchange greetings, and he asks, "What is your decision?"

Christian tells him we've decided to part.

"You made the right decision," the wizard comments.

"Why do we have to part?" I burst out, tears welling up in my eyes. "We broke the curse, we love each other, why can we not stay together?"

"Christian should answer that question."

I look at Christian through a veil of tears. "I am sorry Ann," he whispers. "I was supposed to ask you to marry me. I did not because … because …" his voice lowers even more, "because you are a commoner." He pleads with his eyes. "Please forgive me."

Pain stabs my heart. He would not marry me. I was not good enough for him. With a sad tearful smile I say, "I will forgive you. I am in good training."

"You wanted to know," the wizard breaks in, "if you will remember what happened here. You two will in your own century; the servants will not." Stepping closer to us, he adds, "Now it is time to say good bye."

Christian gazes at me longingly, sadness written on his face.

Damn. I love him.

I fly into his arms and kiss him wildly. I don't care if he messed this all up, I still love him. And always will. He takes my shoulders, and lowers his head, gently planting a kiss on my lips, then, almost inaudibly, whispers, "Thank you, Ann-Marie, thank you for everything." He slips his arms around me, I lay my head on his shoulder. I want to stay with him.

I hear a hauntingly beautiful melody, the kind Christian used to play on his lute, then everything is gone.

Part 2

Twelfth Century

Chapter 10

It is a somnolent late-summer afternoon. Doves coo softly, and a chain creaks as someone draws water from the well. My sister and I are stitching a needlepoint by the open window in our room when a guard's horn shatters the peacefulness. Alarmed, the doves take flight. We leap to the window and see soldiers running to the gate. Moments later they return, dragging a haggard-looking peasant to the keep; one of them is hurrying to the stables, probably to notify our father—the lord of the castle.

I turn to my sister. "Selina, I want to know what is happening."

"I do, too." Her lovely brown eyes are alive with interest.

We put the needlepoint aside and, holding up our skirts, sprint down the stairs to the main hall where loud jabbering greets us. The man is slumped on one of the long benches; there is bread, cheese, and ale in front of him, but he only stares with vacant eyes.

Our father—a large, burly man—arrives. He regards the peasant for a few moments, sits down across from him, and we gather around.

"State your name and your business," Father says in his stentorian voice.

The man begins to rise, but Father beckons him to sit. "Oran, m' lord ... from Moorcrad Castle," he gasps. "... Attackers from the sea ... hundreds ... few of us ... we had no hope … everyone slaughtered … fortress robbed, burned."

"How did you escape?" Father's tone is gentler.

"I was in the forest, sire."

"Why did you not go back to fight?" demands the constable.

"I'm no fighter, sire," the peasant replies, trembling. "I'd been no help … I thought … warnin' the neighbors'd do more good."

Father queries the man about the invaders, and Oran responds the best he can. At the end of the questioning Father stands. "Eat something, then a few soldiers will accompany you to Moorcrad to search for more survivors." Turning to his counselors, he summons them to a meeting.

Selina and I remain in the hall to discuss the event with the excited servants and soldiers, then return to our half-finished needlepoint, still talking about what happened.

Father's meeting lasts a long time. Just before supper, he comes to our chamber. We both rise and greet him but he ignores us, and begins to pace. My stomach tightens. Finally he stops and turns to us. "This part of the country is becoming extremely dangerous. You must move to the castle of your betrothed. Their fortress, Bancloch, is on the north shore away from these raids, and Prince Christian is one of the bravest and most accomplished knights. You will be safer there—"

"Father, I want to stay." I am one of the few people who dare to disagree with him.

"You cannot stay here," he answers sternly and starts to pace again. "Moorcrad was the fourth of our neighbors attacked this summer. Our castle could be next. A fortress under siege is no place for young ladies. You must leave."

I look at Selina for reinforcement but she is staring at Father, dumbfounded.

"Father," I say, "I am one of the best archers and fencers in this castle; if you send me away you will lose a good fighter."

"This is not going to be a friendly joust. This fight will be about life and death."

"I want to stay and fight," I state firmly.

He stops pacing and folds his arms. "No, you cannot. You and your sister are leaving for Bancloch with the next spring tide."

"If the enemy comes by sea, would sending us by ship not expose us to more danger than staying here?"

"No. The raiders come from the southeast, and you will be sailing west and north."

"What about storms? Pirates? Perhaps we should travel by land," I argue.

He frowns and shakes his head. "The journey would be far more dangerous by land. Bandits, marauders, even some castle owners might attack you. You would require more soldiers, and it would take much longer. It is faster and more reliable by ship. We also have family along the shore; you shall visit them." He resumes his pacing.

I try another tactic. "Father, I thought our betrothals were withdrawn. We have had no contact with that family for years. You cannot just send us there."

"I have corresponded with the prince; they are expecting you."

"They are expecting us?" Surprise wells up in me, then anger. "You have written to them, and never said anything to us."

"I've held off the marriage for many years. I cannot do it any longer. You must move, set the date for the nuptial and, God willing, I will join you for the celebration. I would have the ceremony here if not for the attacks, but under the circumstances I have no choice. I explained everything to the prince in the letter."

"Father." I try once more to sway him. "You cannot just send us away."

He stops pacing and squares his jaw. "Ann-Marie, some-times we do what we must. And I want no more arguments."

I do. I want to show him how displeased I am. But I see care and weariness on his face. I could quarrel until he lost his patience—I have done it before. Not this time. He has enough on his mind.

When Father leaves, I'm fighting back tears. "This is not fair. Why do the women have to move?"

Selina, still dazed, shakes her pretty brown curls. "It is the custom."

"Custom?" I spit the word. "No. It is because men make the rules to favor themselves."

Once the initial trauma of the news wears off, I accept my fate. What else can I do? This is the lot of all princesses; sooner or later they leave home to live with (and at the mercy of) a husband. If he is good to her, she is lucky; if not … We were born to a life of duty, not pleasure.

Our young maid, Tara, will stay with us at Bancloch, along with our tutor, Eusabio, and an older knight, Sir Gavin. I am pleased to have Sir Gavin coming along. He's like a second father. He has taught me fencing, archery, and horsemanship. The other soldiers will return with the ship's crew as soon as they have delivered us.

Sailors ready the boat for the trip while Tara, Selina, and I spend our days packing. Since Selina is unusually quiet, and Father is too busy preparing for a possible attack, Tara, who sighs constantly, receives the brunt of my displeasure.

On the day before our departure, I bring flowers to Mother's grave. She has been gone three years now, and I still miss her. I climb to the watchtower to have a last look at the fields, the sea, and the busy courtyard. I have always loved to watch the world below from this tower—the highest point for miles.

In the evening, we have a farewell feast. As I gaze at the

familiar faces of the servants and the soldiers, I can barely hold back my tears.

Everyone comes to the shore to say farewell. After the goodbyes, Father escorts us to the ship and inspects everything. Before departing, he pulls from his pocket a small leather bag and takes from it a silver bracelet with intricate carvings and precious stones. He hands it to me. "This has been passed from mother to first-born daughter for generations. Pass it on to your first-born daughter, and instruct her to do the same."

I feel tears welling up, and quickly blink them back as I glance from the bracelet to Father. "This is beautiful," I exhale. "I will always treasure it." I kiss his bearded cheek, take the bracelet, and slip it on my wrist.

He presents Selina with a large bejeweled crucifix on a heavy gold chain. "This belonged to your mother, and she wanted you to have it."

He hangs it around her neck, then places his hands on our heads and blesses us. His eyes are unusually shiny as he hugs us, turns, and quickly leaves. My vision blurring, I watch as the soldiers row away. I send a prayer and blessings after him.

He waves from the shore, the captain barks some orders, the sailors slowly heave up the anchor while others start to row. With heavy hearts and frantic waving, our journey begins.

~ ~ ~

Our vessel is a modest merchant ship, propelled by a combination of sails and oars. It has only one cabin, which Selina and I share with Tara, and where we usually eat our meals with the captain and Sir Gavin. Everyone else eats on the deck and sleeps in the hold, in hammocks or on the floor.

The first few days bring steady wind and fair weather, and we make good progress.

Selina and I—never the pale and fragile indoor princesses—enjoy spending our time on the deck watching the sailors, practicing with the soldiers, or strolling up and down discussing the little we know about our future husbands.

"I have seen the prince only twice in my life," I tell Selina. "Once, when I was five or six and he was thirteen or fourteen, his family visited our castle. When Mother told me he would be my future husband, I was delighted. At least I was until I asked him to play with me and he said he did not play with little girls. I told him, 'I am not a little girl. I am your future wife.' He sniggered and joined the other boys."

We laugh, though the memory is more poignant than happy.

"I was twelve the next time we met at a tournament. He did very well. I was thrilled to know that this tall, elegant man would be my husband one day. He totally ignored me and presented his prize to another lady. I told Mother I did not want to marry him anymore. She laughed and said the prince would be far more interested in me in a few years' time. And although I remember him on his charger in full armor, I cannot recall his face."

"You know more than I do," Selina sighs. "I have never seen my future husband."

"You must have seen him when they came to our castle."

She shakes her head. "I cannot even remember their visit. I know Father wanted to join our family with that of his childhood friend, I just wish he had befriended someone from closer to home." We turn and walk toward the stern.

"Well, at least I had the good sense to nearly die at the age of four," I point out. "Had they not rushed to betroth you to the younger brother, we would be separated now."

Selina smiles. "Some good comes out of every trouble."

We stop by the railing to watch the waves and the gulls that follow the ship. As we begin to stroll again, I say with a frown, "If our engagements were canceled, why did Father decide to honor the betrothals and resume his correspondence with the prince now?"

"Perhaps because of the attacks," Selina suggests.

"Perhaps," I agree.

We have many similar discussions, and of course do not learn anything new, but they help to pass the time.

Soon we arrive at our first port of call, the fort of our uncle, and his wife—our father's sister—Aunt Eimear. She is a pretty brunette, who welcomes us warmly and invites us to stay for a few days, which we politely decline.

Aunt Eimear assigns a chamber. We bathe and change, then have a private meeting with her. I give her the gifts Father has sent, and she inquires about our father, brothers, and the people she remembers from her childhood at Ryston. We also chat about other relatives, the attackers and the upheaval they are causing, then she asks where we are heading.

"We are sailing to the north," I answer, "to marry the two princes of Bancloch."

Concern appears on her face. "Bancloch? Has your father lost his mind?"

I am instantly alert. "Why? What is wrong with the place?"

"I do not know about the place, but I heard …" She waves her hand. "Better not to talk about it."

"Aunt Eimear, you must tell us what is wrong," I insist. "We should know what to expect."

She pauses for a moment. "I heard—of course, I do not know for sure—that the present prince is the devil's grandson." She wrinkles her pretty brows. "He is hot tempered, a drunkard, a fighter who has killed people for no reason and deflowered many young maidens."

"Sounds like a typical prince," I say.

Our aunt has a good laugh, then turns serious. "He is worse than most of them. I don't know where your father got the idea to send you there."

"He is confident we will be safer at their castle than at home," I explain.

"I hope so." Aunt Eimear sounds unconvinced.

"Do you know anything about the younger prince?" Selina asks.

Aunt Eimear shakes her head. "I have not heard anything good or bad."

Later we visit with our cousins, and in the evening there is a big feast in our honor. In the meanwhile, the sailors and soldiers restock the boat and the next day we sail on.

"A drunkard and a fighter, with a bad temper, who kills people for no reason; he sounds the ideal husband," I say, while we are strolling on the deck. "Probably this is why the engagement was called off. When I asked Mother if the prince had jilted me, she said 'no' but refused to give any explanation. I asked Father ... you know Father ... he simply will not discuss anything he does not want to. They must have found out how evil the prince is."

Selina's brown eyes widen with concern. "Ann, what are we getting into?"

"Do not worry, we will handle it," I answer with more bravado than I feel. "If the prince is as bad as Aunt Eimear says, we will return home."

Selina sighs. "I hope we will have a home to return to." She likes to fret.

"Of course we will have a home."

"What would Father say if we returned?"

I watch the distant shore for a while before saying, "I will take care of that."

A few days later the wind dies down and we have to rely on the oars. This slows our progress. We watch the shore glide by and notice that the further north we travel, the wilder the country becomes.

We visit two more castles on the way. One belongs to our mother's brother, the other to our father's cousin. In both places we receive a warm welcome. We also hear more warnings about the older prince, while no one seems to know anything about the younger one.

I want to discuss the situation with the captain and Sir Gavin during dinner. "Sirs, you have heard all the disconcerting reports about the Prince of Bancloch."

They nod.

"If they are true, we will return home with the ship."

"Your highness," Sir Gavin says steadily, "your father will be angry if you rebel against his will."

"I will handle that," I say with feigned confidence. "I would much rather face an angry father than marry a violent drunkard. I will make my decision when we meet the prince."

~ ~ ~

The remainder of our trip is largely uneventful. We encounter one suspicious ship, which flees as soon as the captain orders all men on board, and for a few days we have such blustery weather both Tara and Eusabio become seasick.

At last we arrive at our destination: a graceful, newly built fortress of pale stone, situated on a cliff above a narrow crescent-shaped beach on which a few fishing dories are pulled ashore. We anchor in the small bay.

"Your highnesses," Sir Gavin says, while we are studying the surrounding country, "with the rumors we have heard about the prince, I wish to visit the castle with a few soldiers first to ensure your safety." He turns to the captain. "If I am not back by tomorrow or if anyone attacks you, you must leave at once without me."

Of course, the bad things you expect to happen seldom do. After a long, anxious wait, Sir Gavin returns and reports that the castle is safe.

The sailors row us to the shore and we climb the hill

with the captain, Sir Gavin, and the soldiers. The air smells different; a pleasant, pungent scent of wild herbs mingles with the salty sea air. I take a few deep breaths to inhale the fragrant breeze.

In spite of the constant wind we are hot by the time we arrive at the castle. Reaching the crest, we see a wide valley and a small village that snuggles in a dip on the lee side of the cliff. The cottages are well kept, but the soil looks poor and rocky, very different from the rich lands around our castle. Beyond the village, an ancient forest runs up the hills that block the view to the south.

Two men in their twenties and a middle-aged woman meet us in the courtyard. My heart skips a beat when I first see them. I did not expect to remember the prince, but I recognize his proud features and noble stance at once. Though I'm thoroughly prepared to dislike him, he affects me as he has always done: I feel a deep yearning to belong to him.

I discreetly scrutinize his face. He does not have the harsh lines of a heavy drinker or a violent man but he is pale and stares at me as if seeing a ghost.

"Let me introduce Princess Ann-Marie of Ryston," Sir Gavin gestures toward me, then motions toward my sister, "and Princess Selina of Ryston." We curtsy.

Confusion, then anguish flit across the prince's face. Is he disappointed in me? He steps forward. "I am Prince Christian of Bancloch." He bows. We curtsy again. He gestures to the man next to him. "My brother, Prince Ryan."

Prince Ryan is slightly shorter and sturdier than his brother. He has shoulder-length wheat-blond hair, and his blue eyes reveal a thoughtful modesty.

"And our Aunt Evelyn." Prince Christian gestures toward the tall, skinny woman with graying brown hair, green eyes, aquiline nose, and a strong chin.

We curtsy. "Good day, Lady Evelyn."

"Call me Aunt Evelyn. Everyone else does," she says. "I am sorry to leave your company, but I must go. I have a great many items to take care of." Turning, she hurries away.

"Welcome to Bancloch," Prince Christian bows again. "Your chamber will be ready in a short time. Until then I would like to offer some refreshments." He holds out his arm for me. As I place my hand on his, a pleasant shiver runs through my body.

I scan the courtyard. The castle is almost square with the keep in the middle, and the kitchen, workshops, and stables lining the outer walls. The few people in the courtyard watch us as we head toward the keep.

We enter the cool interior, and the prince leads us to the dais. Once we are seated, he says, "Lady Ann-Marie, and Lady Selina, your father's letter explained the situation. Let me assure you, you are most welcome, and my hope is that you will feel as much at home at our castle as you did in Ryston."

While he speaks, one servant places chalices in front of us, another fills them with golden mead, and a maid brings a plate of honey cakes.

The prince is very attentive as he asks questions about our trip, our father, and brothers.

To my mortification, I cannot stop gawking at him.

Aunt Evelyn returns to show us to our chamber. Our lodging consists of two rooms: a larger one with two beds, a table and four chairs; and a smaller dressing room with a cot. The soldiers bring our trunks up, but before we can unpack, it is dinnertime. As we join the princes on the dais, Prince Christian introduces everyone of importance: Sir Lorcan, the constable, a large, ruddy middle-aged man; Bishop Henry, the princes' cousin, a lanky fellow in his thirties with a grayish complexion; Mr. Welkin, the steward; and many others.

At the end of the dinner while the people are still sitting around chatting, the prince leans over. "Ann-Marie, how did you get here? You were supposed to return to your century."

"Return to my century? What do you mean, sir?" I feel puzzled not only by his question, but also by his intimacy.

"You do not remember our last meeting," he says.

"I remember it, my lord." I smile at him. "It was six years ago at the king's tournament."

"I am not talking about that time." I am glad he remembers our encounter. "I had hoped you would recall our meeting in the future."

This makes no sense. "My lord, how does one recall an event from the future?"

He seems disappointed. Before we can continue, a soldier interrupts us and whispers something to Prince Christian, who excuses himself and leaves.

I try to make sense of our conversation but cannot.

In the afternoon, while Selina, Tara, and I are unpacking and organizing our belongings, we talk about the first impression of our new home and the people we have met.

"Why have we heard so many bad reports about the prince?" I ask, taking a tunic from one of the chests and unfolding it. "So far he seems the paramount of chivalry."

Selina and Tara agree.

"Both princes are rather handsome," I say. "What do you think Selina?"

Selina blushes.

"Tara, do you think they are handsome?"

Tara blushes too. "Milady," she says, "I—I …"

Selina comes to Tara's aid. "Ann-Marie, it is not becoming to talk so brazenly."

"I do not see anything wrong with discussing the princes. I would bet a florin they are talking about us, too." I put the tunic on the bed and turn to Selina. "I want an honest answer. Do you think Lord Ryan is attractive?"

She blushes again.

"That means 'yes.'" I pick up another tunic. "We must decide by tomorrow afternoon whether we are staying or not."

"Ann-Marie," Selina says, "why are we unpacking if you do not intend to stay?"

"You are right," I laugh. "We should leave everything in the chests until we decide." I shake the tunic. "On the other hand, it is good to air out our clothes and linens, before they become musty."

"I think we should stay," Selina mumbles, folding a linen towel. "Both princes seem genuinely good men."

"Let us wait until we see how they behave tonight." I lift the last tunic. "A bit of mead can do wonders to inhibitions."

We work silently, and I think about the prince. Selina hands a pile of folded linens to Tara, who carries them to the dressing room.

"Selina," I say quietly, "what would you say if I told you Prince Christian believes he has met me in the future?"

"I would say you are teasing me, Sister."

"Actually, I am not. He told me he met me in the future."

"Ann-Marie you cannot be serious."

"I am serious."

Tara returns to the room. Not wanting to discuss this in front of her, we switch to a different subject.

In the evening we join everyone else in the great hall. I sit next to Prince Christian, and we talk about the attackers, tournaments, mutual acquaintances, and our families. He does not mention meeting me in the future.

I enjoy listening to his deep voice, and watching his handsome face. Every time he gazes into my eyes, which he does often, a sweet tingle runs through my body, and I have an overwhelming desire to touch him. He is pleasant company, does not drink excessively, and is polite to everyone. Why did we hear so many appalling rumors?

We listen to a troubadour recite a long legend about some fantastic voyage. A servant comes around with more mead. As the prince reaches for my chalice he brushes my hand, and again a pleasant shiver runs through my body.

Next day the ship is ready for the return trip. Selina and I have decided to stay. We spend the morning writing a long letter to our father telling him about the trip and our pleasant welcome.

The captain and the crew attend a farewell dinner. We accompany them to the shore. As I watch the ship disappear behind a cliff, I wonder whether we have made the right decision. If the prince does turn out to be a monster, we have no means of escape.

Chapter 11

Returning to the fortress, we pass the time fencing and target shooting in the courtyard with Sir Gavin. Shortly after he and I begin a match, Princes Christian and Ryan arrive. They watch us for a while, then Prince Christian says, "Sir Gavin, let me take your place."

The knight glances at me, I nod to him, he steps away, and the prince and I start to fence.

The way he holds his sword shows that he is an excellent swordsman. His moves are fast and light, and he proves a far more challenging opponent than Sir Gavin.

We finish our bout, and he turns to our knight. "From now on I will train with Lady Ann-Marie."

"My lord," I chime in, "you've failed to ask if I want to train with you."

With a small smile and a slight bow, he says, "My apologies, Lady Ann-Marie. May I ask if you would practice with me?" I ponder a way to say "yes" without sounding too eager.

Seeing my hesitation he says, "You will not be sorry, my lady. I am one of the best swordsmen in the country."

"I can tell that, sir." I smile at him. "I will train with you, as long as my sister and Sir Gavin practice with us too."

"Certainly. It will be a pleasure to have Lady Selina and Sir Gavin join us."

We finish fencing and begin target shooting. The targets are thick wood slabs with circles painted on them. I hit the center circle three times in a row. The prince says, "My lady, I can see that archery is not your nemesis anymore."

His remark surprises me. "Archery was never my nemesis, sir. I have been good at it since I was a little girl."

Disappointment flits across his face but in the next instant his warm smile returns. "Would you and Lady Selina be kind to join my brother and me for hunting and hawking tomorrow afternoon?"

We accept his invitation.

Later in the day, we meet with Aunt Evelyn and agree to run the household with her. In the evening the four of us— the two princes, Selina, and I—play checkers, and enjoy a light-hearted witty conversation about everything.

While getting ready for bed, I watch Tara comb Selina's long hair. "We had a lovely time," I tell Tara. "The princes seem rather chivalrous; they even let us win."

"Ann-Marie," Selina laughs, "they did not let you win. You beat them."

"I wanted to see if Prince Christian is a sore loser. He took losing in good stride. It still puzzles me why we have heard so many unsavory reports about him."

~ ~ ~

Next morning I wake up to Aunt Evelyn shaking my shoulder. "Time to get up, young ladies," she thunders in an intimidating voice. "None of this staying up all night singing, dancing, and flirting with the princes, and sleeping late into the morning; not in this castle."

"Aunt Evelyn, it is still dark," I mutter half asleep. "What kind of work cannot wait until the sun comes up?"

"We must check on the bakers and the cooks."

"Don't you have a master to oversee them?" I mumble sleepily, hoping she will go away.

"The master is good for nothing," she booms.

"Then find someone good," I murmur to my pillow.

Aunt Evelyn is not pleased. "Nice mistresses you are. Is this how you ran your household at home? Today's maidens. They are good for nothing. They care only about their clothes, dances, and dallying with the knights."

"Aunt Evelyn," I growl, "could we discuss the short-comings of today's maidens at another time?"

She ignores me. "What will happen to this place when I die? I am afraid the roof will cave in."

Boils. She will not leave until I am wide-awake. I prop myself up on one elbow. "I promise I will take good care of the roof when you die. Now, I want to sleep."

Sitting down, Aunt Evelyn puts the candle on the table. "Why did your father send you here in such an improper way? He should have dispatched a delegation invite the princes to marry you, then sent you away with them."

"We had no time for niceties," I answer.

"No time for niceties," she sneers. "How did he know you would come to no harm here?"

"How would he know we would come to no harm if we married first? Aunt Evelyn, we have been betrothed to those princes since we were born, even before."

"I hope your father has sent some dowry with you."

God, she is irritating. "Of course he did," I answer with great restraint.

"That's good. How old are you?" she asks.

"I am eighteen and my sister is sixteen."

"Eighteen and still a maiden," she gasps, horrified. "What is wrong with you?"

"Could we discuss this at another time?" I say crossly. "I would like to sleep."

"Sleep!" she screeches. "When there is so much work to do. Do you expect me to work myself into the grave managing this castle while you two sleep in late and flirt with those good-for-nothing princes?"

I sit up. "Aunt Evelyn," I use the warning tone I have learned from my father, "you cannot talk to me this way."

"I can talk any way I want," she says haughtily. "Who are you to tell me how to talk?"

By this time, I have had enough. I pull myself up with as much dignity and decorum as I can muster. "Aunt Evelyn, let us be clear. We will respect you, but you must respect us, too. We will work with you managing this castle and follow your routines. However, I do not want you to come barging into our room, ever."

"I mean … I tell …" Aunt Evelyn sputters. "What is this world coming to … you telling me what to do … I never … I never … how repugnant."

I lie down, turn my back to her, and to my relief, after some huffing and puffing about insolent girls, she leaves.

"That was good, Ann-Marie," Selina giggles from the other bed.

I turn toward her. "I hope the bakers appreciate that for once, they could do their morning chores in peace."

Selina and I have a long discussion about how to handle Aunt Evelyn. Since we cannot avoid her, we have to find some other solution. By breakfast, we have a plan. While making our rounds with Aunt Evelyn in the morning, we implement it.

"Selina, look at this room. This is the best organized scullery I have ever seen," I extol as we enter the scullery.

"The wool you produce here, Aunt Evelyn, is so soft and smooth," raves Selina in the weaving room. "It is like silk."

"Selina, look at this embroidery. It is astonishing." I point to a large tapestry in the great hall.

At the buttery Aunt Evelyn invites us to sample the brews. "This is the best ale I have ever tasted," Selina remarks.

"Aunt Evelyn, I cannot find words to tell you how well you run this castle," I enthuse.

"I am very grateful we came here," adds Selina. "We will learn so much from you."

And on and on we go flattering her.

It works.

By dinnertime, Aunt Evelyn tells us that we are the best-behaved, best-taught princesses she has ever met.

"The smartest, too," I say in our room.

"I think she is just starved for praise," Selina says. As usual, she is probably right.

In the afternoon we go hawking with the two princes. Prince Christian is so attentive and courteous—more chivalrous than anyone I have met—it baffles me why his reputation is so different from him.

Later we introduce Eusabio to the two princes. When Prince Christian finds out that he is a scholar from Italy, he sets up a meeting with him to discuss various subjects.

In the evening while Princes Christian and Ryan, Bishop Henry, and Eusabio debate the finer points of the Bible, Selina and I are once again dealing with Aunt Evelyn.

"I heard you went hawking this afternoon," she says.

"Yes, with great success," I enthuse. "Your forest is brimming with wildlife."

"I saw what you brought back." She purses her lips. "I would not call that a good haul. When I was young we used to bring in two or three times as much game."

"I am sure you did," I say as politely as I can. "Aunt

Evelyn, did you grow up in this castle?"

"Yes, I am the sister of the princes' father. My husband died in a tournament and I moved back here. It was about the same time my sister-in-law passed away so my brother asked me to manage the castle for him."

"When was that?"

"A long time ago."

"Do you have any children of your own?" I ask.

She frowns. "My niece and nephews are my children."

"How long were you married?" Selina asks.

"About three years." She stares into the distance as if seeing her past, then looks at us. "When are you two marrying my nephews?"

Selina and I glance at each other. "Maybe we should get to know them first," I say.

"Get to know them?" Aunt Evelyn sneers. "You will get to know them once you are married. All these newfangled notions about courtship and romance are nonsense. Marriage is marriage, not a love affair."

~ ~ ~

Soon our lives settle into the daily routine of making the morning rounds with Aunt Evelyn, training with the princes and Sir Gavin, lessons with the tutor (Prince Christian often joins us and "steals" the discussions), and entertainment or games in the evening.

Some mornings, by the time we finish our rounds with Aunt Evelyn, we are ready to kill her. Once we grumble in front of Tara, who says, "She seems to have a good heart."

From that time on whenever we are cross with Aunt Evelyn we say, "But she has a good heart." Alas, she has no respect for anyone, and no manners.

She never again comes into our chamber before dawn but keeps mentioning that when she was a young girl she had to be up before the sun, and had to learn about baking, cooking, brewing, weaving, sewing, herbs and healing, reading, writing, finances, fencing, archery, horseback riding, hunting, defending the castle … and many more skills. She had no time for idle chitchat, dallying, or sleeping until dinner. We could tell her that all princesses have to learn those skills, and that we do not sleep until dinner, but decide against it.

The princes are much better company than Aunt Evelyn is. Neither of them ever drinks too much. They never get into a fight, other than training with the soldiers, or do anything inappropriate, and they are polite, even to the scullery maids.

They are also charitable. The almoner has an order to give generously to any beggar who comes to Bancloch. Aunt Evelyn often complains about this, too. "A hunk of bread is more than they deserve," she grumbles. "Once the scum find out they can have plenty of food here, every beggar in this country will come to our door, until nothing will be left for us."

Once a month, the prince sends baskets of food and clothing to some of the widows and orphans in the surrounding villages. Aunt Evelyn objects to that too. "Give them free food and clothes, and they will become lazy good-for-nothings. No one will work if they can have all they want for free."

Selina and I are mystified. Why have we heard so many bad reports about the prince?

"Maybe they were talking about Aunt Evelyn," I joke.

Aunt Evelyn asks us every day if we have set the time for the weddings yet. When we tell her we have not, she shakes her head gravely. "Not good, not good at all."

A few times, I chance upon Selina and Lord Ryan alone; they look flustered when I disturb them. But Prince Christian and I never spend any time unaccompanied. He seems to enjoy being with me; we talk about everything (he is wise beyond his age), and sometime he seems to swallow me with his eyes (making my heart burst with joy) but then he withdraws showing no interest in becoming more intimate—and he never mentions marriage.

"What are those boys waiting for?" Aunt Evelyn grumbles. "I will have to talk to them."

~ ~ ~

We have been in Bancloch for about two months when, on a rainy afternoon while we are fencing in the main hall with the princes, two soldiers followed by Sir Lorcan drag in a peasant who has been caught killing a deer. Since the lords also act as judges, Prince Christian is to decide the man's fate.

The peasant, unshaven and disheveled, trembling, falls on his knees in front of the prince and, putting his hands together, begs, "Don' kill me, m' lord, don' kill me as yeh've killed others." I exchange a glance with Selina. So the prince has killed peasants. "Think of me family—wife, children, an' mother—what'll become of them?" the man pleads.

"I will not kill you," Prince Christian growls. "You know that serfs are not allowed to hunt deer."

"Yer highness, it was eatin' our garden." The peasant trembles.

"I am not interested in what the deer did. If it was eating your garden, you chase it away."

"I've tried, m'lord. I've tried," the peasant moans. "It wouldn't move, they know we can' harm them, an' they' not afraid."

Prince Christian glares at the man. "Further impertinence will earn you thirty lashes."

"Mercy, m'lord, have pity on me, yer humble servant," the man wails.

"If I allow you serfs to hunt whatever you wish, the large game would disappear within a few years and we would all go hungry."

"Yer right, m' lord, yer right," the man groans.

"I shall let you go this time," Prince Christian says. "You

must leave the deer in the kitchen. The head cook will give you a couple of rabbits and partridges; you can take them with you to feed your family. If you are caught again you will not get off so easily."

The man gapes at him with disbelief and relief, then throws himself at his feet. "Thank yeh, yer highness, thank yeh. God bless yer goodness."

"Stop groveling," Prince Christian orders him then turns to the soldiers. "Take him away."

The soldiers roughly pull the man to his feet. He stumbles to the door, bowing and repeating, "Thank yeh, m' lord, God bless, m' lord."

"I cannot believe this," grouses Aunt Evelyn, who, of course, had to hasten to the hall—she would probably die if she missed anything important. "He rewards him for killing a deer. What kind of punishment is that? You must be firm with the riffraff, or else they take advantage of us."

"Would you have preferred that I kill him?" Prince Christian asks crossly.

Aunt Evelyn narrows her lips, but says nothing.

In our room Selina and I discuss what happened and are more mystified than ever. Has the prince killed peasants as the man claimed? Why did he let this man go, even give him food? This makes no sense.

~ ~ ~

Next day during our rounds I tell Aunt Evelyn, "On the way here, we have heard many bad reports about Prince Christian, but he is the opposite of what we heard. Could you explain, please?"

"You heard." She waves her hand dismissively. "You cannot believe everything you hear, but in this case, what you heard was true."

Surprised, Selina and I exchange glances.

"He was once the worst devil in the land," she says.

"Everyone hated and feared him. He robbed, raped, and murdered his own peasants. About a year ago, while out hunting, he fell off his horse—many say someone attacked him—and he was as good as dead. Three days later he awoke, a changed man. When he recovered, he travelled the land, apologizing to the families he'd harmed, giving them gifts—a plot of land, a horse, or a cow. At first people thought he would soon return to his wicked ways, but when he did not they started to admire, even adore him. Many believe that while hovering on the edge of death, he went to hell and saw what fate awaited him, and that is why he has mended his ways. Personally, I think he lost his mind. He lives like a monk; he even moved out of the lord's chamber. What kind of lord would do that? He is too generous, too kind. People take advantage of him."

We ask many questions, which Aunt Evelyn eagerly answers.

In our room Selina says, "Father must have known about the prince's bad reputation, and that is why he delayed our marriages as long as possible. Does he know about the prince's change of heart?"

"He must if they corresponded. Why did he not tell us?"

Selina shrugs her shoulders. "It was not our business."

"It was not our business?" I feel anger rising in me. "Whose business was it? Are we chattel? He could have saved us a lot of anxiety, if he had respected and entrusted us with the truth."

Selina sighs but says nothing.

While I am half-asleep, snippets of Aunt Evelyn's tale echo in my mind. "Hovering on the edge of death ... went to hell ... became a changed man."

As I drift off to sleep, Prince Christian and I are strolling across a flower-strewn meadow. I reach out, and as I touch him, the familiar pleasant shiver runs through my entire body. Suddenly Christian is holding me in his arms, his lips hot against my own, then just as suddenly he is torn from my grasp, his anguished face disappearing into blackness.

One morning I wake to find Selina perched on the side of my bed, shaking me. "Ann-Marie, what do you dream about? You keep moaning 'no, no, don't go.'"

I sit up. "I do? It must be the dream." I tell her about the recurring nightmare.

"That explains your thrashing and groaning," she says.

I frown. "Selina, you may not believe this, but on the verge of the dream world I am convinced I have met the prince before. Do you remember the strange thing he told me on the first day about meeting me in the future?" Selina nods. "What if it happened? Maybe I should ask him?" I shake my head. "No, he might think I am mad, or worse."

Selina thoughtfully peers at me and says in a low voice, "You should ask him."

"It is risky. I do not want the prince to think something is amiss with me. What if I misunderstood him?"

"You will not know unless you ask," she answers wisely. "Also, he mentioned it first."

"You are right," I chuckle. "Better to ask than wonder for the rest of my life."

It takes a few more days and tormented nights before I figure out how to approach the prince. At suppertime I bring up the subject. "My lord, maybe I have misunderstood something, but on the first day you mentioned that you met me in the future." I watch his face. What if he denies it? "Would you care to elaborate?"

He smiles at me, and longing grips my heart. "Gladly," he says. "But not here. It is a strange tale, and I would rather discuss it in private."

"In private." I glance around the noisy hall. "Where could we talk in private around here?"

"We could talk in my chamber." His eyes embrace me warmly.

"Aunt Evelyn would die of indignation if I went to your quarters."

The prince laughs. "You are my bride; you are allowed to be alone with me."

At the words "you are my bride," an incredible joy washes over me.

Chapter 12

Next morning only a few servants are moving about, when Prince Christian whispers something to Aunt Evelyn. I cannot hear him, but everyone can hear her reply.

"Shame!" she screeches. "I have never heard such indiscretion. You want to be alone with her in your chamber. You should marry her first. What is this world coming to? I never spent a moment alone with my husband until we were wed."

Selina turns to me. "What is she so upset about?"

"I asked the prince the question," I whisper. "He wants to talk with me in his chamber—alone."

"That explains it," she whispers back. "Aunt Evelyn hates being excluded."

Prince Christian and I leave the great hall under Aunt Evelyn's reproachful gaze.

The prince's chamber—a small room with a table, a bed, two chairs, and many books—is on the top floor. He sits down on one side of the table and I on the other.

His hazel eyes gaze warmly at me. "So, Lady Ann-Marie, you desire to learn how we met in the future."

"Yes." I feel a bit awkward.

"As I have told you, this tale is rather unusual," he says, holding my eyes with his. "You might have heard that I used to be a much corrupted man. Last summer while I was out hunting, a wizard attacked and cursed me and I was unconscious for three days. Folks whisper that I went to hell; I went somewhere, but it was not hell. It was more like purgatory, except I was not dead. I had my body, had to eat, drink, and sleep. I could not return until I had a complete change of heart."

I watch his slender fingers toying with an inkpot, and the vision of a chess figure in his hand flashes through my mind.

"At first, I was furious and railed against the wizard and my fate, although I had no one to blame but myself. However, after hundreds of years my anger subsided and I strove to reform." He releases the inkpot. "To make a long story short, you, or someone like you, came. Her name was also Ann-Marie, but she was born in the twentieth century. I spent 900 years in that enchanted place. We broke the curse and fell in love, but we could not stay together." He swallows. "Sometime I am convinced you are the other Ann-Marie."

A wizard, a curse, 900 years, an enchanted tower, the twentieth century? While I try to gather my thoughts, the prince continues, "I know your father wants us to wed, but I cannot marry you—"

"Because you still love the other Ann-Marie?" I say.

He laughs. "Ann-Marie, will you stop interrupting people?"

"I am sorry," I mutter. "I did not mean to be rude."

"I cannot marry you, because in less than a year I will die."

My heart skips a beat. "No, you cannot die!" I leap to my feet. "You cannot die, Christian."

In an instant he is in front of me, gently lifting my chin. "Ann-Marie, I know you are the same person I met in the tower. I can feel it."

His closeness sets my body on fire. He lowers his head to kiss me, but I turn my head. "What if I am not the same Ann-Marie? I do not want you to kiss me because I remind you of someone else—a phantom, or a vision. If I am the same person, why can't I remember what happened?"

"I do not know." The prince frowns, taking my shoulders. "Neither can I understand why you are here; you were to return to your time." He peers at me with so much love, my insides tighten. "I am certain you are the same person."

"How could I be the same person?" I cry, frustrated.

He smiles. "For one, you keep interrupting me. You also seem to be in love with me since you have arrived—"

"No, my lord," I interrupt again. "I have been—" I stop. I almost said that I have been in love with him since I first saw him at age six.

"You have been …?" he asks, lifting his eyebrows.

"Nothing," I mumble.

He scrutinizes my face as if to find the answer there. "I know you are the same person."

"My lord," I say in a husky voice, "I am not questioning your integrity, but your tale is rather farfetched. I pray tell more about your adventures in that enchanted place."

He releases my shoulders, leans against the table, and relates a woeful tale about princesses failing and dying until he and Ann-Marie broke the curse and fell in love. He talks about her with so much love; jealousy, envy, and sadness grip my heart. Could he ever love me as much as he loves her? Hiding my feelings, I ask many questions, and he answers them thoroughly. The more we talk the more plausible his story becomes. Still, I feel no connection to it.

I sigh deeply. "I wish I knew if the Ann-Marie in your adventure was I or someone else."

In that instant, as if a floodgate has opened, I remember the prince, the tower, and the wizard. I close my eyes, and pictures of our life together flash into my mind: the evenings in front of the fire, the rides, the games, everything; my longing for my family and life in the twenty-first century; our last day at the tower; the wizard's prediction about

Christian dying within two years—and why we had to part.

"Christian." I reach for him, and he pulls me close.

"I knew from the moment you arrived that it was you."

I melt into his embrace. He lowers his head to kiss me—

Somebody knocks on the door and Christian softly curses.

Aunt Evelyn pokes her head in. "I am sorry to interrupt, but this is an emergency. I must talk to Christian in private."

We let go of each other. "I'm surprised she could stay away this long," Christian mutters.

I giggle. "See you later." I wave and leave.

~ ~ ~

I am bursting with excitement, and want to tell Selina what happened. I search the kitchen, the hall, the scullery, the weaving room, even look into the blacksmith's shop, and the stables. She has disappeared. No one has seen her. Finally, I find her with Lord Ryan and the steward going over payments.

Not wanting to disrupt their work, I return to our chamber. I have so much to think about. But as soon as I settle on the window seat Christian arrives.

I smile at him. "Did you take care of Aunt Evelyn's emergency?"

"Emergency? She wanted my advice about some dishes. Dishes! Since when do dishes concern me?" He says this with so much indignation I have to giggle. "I wanted to find you, but it seems you had a tour of the entire castle."

I giggle again. Boils. I am giggling like a love-struck peasant girl. "I tried to find Selina."

"She is with Ryan and the steward."

"I know. I found her eventually." I grin. Where's my dignity?

"We must talk." He sits down beside me on the window seat.

"Yes, we must."

He takes my shoulders and pulls me closer to kiss me, but I place my hands on his chest. "Christian, I want to clear up a few matters first. Why did you not recognize me in the enchanted tower? At least you should have recognized my name."

"Ann-Marie, the last time I had seen you, you were twelve years old. How could I recognize you? Also, do you think you are the only woman called Ann-Marie?" Suddenly, his eyes lighten. "Why did you not recognize me in the tower?"

I swallow. I don't like him turning the tables. "I was from the twenty-first century. I had never seen you before."

He frowns. "Maybe it was the result of the magic, but you were a total stranger to me, too."

"So were you," I giggle. Boils, this giggle. I try to straighten my face. "My lord, maybe you can enlighten me as to why our engagement was canceled."

"It was not canceled, it was suspended. Your father forbade me to visit until I changed my corrupt ways. I wrote to him last year to inform him that I have reformed, and if he were still interested in binding the two families, Ryan would gladly marry Lady Selina. Unfortunately, I could not marry you."

My eyes widen. "You sent him a letter saying that you would not marry me," I gasp, "and he still sent me here."

"Luckily, he did." He beams at me, trying to lower my arms, which are still wedged between us, but I keep my palms firm against his chest. "He appealed to my chivalry, asking me to ensure that both of you are safe."

"I wonder how much you actually love me, if you refused to marry me when I was not a princess. Evidently, title is far more important to you than I am."

His face saddens. "I regretted it more than anything else I have done. The wizard recommended that I marry you; he did not tell me that was the only way we could stay together." He stares deeply into my eyes. "Will you forgive me?"

My first thought is I should teach him a lesson, but as I gaze at his warm, soulful eyes, I have only one feeling: love. Maybe I should punish him, but why play games. "I forgive you," I say solemnly.

In a flash, he lets go of my wrists and pulls me close to him. My hands slide up to the back of his neck, his lips are on mine, his tongue is gently pressing my lips apart. Oh what a kiss this is! It conveys everything: love, passion, forgiveness, gladness. It lifts me all the way to heaven.

We let go and Christian asks, "Lady Ann-Marie, would you do me the honor of becoming my wife? I know I will die next summer but—"

"I would marry you even if you died the week after our wedding," I laugh. "A week of bliss would definitely be better than no bliss at all."

For a reply, he kisses me again.

"This is a dream come true," I whisper to him. "I wonder what Selina will say."

He frowns. "Are you going to tell her about it?"

"Not about the kiss." I smile at him. "I will definitely tell her about our meeting in the enchanted tower." He begins to say something, but I place my finger on his lips. "Selina and I have been honest with each other our entire life. It is the secret of our friendship."

He takes my hands. "Ann-Marie, will you be honest with me too?"

"I am planning to be; what about you?"

"Let's vow that we will always be honest with each other as long as we live."

I solemnly place one hand onto his palm and another one on my heart. "I promise you, Prince Christian of Bancloch, to be honest with you all my life."

He puts a hand on his heart. "I swear to God and his angels I will always be honest with you, Lady Ann-Marie of

Ryston." We seal our promise with another kiss.

This time Selina interrupts us.

"Sorry," she says and is about to leave. Christian stops her.

"Lady Selina, I have something important to announce to you and Ryan. Where is Ryan?"

"He has just left." Selina motions toward the stairs. "He went downstairs," she calls after Christian who is already out the door.

Her eyes wide, she turns to me. "What is happening?"

"You will find out in a moment." I smile at her. "And I will tell you the details later."

Christian returns with Lord Ryan, takes my hand into his, and says, "I have an important announcement to make: Lady Ann-Marie and I will wed soon."

Selina and Lord Ryan glance at each other. "We should wed on the same day. Lady Selina and I were thinking about Christmas."

"Selina, why did you not tell me?" I turn to my sister who is blushing furiously.

"I—I did not want to marry before you did," she mumbles.

"You should not make your happiness depend on what I do. Congratulations." I beam. "To you too, Lord Ryan."

"Perhaps, Lady Ann-Marie," Ryan says hesitantly, "you could call me Ryan; after all, we will be family soon."

"And you can call me Ann-Marie." I smile at him. Christian and Selina also agree to be on a first name basis.

"Why do you want to wait until Christmas for the wedding?" I ask Selina.

"It would leave enough time for Father to come," Selina answers.

I am a bit ashamed; I did not even think of Father. I just wanted to get into bed with Christian as soon as possible.

"Christmas it is then." Christian grins.

~ ~ ~

At dinner we announce our Christmas wedding. Everyone cheers. In the afternoon the four of us meet with Aunt Evelyn to discuss the preparations for the wedding feast.

Aunt Evelyn wants to invite the king, and a thousand guests, and she wants hundreds of minstrels, and jongleurs, and a tournament; and to do it all properly she wants to move the nuptial to next summer. When Christian rejects all her grand ideas, she storms out, telling us that in that case we shall organize the wedding without her. Fine with me.

In the evening I tell Selina, about my "double identity." First she is very skeptical, but after many questions, says, "Though this story sounds implausible, I shall believe you, for I know you as a truthful person."

I cannot sleep. First I replay in my mind our talk with Christian—and the kisses—then I recall our life in the enchanted tower and my life in the twenty-first century.

It is strange. I awoke this morning, as Princess Ann-Marie of Ryston. Right now I don't even know if I am Ann-Marie Ryston or Ann-Marie Burke. Am I in the twenty-first century dreaming I live in the twelfth, or am I in the twelfth century believing I have another life in the twenty-first?

What if I am dead in the future? Nothing I can do about that.

I remember the three magic wishes. It must be due to them I'm here in Christian's time and am able to recall what happened in the tower. But in that case, I must have used up all my wishes.

I sigh. If only I had one more wish I would stop the attack.

Will there be an attack? Will Christian die next summer as the wizard has predicted?

I don't want him to die. I want to live a long life with him, carry his children, grow old together … In that instant, somewhere deep inside I make my decision: if Christian dies, I will die with him.

~ ~ ~

In the following weeks whenever we are alone Selina asks questions about the twenty-first century. She is surprised to learn how different life is. She finds the idea that a machine (I have to describe what a machine is) can fly unbelievable. I try to explain about aerodynamics, without much success.

Eventually our attention returns to the present, and we talk mostly about the wedding preparations and refurbishing our new quarters.

When, despite Ryan's protest, Christian forces him and Selina to take the lord's chamber, which is presently unoccupied, Selina apologizes profusely to me.

I laugh. "I don't care which chamber I get as long as there is a bed and Christian in it."

"You shameless hussy." Selina laughs. "Is this how women talk in the twenty-first century?"

"Sometimes even worse." I tell her that women have a lot more freedom in the twenty-first century than ever before; at least in Western countries. I have to explain to her about Western and Eastern societies, and the round earth, and continents people in the twelfth century never even heard about. She can't stop saying, "This is simply incredible."

Aunt Evelyn, in spite of her initial refusal to help with the wedding preparations, wants to do everything. Daily, she assails us with another suggestion to make the celebrations better, and becomes very offended if we dare to reject her "fabulous" ideas.

"Whose wedding is this, ours or hers?" Selina often protests.

Everything is going well, as well as it can with Aunt Evelyn's constant excitement, but we have a new concern. Although we have sent three letters and a messenger to our father, he has not replied.

Chapter 13

A week before the wedding, Aunt Evelyn and I are in the kitchen when I hear distant horns. "Maybe it is our father," I say, ready to sprint.

"It is not." She holds me back. "It is my niece, Orla."

"How do you know?"

"Only Orla would come with such kerfuffle. I recognize that abhorrent tune her soldiers play." Aunt Evelyn must have good ears; I can't make out any tune. "But we have no time for her," she adds doggedly. "We must finish our round first."

I would have missed my future sister-in-law's arrival if Christian had not fetched me. Aunt Evelyn mutters something about coming as soon as she is free.

Lady Orla's entrance is quite a spectacle. About twenty knights on horses, carrying colorful flags and blowing horns, enter first. Next is a smart carriage, followed by a simpler one, and more soldiers. The procession stops, a servant opens the carriage door and helps a rather plump blond woman from the coach. Once on the ground, she stomps her feet, stretches her arms, and announces, "Ah, the ancestral home."

She is comely. Her features are a mixture of Christian's straight nose and hazel eyes combined with Ryan's high cheeks and light blond hair. She is so smartly dressed; Selina and I look dowdy compared to her.

She warmly hugs Christian and Ryan then, glancing around, asks, "Where are the illustrious brides?"

Christian introduces me, and I curtsy. "Good day, Lady Orla."

"Please call me Orla," she says. Then leaning closer, she whispers into my ear, "Are you the lady who met Christian in that enchanted place?"

What? Christian told her about the enchanted tower? I

did not expect that. As if reading my thoughts she says, "I know what happened while he was comatose." With a laughter that sounds like the gurgling of a little brook, she adds, "What baffles me is how you could endure him."

I smile. "He was much reformed by the time we met."

She laughs again.

When Ryan introduces Selina, Lady Orla says, "What a sweet name. I wish I was young again, so fresh and innocent, and with such a charming name." Scanning the people, she asks, "Where is Evelyn?" She answers her own question. "I know. She is occupied with important matters."

Aunt Evelyn has assigned one of the smallest chambers to Orla.

"My maid sleeps in a bigger room than this," Orla says, smiling irreverently at her. "If that's the best you can offer, I will gracefully accept it. But when these two innocents move in with their husbands, I will take up their quarters."

At suppertime, at Orla's request, we are sitting at a small separate table.

"Why have your husband and children stayed at home?" Aunt Evelyn asks with disapproval in her voice.

"They knew you would give us a cupboard for accommodations," Orla laughs, "and preferred our spacious castle." With a mischievous grin she adds, "They stayed at home because they needed to be away from me."

Aunt Evelyn scowls.

"How many children do you have?" I ask Orla.

"Five here, three in heaven. They range between ages one and twelve."

"You should have brought the youngest one." Aunt Evelyn chides her.

"Definitely not the youngest," Orla says. "The trip would have been too much for her. Also, if I bring one the others would want to come too; it was better to leave them all at home. I have come here to be merry."

Aunt Evelyn's lips tighten.

"By the way, Evelyn," Orla says, "while I am here these two lovely damsels will be my companions. I need their unsullied, refreshing company." Aunt Evelyn's eyes flash, but Orla ignores it. "I know you will miss working them to death, but you will have to do without for this week."

When we show Orla our dresses, she claps her face in mock horror. "No, no. These are not appropriate. They are too plain."

"I like them," I say.

She shakes her head. "You dress for the people, not for yourself. Folks want to see royalty as dazzling, colorful, grand. It makes them happy. Your life is their dream life. You should not disappoint them." She holds up one of the dresses and studies it with tilted head. "We need to add some embroidery, some lace, and lower the waistline."

Next day we work on the gowns in our chamber.

"I hope you enjoy this chamber," she says while browsing through a box of laces. "It used to be mine—a long, long time ago. It was filled with delightful dreams, lofty aspirations, and unrealistic expectations." She laughs.

"What did you find the most challenging about married life?" I ask.

"Being married," she answers with another laugh. "It is all a challenge. When I finally enjoyed him in bed, I stayed with child. Then my first baby was born and I loved him more than I loved my husband. But husbands have this thing about wanting attention or they look elsewhere. After the third child it was easy; I realized that he is much less trouble than the children."

"What would happen if on your wedding night you found out that he has some ugly mark on his body?" Selina asks.

"I don't think it would be of importance," Orla answers

with another light-hearted laugh. "Eventually you'll find worse marks on his soul, not to mention his annoying habits."

"What do you think would ensure a happy marriage?" I ask.

"What do you think?"

"Love and forgiveness," I say.

"Love and obedience," Selina says.

"Obedience?" Orla wrinkles her nose. "Who do you think should be obedient, you or him?"

Selina titters. It is beyond question, the wife has to be.

"Obedience is for dogs—and even dogs are not good at it." Orla laughs. "Never give up your good sense, not for him, not for anyone else. You will only resent and regret it in the end."

"What would ensure a happy marriage?" I ask again.

"Nothing," she laughs. "Keep your humor; keep your spirit, especially in the face of misfortune. My first daughter's death devastated me; life went on. Life wants you to recover and be happy again. Let it make you happy!" She pauses and continues more seriously, "You and I, we are fortunate; we could be one of those wretchedly poor folks whose life is nothing but toil and misery. Every time I see one I thank God for my blessings, knowing well that they could end by a change of fortune. You cannot take anything for granted." She stands up and shakes the dress she is hemming. "Now let us see how these dresses are coming along."

One afternoon, Selina asks, "What if he kept a mistress, as so many do?"

Orla laughs. "It depends on what you want. If he wants you in his bed seven times a week, and you want him only twice, let him have others. If you resent sharing, kick them out, but then you have to supply all his needs. Remember, your husband is the most desirable man in his castle, and it is difficult to keep women away from him, especially if he has an eye for them. But never forget yours will be the only legitimate children."

"No way would I want to share Christian," I say.

She smiles at me. "Keep him interested in you. Do not be a wallflower or a recluse unless he is one. Few of them are and Christian definitely is not."

When we are alone, I ask her, "Christian told me about your dreadful childhood, but you seem so happy. How did you surmount such distress?"

"I moved beyond. I was never too sensitive. That was my mother's forte. She was a timid dreamer. She thought that chivalry was meant for the wives ... maybe for someone else's wife." She laughs. "I am not mocking her memory, but growing up with Father has taught me not to have high expectations." After a short pause she says, "Christian told me how you broke the curse. I forgave too. People think princesses have perfect lives. But life does not care whether you are a princess or not. It will bring trials, triumphs, sadness, happiness, everything. You choose how you react to them."

Orla asks many questions about the twenty-first century. When I tell her about birth control, she is amazed. "Do you mean women do not have to have a child every year?"

"Yes, couples can choose how many children they want and when. Most of them settle for two or three."

"That explains why women have more power and freedom in that age. Birthing and caring for children use up so much of women's time and strength, they must leave the running of the world to men." She laughs. "But when women have more say, the world becomes a better place."

I ask Orla why Aunt Evelyn dislikes her.

"We grew up together," she answers. "Our father was the eldest, Evelyn the youngest. She is only five years older than I am, more like an older sister than an aunt." This surprises me because Aunt Evelyn seems an old woman compared to Orla.

"She was a petulant child.... During her short, ill-fated marriage she had several miscarriages, and when her husband passed away, she chose the tragic widow role, and it has turned her bitter. She is unhappy and wants to make everyone else the same."

We have many other discussions, and I am glad to have met Orla. I am also sad, because she lives too far away to meet often.

~ ~ ~

We still have not heard from our father or the messenger we sent with the invitation. Even Christian, whose words and touch always reassure me, cannot dispel the unease Selina and I feel about our father's lack of response. We pray for our family's safety, send another pigeon, exchange worried glances, comfort each other; nothing helps. Our father's absence casts a disquieting shadow over our happiness.

Aunt Eimear and Uncle Allard arrive the day before the wedding and tell us they also have not heard anything, but the way they glance at each other makes me wonder if they are telling the truth.

This is the last night Selina and I share a room. We reminisce about our childhood and speculate about the future, saying goodnight dozens of times in between.

The night watch changes. This means it is long past midnight, but we still cannot sleep. Finally, we drift off only to be awakened in the next moment—so it seems—by Aunt Evelyn's booming voice.

"You must get up or you'll miss your wedding," she roars.

Good heavens. Today is the wedding.

In an instant we are wide awake.

The morning is beautiful. After many weeks of grayness and rain, we wake to fresh snow that has magically transformed the drab, ordinary world into an ethereal, splendid beauty.

"I take this as a good omen," I tell Selina.

Aunt Evelyn disagrees. "Rain on your wedding day brings bad luck."

"This is not rain," I object. "This is snow."

"It is the same," she says.

We have breakfast in our chamber because according to Aunt Evelyn, it is bad luck to see one's future husband on the wedding day before the ceremony.

Orla and her maid arrive to help us to get dressed, and Aunt Evelyn, using the excuse she must supervise the last minute preparations, leaves.

Both Selina and I have chosen a light-blue gown, the color of the Virgin Mother, thus innocence. I also wear a light blue agate choker and, of course, the bracelet our father gave me. I help Selina fasten her crucifix and we exchange a worried look. Neither our father nor any of our five brothers have come, but there's no time for fretting. A horn blast reminds us that the ceremony is about to start. Tara hands us our bouquets. They are made from evergreens (fine), herbs (fine), and dried flowers, (not fine because, according to Aunt Evelyn, they bring bad luck).

If the common folks want to see princes and princesses as colorful, showy, and grand, they cannot complain about our wedding. With elegant carriages, fine horses, and colorfully dressed servants; the great hall and the bailey decorated with hundreds of flags and shields; non-stop music and entertainment; the lords and ladies arrayed in swishing gowns and glossy tunics adorned with gold, silver, and precious stones— we could impress anyone, probably even the king.

We begin the celebration outside the chapel, where Christian and Ryan are waiting for us. Christian, dressed in midnight blue trousers and a gold-embroidered tunic, is so handsome I cannot stop staring at him.

The bishop says a few words, then Christian takes my hand, turns to the people, and says, "You are my witnesses that I receive Princess Gwendolyn Ann-Marie Rose of Ryston as mine." He turns to me. "From this moment on you are my wife and I am your husband."

His words jolt me. I am his! His wife. We belong together. Gazing at his handsome face, so much love floods me, I can barely say the words: "I receive you Prince Christian John Rupert of Bancloch as mine, so that you become my husband and I become your wife." Christian pulls me to him and kisses me more passionately than ever. In front of all the people.

After Selina and Ryan exchange their vows, we enter the chapel to celebrate our first Mass as husband and wife.

In his sermon Bishop Henry spells out how God-fearing, virtuous Christian couples must conduct themselves. "If you want to avoid burning in hellfire for eternity," he booms, "you must shun the lustful desires of your corrupted flesh. You must refrain from all amatory pleasures such as lewd kisses, fondling, passionate embraces, and entwining of your naked bodies. They are the means by which the devil entraps unsuspecting souls. The reason for the marital act is not hedonism, but procreation—the sacred duty of those who choose marriage over the more blessed and saintly celibate life." He warns us that even married couples must abstain from the carnal knowledge of their spouses during Advent, Lent, Holy Week, Easter, Whitsuntide, Sundays, Wednesdays, and feast days, also on Fridays, because on that day our Lord suffered and died for us. He cites the example of a husband and wife who remained virgin their entire lives "as did the Lord's parents that most holy couple whom we should all emulate." He does not explain how we could fulfill our sacred duty to procreate if we followed his counsel of staying virgins our entire lives.

"Henry, you need to find yourself a good woman," Orla tells him after Mass.

"Women are the devil's instruments to trip men up," he sputters.

Orla, laughing, waves him away. "Men are the devil's instrument to trip women up."

Henry gives her a dark, angry stare.

"Do not look at me so lividly," Orla laughs. "It is not becoming of a representative of Christ." Placing her hand on his arm, she says, "Asceticism is filling your heart with hatred, Henry. Life is good, embrace it."

The bishop jerks his arm away, but before he can reply, Ryan interrupts the exchange. "Lords and ladies, we should return to the great hall."

Inside, tables are set up for the nobles; outside, tents for the villagers and servants. The feast is a great success. It begins with an entire roasted calf, from which a dozen doves escape, followed by one fancy dish after another. Even the dogs have more than enough to eat; ale and mead are freely served; and the entertainment does not stop all night.

Aunt Evelyn, a wound-up marionette, runs around all day. She is everywhere constantly telling everyone what to do.

Around midnight the master of ceremonies, who is so inebriated he can hardly stand, announces that the most important part of the wedding ceremony has arrived: putting the new couple to bed.

I hate this barbarian ritual, but this is not the best time to change the custom.

The master, tottering, leads the procession. Christian and I follow him; Ryan and Selina have to wait for their turn. A group of drunks trail us shoving and pushing, and telling Christian in explicit language what to do, while some of the women, also intoxicated, are shouting advice to me. They push us into our chamber and force us down on the bed. I feel uncomfortable facing those drunks lying down. Suddenly a man whose breath reeks of liquor grabs me. "You must give me one of those passionate kisses, my precious," he roars.

Slam. Christian hits the man so hard he would have fallen if his companions did not catch him. For a second, tension fills the air. Will there be a fight on our wedding night?

"These people are boring. Let's get the other couple," Sir Gavin yells.

"Yes, let's," Sir Lorcan shouts in agreement.

Jostling, the people leave our quarter. The man who tried to kiss me challenges Christian to a fight. His friends shove him out. "Are you mad," one says. "Even if you were sober he would kill you."

Frazzled, Christian and I sit on the bed listening to the raucous noise descending the stairs. The noise level increases again. The rowdy group is climbing up with Selina and Ryan.

As they boisterously push them by our door, which is still open, I can see Selina's frightened face for a second, then Ryan as he is trying to protect her from the unruly crowd. They move towards their quarter, and … Selina screams.

Christian jumps off the bed. "That is enough!" he bellows through the doorway. "Everyone! Out! Unless you want to meet with my sword."

The people grumble about lack of hospitality, but the two brothers, with Sir Gavin and Sir Lorcan's help, clear them out. While they are herding the mob down the stairs, I ask Selina what happened. "Someone grabbed me from behind."

"Perhaps the same halfwit who tried to kiss me," I say.

Our husbands come back. We say good night to each other and retire to our newly furnished chambers.

Finally, Christian and I are alone.

~ ~ ~

We stand in front of the closed door, and I become self-conscious. "What are we supposed to do now?" I ask, probably winning the prize for the stupidest wedding night question.

"We are supposed to consummate the marriage without satisfying the lustful desires of our corrupted flesh," Christian answers, deadpan.

I laugh. The next second, as he is leaning closer, I fall under his spell, and my body tenses up with anticipation. I close my eyes, feel his lips on mine, and …

In the next few days we do everything the good bishop cautioned us not to. We give lewd kisses, passionate embraces, and entwine our naked bodies. We just cannot have enough of each other.

The only people we see are the chamberlain and two pages, who bring food, drink, firewood, and prepare a bath each day, while discreetly keeping their eyes to the floor.

"It would be nice to have running water and central heating," I say after supper when we are alone. "Maybe we should introduce some twenty-first century technology."

Christian laughs. "I thought about it too, but you cannot; there is no knowledge or infrastructure to support it, and most people would reject it as sorcery. Both technological and social advances must come from within the culture. They cannot be forced." He pauses. "If they are forced, as soon as the force ceases, the advances disappear. Even worse, they leave chaos behind."

I had almost forgotten that history is Christian's favorite subject.

"I miss my books, and my magic device," he says. "I used to spend most of my afternoons visiting different parts of the world in different ages."

"That had to be fun. I wish I could have done it. Was it strange to return to this time after learning so much about other eras and cultures?"

"It took some getting used to." He chuckles, then gazes deeply into my eyes. "I have missed you more than anything else. I could not stop thinking about you and about what an ass I was."

"I hope you remembered to forgive and love yourself for being an ass."

"I did not." He laughs. "But I wrote a few songs about how I felt."

"Did you? Could I hear them?"

"If you promise not to laugh."

I promise.

Christian rises, finds his lute, and sings:

My happiness has turned to sorrow, in the night I cry,
And my pillow soaks up my tears; I have lost my treasure,
My princess, my life, without her everything is empty and dark.
I want death to come and console my desperate and lonely soul.

I am deeply touched. "Were you that dejected?"

"I was." His eyes warmly caress my face. "I wanted the attack to come as soon as possible so I could die."

"Oh, Christian, I hope there will be no attack. Maybe the wizard was wrong."

"Maybe, though unlikely."

"Christian if you die, I will die with you."

"Let us not talk about dying. Do you remember any of the songs from the twenty-first century?"

To my surprise, I do. We exchange songs as we did at the tower.

We spend one blissful day after another making love and reminiscing about our life at the enchanted tower. A week is gone by the time we decide to return to "real life."

In the great hall people greet us with enthusiastic clapping, whistles, and shouts.

During breakfast Orla tells me, "I wanted to leave a few days ago but had to find out how long you two would take. You probably hold the record for the longest wedding night."

Aunt Evelyn does not say anything; her prim face tells more than words could.

Orla leaves soon after breakfast, and we promise to write to each other.

Chapter 14

In mid-January, our brother, Brent, arrives with the messenger.

Brent is my favorite brother. He has always been kind to us, his younger sisters. Kieran, our oldest brother, usually ignored us; Fergus, the second oldest, mercilessly teased us. But Brent was chivalrous, even as a little boy. He, like Selina, inherited our mother's brown eyes and unruly brown hair but, unlike Selina, inherited our father's tall, rugged stature.

He is talking with Christian when I enter the great hall.

"Oh, Brent, it is so good to see you." I fly into his embrace. "Tell me, what is new at home?"

Grief tightens his face and I know what we feared the most has come to pass. "Did—did …?"

He nods and swallows hard, but before he can say anything, Selina arrives with Ryan.

She kisses Brent on both cheeks and asks gently, "Were you there, Brent?"

He nods again. He seems weary and much older than he looked a few months ago.

"Brent, would you prefer to tell us about it now," I ask, "or do you wish to rest first?"

"Lord Brent needs to rest first," Aunt Evelyn answers.

Where did she come from?

"Thank you, my lady." Brent bows at her. "But I had better tell my sisters about the fate that has befallen us." We sit down on the dais. Servants bring cold meat, cheeses, bread, and ale for Brent. He cuts a piece of cheese, and breaks a chunk of bread. "It could have been far worse if Father hadn't prepared for the attack. He sent our two youngest brothers, the women, and the children away. He dispatched me to visit the surrounding castles to garner help. I kept him informed about my whereabouts, so as soon as an attack came he could notify me. I had gathered over one hundred knights by the time the messenger arrived. At once we set out for the castle, and reached it in a couple days. The siege was already underway."

Christian takes my hand into his.

"Since we were outnumbered by at least five to one, we decided to split into three groups, hoping to make the impression there were more of us than actually were. First, the group on the east attacked; the invaders turned their force against them. Then the group on the west sprang into action. This confused the enemy, and when the knights from the north stormed out, they panicked, and utter chaos followed. In the meanwhile the defenders opened the gate and joined the fight. We had slain most of the savages, but the victory came with heavy losses. Many of our knights were killed or injured, including our two elder brothers, and Father."

My heart skips a beat. Christian tightens his hand around mine.

"Do you know how they died?" Selina asks.

"Yes," Brent answers, his face darkening. "But I will spare you the details." Searching in his pouch he says, "I have a letter for each of you from our father."

A letter from Father. I eagerly take it. Though etiquette requires that I read it aloud, I do not want to share. Not yet. The letter is short.

Ann-Marie, my beloved daughter,

I am relieved you have arrived safely in Bancloch and find it agreeable. I pray you forgive me if the prince is unpleasant. I could not send you anywhere else.

My dear daughter, I will not see you again—not in this life. Pardon my trespasses against you. I pray that God smile on you and bless your life.

Your Father

Selina reads her letter and begins to weep uncontrollably. I try to comfort her, but she shakes off my hand and runs upstairs. Aunt Evelyn follows.

I cannot cry.

I reread my letter many, many times. Why is he asking me to forgive him? I should ask him to forgive me. How often I pestered him just to have my way. How often I took advantage of his patience and kindness.

If he had not insisted on sending us here, I would never have experienced the bliss of loving someone with all my heart and being loved in return. I wish I could tell him how grateful I am. I wish he could see our happiness ... Maybe he can from above.

"Brent," I say, rudely interrupting the discussion, "when did our messenger arrive in Ryston?"

"Sometime in November," he answers.

"Then you could have attended our wedding, or at least send the messenger back."

"I did not want you to find out about Father's death before," he says, and returns to his discussion with his brothers-in-law.

While I try to decide whether he acted high-handedly or considerately, Aunt Evelyn returns. "Lord Brent, you must have some rest," she says. "Your quarters are ready, and I am certain you could benefit from a hot bath."

Brent leaves, followed by Ryan who decides to see Selina. Christian puts his arm around me. "I am sorry, Ann."

"I hoped for some better news." I smile faintly. "Please

do not think that I am heartless because I cannot cry. I truly loved my father. I—I just … feel empty; no pain, no tears, just a great emptiness."

"I felt the same after my mother passed away." He sighs. "It took nine hundred years before I properly mourned her death."

"Do you think it was considerate of Brent not to let us know about our father's death before the wedding?"

"I think so."

Selina stays in her chamber for supper. Maybe I should visit with her but I want to be with Christian; his steady presence makes me feel better.

After supper, the men have a long discussion about the invaders. Brent explains that the enemy's greatest strength is in numbers and the swiftness of their attack. "By the time you notice them they are upon you. While most castles have fifty or sixty fighters, the invaders come in groups of five or six hundred, maybe even a thousand; it is impossible to kill them all. They are deadly with bows, even more lethal in close combat, and take no prisoners."

"You did well," I say. "With just over a hundred knights you beat an army of more than five hundred."

"When fighting invaders, God is on your side," Christian says. "And you can win against much bigger armies. History is full of such examples."

The discussion turns to weapons and to possible ways to defeat the enemy.

"Before we left," I tell Brent, "our father talked about joining forces with other lords. Had he said anything about it to you?"

"Yes, besides gathering immediate help, I was to persuade the lords to unite against the invaders," Brent answers.

"How much success have you had with it?" Ryan asks.

"It is difficult." Brent scowls. "One problem is that the

raiders strike randomly. For a while they attacked only in the south, then they started to hit castles on the east and the west shores. It is impossible to predict where they will strike next; therefore, we do not know where to concentrate our forces. The other difficulty is that since so far they have only attacked castles along the shore, it is hard to persuade the lords from the landlocked castles to help us. They are more concerned with their petty fights over some lea or hamlet than with the well-being of the county. They do not seem to understand that if the shore castles fall they will be unprotected. Imagine if the enemy decided to settle in one of the defeated castles and raid from there?"

"At least we would know where to concentrate our forces," Christian says, then shakes his head. "They will not settle."

The discussion continues late into the night.

~ ~ ~

To plan a memorial Mass for the repose of the souls of our father, brothers, and the fallen knights, the three of us—Selina, Brent, and I—meet in our old chamber to write a eulogy. Instead of writing we reminisce about our childhood. I find it interesting that though we grew up in the same castle and have the same parents, we have such different memories.

As we talk, I realize something. "Brent, it has just dawned on me that now you are the oldest in our family; you are taking our father's place."

He grimaces. "Something I would rather not do."

"You will be fine." I give an encouraging smile. "You definitely won't be as overbearing as Kieran, or as arrogant as Fergus would have been."

"Now that you are the lord, you must settle down and marry," Selina says.

"Not yet," he answers. "Though it certainly would be nice to have a lady to run the household."

"We can lend you Aunt Evelyn," I say.

"No thanks," Brent chuckles. "She is too shrewish. I would prefer someone more affable."

I laugh. "I am sorry; in that case you have to find your own lady helper. Maybe you do have someone in mind."

"I do," Brent says hesitantly.

"Who is it?" Selina asks.

"The Lady of Abbeydale."

"Do you mean Lady Louise, that pretty redheaded widow?" I ask. "Oh, I hope she returns your affection."

"So do I," Selina sighs dreamily. "Tell us, Brent, what are your chances?"

"We are here to write the eulogy," Brent says and pulls the parchment toward him.

"You are right. We will talk about Lady Louise later." I pick up the quill, and pull the parchment back from him. "We should start by saying that our father was a brave and fair knight."

"And a good father," Selina adds, then turns to Brent. "Brent, you must tell us how Father died."

"I will not tell you," he says.

"You must. Please do," Selina insists, ignoring his discomfort.

Brent swallows and shakes his head. "No, much better if you do not know. It was gruesome."

"Please tell us," she begs.

Brent refuses, but Selina nags him until he concedes.

"Do not fault me if it gives you nightmares." He warns angrily, takes a deep breath, and says, "He fell off his horse, I do not know how. Before he could get up or any of us could come to his aid at least five enemies surrounded him and hacked him to death."

"Cowards." My hand tightens into a fist. "Attack a helpless man on the ground."

Selina starts to weep.

"I think we better write that eulogy," Brent says in a low voice.

With a heavy heart, we return to our task.

"I will read it," I volunteer. "Selina would probably blubber through it and you, Brent, already attended their funeral."

"Why do you not cry?" Selina asks.

I shrug my shoulders. "Our father's death seems so unreal."

How naïve I was to suppose I could read the eulogy without tears. I begin to weep at the first sentence and cannot stop. Brent ends up reading it. As I sit down next to Christian, he puts his arm around me. "I am glad you can cry," he whispers. "I was getting worried about you. Those unshed tears could make you bitter and brittle."

Brent stays for another week. When he again mentions that he would much rather travel around visiting other lords than manage Ryston, I recommend that he train one of our younger brothers to mind the castle.

"They are still too young." He shakes his head. "They have much to learn." With a sigh, he adds, "Even I have much to learn."

With heavy heart, we say good-bye, wish him good luck with his ladylove, and make him vow that he will keep in touch and let us know if something important happens. "As soon as it happens," I add.

Chapter 15

"Ann-Marie," Christian whispers into my ear one morning as we wake up snuggled together, "I cannot allow you to die."

"What?" I turn toward him.

"I cannot allow you to die with me in the siege." He wraps his arm around my shoulder.

"Oh, that's what you are talking about." I nestle closer to

him. "That is up to me to decide."

He frowns. "You must leave when the attack comes."

"Christian, I would much rather die than live without you." I kiss his rough cheek. "I might become a cranky old widow like Aunt Evelyn, and could not bear to be with myself."

He laughs. "You a cranky old woman, I want to see that." Sitting up, he says more seriously, "I am your husband, and I forbid you to stay."

I sit up too. "I am your wife, and I also forbid you to stay. I want to see you as a cranky old man."

It is cold in the room, so we quickly slide back under the warm cover and snuggle close. Boils. I am cozy in the arms of a strong, virile man and we are talking about dying. I have an idea. "If I am with child, I will leave. I would love to raise your child."

He pulls me closer and, plants a kiss on my nose. "Fine. Let us work on it." He rolls me over, and we do.

In the next couple of weeks we have other more serious discussions about the attack. Originally we planned to keep the preparations secret, but soon realized it was impossible. Success requires everyone's willing cooperation. Or, as Christian likes to say, "Those who plan the battle will not battle the plan." With this in mind, one morning after breakfast we have a meeting in the lord's antechamber with Selina, Ryan, Aunt Evelyn, and Sir Lorcan.

"As you have heard from Lord Brent," Christian begins when we settle around the sturdy table, "the enemy has changed tactics and is randomly attacking castles along the shore. I want to prepare for a possible attack—"

"An attack? Holy Mother of God, help us." Aunt Evelyn crosses herself. "How do you know they will attack us?"

"I do not know; however, we should prepare for the possibility; that is why I asked to meet with you," he says. "Since the sea is practically impassable between October and April, we have a few months to prepare. Here is my proposition: the invaders, so far, have stayed close to the shore; therefore, all the women, children, elderly, tradesmen, the serfs, with most of the garrison will retreat to Haukwold, our hunting lodge. It is built with stones and is reasonably defendable. You, Ryan, and you, Sir Lorcan, will lead them—"

"I will not run and hide from the enemy," Ryan interrupts.

"You will not be running and hiding," Christian answers sharply. "Everyone who stays in the castle will die. One of us must carry on the family line."

Ryan stands and places his palms on the table. "I am not a coward. I am staying to fight."

"You cannot stay." Christian stands, too. "Going with the refugees will not make you a coward; quite the opposite. You will have to deal with the aftermath of the attack with hungry, frightened people, mourning and burying the dead, and rebuilding your lives from the ruins. They require more of your strength than dying does. Also, if the invaders attack you at the lodge, you will have to fight them in close combat without the protection of the castle walls."

"Why don't you retreat with the refugees then?"

"You know why."

"No, Brother," Ryan repeats resolutely. "The final answer is 'no.' I am not going to hide at the lodge while you fight here." He sits down.

Selina's face shows that it may not be the final answer. Will she be as obedient as she has planned?

"My lord," Selina says to Christian, "you said that those who stay in the castle will die. Do we have the right to decide which soldiers are to die?"

Christian smiles at her and sits down too. "We will tell the knights what fate awaits those who stay, and ask for volunteers. Sir Lorcan, you will be in charge. Please notify all the knights and the soldiers. Tell them I want to talk to them tomorrow morning—the servants, too, and the serfs."

"Tell the serfs?" Aunt Evelyn interrupts.

"Yes, to ensure their support," Christian says.

Aunt Evelyn shakes her head disapprovingly.

"I will have everyone notified," says Sir Lorcan. "I have a question, though. How much time will we have for the withdrawal when the raiders arrive? Lord Brent said that one of the attackers' strengths is their swiftness. The enemy might be upon us before we can reach the forest. Children, women, and especially the elderly cannot move fast."

"That is true." Christian nods. "The peasants should transfer their valuables to the lodge beforehand, so they will not waste time gathering them the last minute. Also, measure how long it would take the fastest soldiers to get to the top of the hill from the bay, and how far a child and an old woman could progress during the same time."

"We could ask the fishermen to watch out for anything suspicious and give us an early warning," I suggest.

"The enemy's ships are said to move extremely fast," Ryan answers. "Much faster than our fishing dories; therefore, the fishermen may not be much help."

"We could set up sentries along the shore," Christian says. "They could send pigeons to bring the message if they notice anything suspicious."

"We could post some of the young squires," the constable adds.

"I will put you, Sir Lorcan, in charge of this," Christian says. "Also, the two of you—Sir Lorcan and Lord Ryan— will be in charge of training the knights, soldiers, and some of the peasants, too. And kindly estimate and order all the extra weapons we will need."

"Training the peasants to fight?" Aunt Evelyn interrupts. "You cannot trust that riffraff with weapons; they will turn them against you."

"Only if you make their lives miserable," Christian answers sharply. Aunt Evelyn grumbles something, but no one pays attention to her.

"The next topic is provisions," Christian says. "Aunt Evelyn, Selina, and Ann-Marie, please estimate how much food we will need until next year's harvest. You can check the records. Calculate the bare minimum. We must leave part of the supplies for the attackers."

"We are not leaving anything for those devils," Aunt Evelyn huffs.

"We must," Christian answers. "I do not want them to hunt in the forest for their victuals. If they discover the refugees, no one will survive."

"If the attackers come before the harvest, we will not have enough food even for ourselves," Aunt Evelyn says. "And I don't need to go over any old records; I can tell you exactly how much we eat in a year." She rattles off the numbers.

Christian represses a smile. "Also, please take care of the transporting and storing of the provisions at the hunting lodge."

"There is not enough storage space on the main floor of the lodge for a year's supply," Aunt Evelyn says.

Christian frowns. "How much more space would you need?"

"Two floors should be enough."

"That would reduce the available accommodations," I sigh.

Christian glances at me. "We will have extra huts built. Is there anything else to consider?"

"Yes," Selina answers. "We should make our plans to ensure everyone escapes alive."

Christian shakes his head. "Some of us have to sacrifice our lives for others."

"Not necessarily," she argues. "We could recruit an army, as my brother did, and attack the invaders from the forest. We could easily push them back into the sea."

Oh, oh. What's happening to all that obedience Selina was so fond of?

Christian frowns. "Allow me to consider your plan. Let us say that every neighboring lord sends between ten and twenty fighters, since that is the most they can spare. You need to get help from at least twelve lords, probably more, to raise a large enough army. Unfortunately, half of the neighbors can hardly wait to see me dead. You would have to travel quite a distance to find the twelve lords who are willing to aid us. And even if all the neighbors agreed, we are far more isolated here than Ryston is. It would take a week or more before an army could assemble and reach the castle. And who would be the messenger? Can you see the enormity of your plan?" He shakes his head. "I will not waste time on this."

Selina pouts, but says nothing.

~ ~ ~

"Everyone should retreat to the forest and abandon the castle to the enemy," Selina begins our afternoon chat.

We have missed our evening discussions so much, we have started to meet in the afternoon to bring back some of the closeness we enjoyed before our marriages. Though we have soon realized our most intimate moments now belong to our respective husbands.

"Unfortunately, Christian considers that strategy ineffective," I say. "He thinks if we abandon the castle, the attackers will pursue us, unless a small group remains to fight them."

"He should ask for help," Selina says threading a needle. To keep Aunt Evelyn away we decided to embroider a tapestry during our tête-à-têtes. Aunt Evelyn hates sewing.

"I agree," I say. "Christian should ask for help, but since the wizard predicted that he will die in the attack, he will not even consider it."

"Ann-Marie," Selina's eyes grow wide with realization, "if he dies you will be a widow."

I sigh. It's time to tell her about my plan. Feeling nervous, I say, "Selina, I am planning to stay in the castle with Christian unless I am with child." Seeing the horror on Selina's face, I quickly add, "I would rather die with him than live without him."

"You want to die?" Incredulity and concern creases her brow. "I do not want you to die. I want everyone to live."

"I do, too." I concentrate on my stitching.

"You told me you gave up love at the enchanted tower, because your family would have been devastated if you had died. What about me?" Selina's voice is accusatory. "I would be devastated, too."

I sigh again. What can I say? It was a different situation at the tower. Before I have a chance to explain, Selina continues. "Not enough Christian wants to die, so does Ryan, and now you." She angrily glares at me. "I lost my father, mother, brothers, now my only sister, my husband, and brother-in-law want to die too; perhaps I should die with you." She has tears in her eyes.

I put my needle down. "Selina, I am sorry. You are right. What kind of life would await you if all of us have died? You would probably have to leave this castle ... although I am sure Brent would let you move home. He wanted someone to run the household for him ... and you could always remarry."

"Thank you for planning my life for me," she says curtly.

"You are welcome." I pick up my needle. Why do I feel so guilty? "You should try to persuade Ryan to retreat with you to the hunting lodge."

"He is as stubborn as a mule," she answers angrily. "The

more I try to force him the more obstinate he becomes."

"You have already discovered this after a few weeks of marriage?"

She nods, as teardrops run down her cheeks.

A wave of sisterly love washes over me. "I will go with you if Ryan refuses. We can both return home and be cranky old widows like Aunt Evelyn."

She laughs, and wipes away her tears. "You said …You have given me an idea of how to convince Ryan."

"Did I? What is it?"

"I am superstitious. I must keep this a secret for it to work."

"Fine." I smile. We sew silently for a few minutes, until I say, "I think you and I should try to raise an army."

She looks up. "How could we? We cannot request the lords to send fighters, only Christian or Ryan could do that."

"We could ask the ladies of the castles."

"Ann-Marie, what would you do if someone asked you to send some of your husband's soldiers? You could not just send them."

"No, but I could persuade my husband to send them. It might work."

"Yes, it might." She nods, stares at the tapestry, then looks up with a broad smile. "Yes. We should try."

My mind starts to churn out plans. "Some of the servants should know the names of the ladies of the surrounding castles … Do you think Ryan would help us?"

"I will ask."

"Good. Now let us draft a letter. What should we write?"

We put our needlepoint aside and spend the rest of the afternoon composing a letter in which besides asking for fighters—and in return (with tongue in cheek) offering some of ours—we ask our addressee to send a pigeon, so we can quickly notify them when the attack comes.

Next morning while still in bed, I ask Christian, "What would you do if a neighboring lord's wife implored me to ask you to send a few soldiers in case of an attack?"

He studies me with narrowed eyes. "Ann-Marie, I made it clear, I want no help."

"Christian, if you want to die it is you choice." I pull up on the pillow. "What about the soldiers, should they lay down their lives because you want to sacrifice yours?"

"They will gladly forfeit their lives to save their loved ones. Ann-Marie, you cannot ask for help." He sits up on his side to get out of the bed.

"Why not?" I ask.

He stands and turns toward me. "I am in charge of this castle. I am also your husband—"

"So? It gives you no right to negate a perfectly reasonable idea." He's looming too high above me. I kneel up on the bed. "Being in charge does not mean being a tyrant."

"I am not a tyrant," he snarls.

"No, you are not," I agree calmly. "But in this case you are unreasonable."

We stare at each other. He breaks the stare. "Fine. Go ahead, but you are on your own finding help."

"Thanks, Christian." I want to kiss him but he has already turned.

"Hey you forgot the peace kiss," I say.

He swivels back and we have a nice long peace kiss.

~ ~ ~

By breakfast time the castle is buzzing with the news of an imminent attack. So much for keeping anything secret around here, or in any castle for that matter; even the walls seem to have ears.

After breakfast the people gather in the bailey and Christian tells them about our plans. After explaining that everyone who remains in the castle will perish, he asks for volunteers. Every soldier volunteers.

When he dismisses the people, one of the young cooks approaches us. "M' lord," he says, "with yer permission, I'd stay to cook fer the defenders."

"Everyone who stays will die," Christian answers.

"Yeh need someone fer the cookin'," the young man insists.

That is true. We will need a cook.

Christian advises him to sleep on it.

When the cook leaves, I ask, "Why do all men in this castle want to die? Are we women so repulsive?"

Christian laughs. "We want to die to become heroes. There is no greater honor than to lay down our lives for our kin."

"That's not what you told Ryan." We walk toward the keep. "I need a better explanation for why all you men want to die."

He stops and, turning toward me, takes my shoulders. "Ann-Marie, we all die sooner or later. Everyone lives with a death sentence. Somewhere deep down we all know that death is not the end."

I look up at him. "Do you think we would stop killing each other if we believed there was nothing after death?"

"I think we would kill with even more zeal."

I grimace.

We start to walk again. "Christian, you will need someone to take care of the injured, and since I know a bit about healing, the use of herbs, and dressing wounds, I will stay."

"Ann-Marie—" he growls.

"Christian, I told you I will leave only if I am with child. But whether I stay or not, I should collect and dry herbs, and prepare dressings. If I retreat with the refugees, I will pass on the recipes to you."

"Do you think I will have time to brew concoctions?"

I chuckle. "Then I must stay."

"Ann-Marie, you cannot …" He starts to laugh. "Who wants to die now?"

At dinner Selina tells me that she has some good news.

"Has Ryan agreed to leave with the refugees?" I ask.

"No. He agreed to help to raise an army."

That is good news, indeed. As much as I hate to admit this, few people take women seriously when it comes to warfare.

~ ~ ~

Christian, Ryan, and Sir Lorcan work on strategies to hold the enemy at bay. One idea is to make dummies and set them up on the ramparts to give the impression there are more defenders than actually are.

Christian also wants to incorporate some later technologies into the defense. Stonemasons are building arrow slits into the crenellations. The gate, the weakest point in any castle, is strengthened with iron bars. Christian also wants to use Molotov cocktails. To make them we need some special ingredients. Hoping that the local alchemist might have them, we set out to visit his cottage.

"Is it ethical to use such advanced technology?" I ask on the way.

He peers at me. "Ann-Marie, is war ethical?"

I grimace.

When the alchemist finds out what we need the ingredients for he refuses our request. "I am in search for the Elixir of Immortality, not new weapons," he grumbles and from then on ignores us.

Everyone is busy around the castle. The peasants have seeded the crops; builders are working on the huts, and the lodge; the armory is booming with constant hammering; and the soldiers spend all their time training, while little boys imitate them.

The squires, sent to watch the boats, send us a pigeon pretty much every time a ship goes by. Finally, Sir Lorcan gathers them and explains that they are watching for a flotilla.

"What's a flotilla?" one of the young lads asks.

"Twenty or more boats together," Sir Lorcan answers.

The lad's eyes grow wide. "That many boats."

"Yes, and when you see them, you send your pigeon as fast as you can, and head to Haukwold," Sir Lorcan answers. "They are coming to kill us."

The boys promise to follow the instructions and, full of importance, leave for their posts.

Ryan and Selina have recruited about seventy fighters.

However, due to Ryan's refusal to leave with the evacuees, tension is mounting between the two brothers, and between Ryan and Selina too.

One evening when Christian and Ryan get into another quarrel, Selina blows up. She is angry a lot lately.

"Do you know what I think?" she hisses. "I think you two are mad, both of you. What kind of death wish do you have? You are like little boys playing war games, except you forget that in this game you won't just say 'you are dead, fall down,' then get up and keep on playing. You will be dead." She bursts into tears.

Christian and Ryan glance at each other and stop arguing.

About a week later at our afternoon meeting, Selina announces, "I am with a child, and Ryan is coming with me to the lodge."

"That is wonderful." I clap my hands. "When is the child due?"

"Around Christmas—"

"A Christmas baby for a Christmas bride."

"Now it is your turn," she says.

"We are working on it." I laugh. "How did you persuade Ryan to go with you?"

"I told him that their cousin would inherit this castle, if both he and Christian died. Even if our child is a boy, I could not ensure that he receives his inheritance. You should have seen his face." She laughs. "So I added that he need not worry about the child's or my future. I would move back home with the baby; Brent would certainly take us in. It worked."

Gladness and relief floods me. "Well done, Selina."

She laughs. "I have a suspicion that his decision to retreat to the lodge is partly due to the fact he would have the opportunity to lead over a hundred fighters into battle if the attack comes."

"You have over a hundred fighters committed. That is good news."

When Christian learns that Selina is pregnant and Ryan will leave with her and the refugees, he is relieved. The two brothers are on good term again, and Selina is much happier in spite of her morning sickness.

Aunt Evelyn suggests that Selina move to Orla's castle. "She and her husband live inland; you would be away from danger. It would be a safer and more comfortable place for a newborn than the lodge," she explains.

Selina flatly refuses. "I would die of anxiety and would spend all my time wondering whether you are still alive. No. I am staying."

~ ~ ~

Spring has turned into summer, and no attack has come. The people, who were like an overextended bowstring, relax a bit. Since Selina is sick every morning, Aunt Evelyn and I supervise the moving of the provisions to the lodge.

In mid-summer robbers raid the stores. The guards, followed by an angry mob, march the three miscreants to the castle.

The offenders—a disheveled, sorry lot, with a mixture of

defiance and defeat on their faces—are ushered into the great hall.

"Show no mercy this time," Aunt Evelyn hisses to Christian, as he arrives to mete out punishment. "Have the bastards hanged."

Christian with solemn face studies the robbers for a long time. "You scoundrels," he finally says in a low clear voice. Everyone stops talking. "You are robbing your own children, wives, and mothers. The provisions at the lodge are for them, to ensure that they will have food for the winter." He stops in front of one thief, and I recognize the peasant who shot the deer last fall. Christian takes a deep breath. "You scum. I was merciful to you last time. This time ..." His voice trails off. The tension is palpable in the hall. After a long silence Christian hits his palm with his fist. "Damn!" he bursts out. "I've been forgiven for worse offences than this. If I condemn you, I condemn myself. Let them go. Double the guards at the lodge—or triple them if needed."

A gasp goes up from the crowd, followed by an angry buzz.

"You cannot let them go," Aunt Evelyn cries, nettled. "You are a weakling. You must make an example out of them."

"Making an example out of anyone is not justice," Christian says heatedly. He turns toward me, gently taking my shoulder. "Ann-Marie, come with me."

We cross the hall. People send angry or despising glances toward Christian, but step aside without a word. We head to the stables, and in a short time ride out of the castle. We silently canter on the sun dappled, dusty road between the trees. Where is Christian leading me? He turns toward the sea and we arrive at ...

"This is the creek delta, close to the enchanted tower," I exclaim. "Christian, how did you find this place?"

"I came upon it while scouting for lookout points for our sentries."

Overcome by emotion, I stand speechless, drinking in the familiar surroundings, though there is no bench and trail toward the tower. And probably no tower either.

Christian takes a blanket from the horse's bag, spreads it out, and we both sit down.

"Do you think I am weak?" Christian asks.

"No, Christian, you are strong and courageous. You stood up for your conviction in spite of everyone wanting you to do the opposite."

He wraps his arm around my shoulder. "Ann, I love you." In the next moment he is kissing my face, my neck, my breast ...

We make love, first fiercely, then gently. I have never felt this close to Christian.

~ ~ ~

Summer is almost over and still no sign of the enemy. Another month and the fall storms will render the sea impassable again.

"What if the enemy does not come?" Selina asks one evening while the four of us are playing checkers.

"We will be thankful and move the supplies back to the castle," Christian answers.

The peasants harvest the wheat and barley. There will be enough food for the winter. We have never been more thankful for a good harvest.

Two hundred fighters have pledged to come to our aid as soon as the pigeons reach them. This means the defenders have to keep the invaders at bay for about a week.

On a hot, sultry August morning a pigeon arrives from one of the sentries along the shore. A while later the second one reaches us. We estimate the speed with which the boats travel and realize the enemy could be here by the evening.

After a short consultation with Ryan and Sir Lorcan, we decide to send the people away.

A guard blows the horn and the crier bellows, "The enemy is near! Everyone retreat to the lodge!"

In the next moment people are running, grabbing belongings, their children; some are herding animals. Overhead, the pigeons are flying with messages to the other castles.

I still don't know what to do. Should I stay or leave? I am not with child; I do not want to die; and I do not want to live without Christian.

Selina, who is fairly round by this time, arrives in the courtyard with Ryan. He is gently guiding her to the waiting carriage. The tender way he helps her, and the warm smile she gives him, touch my heart.

I make my decision.

I do not want to live without Christian's love. I am staying with him.

Tears flood my eyes.

"Selina, wait," I shout. I run to our chamber, returning with a leather pouch. "You must take this," I pant, placing it into her hand.

Opening it, she draws out our grandmother's bracelet. "But Ann-Marie, Father said it was to be handed down from firstborn daughter to ..." she chokes. Her large eyes are filling up with tears.

"Selina, I am staying for the siege. In case I die, please pass this on to your firstborn daughter, and ask her to pass it on and ..." Tears are choking me. "... love her for me too." Selina is also crying. "Please take care of yourself," I say, weeping openly. "And the baby. And make sure you have many more of them."

She nods, unable to say anything. We hug each other, our tears freely flowing. She climbs back into the carriage, then leans out, waving to me. With a lurch the carriage sets off. I watch until it reaches the trees. Just before entering the forest, it stops. Selina leans out and waves one last time. I wave back and send kisses. Wiping my tears, I stare at the spot where the carriage disappeared.

A young girl, running toward the castle, catches my attention. What has happened?

"My grandfather," she wails, "he won't leave."

"The old fool," someone close by snarls.

"What can I do?" the lass asks.

"You run to the forest as fast as you can," Christian answers her.

"I will take her on my horse," Ryan offers.

Christian is suddenly beside me. "Ann-Marie, what are you doing here? I thought you left with Selina."

I feel hurt. "Christian, who do you think I am? I would not have left without a farewell."

"You must leave with Ryan," he says.

"I have made up my mind. I am staying."

"Ann-Marie," he groans.

I touch his face with the back of my hand. "Christian, I do not want to live without you."

He takes my hand and plants a kiss on my palm. "You should leave."

Ryan interrupts us; he is leading his steed by the reins. "I am going," he says.

"Ryan," I turn to him, "please, take good care of Selina, and the baby."

He smiles down at me. "You take good care, my dear sister. We will be here to help you in a week, or maybe even sooner."

I give him a big heartfelt hug. The two brothers say good-bye. Ryan lifts the young girl onto the horse, mounts up, and gallops away.

Before the gate is closed, Christian tells the remaining soldiers that we have no chance of surviving; if anyone wants to leave this is their last opportunity. No one moves.

Twenty-four soldiers are staying, plus the cook, Christian, and I. I am the only woman.

The drawbridge is raised, and the portcullis is lowered, hitting the ground with an ominous thud.

Chapter 16

The castle is eerily quiet with so few people. The soldiers set up the dummies and we all climb to the seaside ramparts. Though there's not even a single boat on the horizon, the sea seems menacing.

The gravity of the situation hits me. My father's words, "this is not going to be a friendly joust; this fight will be about life and death," echo in my ear.

I feel nauseous. "Christian, I cannot kill anyone," I whisper to him, though there is no need for whispering; only the wind can hear us. "My father was right—a siege is not for young ladies."

He puts his arm around me. "You will feel differently when the fight begins."

"Would killing someone not leave an indelible mark on the soul?" I ask glancing up into his face.

He smiles ruefully. "It probably does."

"Maybe I will just injure people."

"They suffer less if you kill them."

I chuckle. "I am not convinced that killing people is more merciful than injuring them."

"You can stay in the keep, and later look after the injured," Christian says, pulling me closer to him.

Stay in the keep while the others fight? "No, I would rather join you."

We stay on the rampart for a long time, but nothing happens. At dusk we return to the keep, wondering if the squires have sent a false alarm, or if the enemy decided to attack another castle.

Everyone is staying in the great hall. The cook has set up his kitchen by the huge fireplace, and pallets are spread on the floor by the opposite wall. A moonless night arrives. The castle is oddly quiet without the chattering of the servants, barking of the dogs, and braying of the horses. Morning dawns, and still there is not a sound from the surrounding village or from the woods.

The soldiers train as usual. Noon arrives, still no sign of the enemy. The uncertain silence is more harrowing than an attack would be. We keep whispering although there is no need for it. In the afternoon we see the old man who stayed behind drawing water from the village well, and returning to his hut. That is the only life outside the walls.

How long should we stay locked in the castle before we can be certain there will be no attack? Christian decides on at least three days.

Next morning, ear-splitting battle cries roar out from the woods, and at the same time the peasants' huts burst into flame. What happened to the old man? Have they killed him or is he trapped in a burning building? There is no time to wonder.

We rush to our posts. I peep through the narrow opening and see the most amazing and frightening sight: hundreds of drawn bows pointing at us. A dark, deadly wave, the enemy surges toward the castle.

One nearby soldier, crouching down, waves a dummy over his head.

An arrow hits the dummy and we know that the invaders must be within shooting range. Christian gives a signal; the cook hits a drum, and we discharge the first arrows. A few of the invaders fall over. A shower of arrows answers back.

I am relieved to know it is impossible to tell whether I

have hit anyone. Encouraged by this, I shoot frantically into the throng. By mid-morning my arms tire, my pull slackens, my aim becomes non-existent. I cannot keep this up much longer.

Out of nowhere, Christian is beside me. "Ann-Marie," he shouts, "someone is injured, go to the main hall."

The injured soldier is one of the young archers, Sir Donal. An arrow is lodged in his arm. I quickly make two infusions: one to numb the pain, and one to disinfect the wound.

The only way to remove the arrow is to push it through his arm. Sir Donal winces, bites his lip, but does not make a sound. "I have cleaned the wound and tied a poultice to it," I say, while bandaging his arm with a strip from an old cloth. "In case the arrow is poisoned, the poultice should draw the poison out; it will also help the wound to heal faster."

"What am I to do now?" Sir Donal asks when I finish. "I cannot shoot with this arm."

"You should rest," I say.

He grimaces. "I cannot sit here while the others are fighting."

"You can pull the arrows from the dummies, and stand them up again," I recommend.

"I shall ask Prince Christian for something to do," he says and leaves.

I finish cleaning up, organize my jars, then exit the keep. It is hot, smoky, and noisy outside. With the sun mercilessly beaming down from the cloudless sky, the morning coolness is long gone. Our people must be exhausted.

I climb to the barbican to find Christian. "Christian, the people must have a break and eat something," I shout.

"I know," he shouts back. "I will order a third of them to the hall. Have everything ready. And, Ann-Marie, could you bring some water."

I draw water from the well, something I have not done

in a long time. Before I heft up the heavy jug, a strong arm grabs it. "I'll take this," one of the soldiers says. I thank him, and watch as he carries the water up the narrow stairs.

During dinner, Christian asks me to help Sir Donal to collect the arrows. Good job for a page.

As twilight arrives, the fighting stops, and the enemy retreats beyond shooting range.

"I hope they have not found the hunting lodge with the refugees," I tell Christian.

"No, we would see the smoke if they did."

Can the refugees see the smoke from the burning village?

Our soldiers are exhausted. How can they shoot all day? No one talks much. After dinner, they wrap themselves in their blankets and fall asleep.

Next morning the fight starts up again and I join the fighters. The air is oppressively heavy and hot; even the sea breeze has stopped. In the afternoon a storm arrives with such heavy rain and wind, the fighting ceases. We thank God for the relief.

During supper, as we are talking about the attackers, one soldier says, "They aren't very smart. They keep shootin' at the dummies instead of us."

"That's because yeh're hiding behind a wall," another answers.

"Yeh'd think by now they'd figured out that most of our soldiers are dummies," the first soldier says, and we all burst out laughing.

"We must be to stay in this deathtrap," someone mutters.

"They aren't dummies," another soldier says. "They're our most fearless fighters. They just stand there; nothin' frightens them, nothin' bothers them, they never get hungry or tired or injured, and refuse to die."

"Yea," someone else says, "they aren't afraid of flyin' arrows."

"Or death."

"Or the rain."

"Though the wind might knock them over."

"Let's have a drink to our dummies," someone hollers.

After a few drinks, the soldiers tell crude jokes and stories about battles, fights, and women until Christian reminds them that a lady is present.

It is still pouring the following morning. Since the rain renders the bows and arrows if not useless, much less effective, the fighting eases. Most of the attackers have retreated to the forest; we hear their ax blows. Why are they cutting the trees? Are they cutting wood for their fires, or making a ram?

~ ~ ~

Mid-afternoon a terrible accident happens. A pile of stones collapses, crushing Sir Gavin's legs below the knee. His injury is way beyond healing, and far beyond what I can handle.

"We must cut off both legs above the knee; otherwise they will rot," Christian says.

"Better if you kill me," Sir Gavin groans.

"No, Sir Gavin," I cry. "We cannot kill you."

"We leave that to the enemy," someone snorts and spits.

"Get your poultices ready," Christian orders me. "If you can brew up something that takes away the pain and helps him to sleep, prepare that too."

I rush ahead of the two men who carry Sir Gavin to the main hall. A short while later Christian arrives. He forces Sir Gavin to drink half a pint of whiskey and, taking the poultices, orders me to leave. I cover my ears expecting a scream, but hear nothing, until the cook pokes out his head. "You may come back."

Sir Gavin has passed out either from the injury or the whisky or both. Christian is already dressing the stumps, while the cook and I clean up the blood.

Asking me to stay with Sir Gavin, Christian returns to the barbicans. Of course, I am staying; I could not leave Sir Gavin unattended in this state.

As I sit by the injured man—who was always good to me—and see his noble face contorted by pain, I start to sob uncontrollably. All the tensions of the last few days surface in that sob.

How could a loving, caring God allow this to happen? How could he allow good people to suffer, or people who love each other be separated? How could he be loving and permit that I will never see my sister's baby, never have my own? How could God allow so much destruction, so much suffering? How could he let evil destroy goodness?

God must be either cruel or impotent. Why did he create a world so full of tears, suffering, sickness, and dying? I weep—not only for us, but for all the pain in this world—until I have no tears left.

By the evening Sir Gavin has high fever. I stay up with him most of the night, giving him drinks, placing cold compresses on his chest, changing his dressings whenever they soak through.

It is still raining steadily the next day.

By the afternoon Sir Gavin regains his consciousness, and I ask him how painful it was to lose his legs.

"I felt no pain at all," he says in a low raspy voice. "I was numb from the waist down. I feel more pain now. But why have you kept me alive? I am no use and will never recover."

Tears choke me. "Sir Gavin, we do not keep people alive only if they are of some use."

~ ~ ~

In the evening everyone is quiet; there is a feeling of defeat in the air. Even Christian seems troubled. I ask what is happening.

"The attackers are making ladders," he sighs. "We cannot

fight them off if they scale the walls." He draws his hand through his hair. "Even if they make only ten ladders, and they are making far more than that, we will have only two people to fight at each ladder, and that is if we leave the gate unattended." He gazes at me with sadness in his eyes. "Ann-Marie, we are doomed."

"Maybe the help will arrive," I say, hopeful.

He shakes his head. "Not likely."

I sigh. "Why are these people attacking us? We've done nothing against them. They do not even know us." I lean closer to Christian. "Why does God allow this to happen?"

"Ann-Marie," Christian says, "millions have asked the same question and no one has answered it yet."

"Will mankind ever overcome its beastly nature?" I ask, fighting back the tears.

"I doubt it," Christian says. "Look at your century. I remember reading that worldwide you spend more money on weapons in a week than on food in a year. Our weapons are toys compared to what your armies have. We can only kill one person at a time; your military can kill thousands with the drop of a bomb. Some of your bombs could eliminate most life on the earth."

"Hopefully we will never use them."

"Every weapon ever made has been used sooner or later," he says gravely.

"Thanks Christian, you just made my day."

"It is true."

We eat in solemn silence. Obviously, everyone has realized the direness of our situation. After supper, in need of reassurance, we drift to the chapel. Since there is no priest, everyone connects to a higher power in his own way in his own stillness.

Next day the ladders are ready; Christian orders me to stay in the keep with Sir Gavin and the cook.

I pace up and down, look out the window from time to time, and report to Sir Gavin what is happening. I cannot see much, though I can hear shouting and clanking of metals.

Then I see something that stops my heart. The enemy is inside the walls. They are attacking our people from behind. They are pouring in like water over a broken dam.

Suddenly, Christian bursts into the hall. Bewildered, he looks around. "Where is everyone? I ordered them to retreat to the keep."

"No one came," I say. Realization dawns. "I guess no one made it."

Startled, he looks at me for a moment. "Ann-Marie, up the stairs!" he shouts.

"We cannot leave Sir Gavin behind."

Sir Gavin moans, "Just kill me."

"No, Sir Gavin, we cannot," I cry.

The cook is next to us, fear creasing his face.

"Can you use any weapon?" Christian asks him.

"I can use a butcher knife."

"A butcher knife will not help you. Go, and hide," Christian orders him.

The cook runs away in panic. We hear strong blows hitting the thick door of the keep. It should hold up for a while. We return our attention to Sir Gavin.

"Just kill me," he begs. "If you don't, they will."

"Go upstairs!" Christian orders me.

"Christian, no!" I howl.

"Go!" he bellows. "I will come soon. Get your sword ready."

On the stairs I glance out through an arrow slit. The courtyard, a disturbed beehive, is swarming with enemies. The stable is on fire—an acrid smell is mixing with the salt air. I cannot see any of our men.

Christian catches up with me. His breathing is heavy.

"We will stay on the top of the stairs. It is the best place for defense." He pulls me into his embrace. "Ann-Marie, I am sorry it had to come to this. If you survive in your future life, please remember me."

"Christian, the time we've spent together was worth it," I say, leaning close to his strong chest. "I would not give it up for anything. How could I ever forget you?"

He presses his mouth to mine. All the kisses we will not share in the future are crammed into this one passionate kiss.

With a tremendous thud, the door gives way. As the attackers push inside, their shouts carry up though the stairwell. The cacophony increases as more and more of them enter the building. "I will love you forever," Christian whispers into my ear.

"I will love you forever, too." I stroke his raspy face.

We kiss for the last time and take up our positions on both sides of the staircase.

I am surprised. Now that death is certain, I am not afraid of dying. Not at all. Actually, I feel more peaceful than ever before. I thank God for the good life I had, for the love I have shared with Christian. I pray for Selina, her baby, and the people we are leaving behind.

We hear the attackers' footfall on the stairs. They didn't expect anyone else to be alive, so Christian easily kills the first few who come around the turn, but more and more are pushing their way up. It is impossible to kill them all. Soon we are overwhelmed.

I have no qualms about fighting like a trapped tigress. I don't care whether I hurt or kill someone, I send blow after blow. I feel a prick on my left shoulder, ignore it, and keep fighting. I glance at Christian: he is fighting with four men. Suddenly I notice a blade moving toward me.

This will hurt.

It does not. Everything goes black.

Chapter 17

I wake in a small pavilion open on three sides. I'm on a four-poster bed with soft silk sheets, many pillows, and sheer curtains. The pavilion is in a delightful tropical garden with riotous flowers, exotic bushes, trees, and colorful birds darting from branch to branch and calling to each other. A sweet, heady perfume fills the air. In the distance the deep blue ocean shimmers, and I can hear water splashing somewhere nearby, though I cannot see the source. The beauty and serenity fills me with an inexpressible peace. I deeply inhale the fragrant air and sit up, wondering where I am.

"Good morning, Ann-Marie." Christian steps into my view.

My heart jumps and my face breaks into a joyous grin. He is freshly shaved, his hair's neatly tied back, and he's dressed in a white shirt, light khaki pants, and loafers. He looks happier and more relaxed than ever.

"Are we in heaven?" I ask.

He shakes his head. "We are on the wizard's island."

"How do you know this is the wizard's island?"

"I have been here before." He sits down on the edge of the bed, and takes my hand.

"Do you think we are dead?"

"I feel alive." With his free hand, he gently brushes a lock of hair away from my face. "And you?"

"I feel alive too." I smile. "But maybe this is only a dream. Maybe I will wake up in a moment surrounded by enemies. Or maybe the enemies were a dream." Feeling whimsical, I add, "Or maybe everything is a dream."

"Don't get too philosophical," Christian laughs.

"How can I tell this is not a dream?"

"Do you want to test it?" He plants a quick kiss on my mouth.

"That kiss did not last long enough to tell whether it was real or not." I press my lips to his, he pulls me closer, and we share a deep, passionate kiss.

"Okay," I laugh when we let go. "If this is a dream, it is a good one."

"It is." Christian's voice is husky. He lowers me unto the bed and we kiss again.

"Do you have to be celibate on this island?" I ask.

"I hope not," he chuckles, leans on one elbow, and runs his hand down my front, under my shirt, up my stomach to my breast. I gasp, and my pulse quickens.

A small "ahem" interrupts us. We quickly sit up to see a beautiful woman in an elegant gossamer dress. "Excuse me," she says in a soft voice. "The wizard wishes to have breakfast with you. Please follow me."

I'm in a t-shirt and boxer shorts. "I can't have breakfast with the wizard dressed in night clothes. I need something more presentable, like a dress." In that instant I am clad in a light, flowery dress. Wow! How did this happen? "I wish I was in shorts and a tank top," I mumble. Immediately my clothes change. Double wow. "I want to have jeans and a t-shirt on." My outfit changes again.

"I've changed my clothes just by wanting to," I tell Christian. "Watch." I am back in the shorts and tank top.

"I was wondering what this fashion show is about." Christian grins. "Please stop switching your clothes; you look lovely in this outfit."

"Maybe I'll just change the colors. How about yellow top and khaki shorts?" The colors change instantly to the exact hue I had in mind. "This is fun."

"Women," Christian mutters.

"Okay, no more change of clothing for now." I slide my hand into his and we follow the woman on the stone path, which winds its way between an amazing array of flowers, shrubs, and trees. The sun is already warm, though a pleasant breeze off the ocean cools the air. Occasionally we cross a little creek, or have a glimpse of a high waterfall, or the sea. We arrive at an open terrace that overlooks the shimmering, aqua-blue ocean. Under a pergola a table is elegantly set with floor-length tablecloth, porcelains, and silver. Hummingbirds and butterflies flit around a small bouquet in the middle of the table.

The wizard appears out of nowhere. "Welcome to my island." He waves toward the table. "Please join me for breakfast."

We greet him and take our places. He asks what we would like to eat. Christian orders a ham and mushroom omelet and tea. At once the food appears in front of him. I ask for a fruit salad with yogurt, orange juice, and coffee; in the next instant a crystal bowl filled with a mixture of tropical fruits materializes, along with a mug of coffee and a glass of juice. "Wow, this is what I call service," I giggle.

The wizard conjures a crab pâté and coffee for himself. He says grace. For a few minutes we eat in silence. I thoroughly enjoy the peaceful surroundings: the gentle breeze that swings the tendrils of the fragrant climbing plant on the arbor, the soft murmuring of the distant sea, the buzzing of bees, the whizzing of the hummingbirds' wings, the constant chattering of some invisible birds, and the bright light reflecting off the ocean that illuminates even the shadows.

The wizard breaks the silence. "Christian, "I must apologize to you."

Puzzled, we both look up.

"Sir, why would you apologize to me?" Christian asks.

"I made a big mistake when I told you that you would die in the attack. If I said nothing, you would have found a way to survive."

Does it really matter? We are on this splendid island,

eating the most delicious breakfast; who cares about leaving some musty, war-torn castle behind?

"Please remember in the future not to believe anyone's predictions," the wizard continues. "You always have a choice. The future is not settled; you are not following a script. You have the freedom to choose. When you believe in a certain outcome, that belief will influence the outcome. Not by some magic, but by your ability to steer the events into that direction."

Christian places his fork on the side of his plate and reaches for his tea. "Do you mean that we could have survived the attack if I had organized the defense differently?"

"Yes, you could have." The wizard nods. "It was my fault you rejected the idea that could have saved everyone's life."

What idea did Christian reject? I'll ask him later.

"It seems irrelevant," Christian mumbles.

I turn to the wizard. "Sir, may I ask a question?"

"Certainly." His kind face creases into a smile.

"Am I still alive in the twenty-first century?"

"Yes, you are," he says, cutting his pâté.

"How could I be born in the twelfth century if I'm still alive in the twenty-first?"

He looks at me with a small smile. "The answer is the elasticity of time."

"What do you mean, sir?" Christian asks. Christian must know the explanation for everything.

"Time is not set," the wizard says. "Therefore it is easily manipulated."

"Manipulated by wizards, or by anyone?" Christian asks.

"It can be manipulated by anyone."

Christian takes a sip of his tea. "Do you mean we, humans, can also manipulate time?"

The wizard's eyes twinkle. "One day even humans could do it, but it will not happen until they learn to combine physical and metaphysical knowledge. On the other hand," he chuckles, "it is better if people do not know how it is done, because they would be messing around with events, without realizing the danger and the dire consequences of it."

"Combine physical and metaphysical knowledge," Christian mutters.

Before he can ask any more questions, I cut in. "I still don't understand how I could have been born in the twelfth century? And why?"

"You wanted to be with Christian," the wizard says. "How else could I send you there? Drop you out of the sky?"

"Which century was I born in first, the twentieth or the twelfth?"

"The twentieth," the wizard answers.

"Okay," I say slowly. "I was born in the twentieth century, met Christian in the enchanted tower after he was cursed, but I also met him in the twelfth century before he was cursed. How's that possible?"

"The answer again is the elasticity of time. Everything that happened to you in the twelfth century happened after you wanted to meet Christian again."

"Did I end up in the twelfth century because of the magic wishes?"

He nods.

Oh. My heart jumps. "Does this mean … does this mean that I will meet Christian in the twenty-first century, too? My wish was that we stay together in both times."

Christian raises his head with interest.

"If he wants to be with you, you will meet again. He must agree, though. Even magic cannot violate people's free will."

"Of course I want to be with Ann-Marie," Christian says.

The wizard peers at him and nods. "You can be. But since you do not belong to the twenty-first century, you will have to pass three tests to stay there."

Christian is about to say something, but the wizard quiets him with a movement of his hand. "These are the challenges. The first will be to marry Ann-Marie—"

"I thought we are already married," Christian says.

"You will not be married in the twenty-first century. The second challenge will be to make peace with your parents without giving up your dreams, and the third will be to believe Ann-Marie that everything that happened in the twelfth century and in the enchanted tower was real. You will not remember any of it."

"I will—" Christian starts, but the wizard stops him.

"You will have one year from the time you have met Ann-Marie to pass those tests; if you fail any of them, you will die in her time. But if you do not take the challenge, or if you take it and fail, you can be with her all the time invisibly."

"I take the challenge," Christian says, determined.

The wizard nods. "Fine, then you will meet again."

Christian reaches for my hand and we smile at each other.

~ ~ ~

"Let's go for a short stroll," the wizard says after breakfast. We leave the terrace and follow a path that leads up the mountain through the tropical forest.

"Ann-Marie," the wizard says while the three of us saunter in the cool, green shade of the towering trees, "you have asked why there is so much suffering and violence in the world, and why God allows it to happen."

It seems an eternity has passed since I asked those questions. "Yes, I did, but right now they seem totally irrelevant," I say.

"I will still answer them." The wizard strokes his long beard. "You suffer because you—by you I mean every human being—want to suffer."

I stop in my tracks. "We don't want to suffer, sir. Why would we want to suffer?"

He smiles. "It makes you feel stronger, more special. You want to fight and conquer suffering, not realizing that you create it in the first place."

We create our suffering. That's ridiculous. Okay, we do create some of our suffering, like wars, and violence, but not all. "What about natural disasters?" I protest. "We don't create them. What about starving children? Do not tell me they want to starve."

The wizard smiles kindly and starts to walk again. "The earth provides more than enough for every living creature. Your manmade rules keep people hungry. You create systems which make life difficult, then complain that life is difficult."

I sigh. "Yes, sometimes the rulers or the laws are oppressive; still, society couldn't function without them."

He turns toward me. "Ann-Marie, societies are the way they are because people would rather give away their power than be responsible. This way they can blame someone else for their problems, instead of themselves."

"Maybe we do give away our power and let unworthy people rule over us, but what about natural disasters? We're certainly not responsible for those."

"That is true." He smiles. "But every human being has a sixth sense that could warn them of impeding danger or disaster, yet most people ignore it. Even worse, many people deny its existence, and prevent their children from developing this inborn ability."

I don't like his answers. "What about illnesses?" I ask.

"Your body is entirely under your control. You choose your food, thoughts, and the activities that affect your health."

His answers seem too simplistic. "How about death, people losing their loved ones?"

He smiles at me. "People never lose their loved ones, even when they are separated by death."

"Sir, if we create our suffering," Christian says, "we should be able to eliminate it."

"You could." The wizard nods. "But it will not happen until people stop believing in suffering. Many of you are convinced that troubles make you stronger, smarter, or help you grow spiritually—but you do not need to grow. You are perfect and whole as you are. Everything you need is inside you. You don't develop it; you call upon it when problems arise. Humankind is playing games and suffering is part of the game. You are far more powerful beings than you realize. Most importantly, you are the authors of your lives. You cannot blame God or fate, or anyone outside yourself for your predicaments."

"I don't think you would be too popular with these ideas, sir," Christian says.

He laughs. "Of course, not. Denying your power is part of the game."

"But what about children born into poverty, into war-torn countries, or with incurable diseases?" I object.

Sadness flits over the wizards face. "Children, unfortunately, can be victims of their elders' games. But there is more to your suffering. I've heard many people say that they would not want to live in heaven, it would be too boring." He chuckles. "You humans want excitement, challenge. You become dispirited and restless without it. This earth could be heaven if you would not consider life without trials and tribulations too boring, monotonous, or meaningless."

"Is there any way we could stop suffering?" Christian asks.

"There is, but you cannot force it."

We come upon a small wooden bridge that spans a deep narrow gorge and stop to look down into the emerald green chasm. Ferns and small shrubs cling to the moss covered rock walls, which plunge steeply to a shining silver ribbon at the bottom.

"This place is like heaven," I say. "So peaceful and magnificent."

The wizard chuckles. "I hope you will enjoy it."

~ ~ ~

"What else would you like to know?" the wizard asks while we saunter back toward the terrace.

"Could you tell us what happened to the people we have left behind?" I say. "How are Selina and Ryan doing?"

"Selina did very well," the wizard answers. "She became a formidable matron of twelve children; both she and Ryan had a long life."

"Was she happy?" I ask.

"As happy as she wanted to be." The wizard stops, reaching out his hand to a colorful butterfly and watching it land.

"You sound like Orla," I laugh, looking at the folded wings of the butterfly.

"You should say," he chuckles, "that Orla sounds like me."

"How did Orla's life turn out?" Christian asks, also watching the vivid insect.

"In a few years' time her husband died," the wizard answers. "Orla became a merry widow." I giggle. Could Orla be anything but? "Then, to everyone's consternation, she married the man she had loved all her life. She and Selina stayed good friends until the end of their lives."

"And Aunt Evelyn? What happened to her?" I ask.

"She retired to a monastery," the wizard says.

"What?" I burst out. Startled, the butterfly takes off. "Aunt Evelyn joined a monastery? Why?"

The wizard chuckles and starts to walk again. "One day, while collecting berries, she and two of her maids were attacked by robbers. She promised God that if they escaped, she would become a nun. Ryan and a few hunters were close by and arrived just in time to rescue them."

"Did Selina miss Aunt Evelyn's expertise?" I ask.

"Selina managed quite well without her."

I try to imagine Aunt Evelyn as a humble, prayerful nun. It strains my imagination.

"How did the siege end?" Christian asks.

"Ryan and his army arrived a day later and drove away the invaders. The cook survived."

"He must have hidden in a good place," Christian says.

"He did not hide." The wizard chuckles again. "He donned one of the fallen attacker's clothing and kept a low profile."

"Did our countrymen form an alliance?" Christian asks. "Were they victorious?"

"Yes, and yes. They formed an alliance and triumphed in a battle the following summer. But they did not enjoy peace for long; soon other enemies arose."

Christian asks many questions about the battle that drove away the attackers. While the wizard answers, Brent comes to my mind. When Christian and the wizard finish their discussion, I ask, "What happened to Brent? Did he marry his ladylove? Did he have a long life?"

"He didn't have a long life, but he married the Lady of Abbeydale, and their descendants still live in Ryston."

"Sweet."

We ask about the other people we knew until we arrive back at the terrace.

"I'd like to invite you to stay with me before returning to the twenty-first century," the wizard says.

Stay here. Wow. I glance at Christian who glances back at me, then turns to the wizard. "Thank you for your invitation, sir." He bows lightly. "It will be our pleasure to accept it."

The wizard smiles. "Please, make yourselves comfortable and enjoy the island. Feel free to explore it, and meet with my other guests. I have to warn you, though: you have to watch what you wish for while you are here, because everything you want, good or bad, will appear immediately." Chuckling, he adds, "Luckily it will also disappear when you want it to. And please spare some time for me, too. I hope to answer all your questions before you leave this place."

~ ~ ~

Life is good on the island. We enjoy many more discussions with the wizard; explore the shore and the forest; meet with the other guests; practice horseback riding, fencing, and archery; and spend many pleasant hours reading, swimming, and making love.

It's hard to tell how long we've been here—it is impossible to keep track of the days—but lately we are restless, ready to move on. Christian and I agree: it's time to depart.

"We have enjoyed your hospitality, and friendship, sir," Christian says to the wizard in the evening. "We do not want to offend you, but we are ready to face the next challenge."

"Offend me?" the wizard laughs. "Of course you are not offending me. I told you, you are free to leave anytime you wish. When do you want to go?"

"As soon as possible, sir," Christian answers.

"All right." The wizard smiles. "If you are ready you can leave right now."

We thank him for his hospitality, and all the goodness he has shown to us.

"Thank you for staying with me," he says. "Are you saying goodbye to each other, too?"

Christian and I step closer and smile at each other. "See you in the twenty-first century," I say.

Christian cradles my face in his hands. "Remember that I love you." He kisses me deeply, sweetly.

"Christian, I love you, too, and always will," I whisper back.

And then everything is gone.

Part 3

Twenty-first Century

Chapter 18

I am back in the torrential rain on the soggy trail with my companions. It seems not a moment has passed since they—or I—have disappeared. Except no one has disappeared. We are all here, morosely trudging back to the camp.

Did I just have a long moment of insanity imagining I was lost and visiting some enchanted place, or was I in that place?

Was Christian a figment of my imagination? How about the other people? And the places I lived in? Is there such a place as the wizard's island? Or Ryston, or Bancloch?

If I meet Christian, will that prove these events actually happened?

Will I be able to persuade him that we met before? In a fairy tale! Even I am unconvinced.

And if we meet again, will he feel the love that's supposed to connect us?

What about the skills I've learned? Remembering them could be proof too. And I could join a riding or a fencing club.

But what if I have not learned anything?

Then I'd know it was all in my head.

Let's see. How did the ballad about the bards go? I start to hum it, recalling both the melody and the words. Wow. What about the love song? I remember that one too. Double wow.

Do other people have these kinds of adventures?

I've read about people who claim to have been touched by some supernatural events. Every one of them said that it has made him or her a better person. Am I a better person? Has my struggle with forgiveness and love changed me for the better? Has living through that siege—or, to be more exact, dying in it—changed me?

I barely notice the rain that is still pounding us. It's the same rain that drenched me when I found the enchanted tower … how could it be?

Questions and memories twirl non-stop in my mind until we arrive at the deserted camp. The children left yesterday, and we could only stay because we begged and charmed the caretakers until they kindly agreed.

We quickly shower, change into dry clothes, and go for dinner to the local pub, where we spend the entire evening laughing as we recall the most hilarious events of our summer—at least they are hilarious in hindsight.

I want to tell someone about my adventures, but who would believe me? I sure wouldn't. I decide to confide in my sister, and my best friend, Nicole.

Next day on the train home I write down the songs I've learned from Christian, along with names, places, and dates from the twelfth century.

~ ~ ~

No one is at home when I arrive—not that I expected a welcoming committee. I let myself into our apartment feeling as if I've just arrived from another world.

I live with my mother and sister in our childhood home, the only place I can afford while going to school. Mom owns an apartment in an older part of the city, in a hundred-year old Secessionist style villa my father and his company renovated fifteen years ago. After the divorce, Mom decided to stay, because she liked the established, well-heeled neighborhood, the mature trees, and the bright, spacious, high-ceilinged rooms.

The apartment has its drawbacks though; it has only one

bathroom, and two bedrooms, which means my sister and I still share a room. Even if it is the size of a small ballroom, it is short on privacy. Luckily, we have turned the housekeeper's room into a library cum guestroom; so when my sister's long-time boyfriend, Sean, is staying over, they, or I, can take refuge there.

I make a grilled cheese sandwich for lunch, empty the clothes from my backpack into the wash machine, and feel antsy. I want to talk to someone. But still no Sarah. Where is she? During the summer she works the morning shift, from 6 a.m. to 1 p.m., at the local pool. It's almost 2:30. She should be home by now.

Maybe I'll phone Nicole. No, I want to confide in my sister first. I finish the laundry, and I'm just beginning to punch Nicole's number when Sarah arrives. Finally.

While she prepares and eats her ham and cheese sandwich, she updates me on all the latest family gossip: Joe, our cousin, broke up with his fiancée two weeks before the wedding; Ian, my favorite cousin, (he is like an older brother to me) wrecked his new car—luckily, he was not hurt; Aunt Peggy twisted her ankle; Uncle Nick sold his business and made a windfall on it; and on and on until she runs out of news. "How did your summer go?" she asks.

"The usual," I answer. "Trying to keep a bunch of overexcited kids from hurting each other or themselves, answering zillions of questions, making kids feel so welcome they don't want to go home, taking care of scraped knees, upset stomachs, and mosquito bites. Not much out of the ordinary, at least not until the last day when I met an enchanted prince."

"What?" She swings around from shoving her plate into the dishwasher. "An enchanted prince. For real?" she laughs incredulously. "I hope he was good looking."

"He was indisputably good looking. Whether he was real

is still under debate."

She reaches for the coffee pot. "Want some coffee?"

"How old is that stuff?" Coffee has been known to sit around three or four days in our apartment. Our mom seldom craves it, but when she does she brews an entire pot, drinks a cup, and abandons the rest.

"I don't know. It's not turning green yet."

"I'd rather have an iced tea."

"Me too." She grabs two cans of iced tea from the fridge. "Why don't we go to the living room, and you can tell me what happened, and who this enchanting guy is."

Our living room was once the grand salon, but there's nothing grand about it now, except its size and the plaster-work. It is furnished with an eclectic assortment of family heirlooms, which means nothing matches. It looks better than it sounds because the mellow faded colors and finely carved wooden pieces provide a certain charming elegance.

We settle in two armchairs close to the window.

"Spill," Sarah says.

"Okay, but before I say anything, you must promise to keep this secret. This must stay in the family—"

"Wow," she interrupts. "It's that bad."

"You can be the judge, but first swear you will never breathe a word to anyone about what I tell you, not even Sean, or Liv. I know she's your best friend and it won't be easy—"

"You sure know how to wind up the audience." She brushes a lock of light honey brown hair from her face. "I swear I won't tell. Now let me hear it."

I recount the storm, finding the enchanted tower, meeting Christian—

"Am I supposed to believe this?" she interrupts.

"Not really, I have hard time believing it myself. Do you want to hear the rest?"

"Of course I do."

I relate the entire story including the challenges Christian faces.

It takes a few hours to finish, partly because it is a long story, and partly because Sarah constantly interrupts with questions and comments. And I realize that interrupting people is a family tradition.

At the end Sarah says, "Good luck convincing anyone this story is true."

"Thanks for the encouragement. But you're right, it is a rather unlikely tale. To be honest, even I need some proof before I believe it has actually happened."

"What kind of proof?"

"I've learned a few new skills such as shooting with a bow and arrow, horseback riding, and fencing. Before I insist on the truth of the story, I'd like to test if I'm any good at them. No one learns new skills in a dream. I just need to find a place to try."

She brightens. "I know a place where you can try. On a school trip, we went to a medieval festival. You can test all your skills there."

"What kind of medieval festival?"

"The one in Montfield on the last weekend in September."

"Would you go with me? I'll pay." I've earned enough money to be generous.

"Why not?" She shrugs. "Liv and I wanted to go. I hope you don't mind if she, or Sean, comes along. And I will pay for my trip."

"As long as you don't tell them why we're going."

"I will try," she promises.

"Let's find out more about this festival." I drain my tea, bring my laptop to the monster-size desk in the corner of the living room—a hand-me-down from great-grandpa—and we spend the rest of the afternoon planning the trip.

~ ~ ~

The next person I want to talk to is Nicole. We meet for lunch at a small Mexican restaurant close to her office.

She has been my best friend since grade one. We still go to school together, attending the same university. She is majoring in … something different every year. First year it was business, next journalism, then photography. I'm not sure what she's taking this year. She claims the Libra in her makes it impossible to make up her mind.

Nicole works on the weekends at a magazine called *The Female Warrior*, which, as the name implies, is much more concerned with women's issues than fashion. Working at the magazine is one of the few things that truly excite her.

The minute she arrives, she plunges into a story about *The Female Warrior* winning a major publishing prize for their issue on human trafficking, and about attending the gala—the clothes she wore, the food served, and the cute journalist she met.

Nicole is always meeting some cute guy. She draws men like a magnet. It is no surprise. She has light blond locks, flawless skin, a cute nose, shapely lips, large, innocent doe-eyes—the kind that make guys want to protect her, or possess her, or whatever. And she has a perfect figure … and she is witty. I am okay in the looks department, but I sure don't measure up to her.

By the time she finishes enthusing about the awards night and—mostly—the cute guy, her lunch break is over.

"I'm sorry," she says, standing up. "I didn't realize time was going this fast. Did anything interesting happen to you?" She's standing by her chair ready to leave.

"Nothing much." I gather up the bill and the money she left on the table. "I met an enchanted prince, visited the twelfth century. You know, the usual summer stuff."

She laughs. "Do you mean you met the love of your life?"

"I'd say so." I stand up, too. "In a rather extraordinary

way, I should say supernatural way."

"In a supernatural way?" Her eyes widen. "Tell me quickly what happened?"

"At another time. It's a long story, and you are supposed to be back at your office in a few minutes."

"I want to know about this guy and how you met him." She sits down, whips out her cellphone, calls her office, and tells the secretary an emergency has come up and she won't return for a while.

"An emergency?" I ask and sit down too.

"My concentration has been shattered. I can't focus on anything until I find out what happened to you. That's emergency enough." She waves to the waiter, asks for the dessert menu and more coffee. "Now we have a good excuse to eat something sweet, and you can tell me about your new guy."

"Okay. But promise you will not think I am nuts."

"I promise."

Without going into too many details, I tell her what happened.

"I always knew you had good imagination," she says when I'm finished.

"Here is the scoop," I say, dumping my leftover melted ice cream into my coffee and stirring it. "I have learned horseback riding, archery, and fencing during my adventures. To find out if I am still any good at them, Sarah and I are planning a trip to the Montfield Medieval Festival. Would you be interested in joining us?"

"Ann-Marie, you can't be serious. These sort of things don't happen—"

"Exactly my sentiment. That's why I want to test if I've learned anything. You and Sarah are my witnesses I've never before ridden a horse, shot with a bow and arrow, or had a sword in my hand. And I swear I didn't learn any of those skills at the children's camp."

"You didn't. How can you prove that?"

"You can phone the caretakers at the camp and ask."

"This sounds interesting. I'll see if I can take the days off."

~ ~ ~

School starts the following week. King's College was established in the fourteenth century, and now has close to ten thousand students plus the faculty. It is a small city within the city with a mixture of old noble architecture, modern buildings, high-rise student housing, parks with large old trees, and grassy banks that lead down to the river.

As part of our program, we provide free labor to one of the university's libraries. It's called internship. We can choose which department to benefit. Scanning the list of possible places, my eyes fall on the history department's library, and I sign up for that job.

"I thought you wanted to be a school librarian," Mom remarks on Saturday morning while making waffles for breakfast. She's rarely at home on Saturdays and hardly ever makes breakfast.

"I've changed my mind. During summer I became interest-ed in history. It's—"

"Please set the table," she interrupts.

As I move a pile of mail to the side to make room for the place mats, my eyes fall on a brochure from a bus-tour club Mom belongs to. Once a month they visit some obscure place, typically old ruins, then sample the local cuisine and beverages (mostly the beverages) until late into the night. I accompanied her once when I was fifteen and swore never to do it again. The average age of the participants is around sixty if not older. The tour guide and I were the only two people under twenty-five.

The brochure is advertising an excursion to tower houses along the north shore on the weekend following the medieval festival. Perfect. "Mom, could I go with you on this trip?"

"Which trip?" She turns to me.

"The one to the tower houses on the north shore, first weekend in October."

"If you want to." She shrugs her shoulder and turns back to the stove. "Will is planning to come too."

Will is my mom's gentleman friend. I used to call him Mom's boyfriend, but she insisted that he is a gentleman friend.

"What's the difference?" I asked cheekily. I was a not-so-sweet-sixteen at the time.

Mom's Spartan explanation: "A lot."

"You mean a gentleman friend is someone who will never marry you?"

"I told you before; I will not get married until you girls leave home."

Will is all right. Maybe because he already has three adult sons, he never tries to father us. Sarah and I both appreciate that.

"I don't mind going with Will."

"If you promise for sure you will come, I'll make reservation for you."

With a theatrical gesture, I place my hands on my heart. "I solemnly swear I'll go with you on that trip. I will pay, too." Feeling light and happy, I set the table.

~ ~ ~

The following Monday I join the history department's library. It is in one of the older buildings, with dark oak paneling and shelves, tall windows, oak tables polished by many years of use, and colorful plastic chairs.

At the checkout counter I ask for Mrs. Quinn, my supervisor.

"I am Mrs. Quinn," the woman answers in a high-pitched voice that makes her sound like a little girl, which she is not. She is middle-aged, slightly overweight, with reddish-brown hair, thick glasses, and a narrow, pinched mouth.

"I am Ann-Marie Burke." I smile at her. "I'm supposed to do my training at this library."

She opens the gate, ushers me into her office, and picks up my application from her desk. "You don't have any history credits. Why do you want to work in our library?"

"I've become interested in history, and hope to learn more about it by taking this job."

With narrowed eyes she gives me a once over. "You will have a hard time working here."

She's so encouraging. "I want to do some private research about castles," I say, trying to impress her. "Ryston and Bancloch in particular. Do you know anything about them?"

"Ryston," she says archly, "is a famous tourist destination. My dear, you will really have a hard time here."

So much for impressing her. "I will learn. I'm a quick learner," I mumble to reassure her—and myself. "Actually, I know a lot about both Ryston and Bancloch but want to find out more." I've already searched Ryston on the internet and two million plus hits came up, but nothing about Bancloch. "Have you heard about Bancloch?" I ask.

"I have not." With a stern face, she says, "I hope you realize you will have to do your research in your free time."

"I know that." I smile with my most charming grin.

"Today you will work at the check-in counter," she says then explains how to use the computer, the scanner, and sort the books, as if I were a total greenhorn. It is a slow morning, so while we are alone Mrs. Quinn tells me about the rules concerning who can borrow what. The library has a restricted section with rare books, prints, and other material, which only faculty or people with a special permit can take out.

Just before I leave at lunchtime, Mrs. Quinn hands me a large folder. "This catalogue, compiled by one of our retired professors, has the most extensive information about castles.

It is restricted material, but you can take it with you, as long as you return it by the end of the week. We also have a few other books that could be of interest to you. You can find a list of them in the bibliography of the catalogue."

I take the folder feeling as if someone has just handed me the moon. "Thank you, this is wonderful." I beam.

"It could be difficult to find a castle from the twelfth century. It might be leveled to the ground, or could have changed names many times." She cracks the tiniest smile. "If you run into any problems in your research, you can always ask me."

"Thanks," I say happily. I've always known if you're searching for something, everything conspires to help you—at least it seems that way.

In the next few days, I study the catalogue Mrs. Quinn gave me. It's called the Rosenthal Catalogue, named for the professor who compiled it. It's a well-researched, comprehensive work—it even includes places which are only a rock pile nowadays—with pictures of every castle, the date they were originally built, who built them, which families owned them, and how and where to find them. In addition, it incorporates legends and stories associated with each place. I find the catalogue fascinating.

The first castle I read up on is Ryston. It was a stronghold from the Stone Age, attacked and damaged many times throughout its history, and owned by the same family since the tenth century, although they temporarily lost it in the sixteenth.

On the internet site, I find the genealogy of the owners. Unfortunately, the list begins with the thirteenth century.

I cannot find any information about Bancloch. I carefully study the pictures of every castle along the north shore, read the history of each one, but nothing turns up. Undeterred, I make a long list of reference books.

Chapter 19

Late Friday afternoon Liv, Sarah, Nicole and I drive to Montfield in Nicole's BMW. The ads for the festival have promised many interesting activities: competitions, demonstrations, kids' events, and a medieval dance on Saturday evening. Visitors can also sample medieval food and buy antiques, replica medieval clothing, jewelry, pottery and many other craft items.

We stay at a B&B, a romantic, musty old building with geraniums in window boxes and quaint shutters which cannot be closed because of the geraniums. It's a long way from the castle, and has only one washroom for the three upstairs guest rooms, but it was the only reasonably priced accommodation left.

"It could be worse," I tell Nicole when she complains about the washroom situation. "It could have an outhouse and it could be raining."

On Saturday morning after a hearty breakfast we head to the fair that is held at the partially restored Montfield Castle. The day is pleasant and sunny. At the gateway two young women dressed in medieval clothes hand us maps and event schedules.

"Let's begin with archery," I recommend after studying the map. "The field is just around the corner and it will soon close for a competition."

The archery field is a long grassy stretch by the castle wall. Rolls of hay at one end are the targets.

"Have you used a bow before?" asks a middle-aged man dressed in a medieval tunic and not-quite-medieval jeans.

What can I say? "Yes … I think."

"What type of bow would you like to use?"

I choose a longbow, and as soon as I pick it up, I know I'll be fine.

"The center of the middle bale is the bull's eye, but any arrow that lands in the bale will win a prize," the man explains.

Two of my arrows hit the center circle, and one comes close.

"Wow," says Liv, her green eyes wide. She's a timeless beauty with soft features and the most radiant smile of all the people I know. "When did you learn archery?"

"This summer." I beam.

"I have to try this." Nicole hands her tickets to the attendant who shows her how to nock the arrow.

She pulls the string and says, "This isn't easy."

Tell me about it.

All her shots lands in the bale. Damn, she's better than I was.

Sarah, too, wants to try. She asks me to show how to do it. I explain—the way Christian taught me. When I step back, the attendant says, "Good way of teaching. Which club do you belong to?"

I smile. "Thanks for the compliment. I don't belong to any club." An idea hits me. "Would you know an archery club in Kinsborough?"

"So you're from the capital." He grins.

He has a directory of every archery association in the country, and gives me the name and phone number of the contact person in Kinsborough.

For the rest of the morning we wander around the noisy castle grounds. It is crowded with minstrels, jugglers, jesters, knights and ladies, vendors, and visitors.

We stop at a spinning and weaving demonstration, watch a potter throw his clay, then a baker working bread dough by hand. We visit the medieval bazaar, where Liv buys a small alabaster container, Sarah and Nicole purchase some silver jewelry, and I buy a set of four splendidly hand-embroidered handkerchiefs with medieval design. I have no idea what I'll use them for. Definitely not to blow my nose.

At one of the stalls a man is selling plastic swords, shields, toy knights, even a plastic suit of armor.

"I did not realize plastic was this common in the Middle Ages," Nicole says.

We watch a medieval weapon demonstration, then a mock fight with spiked one-ball flails and shields between two very agile modern day knights.

We listen for a while to a bagpipe contest (hard on the ears) then visit the food court, where authentic medieval food (or to phrase it better, food prepared according to authentic medieval recipes) is offered. The delicious aromas are enough to make anyone hungry. To try as many of the exotic-sounding dishes as we can, we buy four different dinners and a dessert and share everything.

We head to the fencing competition, after which the public can try their hand at fencing. As we watch the participants while they warm up, one of them, dressed in a yellow and red tunic with a dragon in one field and a fleur-de-lis in another, catches my attention. He reminds me of Christian. My heart speeds up. Could it be him? Hard to tell since his face is hidden behind a mask.

"That guy in the yellow and red tunic will win," I tell Nicole.

"How do you know?"

"He's good."

The competitors are introduced. His name is Christian Seymour. Christian. Omigod. It must be him. I feel a mixture of elation and nervousness. As I watch him, I am almost a hundred percent sure he is Christian. He wins the tournament.

While an announcer tells the audience where they can fence with the competitors, something very upsetting happens. A very attractive, very pregnant woman with a toddler on her arm appears beside Christian. He takes his helmet off, but turns his back toward me. Even his hair is the right color.

The woman tells him something and he nods, she kisses him on the cheek, he says a few words to the kid, and she leaves. Damn. He can't be married.

There's no time to be upset; if I want to fence with him I'd better hurry.

I find Christian Seymour's group. A line is already forming, and more people are arriving. An attendant announces that only thirty people can fence with each contestant, and the match ends when one of the competitors scores or after sixty seconds. I am the eighteenth in line. Phew.

The man in the yellow-and-red tunic eliminates his challengers in record time. When it is my turn, I put on a mask and vest, and we start to fence. His moves are fast and light just as Christian's were. I am pleased to find out that I can fence as well as I did in the twelfth century. When the minute is up, the man takes off his mask, and I almost faint.

Christian!

I take off my mask, shake out my hair while trying to regain my equilibrium and wipe the stupid grin off my face. We shake hands.

"Where did you learn fencing?" he asks, peering at me.

Good question. I just don't know how to answer it. "I— I learned it … from a friend," I stammer trying to hide the tempest inside me.

"Your friend taught you well." He smiles, still holding my hand. "Interesting technique."

"Thanks." I look into his eyes and feel as if some kind of recognition has passed between us. That's impossible. He's not supposed to remember me. His hazel eyes, warm and friendly, hold mine. "Nice meeting you."

"Nice meeting you, too." I reluctantly release his hand.

As I find my way out, my heart is racing wildly. Get a grip.

"Yoo-hoo, we're here," Nicole calls as I stumble out of the arena.

"You look like you've just seen a ghost," Liv remarks.

"I think I just did," I say, taking my purse from Sarah.

"Where else do you plan to show off?" Nicole asks, "You don't need to anymore. You've made your point. I believe you've learned a thing or two during the summer."

"I'd like to try horseback riding, if it's okay."

The stables are in the outer bailey. On the way I scan the grounds, hoping to get another glance of Christian, but I don't see him or the woman with the toddler anywhere.

I sign up for the experienced rider group, which consists of five riders. First, the leader makes us walk, trot, canter, and gallop, probably to ascertain we know what we're doing, then we canter off into the small forest that surrounds the castle.

The earthy scent of the trail and the thumping of the horses' hoofs make the memories of the time with Christian more real, but instead of cheering me up, they fill me with a sad longing.

~ ~ ~

We spend the rest of the afternoon getting ready—okay, primping—for the medieval dance, and arrive a bit early at the restored, almost empty, great hall where the dinner and dance is held. Long tables that seat eight people are arranged along the walls, leaving room for a dance floor in the center. Candles, water glasses, and silverware rolled into napkins are set out on each table on burgundy or dark blue tablecloths. Band members dressed as minstrels are tuning their instruments.

A few minutes later, Christian enters with three other guys. My heart jumps. He's dressed in casually elegant slacks, shirt, and a wool sweater. They stop by the door, scan the room, have a short discussion, then head directly to our table.

"Are these places taken?" Christian asks, pointing to the empty chairs.

"I don't see anyone sitting there, do you?" Nicole says.

Christian answers, "In that case, I hope you don't mind if we take them."

We don't mind at all. In fact, we stop slouching and generally look far more lively and perky than only a few seconds earlier. "I'm Chris," Christian introduces himself. "Kevin," he points to a blond sturdy fellow, who reminds me of Ryan, "Luke, and Grant." Luke has nice brown eyes; Grant is tall and gangly.

While we introduce ourselves, I peek at Christian's fingers. He has no wedding band on. That doesn't prove anything. Many people don't wear their wedding ring.

He sits down across from me. "You have interesting fencing technique," he says. "Where did you say you learned to fence?"

I am tempted to say "I learned from you," but decide against it. He might think we are escapees from the local mental institute. "I learned it from a friend," I say.

"Where does your friend live?" he asks

"I lost touch with him." This is mostly true. "Why are you asking?"

"I am the coach of the medieval fencing club at Kings. We invite instructors from different clubs to lead workshops. Your friend would be a good candidate."

If he's the coach ... "Are you attending Kings?" I ask.

"I am," he says.

"So are we." I beam. "Is there a fencing club at the university?" What a stupid question. Of course, there's one if he's the coach.

"Yes," he says with a smile that makes my heart skip a beat. "And you should join it."

"I probably will." I'd join any club if he invited me, even the chess club. "What made you learn to fence?"

"I'm likely the reincarnation of a medieval lord," he answers deadpan. "Either that or a medieval knight got lost inside me."

"Great." I grin. "I used to be the lady of a castle in the twelfth century."

"Is that where your ladyship learned fencing?"

"I learned at a tower house. What are you studying at the university?"

"History," he says.

I should have guessed. "I'm taking library arts."

He nods. "You haven't told me the name of your master yet."

To my relief, a waiter arrives at our table to take the drink orders. I ask for a glass of house red.

At his turn, Christian says to the waiter. "Please bring a bottle of (he names some French wine) and cancel milady's order." He indicates me. "I am buying wine for her too."

"You don't need to," I protest.

He smiles at me disarmingly. "I am not being totally altruistic. I hope to entice you to tell me your master's name and at which tower house you've learned to fence."

It feels stupid to be so secretive. But what can I say? This is no place to talk about enchantments. "Are you trying to get me drunk to pry out that information?"

"There's a plan," he laughs.

"Sorry to disappoint you, it won't work. I've never been drunk in my life."

"There goes plan A."

"What's plan B?"

"I don't know yet."

"Believe it or not," Nicole cuts in, "she's learned fencing out of this world."

Thanks Nicole. I can see on her face that she is ready to charm Christian. Great.

Christian looks at me questioningly. "Out of this world?"

"It's not out of this world," I say. "The place is called

Bancloch."

Christian frowns.

Omigod. How familiar that frown is.

"Bancloch," he says. "I haven't heard of it before. Where exactly is that place?"

"On the north shore. Are you good at archery too?"

"Why are you asking?"

"You said you're the reincarnation of a medieval knight. I thought you might be interested in other medieval sports like archery and jousting."

He peers at me. "I am good at both. Are you?"

"I'm good at archery. I've never tried jousting."

"She learned archery at Bancloch, too," Nicole says.

I wish Nicole would stay out of this.

With another charming smile, Christian asks, "What else have you learned at Bancloch?"

"Horseback riding, medieval songs and dances, a bit of history." To love you, I add silently.

"Is Bancloch some kind of medieval boot camp?"

I laugh, but before I can answer, the waiter arrives with our drinks. Christian pours wine for me and him then lifts his glass. "To Bancloch."

"To Bancloch." I take a sip. "Is there an archery club at the university?"

"Not at the university, but I belong to a club. Are you interested in joining?"

"Yes." This sounded a bit too enthusiastic.

"Good." He touches his lips with his tongue.

Involuntarily, I touch mine too.

Our food arrives. While we eat, two things happen: every time I glance at Christian he is looking at me. And I have to admit I glance at him more often than I should. Second: Nicole gets into high gear, and entertains Christian so charmingly it makes me sick.

After dinner a dance group demonstrates medieval dances.

"Do you know any of these?" Christian turns to me.

"Not these ones, but I know a few similar ones." At least I think I do.

"Maybe Ann-Marie could give us a demonstration," Nicole says.

Christian smiles at me and turns back to watch the dancers. When the performance is over, people are invited to learn a medieval dance.

"Do you want to give it a try?" Christian asks me.

"Yes." Again I sound more eager than I want to. Rats.

When I'm next to him, Christian offers his arm just as he has done many times. His movement is so familiar my breath catches in my throat. I place my hand on his and look up into one of his captivating smiles.

"Do you like dancing?" I ask while we join the group in the center of the dance floor.

"I'm not much into dancing."

For someone "not much into dancing," he is good.

We finish the medieval dance, and he asks with a theatrical bow, "May I have the next dance, too, my lady?"

"Yes, my lord, you may," I curtsy.

The band switches to twenty-first century music. After two fast pieces the third dance is slow. Christian pulls me close to him and leans his head against mine. To prevent myself from melting into him, I recall the woman with the child. Who is she? It is hard to worry about her while in Christian's arms.

When we return to the table, Christian asks Nicole for a dance. I watch them. He laughs as she talks to him animatedly. At the next slow dance, Nicole is burying her face in his neck. I bite my lip.

Obviously, she is after Christian. I could tell her to lay it off, but that would probably make her even more interested.

Damn. If convincing Christian that the impossible actually happened—and beguiling him enough to marry me—wasn't enough challenge, now I have to contend with Nicole too.

"May I have this dance?" Grant interrupts my thoughts. We are the only two people sitting at the table.

"Yes," I say. Anything is better than watching Christian and Nicole. Grant is even taller than I thought. My head ends just below his chin. "Are you going to Kings too?" I ask to start a conversation.

"No, I work at an engineering firm."

"How did you meet Christian then?"

"At school."

"What kind of school?"

"Boarding school." So Christian went to boarding school.

"Do you fence too?"

"Yes."

"Where did you learn fencing?"

"At the boarding school."

"What kind of engineering firm do you work for?"

"Richardson."

I've never heard of the company. "What does the company do?"

"Plans highways and bridges."

In the above style, I learn that he's an infrastructure engineer; likes sailing, operas and poetry; is an only child; and has known Christian since age ten. I'd like to ask if Christian is married, but decide against it.

As our entire conversation consists of me asking questions and Grant giving the shortest possible answers without asking any questions about me, I feel like an inquisitor. The conversation peters out by the end of the second dance. We return to the table and, without saying another word, watch the dancers. I try to find Christian and Nicole in the crowd, but cannot see them until they return to the table.

For the rest of the evening Nicole dominates Christian, Grant broods alone, Liv and Luke disappear halfway through the evening, Sarah dances almost constantly with different guys, and I … I fume.

The dance ends at one in the morning. Liv and Luke are back, and the guys accompany us to Nicole's car; even Kevin, whom I have not seen since dinner, reappears. Before I climb into the back seat, Christian leans close, and whispers in a husky voice, "Make sure you come to the fencing class on Thursday." He lightly brushes my forehead with his lips.

Omigod.

~ ~ ~

I lie awake for a long time. I can't chase from my mind the vision of Christian and the woman—and Nicole charming him. Can I stop her from stealing Christian? When I finally drift off, I have restless dreams in which Christian and I almost touch, but people keep coming between us.

The day is cool and windy with intermittent rain; rather unpleasant for wandering around.

"The organizers were lucky to have such good weather yesterday," Liv remarks.

We watch a horse show, check out an exhibition about the castle's history, and learn that the proceeds from the festival will help to restore the armory. We have another medieval lunch, and attend the closing ceremonies during which the winners receive their prizes.

With Liv's theater binoculars, I search the spectators for the pregnant woman with the toddler but can't see her anywhere. Christian receives four medals, then takes off with his friends. I'm a bit disappointed. I had hoped to talk to him again.

On the way home the four of us discuss the fair and the guys we met.

"Where did you disappear to?" Nicole asks Liv.

"That's none of your business," she retorts. "How about you and that Chris guy?"

Nicole and Christian. Did Christian show more interest in Nicole than me? He definitely spent more time with her, but only because she would not leave him alone. I hope.

"He's invited me to fencing," Nicole says. "But I'll let Ann-Marie do the fencing part. I'll go for something more exciting."

Sometimes I hate Nicole. Did Christian invite her with a brush of his lips? Better if I don't know.

"He's cute," Liv says.

Nicole agrees. "How about Grant?" she asks, glancing at me through the rear view mirror. "Did you find him attractive?"

"He seems a nice fellow," I say. "But he's not my type."

"I could tell." Nicole smirks. "You kept gawking at Chris."

"I did not gawk."

"You sure did."

Before I could answer, Sarah puts her hand on my knee, waving a "leave it."

When we arrive at home Sarah says, "He was far more interested in you than in Nicole."

"Who?" I ask.

"That Chris guy," she answers, turning her backpack upside down, dumping its contents on her bed.

"Thanks, Sarah." I smile at her. "I just hope he's more interested in me than my fencing instructor. Also, he might be married."

"Married?" she asks, surprised.

"Yes." I tell her what I saw at the fencing competition.

"I don't know," Sarah says, uncertain. "He definitely kept his eyes on you."

"Sarah, do you know who he is?" Without waiting for a

reply, I say, "He's Christian from the enchanted tower."

Sarah straightens. "Is he? Are you sure?"

"Of course I am." I drop a pair of sandals on the floor. "Nicole's after him. What if he chooses her?" I angrily pull a pair of jeans from my bag. "Or what if he already has a family? We're supposed to get married or he'll die."

"Die?" Sarah's eyebrows shoot up.

"Who will die?" Our mother pokes her head into our room. I didn't realize she was home. How much of our conversation has she heard? From her tousled hair and wrinkled clothes, I assume she's just woken from a nap.

"No one is going to die," I say. "Well, actually, everyone will … one day."

She laughs and asks how our trip was. We tell her it was great.

Chapter 20

In the next few days I find it hard to concentrate on anything. Christian occupies my every waking thought and many of my dreams.

On Thursday I arrive a few minutes before fencing starts. When he notices me his face brightens, and he gives such a warm smile my heart does a little dance.

I fill out the necessary forms, and Christian promises to drop them at the office.

Eight men, including Kevin and Grant, and two women are in the class—three counting me. We warm up, do foot work, and practice different moves. During the class I notice that both girls flirt with Christian. Great. I try to talk with them (they introduce themselves as "the K-girls, Kyla and Kim"), but they prefer to giggle and chat among themselves.

In the second half of the class we have an in-house tournament. As Christian pointed out in the enchanted tower, you can learn a lot about the opponent's personality during fencing. You quickly find out whether he or she is confident or unsure, easy-going or aggressive, friendly or distant, nervous or relaxed.

Grant lets me win without a fight. Kyla becomes rather annoyed and aggressive when she realizes I am good, too. Christian is challenging and friendly, but he doesn't let me win. While we're shaking hands at the end of the match he says, "I should not ask who your teacher—"

"No, you should not," I interrupt.

"Whoever taught you was good."

"How about giving me some credit too?"

"You're good too," he says in a way that makes me wonder if he's talking about my fencing.

At the end of the class while I am returning my mask, vest, and sword to the club's locker, Christian corners me. "We usually go for some refreshments after the class. Do you want to join us?"

I'd love to but I have a study group in about five minutes in another building. "I'm sorry, but I can't." In that moment Nicole walks in. What is she doing here? Maybe I'll skip the study group. Nah. I am in no mood to compete with her for a guy's attention—even if that guy is Christian.

~ ~ ~

On Friday I am off on the bus tour with Mom. Using some emergency at work as an excuse, Will misses the trip. I suspect he does not want to interfere with our mother-daughter bonding.

"Have you packed everything you need?" Mom suspiciously eyes my carry-on bag; it is half the size of her suitcase.

"Yes, Mom." I grin at her. "How much stuff do you need for two days?"

Actually, Mom—who is rather pretty, with thick brown

hair, large brown eyes, a figure many younger women would envy, and is always elegant and well groomed—needs a lot of stuff for two days.

"I've told you," she says. "You need two changes of comfortable clothes for the bus, two dresses for dinner—a different one for each night—comfortable shoes for walking, elegant shoes for the evening, an extra set of clothing in case you get wet, umbrella, nighties—"

"Mom, trust me," I interrupt. "I've packed everything you've told me, along with a change of underwear, socks, spare shoes, toothbrush, comb, and whatever else I might need, including the kitchen sink."

"You could fit them all into that small bag?" Her eyes narrow.

"I'm good at packing." This is true. I'm also taking less than half of the stuff she thinks I should, but she doesn't need to know that.

The wail of the entry buzzer interrupts our discussion; the taxi has arrived. It is rush hour and the trip to the bus depot takes longer than we expected. Luckily, we are still on time. While Mom keeps fussing over her suitcase, I board the bus and take the window seat.

She sits down next to me and drums her well-manicured fingers on the armrest. This is an indicator that she is annoyed about something.

"What's the problem, Mom?" I turn to her.

"You should have shown a bit of courtesy and asked if I'd like to have the window seat."

A few months ago I would have been up in arms; now I just say, "Okay, Mom. Would you like to have the window seat?"

She titters. "Not now; we can switch at the first stop."

When everyone is seated, the tour guide introduces herself and hands out an itinerary to each passenger. She tells us when and where the stops will be. I study the names of the places and wish I could have brought the Rosenthal catalogue with me. Mom starts to read a novel, and I stare out the window thinking about Christian.

At the first stop Mom meets someone from work. They get into a gossip session that takes much longer than our break so Mom joins her friend, who has an empty seat beside her, and I end up with the window seat again. Not that I mind.

The third stop is our final one for the day. We are staying at a large manor house. I like the place. Our room is furnished with antique-looking furniture; the bedding smells clean and fresh; dinner is served on fine china; and we don't have to cook or do the dishes. You can call me self-indulgent, but I could live like this.

During supper I talk with our tour guide to learn what qualifications are required for her job. Maybe I could become a tour guide. It would be fun. She tells me the job is anything but glamorous and the pay is a pittance. I learn that she's attending Kings too, taking history as a part time student. I ask her if she knows anyone named Chris Seymour. She doesn't.

Next day, in pouring rain, we reach the north shore and stop at many tower houses. We learn that most of the towers were built between the tenth and fifteenth century to protect the shores from pirates and invaders. Some of them are still in use today as first or second homes. None of them is Bancloch, and none of the shorelines is familiar.

On Sunday before the return trip, we have some free time in a picturesque medieval city called Norbury. Instead of shopping, Mom and I visit a charming coffee shop. We order two espressos and some dainties.

"Where did your sudden interest in history and castles come from?" Mom asks after we settle at the table with our goodies.

In a moment of impulsive honesty, I decided to tell her the truth. I like to shock her. "During summer I had a remarkable experience. I lost my way during a hike and discovered an enchanted tower with an enchanted prince." To her credit she doesn't even blink. "He taught me how to ride a horse, fence, and shoot with bow and arrow—skills which I still remember." No reaction. "History was one of his favorite subjects; he made history so fascinating I want to learn more about it." Mom's watching me, her mouth agape. "That's not all," I continue. "I met him again, in his time, in the twelfth century. We married but died in a siege shortly after. I am searching for the castle in which we lived. Its name is Bancloch."

"Do you know," she says in a low, stunned voice, "when I was a child I could visit another place and time too?"

It is my turn to be surprised. "Could you, really?"

"It was shortly after my father passed away. I was an only child at that time and had to play a lot by myself. I had a little hideaway behind some overgrown currant bushes, and whenever I hid there, I could travel to a castle in the sixteenth century." She stares into her coffee as if she could see the place there. "When I told others about it, everyone thought it was only a child's fantasy. It was not. It was real. I was really in that castle."

"Mom," I smile at her, "I never thought you'd have such an amazing secret. Have you tried to find that place?"

"Yes. I've found it. It is a well-known fortress in Italy; I recognized it at once."

"Wow." I grin. "Can you still visit the sixteenth century?"

With a sad smile, she shakes her head. "When Mother remarried and we moved to the city, I couldn't visit any more. It seems I could only reach the castle through my childhood hideaway. I went back years later to find the house; both the building and the garden were demolished, replaced by an apartment and a parking lot."

"So you believe I was in another place and time?"

"I do," she whispers leaning toward me. "But better keep it a secret, and please don't tell anyone what I've told you."

"I don't know." I grin at her. "I've planned to take out a half page ad in the paper and let everyone read about it."

Mom laughs. "When I was a teenager, I confided in my best friend about my visits." She stirs her coffee pensively. "She thought I made it all up to be special."

"That's why I only told Sarah and Nicole about my experiences. I must convince one person, though—the prince. He cannot stay in this century unless he believes me, and I have only until next October to convince him."

Mom frowns. "A prince? From the twelfth century?"

"Yes and no. He is from the twelfth century, but he was born here. It's complicated, and there isn't enough time to explain it now." I take a dainty and stuff it into my mouth, then offer her the plate.

"How could he be here?" She waves away my offer.

"As I said, it's complicated."

"I'd like to hear more about this."

I smile at her. "If you tell me more about your visits, I'll tell you more about mine."

She looks at me solicitously. "Let's see when we could get together. Monday is out. Tuesday's taken too. Wednesday—"

"Mom," I interrupt, "we don't have to make an appointment right now. Just try to squeeze me in before Christmas."

She laughs. "Hopefully, I can."

Chapter 21

Nicole shows up just before the end of the fencing class. Christian is talking with Grant by the door, and Nicole joins them. I'm very tempted to stay for the refreshments. No. I know from previous experiences if she came to charm Prince Charming she will ignore me or, even worse, use the occasion to make me look ridiculous. Anyway, I refuse to compete for a guy's attention: I'd rather study. (Ha, ha, ha.)

As I am leaving, Christian stops me at the door and asks, "Are you coming to the coffee shop?"

"I can't, I have a study period."

"Fine. In that case I want to talk to you now."

"Okay." What's so important that he must discuss it right now?

Christian turns to the K-girls, Grant, and Nicole. "I'll catch up with you in a minute." Reluctantly, they leave, except for Nicole who only takes a few steps and stops.

"You mentioned that—" he says then notices Nicole eavesdropping, and tells her in his customary imperial manner, "I'll meet you at the coffee shop." She leaves reluctantly. Christian watches her go, his face inscrutable, then turns to me. "Are you still interested in joining the archery club?"

"Yes, I am. I just haven't had a chance to look it up."

"You don't need to. I'm going this Saturday morning and I want to invite you." I cannot repress a happy grin. Damn. "The practice shooting is between eight and ten," he says with a smile. "Do you know where McGregor's Field is?"

I shake my head "no."

"It is at the east end of the city. Do you drive?"

"Yes, but I don't have a car."

"Good, I wanted to give you a ride. Where do you live?"

"On the west side. Where do you live?"

"I live a few blocks from the university." The university is on the east side of the river.

We decide to meet at the campus bus stop.

On Saturday morning low clouds chase each other over the rooftops. I step off the bus and notice Christian leaning against a beat-up dark-blue Rover, his arms crossed over his chest, his long legs crossed at the ankle. He's dressed in jeans, a t-shirt and a black bomber jacket. Damn, he's sexy. As I approach him, he gives me one of his heart-stopping smiles.

"Have you been waiting long?" I ask, pretending to be unaffected by his charm.

"Not at all." He pushes himself away and opens the door for me.

"This is a pretty macho car," I say when we settle in our seats. "Do you do lots of four-wheel driving?"

"At home I do."

"At home? Where is at home?"

"In Norbury." He turns the key in the ignition.

"I was there last weekend on a tour," I exclaim. "It's a lovely city."

He mutters something, pulls away from the curb, then, glancing at me, says, "Now that I have you alone, please tell me the truth about where you've learned fencing and the name of your master."

I swallow hard. Is this the only reason he wanted me to come with him? I hate to admit I was hoping ... never mind. "Do you want to know the truth or do you want me to come up with an acceptable explanation?"

He send a sideway glance toward me. "I would like to hear the truth."

Should I tell him? I will have to, eventually. "Okay. I'll tell you the truth, but you must promise you will not think I'm off my rocker."

His mouth twitches lightly. "I promise."

"A few months ago, somehow I stepped outside time and found myself in an enchanted tower and later in the twelfth century. That's where I learned fencing, archery, and horseback riding."

All right, so this wasn't the entire truth, but I'm not ready to tell him he was there too.

He doesn't reply.

We turn onto the freeway that leads out of the city. I watch the other cars. There's little traffic this early on Saturday morning.

After a long silence Christian says in a low voice, "I have very vivid dreams." I look at him, but he's keeping his eyes on the road. "If you can call them dreams... I live in a castle ... it is always the same castle ... and that's where ..." He glances at me uneasily. "Why am I telling this to you?"

I smile at him, but his eyes are back on the road. "We had similar experiences. I am sure I visited the twelfth century, but how many people would believe me?"

"That explains why you fence differently," he says.

"Do I fence differently?"

"Somewhat."

We ride in silence. I think of Mom's confession, wondering how many people visit other times but never talk about it. "Actually, Christian, we may not be as unique as we think. I met someone who told me she could go to another time when she was a child."

He makes a face. "I know a club full of people who claim they can visit other times or planets."

"Is it the mental asylum?"

He laughs, and turns the windshield wipers on; it's started to rain. "It is a club full of seemingly normal people. They meet once a month to discuss their travels."

"How do you know about them? Do you attend their meetings?"

"I've been only a couple of times." Christian frowns. "If you're interested we can visit."

"Of course, I'm interested," I say.

"Fine. I'll let you know when we can go." Glancing at me sideways, he says, "You still haven't told me who your master was."

You, I think. "His Royal Highness Prince Christian John Rupert of Bancloch."

"A prince has taught you," he says in a way that makes it hard to know if he's teasing me or is taking me seriously.

"Yes, I only take lessons from the best."

"Didn't he have anything more important to do?"

"I guess not."

We leave the freeway and are out in the country. Christian turns to a winding driveway that leads to a long, low building. "This is the shooting range," he says, shutting off the motor.

Only a few people are in the building. The session we attend is an early morning practice, not a class. Because of the rain, we decide to use the indoor lanes.

Christian has his own bow and arrows, but I have to borrow. I test a few of the bows before finding the right one, and then choose the arrows. Christian watches me with amused interest.

"It seems you know what you're doing," he remarks. "Have you also learned archery from the Prince of Bancloch?" There's light mocking in his voice.

"Yes," I say, tying the quiver and picking up my bow. "Are we going to shoot?"

We decide to use the same lane, taking turns.

"Ladies first." Christian bows.

As I'm nocking the arrow, I feel Christian's eyes on me.

Focus on shooting.

All three arrows land close to the center.

"You're good," Christian says. "I hoped to give you a shooting lesson, but it would be redundant."

"If your heart is really set on it," I say, remembering our lessons at the tower, "you can teach me."

He steps closer. "It's unnecessary." He traces my cheek with his finger, then his eyes wander to my mouth. Desire wells up in me. He leans closer, and I am sure he will kiss me …

No such luck.

He straightens. "Please stand behind the safety line. It's my turn."

We have a good time at the shooting range, taking turns, adding up points, joking, laughing while congratulating each other. All the old intimacy has returned.

"How about a moving target?" he asks with a grin.

"Christian, you know I was never good at moving targets." Seeing surprise on his face, I realize what I said. He studies me with such intensity, it brings heat to every part of my body. "You remind me of the other Christian." I shrug.

"The prince in your fantasy?" he asks.

"It was more than a fantasy."

"We will shoot at moving targets another time," he says. "We should call it quits for today. Would you join me for breakfast at my favorite coffee shop?"

Of course I would.

It is pouring outside. Pulling my hood over my head, I run to the car, getting soaked. Laughing, I climb into the Rover.

~ ~ ~

"Christian, what does the castle you visit in your dreams look like?" I ask on the way back to the city.

"It is on a cliff by the sea." He gives a perfect description of Bancloch.

Damn. I've made a big mistake. I should have told him what Bancloch is like. What a missed opportunity!

When he finishes, I say, "It sounds like Bancloch, the castle I lived in during the twelfth century."

He glances at me. "I am trying to decide if you are for real or putting me on."

"Are you married in your dream?" I ask.

"I'm single."

"How about in this life?" Good grief. When will I stop to think before I speak?

His mouth twitches. "Neither am I married in this life."

I want to ask about the woman at the competition. Better not. "Christian, can you visit that castle any time you want to?"

"Yes, but I don't want to."

"Why not?"

"Ann-Marie, I'd rather not talk about my dreams," he says in his cold, imperial manner.

"Why not?"

He shrugs.

When he half-joked about being the reincarnation of a knight, I thought it would be easy to discuss the subject. His curt refusal shows otherwise. I sigh. The challenges seemed so easy on the wizard's island. I should have known there would be some twists to them. I wonder what problem he has with his parents. Maybe I can find out later.

We arrive at the café—a pleasant place with dark leather armchairs, sofas, earth-colored walls, and many modern paintings. Small accent lamps light each table casting a friendly glow in the rainy gloom.

"These people make the best latte in town," Christian says while guiding me to the front. We order two lattes and two croissants.

"Are you a coffee connoisseur?" I ask as we take a table close to the window.

"I like good coffee."

"I drink my coffee with so much cream and sugar, I can't tell the difference." I smile at him. "Tell me something about yourself."

"What would you like to know?"

"Anything. Everything."

He laughs. "Better if you don't know everything."

I take a sip of my coffee and break a piece off the croissant. The coffee is strong, but the croissant is heavenly. Soft and warm, it melts in my mouth. "This is the best croissant I've ever tasted," I say, smearing some kind of homemade marmalade on it. "Tell me about your family."

He makes a face. "My parents live in Norbury. My father takes care of the family business and Mother is the PR person. I have an older and a younger sister; both are married."

"Do you get along well with your parents?"

He looks at me with surprise. "Why are you asking?"

Feeling myself blush, I force a smile. "You don't have to answer."

He studies me for a few seconds than says, "I don't have the greatest relationship with them."

"I think it's hard to have a great relationship with our parents. We know them too well." I take a sip of my coffee.

"Maybe that too," Christian agrees. "My father wants to dictate every aspect of my life—"

"Welcome to the club," I interrupt with a grin. "My parents also think they could run my life better than I can. It must be a parent thing."

"My father wants to control everything: what I study, who I marry, where I live, what work I do?—" he suddenly stops, glares at me with narrowed eyes. "Why am I telling you this?"

"I promise I won't tell anyone anything we discuss here."

He frowns. "I've never met a girl who doesn't share everything with her chatty friends."

"Hey, that's nasty."

"I've riled you, haven't I?" he laughs.

"I can assure you, women have a few secrets too."

"Maybe about themselves, but not someone else."

I ignore the remark. "So, are you studying history in accordance with your father's wishes, or against them?"

"Against. He is convinced history is the most useless subject." Christian's hands tighten around his cup. "He is a businessman. He took a dying family business and turned it around, and he wants me to follow in his footsteps."

"And you don't."

He frowns.

"What year are you in at the university?"

"I'm working on my doctorate."

"Wow. You must be smart." He represses a small smile. "When did you become interested in history? Or were you born with that interest, too?"

"In high school, as we learned about empires in social studies, I saw a pattern in each society's rise and fall." He takes a sip of his coffee. "All politicians and business leaders should study history. They could recognize the forces that build and destroy societies." He takes another sip. "Amazing how little humankind has learned from its own mistakes."

"What kinds of mistakes?"

"Let's take an oversimplified example of the economy. If too much wealth is concentrated in a few hands, societies collapse. Still, the rich cannot stop grasping for more."

"I thought we all grasp for more. Do you think people can ever be satisfied?"

He laughs. "Do you grasp for more?"

"I don't know." I shrug. "I've come from a middle class family; we always had a comfortable life. My parents have worked long hours, but I think they enjoy it." I pause. "Having more things was never important to me. I am far more interested in making this world a better place, and becoming a better person."

"I can relate to that," he says. "So what made you choose library arts?"

"I've been a voracious reader all my life, and I love children. I want to be a school librarian to instill the love of books in children."

He smiles. "That's a noble notion. I've told you about

my family, now you tell me about yours."

We talk about our families. After a while Christian glances at his watch. "I am afraid I'll have to go soon. But I have enough time to give you a ride home."

I planned to do some shopping to buy a gift for my father —his birthday is tomorrow. Maybe I'll ride home with Christian then come back. Nah. That would be silly. "I'll take a rain-check on the ride," I say. "I want to do some shopping. Before we go, could you tell me if you know of any riding club or stable where a student could afford to ride?"

"I know one place where you could ride for free," he answers.

"You do?"

"My uncle, who is a world traveler and is hardly ever at home, lives just outside the city. He lets me ride his horses anytime. His property is close to the shooting range. We could go next Saturday after shooting."

"That sounds great." Wow. Another invitation.

He finishes his coffee, and we exit the coffee shop. At his car, without any prelude, he leans down and plants a friendly little kiss on my lips, the kind one would give to a close friend or relative. "See you on Thursday," he says, wheels around, and strides to the driver's side.

I stand stunned, watching as the back of his Rover disappears into traffic.

Chapter 22

On Sunday, Sarah and I are on our way to Father's birthday lunch. I haven't visited him since returning from the camp, though we talked on the phone a few times.

Dad and Martina live on the top floor of an elegant, modern apartment building his firm designed and built. It has a stunning view of the city through its many large windows.

Martina had it professionally redecorated just last spring, mostly in grays and blacks (the grays emphasize her gray eyes) with the occasional red and white accent. The place is the antithesis of our apartment.

"I hope they have other guests, too," I tell Sarah in the shiny elevator.

"Me too."

As soon as we arrive on the top floor, a maid opens the apartment door. She ushers us into the expansive living-dining room, where the table is set for only four people.

Rats.

Martina, tall and slim in a black and white Chanel suit, bursts in from the kitchen. "Look at your hair. It's awful." I touch my hair, but she's talking to Sarah. From Martina's reaction you'd think my sister has colored her hair purple or something, when she's only cut it short with bangs.

"I like it," I pipe up to support Sarah.

"I like it, too," says our father, with twinkling eyes, as he enters the room. "It suits you." He would adore Sarah even with purple hair. Then I notice that the jealousy I usually felt when my father commended my sister is absent.

"Hi, Dad." I swivel around, and give him a hug and a kiss. Father is about the same height as Christian, but has gained some weight in the last few years. He's still attractive with hair graying at his temples, square jaw, and laugh lines around his smiling blue eyes.

"Hello to you, too," Martina says sharply.

"Hello, Martina." I give her a politician-kiss on the cheek. Martina has the smoothest skin. She should. She probably spends more money on organic facials in a week than a librarian makes in a month. She believes in organic. Only organic food, clothes, cosmetics, cleaning supplies, etc. can enter her apartment.

"I must go check the kitchen," Martina says abruptly.

"Can we help with anything?" I ask just to be polite, knowing the answer will be "no."

"No," she says. "You should visit with your father, since you so seldom take time to see him." She trots to the kitchen.

"What would you like to drink?" our father asks, opening a door that blends into the paneling, but hides a well-stocked bar.

I have a Martini Rossi.

The three of us settle in the living room, and talk about school and work.

"Have you solved your problem with that unreliable PA?" I ask.

"We had to let her go," he says. "It wasn't easy. It is never easy to tell someone they don't measure up."

"I hope Mrs. Quinn won't think I don't measure up," I say. Martina chooses that moment to returns to the room. "She is convinced that without history credits it's impossible to do a good job in the history department's library."

"Not everyone is smart enough for university education," Martina says.

Dad frowns. "Ann-Marie is smart enough."

As far as I know, Martina only made it beyond her freshman year because her father threatened to withdraw his substantial donation to the university. She spent most of her campus days partying and shopping. Come to think of it, she still spends most of her days shopping and partying, only the parties are called galas, fundraising dinners, and balls. She also meets her friends for lunches, goes to the gym and health spa, and attends premiers. Luckily, she never wanted to have children.

"I better check on the kitchen," Martina says and leaves. The three of us continue to talk about Dad's business and school until Martina comes back to announce that lunch is ready.

We move to the table. The maid serves the appetizers: mushrooms stuffed with some tasty cream cheese.

"Why have you not visited your father since you've come back from your summer vacation?" Martina asks me.

"I was not on a vacation," I answer. "I worked at a children's camp to pay for school."

"You don't have to work to pay for your school," Martina scowls. "Your father provides you with more than enough money." That's true.

"The work experience will look good on my resume," I answer.

"You've been back for two months," Martina says, giving me the evil eye. "You could have saved a couple of hours for your father." Pointing at Sarah, she adds, "You too." She turns back to me. "What's your excuse for not coming?"

"Between school, studying, internship, fencing, and archery practice, I barely have time for sleep," I answer.

"If you are so busy," Martina says, "you should drop your fencing, and archery, and visit your father instead."

The maid enters from the kitchen and takes our empty appetizer plates.

"When did you take up fencing and archery?" Father smiles at me.

"Last summer, during camp; I've learned horseback riding, too." With an insolent smile to Martina, I add, "And I am planning to continue."

"Do you want to be a cowboy?" Martina sneers.

"No, I prefer to be a knight."

The maid returns with the soup, some kind of consommé.

When she exits, Martina asks Sarah, "What's your excuse for not coming?"

"I have no excuse," Sarah says. "I am here when I have time."

"You don't seem to have much time for your father."

Suddenly, I realize the game Martina is playing. She wants to keep us away by making our visits unpleasant, while at the same time proving to our father we don't care. "Martina," I interrupt with a sweet smile, "you haven't told us about your South American trip yet. How was the cruise?"

"It was fine," she snarls.

"We'll show you pictures after lunch," Father says kindly.

We eat in silence for a few minutes.

"I've read in the paper," Martina drawls, "it's unhealthy for young people to live with their parents after their teen years. It stunts development."

"It seems," I answer, "most people throughout the centuries and even today live with their parents all their lives. Do you mean they are all stunted in their development?"

"If researchers say so it must be so," she says.

I leave it at that.

Somehow, we get through lunch. Later Martina and Dad show us, on their 80-inch TV in the media room, hundreds of pictures of their trip. While reminiscing about the voyage, even Martina enjoys herself.

Father offers to drive us home. "It's time you two learn to drive," Martina grumbles.

"We know how to drive," I say cheerily. "We just can't afford a car."

On the way home, as always when only the three of us are together, we joke and have a good time.

At home I tell Sarah, "It was much easier to forgive Martina in the tower than to put up with her while she's bugging us and trying to ruin our visit. I think she's doing it to keep us away."

"Why would she do that?" Sarah asks.

"I don't know." I shrug. "Maybe out of jealousy, or guilt, or an inferiority complex, or she believes scolding is good parenting. Maybe that's how her mother treated her."

"Which one of her mothers?" she asks. "Her father is on wife number five. But I know she was always compared unfavorably to her sisters."

How does Sarah know that? She seems to know so much more about people than I do. "That's enough to make anyone feel a loser," I say.

Sarah agrees, and we spend the next half hour psychoanalyzing Martina. It makes us feel a lot better.

~ ~ ~

The following Monday, for the first time since I began to work at the library, Christian shows up. He is surprised to see me. "I did not realize you worked here," he says. "Is this where school librarians train?"

"Nope, this is where people who want to do some historical research train."

"Searching for Bancloch, I imagine." He smiles.

Damn that smile. It makes me want to kiss him. "Among other things." I nod, then, trying to act professional, I ask, "What can I do for you, sir?"

He hands me a piece of paper. "Please find a few articles for me."

"I am sorry," I apologize with cool professionalism. "We only find articles for the teachers."

"I am a teacher," he says.

"You said you're working on your doctorate."

"Yes, I am. I also teach."

"I thought only professors …" I realize how silly it is to argue with him. "Let's see what articles you are searching for." I take the list, read it, and nod as if I know what the books and articles are. "We will give you a call when we have retrieved them."

"Thanks, Ann-Marie," he says with another heart-melting smile.

In the evening when Sarah arrives I greet her with, "You

won't believe this. Christian teaches at the university."

"Nice." Her mind is obviously somewhere else. I can't blame her for not getting excited about Christian. I've only talked about him a zillion times. I'm surprised she's still willing to listen.

I have a sudden inspiration. "Would you be interested in sitting in on one of Christian's classes with me?" Maybe I should have asked Christian first, if it was okay with him.

"If it won't conflict with my schedule," she says.

"I'll find out and let you know."

Next day Christian comes to the library to pick up his books, and I ask him if it would be okay to visit one of his classes.

"Of course," he says. "You are the first person who's asked permission to come to my class. Normally, people ask if they could skip." He grabs the note pad from the counter, writes something on it, and hands it to me.

"You have a very early class," I say after reading it.

"Being on the bottom of the pecking order, I had to choose between one of those early-bird classes, when everyone is still half asleep, or a very crappy classroom."

"Is it okay if my sister comes with me?" I ask.

"The more the merrier," he answers.

In the evening Nicole stops by our apartment. "We haven't visited for a long time," she says.

That's true. We've only exchanged a few words on Thursdays after fencing. "Come on in," I usher her into the living room where Sarah is playing the piano.

"Anything new with you?" I ask as we sit ourselves on the living room sofa.

"I am falling in love," she answers with a coy, theatrical grin.

I have a bad feeling about this. "Who's the lucky guy?" I ask. The last interest I heard about was that "cute journalist."

She dreamily turns her eyes toward the ceiling folding her hands in front of her heart. "Chris Seymour."

"Christian?" I choke. "Is—is he interested in you?"

"Of course, he is." Nicole smiles indulgently and spends the next while raving over Christian.

Sarah, who kept playing, stops. "Talking about Christian, Ann-Marie, have you found out about his schedule?"

Sometime I wonder about Sarah.

"Whose schedule?" Nicole stiffens.

Rats. I didn't want to tell Nicole about visiting his class. "Christian teaches a course at the university," I say. "I asked him if we could sit in on one of his classes."

Nicole's eyes narrow. Studying her perfectly manicured fingernail, she says in a bored voice, "He invited me before, but I couldn't make it." Sarah and I glance at each other, then at the ceiling. "When are you going? Maybe I can make it this time."

"We haven't set a time yet, probably on Thursday morning."

We tentatively agree on Thursday, and I promise Nicole I will let her know.

"When did he invite you?" she asks with feigned indifference.

"He didn't invite me. I invited myself, and he kindly agreed." I tell her about our meeting at the library.

"Oh," she says.

"How are your classes going?" I ask. This year she's taking science. We talk about our classes until she leaves.

On Wednesday morning when Christian shows up with another list of books, I ask, "Is it okay if Nicole visits your class, too?"

His eyes narrow for a moment. "Fine, but please do not turn this into a public event."

"I promise no one else will come."

I am wrong. Liv joins us, too. We slip into the last row of

the auditorium. Since about a hundred students are present, four more shouldn't make any difference.

Christian's lecture is first-rate: logical, entertaining, peppered with questions, anecdotes, and jokes. He has a strong presence and an instinct for engaging his audience.

As I listen to his voice, the memories of our evenings together flood me. I close my eyes to let them flow freely. All of a sudden, everyone laughs. I open my eyes and ask Nicole what's happened.

"You're supposed to listen in class, not daydream," she whispers.

"Is that what he said?" I whisper back.

"I am not going to repeat what he said. Listen next time."

"He's good," Liv says, when the lesson is over and we are standing in the hallway. "He actually makes sense instead of just using big words. I wish more instructors were like him." She giggles. "He seems the perfect male specimen: good looking, smart, entertaining. I wonder what his short-coming is."

A few hours later I have an answer for her question. He's a damn flirt. During fencing the K-girls seek his attention more than usual and he just goes along. Nicole arrives, and the K-girls send dark glances toward her. I guess they don't like the competition. Neither do I.

When it is time to leave, Christian is talking on his cell phone. I wait around a bit chatting with Nicole, but he seems so engrossed in his call, I just wave good-bye and leave. Later I realize we had not confirmed our meeting on Saturday. Should I just show up? Should I call? No. I don't want to seem too anxious.

On Friday morning I am shelving materials and Mrs. Quinn is minding the desk when Christian shows up. He leaves his request with her. On the way out he stops by me and says in a low voice, "See you tomorrow morning, same time same place."

"I'll be there." I smile, relieved, then notice Mrs. Quinn is watching us.

~ ~ ~

Saturday morning dawns cool, bright, and windy. Christian is waiting for me when I arrive at the bus stop.

"I enjoyed your class," I tell him in the Rover.

"I enjoy them, too. I can feel smart and important while lecturing."

I laugh, and we talk about classes and teaching. I learn that Christian is debating whether tenure is for him. He'd much rather write well-researched historical novels because through them he could reach a wider audience.

I tell him I find history so fascinating I'm tempted to stay in that field. We talk non-stop until we arrive at the shooting range.

"Want to have fun shooting outside?" Christian asks while I'm searching for "my" bow.

"In this wind? Sure."

We are the only people outside. Shooting in strong wind is challenge enough, shooting in strong gusting wind is beyond challenging. You compensate for the wind, and it suddenly stops or picks up and as a result your arrow flies totally off course. Our final score is about a third less than it was the previous Saturday. Not that we care. What we care about, at least what I care about, is being together.

"Are you ready for horseback riding?" Christian asks, windblown and in high spirits, as we return to the building.

"Yes, sir."

We drive in the opposite direction from the freeway then turn so many times, by the time we stop in front of a tall wrought-iron gate, I'm totally disoriented. Christian gets out and punches something into a security pad. A long paved drive leads to an elegant Georgian house, the size of our apartment building, but we don't follow it. Instead we turn onto a gravel road that winds its way to the stables.

A middle-aged man greets us. "Good morning, sir," he says. "I have the horses ready for you."

"Thanks, Kline," Christian answers, then introduces the man to me. "Roan Kline, the stable master. Miss Burke." He gestures toward me.

"Nice to meet you," I shake Roan's strong, calloused hand.

A teenage boy, a younger image of Roan, leads two horses to us. "Another riding student." He grins insolently. "I should give riding lessons, too." His father shoots him a warning glance.

As always, I enjoy the ride. We travel the country lanes, jump over fences, canter, gallop, and trot until we arrive at a small brook where Christian stops his horse. "Let the horses take a break, while we eat something."

We dismount. He pulls a small quilt and tarp from his saddlebag, asks me to spread them on a flat rock, then takes a couple sandwiches, a thermos of hot tea and two plastic mugs, gives me one sandwich and a mug of tea, then sits down on the rock. I remain standing.

"There's enough room for both of us." Christian pats the place next to him.

Barely. He moves over a bit and I sit down beside him. Our hips touch, sending tiny ripples of pleasure through my body. "Have you brought other girls here?" I ask, taking a bite from my sandwich.

"What makes you think so?"

"The remark Roan's son made."

Christian laughs. "I've been here with some other riders, none of them as good as you."

Is he talking about my riding? "Does that huge house belong to your uncle?"

He blows into his hot tea. "A better way of putting it would be my uncle belongs to the house. The house comes with the family business."

"What kind of business does your family run?"

"You name it, and my family will have a share in it. My father insists on diversifying." Christian's family must be rich.

"Is your uncle your father's brother, or your mother's?"

"He's my mother's oldest brother."

I'd like to learn more about the family business, but Christian steers the conversation away from the subject.

Clouds have moved in since the morning. With the sun gone and the wind still strong, a shiver runs through my body. I should have brought a warmer jacket with me.

"Are you cold?" Christian asks.

I nod.

He puts his arm around my shoulder. "Is this better?"

It is. Suddenly I feel hot. I drain my tea. "We should go."

He takes the cup from my hand, puts it on the ground, turns back, pulls me closer to him ... and I know he will kiss me. His lips are soft, tentative, I open my mouth, and our kiss deepens.

"This was nice," I sigh when we let go.

"Only nice?" he murmurs. "We have to try harder."

We do.

When we let go again, I ask. "Is this part of every riding lesson you give?"

"No, this part I save for special students," he answers deadpan.

Oh. "Do you have lots of special students?" What a stupid question, as if he would tell me.

"No." He smiles. "I am choosy." He kisses me again.

I feel a raindrop on my hand; it's soon followed by others. Damn rain.

We pack up and return to the stables then Christian gives

me a ride home. "Would you like to come in?" I ask when we arrive at my apartment building.

"Not today, but ..." He reaches over the console and pulls me into another kiss.

"Whoever came up with the idea of a console in the middle of the front seat was an idiot," he mutters when he lets go.

In the next few weeks Christian comes to the library almost every day. We also meet on Thursdays for fencing and Saturdays for shooting, after which we either go horseback riding, or visit Christian's favorite coffee shop. Our Saturday outings become the highlight of my weeks. We talk about everything. We see the world much the same way, except the supernatural. Whenever I bring it up, Christian becomes uncomfortable, and changes the subject. We're both good at changing subjects.

On one Saturday Christian joins Sarah and me for lunch at our apartment, and the three of us have a great time. Mom, as usual, isn't home.

"Finally, you're dating a normal guy," Sarah comments after Christian leaves.

Chapter 23

On the last Saturday in November, Christian and I visit the Time and Space Travelers' Club. The meeting is in one of the small conference rooms at an expensive hotel. When we arrive, about twenty people are present in the dimly lit room, glasses in hand, talking in groups of two or three.

"Dahrling!" someone shrieks as we enter. A curvy woman—draped theatrically in a flowing star-studded purple and mauve muslin dress with a magenta sari over it— hastens to us. Hard to tell her age; it's somewhere between forty and sixty-five. "Christian," she exclaims. "How good to see you, my boy." She grabs Christian's hands, and a cloud of perfume envelops us. "How's your mother? I must visit with her when she is in town again. And your grandmother, how's she doing? And what's going on with you? Has anything extraordinary happened to you lately? Just wait until you hear David Little's latest adventure. I've missed you, my boy. How's school going?" She notices me. "Oh, you've brought a visitor. Splendid. May I know who this young lady is?" Without waiting for a reply she continues, "I remember now, she's the one who claims to have had some extraordinary experiences. I can hardly wait to hear it." With ring-covered hands she grabs my hand. "So nice to meet you, my dear, my name is Madame Royale." Finally, she stops to breathe.

"Nice to meet you," I say. "I'm Ann-Marie Burke."

She lets go of my hand. "Splendid, Ms. Burke. Are you Christian's girlfriend?"

Am I? "A friend," I mutter.

She gestures toward a portable bar and a table spread with finger food. "I must leave you; I have some business to attend to. Please, serve yourself."

While Christian and I saunter to the bar, I say, "You said you've been here only a couple times. How come she greets you as if you were a close friend?"

"She's family." Christian grimaces. "She's my mother's cousin."

Oh.

"What would you like to drink?" Christian asks at the bar.

"I'll have red wine."

He orders two glasses of red and with drinks in hand we step over to the food table.

"How many people do you know here?" I ask, placing a skewered shrimp, a few pieces of raw vegetables, some dip, and a bite-size quiche on my plate.

"Only my aunt," Christian says, piling a bit of everything on his plate.

A well-dressed, slightly chubby man in his early thirties with dark hair and gold-framed glasses stops by me. "You must be new here. I'm Marcus Middleton, lawyer and space traveler. What adventures have brought you here?" He reaches out a hand.

How can I tell him? And how can I shake hands? I have a plate in one hand and a wine glass in the other. "Sorry." I smile apologetically and quickly place the glass on the table.

Christian steps closer to me. "I'm Chris Seymour. What kind of space traveler are you, Mr. Middleton?"

"I travel to the Andromeda Cluster."

I don't have the slightest idea where or what the Andromeda Cluster is, so I ask Mr. Middleton. While he explains it, a woman interrupts us. "Are you new here?"

I turn toward her. She's in her thirties, slim with bobbed brown hair and long false eyelashes. I learn that she can visit the court of Henry the Eighth. We also meet a man who in his free time is a Samurai in Edo period Japan.

"How are you able to fit in with your European features?" I ask but never hear the answer because Madame Royale rings a small bell and announces it's time to start the meeting.

What meeting? I expected the whole evening to be a cocktail party.

Everyone takes a chair around a square conference table. The secretary of the group reads the minutes of the last meeting and the treasurer reports. Then the agenda is read, and to my dismay, I find out I am one of the items on it.

"We have a visitor with us tonight," Madame Royale says, gesturing toward me. "Would you please introduce yourself?"

"Ann-Marie Burke." I force a smile, as I look at all the faces turned toward me.

"As I understand, my dear," Madame Royale grins, "you had some interesting experiences but are unsure about their nature. Please, darling, tell this group what happened."

I want to wring Christian's neck. He must have known this evening was more than just chatting with a few eccentric people. He didn't tell me I have to talk about my adventures.

Fine. I'll teach him.

I glance at everyone around the table. "It all started on a dark, stormy night, when I became lost and wandered into an enchanted tower. At the tower I met a rather obnoxious, cursed prince. To make describing him easier, you just need to look at Christian here, the prince's appearance was much the same, and, incidentally, he also had the same first name." He shoots a murderous glance at me. Obviously he is not pleased. Neither am I.

"What happened at that tower, my dear?" Madame Royale asks.

I narrate the rest of the story, including Christian's challenge. While I talk the scowl on his face deepens.

I have mixed feelings about him and about recounting my tale. On the one hand, it feels good to share what happened with a group of people who, I hope, don't think I'm totally nuts. On the other hand, I feel uncomfortable revealing my secret to total strangers.

"An interesting adventure," Madame Royale says when I finish. "Would anyone like to ask any questions before we rate this voyage?"

People ask about small details: what color were the butler's eyes; what did a medieval fishing dory look like; what underwear did people use.

"Have you met the prince in our time, yet?" one woman wants to know.

Should I tell the truth?

"Yes, I have," I say and smile innocently at Christian. Every eye turns to him. He looks at me, furious.

"Have you told him about your adventures?" the woman

asks looking at him.

I just did. "Not yet," I say.

To my surprise, the members vote on whether my story is real or not. I pass.

In the last part of the meeting, the other members report about their latest journeys to other time or outer space. The meeting ends around eleven.

As we leave, Madame Royale invites Christian and me to the next meeting, the group's Christmas dinner in mid-December.

Thanks. I am certain I will not attend.

~ ~ ~

An unfriendly silence enwraps Christian and me as we wait for his car.

"Why didn't you warn me I would have to tell my story?" I burst out in the Rover.

"Why did you insinuate I am the Christian in your story?" he asks at the same time in cold, imperial voice.

"Because you are the same Christian," I sputter. "And if you'd had the courtesy to warn me, I would have told you about our encounters before the meeting."

With tires screeching, he enters the traffic. "So I must marry you. Hah, that's a good one. And my relationship with my parents is none of your business," he adds frostily.

"You don't have to marry me," I retort, seething. "You don't have to do any of the three challenges. You never had to do them. And no one is forcing you now. You could have stayed on the other side and you can—"

"Do you expect me to believe all this nonsense?" he asks in his haughtiest manner.

"I hoped you would," I shoot back vehemently. "I know this is shocking to you—"

"It is not shocking. It is nonsense." He's frantically weaving his way between cars. "N-o-n-s-e-n-s-e."

I don't answer. Why is he so closed to the idea of us meeting on the other side? If he has dreams of the twelfth century, how can he say this is all nonsense? What am I to do? I must convince him or he'll die. We must stay on good terms. I must make peace with him somehow.

"Christian," I say in a calmer voice, "I know it is hard to believe this story ... to be honest, I had problems believing it myself ... I needed some proof first." I pause. "One is that I've learned fencing, archery, and horseback riding. You can ask my sister; half a year ago I knew nothing about those sports. And you cannot learn those skills in a few weeks, not at the proficiency I have." I would like to tell him meeting him is one more piece of evidence, but I know he'd reject it. "I also have names of people, places, and dates from the twelfth century. One reason I joined the history department's library is to research them ..." I trail off.

He's silent for a while then asks more amiably, "Have you found anything?"

"I haven't had time for serious research."

He doesn't answer. As we ride silently, I watch the streetlights' reflections slide on the wet hood. I can feel the tension dissipating.

"So, according to you, in the twelfth century I was a sociopath." Christian snickers. "And we were married. And I studied history, philosophy and religions for ... what did you say? ... nine hundred years ... no wonder I am so good at it."

"Christian, I didn't want you to find it out this way," I say softly.

"It was probably better this way," he says. "You could not have finished your story if I could interrupt."

I smile faintly, appreciating his honesty.

"Is this Time and Space Travelers group some kind of secret society?" I ask.

"It is by invitation only."

"Did you find out about them because of your dreams?"

"My mother is a member."

"Your mother. Is she a time or space traveler?"

"I'd rather not talk about it."

I'd like to ask more questions about his mother, but I have a feeling this is not the best time.

We arrive at my apartment building. Christian shuts off the motor. Will he kiss me? He doesn't move.

"I guess, we are here," I say tentatively. Could I have said anything more stupid? Of course, we are here. Christian sits silently. "Thanks for the ride ... and for the evening."

"It was undeniably entertaining." He frowns, his hands resting on the steering wheel.

He, obviously, isn't going to kiss me. I quickly reach for the door latch. I don't want him to think I'm waiting for his kiss. "Thanks again." I climb out, and slam the door with more force than I expected.

He starts the engine and takes off.

Damn.

~ ~ ~

"Are you okay?" Sarah asks when I enter our room. She's in bed, reading.

"I'm fine," I mutter. I don't want to discuss the evening with her. Not yet.

"You seem upset."

"No, truly, I'm fine."

I am not fine. Christian left without a kiss. He didn't ask about next Saturday. How could I be fine? Maybe this is it. The end of our relationship. Since fencing has ended for the semester, I won't see him unless he comes to the library.

He doesn't visit the library all week, not even once. As the week progresses my mood becomes darker and darker; by Friday night I am in the depths of despair and in a huff.

Dammit. I didn't need this emotional upset just before

the exams. I should concentrate on studying, instead of thinking about Christian.

What if he thinks I am a lunatic and this is the end of our relationship? I sigh. Could I just go back to fencing and pretend nothing's happened? I'll have to, unless I want him to die.

Stop thinking about Christian. Study. I begin to read my notes.

His challenges seemed so simple when the wizard told us about them. Marry: we were already married, we were in love, of course we'd marry again. Make peace with his parents: we all have to make peace with our parents. It's a sign of being a grown up. Believe what happened was real: that's the tough one. Nowadays we want proof. Throughout the centuries, people's inborn faith in the supernatural has been abused and exploited by so many unscrupulous men and women, we became cynical. Either that, or we want the mind to prove what only the heart can know.

Stop thinking about Christian. Study. I start to read again.

Maybe he's busy working on his dissertation or preparing exams.

What can I do to make peace with him? Nothing right now. Concentrate.

I spend as much time thinking about Christian as studying for the exams.

Sunday evening the phone rings for about the tenth time since noon. Normally we have ten calls in a week.

"Are we popular today or what?" I grumble.

"I'm not answering it," Sarah says.

"Fine, I will."

I pick up the phone. "Hello," I bark into the receiver.

"Hello, Ann-Marie," a male voice says, and I almost drop the receiver. It's Christian.

I can barely breathe a "hi."

"Would you join me for a Christmas dinner on the eighteenth? I won't have time to see you before."

I am torn. I want to have dinner with him, and I want to let him know …

Let him know what? I was all upset and have made myself miserable because I thought he had broken up with me.

"So?" he asks.

"Okay," I say, keeping my voice calm. "Thanks for the invitation."

"I'll be at your place at seven on Saturday the eighteenth. And …" A short pause. "It's an elegant restaurant, so please dress accordingly."

Happiness burst through me. Christian is taking me to an elegant restaurant. "Thanks Christian," I say as calmly as I can manage. I hang up the phone and dance around the living room. "Christian's invited me to a fancy restaurant. Christian has invited me. Hurray. Hurray."

Sarah looks up from her papers and rolls her eyes. "Any chance of studying in peace in this place?"

The next two weeks fly by in a whirlwind of activities and sweet anticipation. Between studying and exams I barely have time for sleep.

The exams are over, and the four of us, Liv, Nicole, Sarah, and I go to a nearby bakery to celebrate with mega-calories. We discuss the exams, then our conversation turns to Christmas and New Year's celebrations. "Who would like to go to Eigth&Eight on New Year's Eve?" I ask.

"To Eight&Eight," Liv says. "You must make reservations at least two months ahead to get in."

"Not when the owner is your uncle," I answer. "Though, family or not, he still wants us to pay their overinflated New Year's Eve price." Uncle Ted believes if he'd let family members attend for free, he'd have no room left for anyone else. He's probably right.

Liv declines the invitation; she'll be out of town. And Nicole won't know until after Christmas.

The marks are posted by the end of the following week. I finish between 85 and 92 percent in every subject except my internship. Mrs. Quinn gave me 78.

I march to the library. "Mrs. Quinn, could you tell me why you gave such a low mark? Was I that bad?"

"Seventy-eight percent is a good mark," she says.

"Not for me. In every other subject I finished over eighty-five percent," I say politely. "Could you tell me what I did wrong to deserve such a low mark?"

"I took off 10 percent because you flirted with the users," she says.

"I did not flirt with anyone," I protest.

"Except that handsome history instructor who only comes when you are here. I do have eyes, my dear."

"Mrs. Quinn, I was not flirting with him. We are friends." I hope.

"You didn't act like friends," she says. "You must behave as a professional, with everyone, even with friends."

I tighten my lips. No point arguing with her. Maybe it wasn't such a hot idea to work in the history department's library.

When Sarah finds out about my mark, she asks, "Are you going to contest it?"

"Nah." I shake my head. "I am not going to waste time or energy on it. I will just try to be a better slave next semester."

My mother's comment is, "When you apply for a job, it won't look good that your lowest mark is in practical."

What can I do?

"She's jealous because no one wants to flirt with her," Nicole tells me over the phone. "So that's where you sneak in meetings with Chris."

"I don't sneak in meetings," I say. "He comes to the library and we say a few friendly words to each other."

"Maybe I could transfer to history major," Nicole says.

I roll my eyes.

Chapter 24

Saturday afternoon I have all Sarah's and my elegant clothes spread out in our bedroom. I'm trying to find something that's stylish and sexy—but not too sexy. I settle on black silk trousers and a white silk blouse.

Sarah and Liv arrive, and when Liv finds out about my date with Christian, she shakes her head. "That cute teacher, and you want to go in black pants and a white blouse. You need some help, girl." She willingly provides the help. Liv has such good fashion sense she can look stunning in a sweat suit, runners, and a few accessories.

She thoughtfully studies me, studies the clothes spread out and says, "Try on that black spaghetti-strap dress, and this purplish jacket." I put them on and they are exactly the mien I am after. "Now let's find some shoes and jewelry to compliment them." We settle on my sister's high-heeled pumps, and Mom's choker with matching earrings. I will ask for Mom's permission later.

Liv styles my hair and helps with the make-up. I glance in the mirror, and cannot believe the transformation.

"Liv, you should be in fashion," I say.

"My parents would think it totally undignified," she laughs. She, like Sarah, is studying to become a pediatrician.

"You should always wear some make up," Sarah comments looking at my reflection in the bathroom mirror.

I agree. I should. But it does not mean I will.

To my relief, Christian arrives in a suit and a tie. I was afraid I might be overdressed. He looks good in a suit. Actually, Christian looks good in jeans and t-shirt, too, and if my memory does not fail me, he looked just as good in medieval clothes … and without …

Never mind.

He jokes with Liv and Sarah while I get my coat and purse. As we're leaving, Sarah crosses her fingers to wish good luck. She can wish me good luck again a minute later, because as soon as we reach Christian's car, I realize I left his present at home, and run back to get it.

"It's bad luck to run back for something you've forgotten," Sarah says.

"It's worse luck not to give Christian his present," I answer, running out the door.

Once in the car, I tell Christian about the grade Mrs. Quinn gave me, and her explanation.

"Not good," he mutters, and I realize flirting with me could be a problem for him too.

"I think there's more to it," I say. "Mrs. Quinn believes that without history credit, I cannot possibly do a good job."

"You have no history credit. Then why did you take this assignment?" Christian asks.

"To do some research," I answer. "Also, when I met you in the enchanted tower you talked a lot about history and I became interested. You make history sound fascinating."

"It is fascinating," he says, without commenting on the enchanted tower part.

We turn to the main road. The streets have a festive atmosphere. They are brighter than usual because colorful Christmas lights are twinkling everywhere: in windows, on lampposts, and reflecting back from the wet pavement. The sidewalks are crowded with shoppers. I notice four children with noses pressed to a toy store window and memories of the magic of childhood Christmases flash through my mind. "I love Christmas," I sigh.

With a smile, Christian glances at me. "What are your

plans for Christmas?"

"Visit with family and catch up on gossip, eat more than I should, drink more than I should, then try to lose the extra weight. What about you?"

"Much the same. Only I will be in Norbury. I will have to stay for a New Year's Eve ball, too." He sounds anything but pleased.

I guess we won't be spending New Year's Eve together. "You don't seem too happy about your visit."

"If you knew my family you wouldn't be surprised."

"Why?"

Christian grimaces. "My father uses every opportunity to let me know what a disappointment I am."

Oh. His father thinks he's a disappointment. "What does your father want? You're smart, pleasant, and talented." Not to mention sexy. "You must have an indomitable spirit, too. Usually kids whose parents are too critical tend to become withdrawn, and shy, which you are not." Christian has a peculiar expression on his face. I shrug. "I read that somewhere about the kids."

"You make me blush," he says, though he's not blushing at all. "I spent most of my life in boarding schools, where I happened to be popular with both the kids and the teachers, and during the vacations I stayed with my grandmother who, just like you, has an excessively high opinion of me. And of course, when I was a kid I actually believed her."

"God bless grandmothers," I say. "I also have a wonderful grandma."

We arrive at our destination: a small, elegant hotel. A valet opens my door to help me out. Christian gives him the car key, and ushers me to the well-appointed lobby. The dining room is intimate and elegant, with low light, white linen tablecloths, velvet-upholstered beige chairs, tasteful Christmassy centerpieces, and soft piano music.

"Good evening, Mr. Seymour. Good evening, Miss Burke," the host greets us then leads us to our table. He pulls out the chair for me and places the velour-covered menu in front. I open the menu. It's written in fancy calligraphy, and I realize no prices are printed. One waiter pours water and another one puts a basket of bread rolls and a small dish with oil and balsamic vinegar on the table. Christian orders a bottle of French wine.

The food is delicious, the wine is excellent, the company is even better, and the subject of our discussion: the people I knew in the twelfth century. Christian becomes excited when I tell him I have all the names and particulars written down and he can have a copy of it.

While we wait for dessert I hand him his Christmas present.

"May I open it now?" he asks.

"No, you must wait until Christmas Eve."

I bought a book for him. One of my favorite hangouts is a used bookstore close to the university. While browsing I checked the history section, and came across an old book by a famous history scholar of the early twentieth century. When I showed it to Mrs. Quinn, she told me it was a rare book indeed. I hope Christian will appreciate it.

At our apartment building Christian wants to wait in the foyer. I run inside, quickly make a copy of my notes. By the time I return to him the lobby is dim. To save energy the lights turn on only when someone opens the door and automatically turn off after a few minutes. The streetlight streaming through the glass wall keeps the lobby from becoming pitch dark. I reach for the lights, but Christian stops me. "It's bright enough," he says.

"Here are your papers." I hand him the sheets. He slides them into his coat pocket. "I guess I should go," I say reluctantly. "Are you sure you don't want to come in?"

"No." He shakes his head, pulls a small box from his

pocket. "I have a little present for you, too." He hands the box to me. "You're not allowed to open it before Christmas Day."

"Thanks, but …"

I can't finish the sentence, because Christian pulls me into a kiss. This kiss is far more passionate and demanding then any kisses we've shared so far. My body quickly reacts to it. He backs me into the corner, and our kissing becomes even more passionate. "You feel so good," he mutters, pulling me against his firm chest. The chemistry that has always existed between us works its magic. His hand is caressing my back under my coat. He lets go of my mouth and kisses his way down the sensitive skin of my neck.

"Oh Christian," I murmur and bury my fingers in his thick wavy hair. Christian's mouth finds my breast. "Are you sure you don't want to come in?" I whisper.

"No, not tonight," he moans. "When I come back." His hands cup my bottom pulling me closer and I can feel his hardness. I want to kiss him, but his lips are busy somewhere else.

Suddenly the lights are on. Damn.

It's Mom. Double damn. We both blink in the sudden brightness and I quickly straighten my dress. When I regain my composure, I say with as much dignity as I can muster, "Mom, this is Christian Seymour."

Christian says an impeccable "How do you do."

Turning to him I say, "Christian, this is my mother, Meghan Cooper."

"I'm pleased to meet you," my mother says, though she seems anything but pleased. "Would you like to come in?"

"At another time," Christian answers. "I am leaving early tomorrow morning. Nice to meet you." He smiles at my mother, leans down and kisses me on the lips.

"I'll walk you to your car," I say to delay the confrontation with Mom.

We kiss again for a few minutes by the Rover. "Have a good Christmas," Christian whispers. "And see you in the New Year."

~ ~ ~

"I don't think the entrance is the best place for making out." Mom confronts me as soon as I enter our apartment. She's been waiting in the entry hall.

I am too happy to argue with her. "Mom, I am sure you've never kissed anyone in a public place." I take off my coat, twirl with it as if it is a dance partner, then hang it in the closet.

"Who is this man?" she asks fuming.

"One of the teachers," I answer light-heartedly.

"You're dating a professor?" she says horrified.

"I am not dating him. We just do fencing and archery together," I trill happily.

"You are not dating him; just practically having sex with him by the entrance." She glares at me, hands on her hips. "What if someone else came in, what would they think?"

Mom is right; we shouldn't have been so carried away in the foyer. But I won't admit that I agree. I shrug my shoulders. "They would know I'm interested in guys. And we weren't having sex. We were only kissing."

Mother swallows hard. "You should not be dating any of the instructors."

"Mom, first, he's not my instructor," I say in a pacifying voice. "Second, he is Christian from the enchanted tower. We married nine hundred years ago; we're allowed to kiss in public." I open the door with a deep, butler-like bow. "Ma'am, could we discuss this in the comfort of the living room?"

"How old is he?" she asks, stalking through the doorway.

"Let me see." I close the door. "He was born in 1080 A.D. so he is nine hundred—"

Mom makes an irritated move and I know I'm at the end of her patience. "Ok. He's thirty."

"What does he teach?"

"He's working on his doctorate in history." This should impress her. It doesn't. I can see on Mom's face that she wants to fight, but I don't. "I am ready to retire," I say, heading for the bathroom.

"Where does he live?" Mom follows me.

"I don't know." I search for a cotton ball to wipe off the make-up. "Somewhere close to the university."

"He's never taken you to his place?"

"No," I say. And it's for the better because if we started to kiss like today, we probably wouldn't stop at kissing. "We usually go to the shooting range, to a coffee shop or horseback riding. He has some other commitment on Saturday afternoon." I wipe away my mascara.

"What commitment?" She's standing behind me, and I can see in the mirror her face is flushed with annoyance. "If you've never been to his place, how do you know he's not married?"

The woman with the child flashes through my mind. "He told me so." I turn on the water.

"And you believed him."

"Why shouldn't I believe him?" I splash water on my face. "Mom, relax. We only kissed. It's not like I'm pregnant with his child," I say between splashes.

Mom doesn't answer. I know exactly what she's thinking. She's thinking about our father. "Mom, not every man cheats on his wife."

"According to statistics, half of them do," she argues.

"I know." I reach for the towel. "And the other half is lying."

Mom titters.

"Mom, you must have more faith in men. Just because

our father was unfaithful—"

"No man can be trusted," she interrupts me.

"Fine," I mutter, squish toothpaste on my toothbrush, and brush my teeth. Mom is standing behind me, lost in her thoughts.

Will she ever regain her trust in men? What would I do if I were in her place? Hard to tell.

"It's close to midnight," I say after I rinse my mouth. "Let's talk about this at another time." In our family, "another time" usually means "never." Mom and I still haven't shared our fantastic adventures.

"Fine," she sighs. "Promise not to kiss in the entry again."

"I will try."

She sighs again.

Once in bed I relive our kiss a million times. It feels so good.

Chapter 25

Mom's family is coming to our place for Christmas Eve dinner. She and her siblings take turns hosting, and this is our year. Everyone brings a dish or two, which means we don't have to cook for seventeen people, but we still have a lot to do: clean, decorate the tree, and set up the table. Our table doesn't sit seventeen, so we extend it with homemade extensions, which are rather tricky—no, frustrating is a better word—to set up.

Aunt Peggy, with her teenage son and daughter, arrives in the early afternoon ready for action. Nineteen-year-old Allen carries in boxes of china and folding chairs. As if we needed more chairs. Once, Sarah and I counted all the chairs in our apartment; the total was twenty-five—for three people. My aunt has a dinner set for twenty-four and it's a tradition to use it at Christmas time. No one dares to refuse her. Sarah and I set the table with help from cousins Allen and Peggy, and we chat about school. Allen started university this year. He is studying to become an accountant—like his mother, uncle, and grandpa before him. In mom's family everyone is good with numbers and finances. I am too, but I find numbers boring.

More aunts and cousins arrive. Mom has three divorced half-sisters, and a married half-brother. They all come with their kids. The youngest grandchild, Simon, my uncle's son, is only four years old. He loves the attention he receives from his teen and pre-teen cousins when he joins us in our bedroom where the discussion is about the latest hits, fashion, TV-shows, movies, and boys. All my cousins, except three, are girls. Allen and Alex, the two older boys, disappear; they're probably hiding in the library.

Except for my uncle and three cousins, everyone present is female. None of my aunts has any intention of remarrying. I am sure there would be volunteers—after all, they are attractive with their brown hair and eyes, are well educated, and have good jobs—but they don't seem interested in tying the knot again.

My widowed grandma takes her place in one of the arm-chairs in the living room, and from that vantage point advises everyone as to what to do and how.

To mom's family elegant perfection is next to cleanliness, which is next to holiness. The table is picture perfect, the Christmas tree is picture perfect, the carefully wrapped presents are picture perfect, and so are we, in our Christmas finery. Soft classical music is playing on the stereo to set the perfect genteel Christmas mood.

Perfection is absolutely imperative. What else can you expect from a bunch of accountants? (Maybe that's why there are no husbands. They did not fit the perfect image. One liked booze too much, one liked women too much, one was too loud and quick-tempered, and the fourth … I am not sure what was wrong with him.)

During dinner no one drinks too much, no one eats too much, and we talk about appropriate subjects such as theaters, concerts, books and authors, extended family—Aunt Lydia ran into some second cousin—and long ago Christmases with grandpa.

What would Christian think of my "perfect" family? Does he have a "perfect" family?

Dinner is a long drawn out affair. We open the presents in a well-organized manner. Christian gave me a pair of diamond earrings. I know I will cherish them as long as I live.

Aunt Lydia, the only religious member of the family, who at one time wanted to be a nun and now works at the chancery as an accountant, invites us all to midnight Mass, which, by the way, starts at ten o'clock. I am the only one who willingly accompanies her—her kids have no choice. The four of us take her car to the cathedral, which is packed with people. I love Christmas Eve Mass. It's so romantic with all the candles and organ music. It sure beats doing dishes.

By the time we are back everything is cleaned up, the dishes are washed, the youngest ones are asleep, and everyone else has moved to the living room to sing Christmas carols accompanied by Aunt Peggy on the piano—even if Sarah is a better piano player. We wrap up the evening around midnight, by which time Grandma is asleep, too.

~ ~ ~

Next day's dinner at my paternal grandparents' house is a very different affair.

While my mother's family is predominantly female, my father's is predominantly male. My grandparents had five sons, then gave up trying for a girl. I was the first female grandchild and because of that, I am my grandpa's favorite. He still calls me his princess.

Grandpa owns a few garages around the city—now Uncle Joe manages them—and has a larger-than-life presence that all his sons inherited.

Grandma is close to eighty, short—maybe five feet tall—with smile-lines all over her face, twinkling eyes, and wispy white hair. She has a special talent for encouraging people and making them feel good. When in doubt the person to talk to is Grandma. I'm sure that's one of the reasons why her sons, each around six feet tall and with their own businesses, have so much affection for her.

You can call my father's family many things; quiet is not one of them. When Sarah and I arrive, the women are busy in the kitchen getting dinner ready while the men sit around in the living room drinking and loudly talking about the three forbidden subjects of civilized company: politics, money, and sex. Sometimes the conversation turns to sports, business, and cars. My uncles and cousins never see eye to eye on anything. I often suspect the reason for their differing views has less to do with ideology and more with the fact they love to argue.

When we enter the room, all attention turns to us. Sarah and I receive many bear hugs and compliments about how beautiful we are.

The kitchen is just as noisy, with pretty much everyone talking at the same time. Here too, we receive many kisses, but no one tells us we are beautiful. Grandma asks us to help with peeling potatoes. The aunts and Martina are chopping vegetables for salad, while discussing the best hairdresser, the best place to buy prosciutto, and who has the most annoying neighbors. After we finish with the potatoes, Sarah and I arrange the sweets on a platter.

Ian brought his girlfriend, whose name is Melanie. Since she seems lost and bewildered, Sarah and I befriend her.

It takes half an hour to settle at the table. The food is

passed around, and everyone talks at the same time. Suddenly I realize while all my aunts are divorced, all my uncles are married.

Close to the end of the dinner Uncle Joe and Uncle Nick argue about a business venture that went belly up twenty years ago. Booming and red in the face, they blame each other for the failure. Since this argument is repeated at every family gathering, no one pays attention to them except Melanie, who seems appalled. Sarah and I try to reassure her we are not a bunch of crazies, even if we look that way.

"Is your family always this loud?" she asks when we ferry leftovers to the kitchen.

"No," answers Cousin Joe, who is carrying the remains of the turkey behind us. "This was a quiet dinner. We haven't even thrown any plates."

"We never throw dishes at each other," I say.

"Only knives." Joe winks.

Next the presents are distributed. We only buy gifts for the closest family members; no one is expected to buy twenty-seven presents. It takes a long time to pass out everything. Grandma receives the most gifts—she deserves it—but I get the biggest one. My father bought a car—and insurance for the first year.

Wow. I am so surprised, for a few seconds I am speechless. "Thanks, Dad," I finally stammer. "What's the occasion?"

"This is your graduation present too," Father says, while handing me the keys and the insurance papers. "You can pick up the car tomorrow at my place."

"I wish my dad would buy me a car," Cousin Steve says. He just turned sixteen a month ago. "Can I borrow yours?"

"Absolutely not," thunders Uncle Steve, his father. I'm glad he saved me the trouble of refusing him.

The gift giving is followed by telling mostly X-rated jokes. By the time the jokes are finished, Melanie looks horrified.

Family wisdom has it only a woman madly in love would marry a Burke. I can see why.

~ ~ ~

On New Year's Eve, Nicole arrives close to seven. She looks stunning with sequined top, short black skirt, and four-inch heels.

"I have a present for you under the tree," I tell her. "Go ahead and find it while I finish my make-up."

When I return to the living room Nicole is reading Christian's card. Damn. He signed it "with love, Christian." She quickly sets the card back on the mantle.

"Was Santa good to you?" she asks.

"I don't know about Santa, but my dad gave me a small Ford with the insurance paid for one year."

She whistles. "That's generous."

Sean arrives. He is a med student. Everyone in his family is a doctor—his parents, his sister, and his older brother. We've known them ever since we were kids because his family has a country house next to Grandpa and Grandma Burke's property. He and Sarah have been in love since God knows when—since they could talk and walk or even before. Sean is tall, has sunny-sky blue eyes, and is handsome, in spite of his already thinning hair.

I volunteer to be the designated driver.

Uncle Ted promised to save a parking spot for us at the back of the restaurant, but there is no free space left. Reluctantly, I drive on. The closest parking is four blocks away. It's hard to walk in four-inch heels on the wet pavement.

After we've waited half an hour in line, the bouncer doesn't want to let us in. "You must have tickets," he says.

"Tickets?" Uncle Ted did not give us tickets.

"No ticket, no entry," he says.

"Why don't you go and fetch the owner or find Mark or Ian," I say. "They can tell you that we paid."

"I am not a messenger," the bouncer growls, "Now move over."

People are watching our exchange, some with smirks on their faces.

"Not until you get one of the owners," I answer.

"I am not getting any owners." He moves menacingly. "And if you don't move, I will have to force you." By this time everyone is watching us.

"Let's go to the back door," Sarah suggests. She hates scenes.

"Hi, Ann-Marie. What's the problem?" someone says behind us. I wheel around. It's Grant.

"Nothing," I answer.

"I have an extra ticket," Grant says. "My friend cancelled at the last minute. You can come in with me."

"What about the others?" I say.

"I'll come with you." Nicole smiles at Grant. "I'm not walking anymore in these shoes."

"Fine," I huff. "See you on the inside."

With heads up we march around the block to the back door where one of the kitchen staff doesn't want to let us in, but at least he fetches our uncle and finally we're admitted.

"You have a few overzealous bouncers at the front," I tell my uncle.

"I told you to park in the back," he says.

"There is no parking left. And why didn't you tell us we need tickets to get in?"

"You were supposed to come to the backdoor." I don't remember him telling me that. "Didn't you say there would be four people?" he asks.

"Our friend bummed a ticket from an acquaintance when we couldn't get in," I say.

Our uncle bellows for Cousin Mark to usher us to our table and scuttles away. As soon as we leave the kitchen, we step into deafeningly loud music. The restaurant is dark; the only illumination is provided by colorful lights under the dance floor, and spotlights over the tables, which are on three levels in a circle. Our booth is on the highest level in the back, a wonderful place for lovers who don't want anyone to notice them.

"I'm glad you didn't put us on the roof," I shout to Mark. "Are you going to join us?"

"Not a chance," he yells back. "I'll stop by later."

"Could you turn the music down a notch?" I holler at the top of my lungs.

He gives me an incredulous glance and leaves.

"Now we just have to find Nicole," Sarah shouts.

Nicole shows up a few minutes later with Grant and his friend. "So you did get in." Grant grins. "Does your uncle really own this place?"

Before I can answer, Nicole asks, "Could Grant and his friend join us at this table?"

The booth will be cozy with six, but it's doable. Sarah and I glance at each other. "Why not." Sarah shrugs.

Grant's friend, Mike, is quite good looking, and totally enthralled by Nicole.

After the buffet dinner I dance with Sean, Mike, Grant, and Cousins Mark and Ian, who are helping their father tonight. "I heard you were hustled at the door," Ian laughs as we head to the dance floor.

"Yes, and you owe us a drink for that," I answer.

"Okay."

"Has Melanie broken up with you yet?" I ask.

He looks at me surprised. "How do you know she's broken up with me? It only happened this afternoon."

"She wasn't impressed with our family," I explain.

"I know." He grins. "If I want to break up with someone, all I have to do is introduce them to the family."

I laugh. "If I want to break up with someone, all I have to do is introduce them to Nicole."

~ ~ ~

I didn't expect an exciting night, but definitely something better than being hidden in a corner booth trying to strike up a conversation with Grant who keeps gazing at me as if I were dinner. It's hard to chat with him; he's not exactly loquacious. I ask him about his Christmas.

"It was all right," he says unenthusiastically.

"Did you spend it with your family?"

"Yes."

"In the city or the country?"

"In the city."

"Does your whole family get together for Christmas?"

"Sometimes."

Christian told me Grant is one of his best friends since childhood. How they can be friends is beyond me. Maybe Grant is more open with Christian. Or maybe they understand each other without words. "You told me you went to school with Christian," I say. "What school did you go to?"

"Glendorf," Grant answers.

Glendorf is the most exclusive and expensive school in the country. "You went to Glendorf?" It's hard to curb the surprise in my voice. "Are you one of the superrich or one of the nobles?"

"My father is the Earl of Invermere."

Here is a shocking revelation. "How about Christian, is he superrich or noble?"

"He's the future Duke of Norbury," Grant answers.

What? He's never told me that. What else is Christian not telling me, that he has a wife and a kid? I feel dismayed by his lack of honesty. I believed that … Tears well up in my eyes.

Grant puts his hand on mine. "Ann-Marie, you shouldn't be in love with Chris," he says.

I pull my hand away. "What makes you think I am in love?"

"You shouldn't trust him." He scowls.

"Why not? Is he married?"

"No, he's not married. Neither is he interested in any long-term relationship. Actually he—"

I never hear the rest of the sentence, because Sarah and Sean return to the table. Sarah takes a glance at me and says, "Let's visit the little girls' room."

I am glad to escape with her.

"What's happened?" Sarah asks when we enter the brightly lit, elegant washroom. "You seem upset."

"I've just found out Christian lied to me all along," I sigh and plop down into one of the four armchairs in the front room. Sarah takes the other chair.

"Is he married?" she asks with concern on her face.

"According to Grant he's not, but he is the future Duke of Norbury." I sniffle. "He's never told me that." Tears run down my cheeks. "We talked about everything: his family, his plans, but he's never once mentioned something that important." I wipe my tears with the back of my hand.

Sarah grabs a few tissues from the box on the table and hands them to me. "How does Grant know?" she asks.

"They went to Glendorf together." I dab my eyes. "Apparently, Grant is the son of the Earl of Invermere."

"Oh here you are." Nicole enters the room. "It's almost midnight. What are you two doing here?" She notices my smudged face. "What's happened? Is Grant boring you to tears?"

I chuckle in spite of my inner turmoil.

"No," Sarah says. "She's just fund out …" I quickly nudge her leg. She glances at me, looks back at Nicole, and continues, "She's just found out that Grant is the son of the Earl of Invermere."

"And she's crying about that," Nicole says, obviously not

believing us. She sits down, too.

"No, I just have some cramps," I say.

Nicole shakes her head. "You never have cramps."

That's true.

"Oh, I see." She pouts. "You don't want to tell me. Fine."

I should tell her. But I would have to confess about our Saturdays with Christian, and our dinner, and why I never told her about it before. "Honest, I don't know why I'm crying." I wipe away the tears. "Maybe I have the Christmas blues, or PMS, or whatever."

"Are you saying Grant is a future earl?" Nicole asks.

"Yes," I answer, dabbing beneath my eyes.

Our discussion is interrupted by people shouting the countdown to the New Year.

"Come on," Nicole says, "you don't want to greet the New Year in the washroom."

Definitely not.

There's no time to touch up my make-up. It doesn't matter, the restaurant is dark enough. We exit the washroom, wondering if we have enough time to find Sean and Mike. No need to worry, they are lurking close to the entrance of the hallway that leads to the washrooms. Sean looks at me questioningly.

"An emergency meeting." I smile at him.

We join the countdown on the dance floor. "Ten, nine, eight, … four, three, two, one, New Year."

While the band is playing "Auld Lang Syne," people hug and kiss, wishing happy New Year to each other. Sarah and Sean are lost in a kiss. Nicole is kissing Mike. Cousins Mark, Ian, and Uncle Ted appear at my side with a bottle of champagne and flute glasses. "It's on the house," Mark shouts, "for being hustled at the door." He hands a glass to each of us, and pours the champagne. "Happy New Year."

Happy New Year.

Chapter 26

"Here's what I've found," Christian says, opening a folder. We are sitting close to the window in his favorite coffee shop. The day is so gloomy it feels like dusk although the time is only two thirty in the afternoon. "I couldn't find Bancloch or any reference to it, but I found a princess named Selina." He takes the top page, and turns it toward me. "She was born in Ryston and married the lord of Haukwold, a prince named Ryan."

"Haukwold?" I say surprised. "Haukwold was the name of the hunting lodge to which the refugees retreated. Why would Ryan change to that name?" I notice it has started to snow.

"Do you mean Haukwold was close to Bancloch?"

Oh my. I am not very sharp, am I? Why didn't I think about this sooner? "Christian, I should have searched for all the other principalities around Bancloch, and I could tell you exactly where the castle was. I knew that your…" He scowls. "… Christian's mother was a princess of Norbury, why didn't I make the connection sooner?" Excited, I take a sip of my coffee, "Norbury was only a day's ride east of Bancloch."

Christian smiles. "If you could find a lost castle, it would make you famous among scholars."

"Would you believe me then?"

His smile fades. "Ann-Marie, it's a long way from finding a place to believing you lived there in the twelfth century a few months ago."

I sigh. "How else could I explain knowing about the castle?"

He studies his cup with a frown then looks at me. "You should never tell anyone you've learned about the castle by living there. No one would take you seriously after that."

"You're the only one I want to convince." He makes a face. "Christian, you must believe me."

"How could I believe you? Can you prove that you were there?"

My mind whirls at the speed of thousand thoughts per millisecond to come up with a convincing argument. "If I told you I visited the zoo yesterday, you would believe me even if you couldn't prove it?"

"I would believe you because of probability. The probability you went to the zoo is high; however, the probability of you living in the twelfth century a few months ago is zero—zilch, nada."

"Why?"

He takes a sip of his coffee. "Anyone can visit the zoo any day, but as far as I know, no one can visit the twelfth century."

Another argument pops into my mind. "Do you believe humans landed on the moon?" I ask. "Except for a film clip we really have no evidence for that."

He laughs lightly. "No, we don't, but we know technology behind it, and could repeat it any time."

"So if we don't know how something happens, we just say it cannot happen."

"If there's no physical evidence it's happened, it is nothing more than hearsay. And personally, I don't believe in hearsay."

I ignore his condescending tone. "Do you believe in anything that cannot be proven?"

He stares at the papers in front of him, then looks at me. "No. Do you?"

Do I? I recall how I needed proof about my experience before I truly believed it happened. "No, not really, but I have an open mind. I don't say if it cannot be proven, it could not happen."

After a short pause, he asks, "Do you want to hear more about what I found?"

"Of course."

"Fine." He picks up the paper. "Ryan had an older

brother, Christian, who died at age twenty-seven without an heir or ever being married."

"Christian, that was you."

"Ann-Marie," he growls. "Please refrain from ever mentioning you met me in the twelfth century."

"I can't. I must convince you."

"You will not convince me."

"Not even if we find Bancloch?"

"Not even if we find Bancloch." With a frown, he looks down at the paper in front of him. "I've found information about Princess Orla, too." He pulls out another sheet from his folder. "She was married to a Prince Paxton. They lived at Caerburn Castle and had nine children."

"Yes, she is Princess Orla, your sister—" Christian lifts his eyebrows. "I mean, Christian's sister. What else have you found?"

He takes out the next sheet and for the rest of the afternoon we talk about the people from the twelfth century.

"Have you found anything about Ann-Marie Ryston?" I ask when we finish his list.

He gives me an enigmatic smile. "I want you to have the pleasure of researching her. I've written down where to find the information." He straightens the papers and puts them back into the folder. "I plan to finish and present my dissertation this spring. I won't have time for your research, but if you need help you can always ask me." He hands me the folder.

While we talked a good two inches of snow has accumulated on the ground.

"We should go for a walk," Christian says looking out into the snowfall.

"Yes, let's. But I need to change into something warmer."

We agree to meet at my apartment in half an hour.

~ ~ ~

By the time Christian arrives the snow is an inch deeper and is falling more heavily than before. It is softly veiling the houses and the trees, muffling the city noises, outlining tree branches and railings. As the bluish darkness descends, the street takes on a magical quality. Streetlights glow silkily illuminating the millions of snowflakes waltzing around them.

We head to a playground a few blocks from my apartment building. The street is deserted. It feels as if Christian and I are the only two people in the world. First I try to catch snowflakes with my tongue then Christian makes a snowball, throws it at me, and we have a snowball fight. At the playground, we decide to build a snowman.

"To be more politically correct we should call it a snowperson," I say.

We've rolled the snow into a large ball when a young couple, pulling two kids on a sled, amble by. The kids, too, want to make a snowman. Soon, the six of us are enthusiastically building "the biggest snowman in the world," as one of the little girls puts it. We stack the three large balls, the two kids bring branches for the arms, Christian plucks three pinecones for eyes and nose, and the girls' mom draws the mouth using her lipstick. We admire our masterpiece for a while then say a friendly goodbye to the family and go our separate ways.

On the way home I waltz around Christian singing *I Could Have Danced All Night*.

"Is this some kind of numinous dance?" Christian asks.

"Numinous?"

"From the Latin, numen, awe-inspiring, of the divinity; a numinous dance is a sacred dance," he says, professorially.

"Ah, then yes. This is the sacred snow dance of the ancient druids."

"Including the song," Christian adds.

I laugh. "Including the song." With a curtsy I ask, "May I

have the next dance, please?"

Christian takes my hand, slips his other arm around my back and we waltz in the snow. A man with a briefcase, hurrying, head bent against the snow, turns onto our street, notices us, and taps his temple to show his opinion. We laugh, and keep on sashaying.

At the corner we almost collide with Mrs. Mendelsohn, an older woman who lives in our apartment building. We apologize profusely. She sighs, "I wish I could be so young and happy again," then plods on.

As we twirl, I hit a branch and all the snow tumbles onto my head, neck, and shoulders. It finds its way to the inside of my collar and the snowmelt trickles down my back. Christian pulls off his glove and rubs the back of my neck. The next second he's kissing it. My body tenses with sudden pleasure. He twirls me around, pulling me close to him, and his lips bear down on mine. I press closer, lost in the delight of our kiss.

A car stops next to us. Glancing sideways, we realize it's a police car. "Is the man bothering you?" the officer asks through the rolled down window.

"No," I say, still locked in Christian's embrace. The officer suspiciously surveys Christian.

"She's my wife," he says, looking innocent.

"You should kiss her at home then," the policeman grumbles, rolling up the window. The car cautiously inches forward and soon disappears in the snowfall. We look at each other and laugh. Christian's eyes wander to my mouth; I tilt my head upward and press my lips against his. He moans and we kiss again.

"Do you want to come in for something hot?" I ask when we arrive at the apartment building.

"Something hot?" Christian whispers into my ear. "Yes, I'd like to have something hot."

"I meant a drink," I say huskily.

"That too," he says and kisses me again.

Sarah is playing the piano when we arrive. While I make hot toddies in the kitchen, Sarah entertains Christian—though from her carefree laughter, it sounds more like Christian's entertaining her. I bring the drinks to the living room, and while we sip them, we have a pleasant chat.

Christian and I retreat to the library, where we settle on the sofa. He puts an arm around my shoulder, leans across me to turn off the light, and we start to kiss again. Our kissing quickly becomes intense, our hands and mouths exploring the other's body, and I know if we don't stop now, we won't be able to stop. Do I want our first love making to be a quickie in the guest room? No. I want something more special. As if reading my mind, Christian pulls away. "I'd better go," he whispers huskily. "Before the roads become impassable."

Maybe I should invite him to stay for the night. "Yes, you should go," I say.

He plants a little kiss on my lips before standing up. I accompany him to the gate. Before saying good-bye, Christian pulls me into his embrace and kisses me slowly, lovingly. I ask him to phone me when he arrives at home (gosh, I'm acting like my mother) and watch until his car fades into the snowfall.

Sarah is still playing the piano; she stops when I enter, stretches her arms, and says, "I should take a break. Would you like another hot toddy? I'll make it this time."

"Sure," I say and plop down on the sofa. What's wrong with Christian and me? Why did we stop? Now I wish we hadn't.

Sarah returns with the drinks. "How was your walk?"

"Magical," I sigh.

"Have you asked Christian about being a future duke?"

"No, but I will when the occasion presents itself."

A short time later the phone rings. It's Christian letting me know he made it home. The phone rings again. This time it's our mother. "The roads are impassable," she says, sounding as if she has a cold. "I'm spending the night at Will's apartment. Are you two going to be all right?"

"I am pretty sure we can take care of ourselves," I answer. "I think you're a bad influence, Mother, spending the night with a man."

She titters.

I wish I could spend the night with … Why did I chicken out?

~ ~ ~

"Look at this," I tell Sarah who is reading at the large desk in our living room. I'm sitting on the sofa, searching the websites Christian gave me. "I've found the names and birth years of the Rystons in the eleventh—" I suddenly stop and stare at the screen with dismay and disbelief.

According to the genealogy, Ann-Marie Ryston, Selina's older sister, died at age four.

What? That's impossible. She was sick, but recovered. How could …? Did the wizard …?

Ohmigod. Was everything that happened my imagination?

It couldn't have been. Christian is here, he is real, and he is the same person I knew in the enchanted tower and in the twelfth century. His appearance, his movements, his interests, even his occasional haughty reactions are the same. And I have all these new skills. And how could I know the names of so many people in the twelfth century? I was never interested in history. It couldn't have been a dream.

"What do you want to show me?" Sarah interrupts my thoughts.

"Nothing," I mumble.

She returns to her reading.

I am sure Christian saw that the eleventh-century Ann-

Marie died in childhood. Probably that's why he told me to find her on my own. Damn. This will make it even more difficult to convince him.

My attention returns to the genealogy tables and I discover that Selina named her first-born daughter Ann-Marie. Why would she, if her sister died when Selina was still a baby and her mother's name was Gwendolyn?

I keep studying the family tree and find out that in the early fifteenth century the Haukwold family line died out. The last direct descendant was a spinster, ironically, named Ann-Marie.

I lean back and stare into the soft whiteness outside the window. Two feet of snow have fallen during the night, shutting down the entire country. There is no traffic at all. Later I hear children's delighted laughter, and the scraping of a snow shovel as the caretaker is clearing the sidewalk.

We spend an extremely peaceful morning with Sarah reading and me surfing the 'net. Our peace is shattered with a slam of the front door. In the next second our mother staggers into the living room, collapses into one of the imitation Louis XV armchairs, lifts her head toward the ceiling, and closes her eyes in distress.

"What's the matter, Mom?" alarmed, Selina and I asks at the same time.

She is silent. Oh yeah, she *can* be a drama queen. Sarah and I glance at each other. Finally, after the perfect dramatic break, our mother says, "Will has been transferred. He's got a promotion. He'll be in charge of the entire eastern division … but he has to move to Dunham."

What?

Our mother closes her eyes again, and says in a tragic voice, "He wants us to get married and move together."

"Oh, mother," Sarah cries.

"And you?" I say.

"I can't move," our mother whispers. "My family, my job, my entire life is in this city."

I feel sorry for her, and somewhat angry with Will. What would I do if Christian asked me to move with him to Norbury? That's a whole different story. "Mom, would you move away, if you had the promotion?" I ask.

She glances at me sharply. "Let's not deal with hypothetical questions."

"Okay." I shrug. When our mother is in this mood, it's best to leave her alone.

She rises with a sigh. "I need a hot bath."

I return to the internet but can't concentrate on it anymore, so I go to the kitchen to make tea. I know for sure what mother will decide. She will give Will up. It will be hard on her. It will be hard on us, too, because when she's upset she picks on Sarah and me.

Mom enters the kitchen with a towel wrapped around her head. "We should talk about your adventures in the twelfth century," she says, sitting down by the window. "Today would be a good day for it."

I want to talk about her problem. "Mom, what do you think you will do?" I ask, pouring a cup of tea and handing it to her.

She studies her cup for a while. "Will wanted this promotion." She shrugs. "Nothing would stop him from accepting it. And he knew he would have to move."

"Maybe you could have a long distance relationship," I say, blowing into my still-too-hot tea.

"Sure, he'll just drop by for a drink after work," she says sarcastically. With a sad smile she adds, "Long distance relationships are not my forte."

"Have you tried it before? You've always told us we never know what we can do until we try."

"I tried it in college. It did not work."

"That was long time ago, Mom. Maybe—"

"Ann-Marie," she interrupts edgily, "I want to hear about your adventures."

"Okay, just one more question?" Before she can object, I ask, "You've been going out with Will for ten years. That's an awful long time for dating. Why didn't you marry? It had to be more than just waiting for us girls to grow up."

Her mouth tightens. "There's no point in discussing this. Tell me about your adventures."

Why are people so reluctant to talk about uncomfortable subjects? Or is it only Mom and Christian? "Okay. Where should I start?"

"How about the beginning?"

We spend the afternoon talking about our adventures "in the alternate world," as Mom calls it.

She is much happier and more relaxed by the time we finish our stories.

Chapter 27

Since school does not start for another week, I've hoped Christian and I would meet; I don't hear from him until the phone rings on Friday. "Do you want to go shooting tomorrow?" When I agree he adds, "Do you mind if your friend, Nicole, joins us?"

Jealousy shoots through me. When did he talk with Nicole? The only times Christian and I spend alone are Saturday mornings. Now Nicole will join us. Great. Just great. Swallowing my jealousy, I say, "I guess it's okay." I must be crazy.

"Meet you at the usual place, the usual time." Christian hangs up.

I glare at the receiver for a long time. What the hell is going on? Maybe I'll phone Nicole. No, better not, I would probably have a fight with her.

On Saturday morning Nicole is late. I don't mind. I enjoy the faint winter sun on my face and the little chat with Christian.

"Am I late?" Nicole asks, when she arrives, all charm and good cheer.

"Yes," Christian says frankly.

"I am so sorry." Now she's all contrition, as she puts her hand on his arm.

"Let's get going." Christian moves away from her to open the front door.

Nicole hops in and I, having no choice, take the back seat.

"It will be so exciting to learn to shoot with a bow and arrow, especially with a wonderful teacher like you, Christian," Nicole trills.

I roll my eyes.

She chatters about *The Female Warrior* all the way to the shooting range, and, to my annoyance, Christian encourages her by asking many questions.

Run this by me again, why is Christian bringing Nicole along?

At the shooting range, they ignore me while Christian explains how to choose a suitable bow, how to tell if an arrow is well balanced, and how to adjust if it is not. She even asks for instruction as to how to tie the quiver. Oh for the love of God, grow up, Nicole.

Finally, she's ready. Christian demonstrates how to shoot and tells her to try. She stands, nocks her arrow, pulls the string, then with a saccharine smile turns to Christian. "Am I doing this right? Do I need any correcting?"

"You're fine." He sends her one of his killer smiles.

My stomach tightens. On Monday night we had a most romantic evening, and today he's flirting with Nicole. Damn. I would stop dating him right here and now, if he wasn't Christian.

"That was not a very good shot," Nicole says when her arrow lands on the floor in front of the target. "Christian, could you help me with the next one?"

I roll my eyes. Christian helps. He adjusts her arms, gently tilts her head … I'm not going to watch this.

"I'll just do some shooting on my own," I mutter, stalking to the farthest lane.

Twang. Twang. Twang. I shoot angrily, taking out all my frustration on the target.

Christian is next to me. "What is going on here?"

"Nothing," I snarl. "I am practicing."

He gives me an odd look and leaves. I keep shooting.

Next week I'll bring my car. If I even come next week. Come on. Am I going to give up shooting because of Nicole? I bought an annual membership just before Christmas. Twang. Twang. Twang. Am I coming here to be with Christian or to shoot? Oh, damn. Be honest, would I come without Christian? Twang. Twang. Twang.

Christian appears again. "Are you trying to kill the board?"

"Yes," I growl. Better the board than them.

He watches me for a while then leaves. Later he is once more beside me. "We are ready to go," he says. "Are you ready?"

"Is there any bus service out here?"

"No." He shakes his head with an amused frown and gives me a warm smile. "Come on, Ann."

When we exit the building, Nicole purrs, "Wasn't this fun?"

I roll my eyes. I sit in the back—again—staring out the window and ignoring Christian and Nicole as much as I can. This is the last time I'll come to archery with them.

We stop at the coffee shop.

The coffee shop. No way.

"Thanks for the lovely morning," I tell Christian, when I

get out of the car. "I can find my way home from here."

"Ann-Marie, please stay," Christian says quietly, putting his hands on my shoulders, his eyes warmly caressing my face. Or maybe I'm only imagining it.

"What for?" I ask, fighting back my tears. "I don't particularly enjoy being a third wheel."

"How is your research coming along?" He has a friendly little smile in his eyes. "Do you have any questions?"

"I'll phone you if I do. I am going now."

"Fine." He leans down and plants a light kiss on my mouth. Behind him, I see Nicole's eyes narrowing with jealousy.

Damn. How can his one stupid little kiss make all my anger evaporate? Have I no pride?

~ ~ ~

"I don't understand why you're friends with her," Sarah says, throwing herself into one of the armchairs with a can of soda in her hand. "This is not the first time Nicole has wanted your boyfriend."

"Maybe she's in love with Christian," I say.

"She's not. She's in love with Nicole."

I scowl. Although Sarah is younger than I am, sometimes it feels as though she's the older one. She's definitely wiser. "You should avoid her; she's not a true friend."

"We've been friends since we were kids." I pick up the antique silver cigar box that's now our candy dish and snap it open. It's empty. With a grin I say, "She also helps to sort out who cares about me and who doesn't. Anyone who falls for her charms is out. I just did not expect Christian to be one of them." I snap the lid closed. "It sure would be nice to find someone who would prefer me to Nicole." Putting the box down, I sit up straighter. "Why am I attracted to damn flirty guys?"

"Because our father is one of them," Sarah says. "You want to win where our mother has failed. Our mother had an attractive and popular husband she couldn't keep, so you want someone attractive and popular and you want him to stay faithful to you. You even keep the competition close by."

"I've heard that theory about trying to win where our parents have failed. It hasn't stopped me from being drawn to the wrong kind of guys." I pause for a second. "Anyway, I am friends with Christian because I met him in the enchanted tower, not because he's—"

"Ann-Marie, face it," Sarah interrupts. "You are attracted to the flamboyant type."

"Am I? Okay. Let's see what type catches my fancy." I place my finger on my lips, then take it away. "He has to be good looking … intelligent … a leader … caring and honest." I pause. "He also has to be strong, able to stand up to me, and he must have enough confidence to listen and compromise, and his kisses should be at least as good as Christian's."

Sarah laughs. "You didn't mention faithfulness."

"Faithfulness is so fundamental it doesn't even need mentioning."

"Are you willing to compromise on any of those requirements?" Sarah asks.

"If I have to. I won't compromise on the kisses, though."

She laughs and finishes her pop. "Sean will be here soon; I should get ready."

~ ~ ~

During the week Christian doesn't come to the library at all, not even once. Is it because Mrs. Quinn thinks we are flirting, or because he doesn't care about me anymore?

On Thursday, at the end of the fencing class, he corners me by the lockers. Some guys can stand by you as if they own you, and that's exactly how Christian stands in front of me. "I'll pick you up on Saturday," he says.

"What makes you think I want to go?"

"Please come." He leans against the locker, his hand

beside my shoulder, making my heart beat faster.

"Is Nicole coming, too?"

"Yes." He does not sound too thrilled. Or maybe it's just my wishful thinking.

"Then what do you need me for?"

"For your company. I like your company."

His face, only inches from mine, is making my heart thump even more wildly. Still, I am going to say no. "Okay," I say. Rats. "I'll come but you must promise you won't ignore me."

"I promise," he says and lightly kisses my forehead, melting my heart again.

On Saturday Christian keeps his promise—most of the time. While the three of us have coffee, Nicole flirts with him and I sulk.

Suddenly, my sister's words echo in my mind, "You want to win where our mother has failed ... you even keep the competition close by." I see the pattern. Other women have been upstaging me all my life, starting with my sister. I was a cute baby; my sister was a doll. Once she appeared, no one even noticed me. Martina came and upstaged all three of us; Nicole upstaged me with Tom, and with some other guys; she might succeed with Christian, too.

I heard somewhere that our problems will follow us throughout life until we are willing to face them. Okay. I will face this problem.

How?

I will stand up for myself and tell Nicole it's disgusting to steal other people's boyfriends. I will be firm and diplomatic. I will also give Christian the ultimatum: choose between flirting with Nicole or me. Yes, I will tell them that their behavior is unacceptable. I am going to stand up for myself, and show some backbone. I will.

Soon.

~ ~ ~

I have a spare class and decide to use it to research Bancloch's neighbors. One morning while we are readying the library for opening, I ask Mrs. Quinn if I could borrow the Rosenthal Catalogue again, and if she knows about any 12th century map that shows principalities.

"Are you still searching for that castle?" she asks.

"I haven't had much time for research," I answer, turning on the computers and entering the passwords.

"How did you learn about that place? Bancloch, was it?" Mrs. Quinn asks, while scanning the returned books.

"I read about it in a novel."

"Oh my dear," she say. "Writers come up with all sorts of fictional names and places."

How stupid does she think I am? "It was supposedly a historically accurate novel," I say, hoping she will not ask for the title. If she does I'll just say I don't quite remember it.

The phone rings. Thanks goodness. After returning, she says, "You can borrow the catalogue. As for the map, the National Archives has one. The original is very fragile but you should be able to get a photocopy; just give them a call, and have it sent over."

Will I ever know as much about historical resources as she does?

We work silently for a few minutes. When I finish with the computers, I return to the desk to check in books.

"I haven't seen that handsome history teacher lately," Mrs. Quinn says. "Are you still friends?"

"What history teacher?" I feign ignorance.

"The one who could not keep his eyes off you; Mr. Seymour," she answers.

I blush. I hate blushing. "Oh him," I say as coolly as I can manage.

"Most professors think that he is a genius," Mrs. Quinn continues.

"That's nice," I mutter. I rather not discuss Christian with her.

"He has a great future in academy," she continues.

"I don't know," I mumble and grab the book trolley. "I should shelve these."

"Not yet." She holds the trolley back then, in spite of my feigned disinterest, keeps talking about Christian until we open.

The copy of the map arrives the next day. I study it during my spare. I find Haukwold, or I think I have found Haukwold. The map is not to scale, and it's hard to read because it's fuzzy and because the words are written in "insular miniscule," an ancient script that barely resembles today's letters.

I also realize if Ryan has changed the name of the principality, I should have asked for an eleventh century map. There's a smudge where, I think, Bancloch's supposed to be. I enlarge the smudge to see what it is. I end up with a bigger smudge.

I find Haukwold Castle in the Rosenthal catalogue and learn that originally it was a wooden fort replaced by a stone building expanded in the first half of the twelfth century and again in the fourteenth. It was the Haukwold family's main residence until the last direct descendent passed away, at which time it reverted to the crown.

Years later it was bequeathed to the Duke of Norbury, in return for developing roads and postal service in the northern parts of the country. For a while it was leased to lesser nobles but eventually fell into disrepair, and was finally abandoned when a new manor house was built close by. Mr. Rosenthal believes the picturesque old ruins are worth a visit.

The Duke of Norbury. Christian's family. Are they still the owners?

In the evening I search the area on Google Maps. I find Haukwold Castle then scan the shore north of it; I cannot find any sign of Bancloch or other familiar landmarks. Of course, due to wind and water erosion, the shore has probably changed in the last 900 years. I search for the Duke of Norbury and learn about Christian's family history and that his family home is called Ashton Hall.

Out of idle curiosity I look it up on Google Maps, then absent-mindedly follow the shore until three islands catch my attention. They remind me of the islands close to the enchanted tower. And there's a tower house on the shore!

Wow. I want to tell someone what I've found but I am alone. Who could I talk to? Sarah and Sean are at the theater; she wouldn't appreciate my call. Mom ... no; she would not appreciate my call either, wherever she is. Nicole ... no. After some deliberation, I decide to call Christian.

"Christian," I say excitedly when he answers the phone, "I think I've found the location of the enchanted tower."

Long silence.

"Are you still there?" His answer is a growl. Did I just wake him? "I think it is on your family's estate—"

"My family's estate—" very uncharacteristically, he interrupts.

"Yes, I think the land belongs to the Duke of Norbury ..." Oops.

Silence. "Ann-Marie, how do you know about my family?" he asks in a cold, haughty voice.

I ignore his haughtiness. "Grant told me at the New Year's Eve party."

Christian bursts out a four-letter expletive. "What else did Grant tell you?"

"That I shouldn't trust you. Christian, are you married?"

More silence. My heart races. Finally, he says, "Ann, who do you think I am? I would never cheat on my wife. If I were married, I would not date you." Are we dating? We haven't even kissed since Nicole is coming along to archery. After a short pause he adds, "Can you meet me this evening?"

It's nine o'clock. "If you don't mind coming here—"

"You're not in bed, are you?"

"No." And even if I were, I would get up.

"I will be at your place shortly," he says and hangs up the phone.

While waiting, I make tea.

"What did Grant tell you?" he asks as we settle in the library, Christian in an armchair and I on the sofa.

I recount the conversation with Grant. "Christian, why didn't you tell me about your title?" Horror of horrors, I use the same accusing manner my mom does when upset.

He peers at me. "I don't tell people about the family title because it makes no difference to who I am."

"Of course it makes a difference."

He grimaces. "You're right, it does to most people. As soon as folks find out about my family, they behave differently." Looking straight into my eyes, he says, "I've told you everything I consider important about my life. I told you my father took the family business and turned it around. I told you that once I earn my doctorate I want to write books. I don't want my only accomplishment to be that I was born the son of a duke. I want to be respected for my own achievements. Would it have made any difference to you if you knew that in twenty or thirty years I might be a duke?"

"I don't know." I shrug. "My interest in you originates from beyond."

"Is that the only reason you are interested?" he asks, his eyes burning into mine.

"No." I shake my head. "I like you." Okay, I love him, but this is not the time to discuss that. He regards me with such intensity, I blush. "Christian, the only reason we met in this life is because we met in the enchanted tower. I wouldn't have gone to the Montfield festival, or taken up fencing, if not for those adventures." He may not even be here if not for our encounter. I don't mention that. "Anyway, I thought we were friends, and that you would have trusted me enough to share something this important."

With an apologetic smile he says, "I would have told you, eventually."

We sit quietly until Christian breaks the silence. "My grandfather, who was interested only in hunting and gambling, died in a riding accident thirty-five years ago and left my father and grandmother with tremendous debt, a title, and a property on which the upkeep is astronomical. My father had the drive and willingness to work hard to change the family's fortune. He's done much for the northern region. His investments provide employment for the locals; he supports small entrepreneurs, schools, theaters, hospitals. He has left his mark on the world and made it a better place." After a short pause he continues, "I want to leave my mark, too. I want to do it my way, using my talents. I don't want to live my life in my father's shadow."

"So you want to pretend you're not a duke."

He laughs. "I am not a duke. I could use a lesser title, but prefer not to. Ann-Marie, have you told anyone about my family's title?"

"Only Sarah."

His face falls.

"She has never betrayed my confidence."

"Would you please keep it a secret?"

"Is that why you rushed over here, to ask me to keep this a secret?"

He nods. "Partially."

"Your secret is safe with me," I promise. "I'd like to ask a favor, too. Any chance I could visit that tower with you?"

"Show me what tower you're talking about."

I bring my laptop. While I search for the place on

Google Maps, Christian moves from the chair and sits by me on the sofa, making my heart speed up. Why can't I just stay normal next to him?

"That tower," he says, when I finally find the image, "was built in the early nineteenth century as a family retreat-slash-folly. A fire destroyed most of the interior at the beginning of the twentieth century, and it has been neglected ever since. It is pretty much a ruin by now. It's also supposed to be haunted."

"Could we visit it?"

With a sideward glance he smiles at me. "We could visit it after I hand in my dissertation. I will not have time before. However, you must promise you won't tell my mother you think the place is enchanted."

Gladness fills me at the prospect of seeing the tower. I place one hand on my heart and hold up the other. "I swear, I will not breathe a word to your mother about the tower being enchanted." That should be an easy promise to keep.

"Thanks." He smiles. "I have to go now; I still have lots to do."

"You're not having any tea?" He hasn't touched his tea or the sweets.

"Not tonight, thanks."

I accompany him to the main entry. Cupping my head with both hands, he gives me a little kiss, which quickly turns into something far more passionate. Our kisses always become intense.

That's when my mother arrives. "Hmm." She clears her throat. "May I go by?"

"Works like magic," I mutter to Christian. "Kiss me by the entrance, and my mother will appear."

~ ~ ~

For the next (too many) Saturdays, we visit the shooting range as a sweet threesome. I must be the greatest wimp in the world. Why don't I tell Nicole and Christian to shove it? Why do I join them against my better judgment? I tell myself I'm only doing this for Christian's sake. I must befriend him. I must help him with his three challenges, especially since he cannot complete two of them without me. Deep down I know this is only an excuse, but it makes me feel better.

Or maybe I am a masochist. I just love being spurned by the man I'm in love with. Occasionally, Christian throws me a heart-warming smile, or touches me with so much gentleness and affection, or gazes at me with so much intensity, my battered heart—disgustingly—fills with hope and love. Especially when I realize he only gives those signs of affection to me, never to Nicole. Or is he such an expert flirt he knows how to keep both of us hooked?

I rehearse a thousand times what I am going to say. I just never say it—to him or to Nicole. Finally, one Thursday, I gather enough courage. After class while he is organizing the fencing club's locker, I sidle up to him. "Christian, I want to talk to you." Why is my mouth suddenly dry? "Alone," I add.

"That's good." He smiles at me, then straightens, concerned. "Any problem, Ann-Marie?"

What expression is on my face? "I'd like to talk to you alone in a quiet place."

We find a secluded corner in the coffee shop. The other fencers sit at another table and covertly watch us. Christian sits down across and lovingly gazes at me.

Come on. Courage. "Christian." I swallow. "I—I …" How could I say this? It's so much easier to say it in my head. "Christian, I will not go with you to archery as long as Nicole comes along. I don't like you flirting with her." I swallow again. "You have to choose between Nicole and me."

He turns red. "What?"

"I want respect," I say more confidently than I feel. "Flirting with Nicole while I am there shows no respect; not to me, not to Nicole, not even to your own self."

"Ann-Marie—" he growls.

"I must go now." I rise quickly. "You make your decision and let me know. You can choose Nicole or me, not both." I rush out of the cafeteria.

Doubts assail me as soon as I leave. What if he chooses Nicole? I'll have to accept his decision, even if it breaks my heart. As much as I dread Christian's answer, I also feel relieved. I've done it. I stood up for myself. Now it's time to tell Nicole, too, to stop chasing after my boyfriends. Or maybe I should have talked to Nicole first. Too late for that.

All through the next day, every time the phone rings my heart jumps. When the caller turns out to be other than Christian, I feel a curious mixture of disappointment and relief.

Friday night arrives and still no call. Not wanting to think, I read until I fall asleep. At least he should have had the courtesy to tell me he'd chosen Nicole.

I linger in bed on Saturday morning. There's no reason to get up. I take a book and keep sighing over it.

The doorbell rings. I know it's Christian and cannot repress a happy grin. Wait. What if he came to tell me he has chosen Nicole? That thought stops my grinning. I am not going to answer the door.

"Ann-Marie," Sarah shouts from the entry, "you have a visitor."

I hop into a pair of sweat pants, pull on a sweatshirt, and head to the entry. "Hi," I greet him, wondering what he has to say.

"Hi, Ann-Marie," Christian says awkwardly. "Nicole will not come to archery anymore. Will you come?"

"Yes, I will." I can't hide my joy and relief. "Give me a few minutes to get ready."

"Do you mind telling me what's happened?" I ask in the Rover.

"You can ask Nicole if you want to know," Christian says curtly. "I'd rather not talk about it."

Now I'm even more curious. Why does Christian not want to talk about what happened? What did he tell Nicole? Did they have a fight? Are they meeting some other time? We travel in silence while all sorts of scenarios play out in my mind.

Christian breaks the silence. "I know it is not my concern, Ann-Marie," he says. "You should not be friends with Nicole."

"Why?" I look at him. "What's happened?"

"Ask her," he answers, keeping his eyes on the traffic, which is heavier than usual. The warm spring weather must have lured people out of their homes. "All I can say is that you deserve a better friend than she is."

"We've been friends since we were six years old," I say. "Nicole and Sarah are my two closest friends."

Christian makes a face but does not answer.

"Why did you invite her to archery in the first place?" I ask.

He frowns. "She invited herself, and since she's your friend, and I did not know what kind of person she is…. I mean I knew she's flirty, but … anyway I saw no harm in her joining us."

I grimace. No harm to bring someone to the only time we could spend alone? What a loving gesture. "How did she find out about our archery time? I never told her about it."

"Neither did I." We exchange a glance. "It must have been Grant," Christian says.

Do I miss Nicole at the shooting range? No. Not at all.

~ ~ ~

Later in the afternoon, Nicole calls. "I did not go to archery with you," she says, "because I never want to see Chris again. You should not date him at all. You know what he did? I went to his place to borrow a book and he tried to force me to have sex with him. I should report him at the university."

Oh, no! I might jump to conclusions, but I am convinced Christian would not try to force sex with anyone. Why would he? He can have all the volunteers he wants. If Nicole accuses him, even if he clears his name, it would ruin everything he has worked so hard for. Is this Nicole's revenge? I must talk some sense into her. "Could we meet today?" I ask.

"I am busy today."

In January, Nicole told us her hours at *The Female Warrior* were cut back to Saturday afternoons. "I can meet you after work," I suggest.

"I've changed my hours to the morning," she answers.

After a short back and forth she agrees to meet with me at the small Mexican restaurant.

Sitting across from her at the restaurant, I ask, "Nicole, please tell me honestly, what's happened between you and Christian?"

Her long finger follows the checkers on the red and white tablecloth. "I told you, he invited me to his apartment and tried to have sex with me."

I carefully scrutinize her. "He did. And you resisted him." I doubt that she would. "I think Christian has too much to lose to force sex with anyone. He has always been a gentleman with me."

"You think because he doesn't want you, he doesn't want anyone else," she scoffs.

I ignore the snub. "Would you tell me what happened?"

"I've told you, he offered to give me a few books about history; now I know he only used that as a pretext to lure me to his place."

Christian has never once invited me to his apartment. "Did he invite you?" I ask.

The waitress arrives with our coffee.

"Nicole," I say while adding sugar and cream to my mug, "do you really want to report Christian? Do you want to attend hearings and maybe even go to court? Do you want to drag his name through mud and dirt?" She purses her lips. "If you report him, I won't support you. Also, if you report him, and Christian clears his name, he could sue you for libel. Is that what you want? Why do you want to do this?"

Nicole's eyes narrow. "You wouldn't support me. You'd take his side. You'd betray me," she hisses. "And you call yourself my friend." I try to say something, but Nicole drowns me out. "You think you are such goody-goody two shoes. Ann-Marie ... the saint ... on the moral high ground." She glares at me. "There's nothing special about you. Why do *you* attract guys like Chris, or Tom, or the others?"

"I don't know," I shrug, but my words are lost in Nicole's furor.

"You know what? I've had enough of you. I've had enough of your false friendship." Rising, she slams her napkin on the table. "I am not your friend anymore." She storms out.

A second later the waitress arrives at the table with our orders.

I smile at her. "I guess it will be two take out dinners."

She grins and returns to the kitchen.

~ ~ ~

"I know this is hard," Sarah says while we're eating the Mexican food at home. "But you are better off without her."

"Nicole is such an important part of my life," I moan. "We shared so many secrets and dreams. I love her. I even forgave her stealing my boyfriends. I hoped with age she'd smarten up or fall in love or something." I sigh. "And what if Christian tried to have sex with her?"

Sarah rolls her eyes to the ceiling. "She would be here dancing a victory dance, instead of hopping mad. I think Christian told her about your request, and she did not like it."

I sigh. "I will miss her. I will miss her witty remarks, her spot-on observations. Maybe if I didn't force a meeting when her hurt was so fresh, we'd still be friends." Sarah doesn't answer. "Maybe I'll call her in a few days and apologize."

Sarah stares at me with disbelief. "She tries to steal your boyfriends, she gets mad at you, and *you* want to apologize to her. Now, that's what I call dumb."

Sarah can be so right.

Chapter 28

It's April. Six months have passed since I met Christian Seymour. Half of our allotted time is gone. And what have we accomplished in that half year? Nothing.

Our relationship is at a standstill. I know Christian is attracted to me. I can feel it. Whenever we are together there's such a strong pull between us. But he is holding back. Why? Maybe he has someone else.

As for believing our adventures in the enchanted tower, that's even more hopeless. He doesn't even want to talk about it.

And his relationship with his parents: I have no clue. I know his father must be a controller. I have no idea what Christian could do about that.

The end of the semester arrives, and the finals. If studying for the finals wasn't enough, I also try to find a job at the same time.

I have a few interviews. I am either overqualified, or under qualified, or don't have enough experience.

No kidding. How will I get the experience if no one hires me?

I send an application to the school board for a school librarian position. They promise to keep it on file. Thanks.

The courthouse is looking for a junior librarian, legal

experience required. The National Historical Museum wants a temporary, part time library assistant, student preferred. Would I still qualify as a student? I don't know. I apply anyway.

I get a call from the history museum; they want an interview the following Wednesday at one thirty. Perfect timing. I have an exam in the morning and another one on the following day.

I finish the exam at twelve then, eating on the run, rush to the museum. The personnel office is in the back of the building, looking out into the surrounding park. The window in the office is partly open; through it, the breeze carries in the sweet fragrance of the opening buds, shouts of children from the close by playground, and the constant humming of the traffic. I wouldn't mind working in this pleasant place.

Two people are at the interview, the personnel officer, Mrs. Sharman, and my potential future boss, Pari Bloomberg. She tells me to call her Pari. She's in her early thirties, and with her slender figure, long, dark hair, and an elfin smile she reminds me of a fairy. I like her.

As it turns out, she used to work with Mrs. Quinn when she attended university "a hundred years ago," as she puts it.

"How do you get along with Mrs. Quinn?" Pari asks, tossing back her hair.

"We seem to get along fine," I say, without mentioning the ten percent. Mrs. Quinn took off for flirting.

"She can be rather vexing." Pari laughs. "She almost failed me because of a small stupid mistake." Then she asks me about the other teachers.

The interview takes an hour, most of it spent talking about Pari's school memories. At the end Mrs. Sharman tells me they will let me know after two weeks whether I'm hired or not. An improvement over most places, which simply told me "if you don't hear from us don't call."

In the museum garden, the daffodils are in their full glory and so are the cherry trees. Although I should be studying, I succumb to the temptation to linger and enjoy the pleasant spring day. Sitting on a bench, I watch the people—mostly young mothers with little kids, and elderly folks—saunter by.

Then I see the woman. The woman Christian talked with at the fair. She's pushing a stroller. I also recognize the toddler. They stop at the playground. The little blond boy grabs a bag of sand toys from the bottom of the stroller and runs to the sandbox while the woman settles on a bench. Here's my chance to find out who she is.

"Do you mind if I sit down here?" I ask.

She smiles at me. "Not at all, go ahead. What a beautiful day."

"Yes, and this park is lovely," I agree. "Do you often come here?"

"When we are in the city," she says. "Do you?"

"Not really. I may in the future. I just applied for a job at the museum. If I get it, I'm sure I'll be a regular here."

"What kind of job?" she asks while adjusting the blanket on the sleeping baby in the carriage.

"Library assistant. I'm Ann-Marie Burke." I hold out my hand. I feel a little odd giving my full name so soon, but I want to know her name.

"Ann-Marie Burke." She turns toward me with interest. "Do you know Chris Seymour?"

"Yes," I say, surprised.

"I am Kimberley Seymour-Harding, Chris's sister." She takes my hand. "Chris has mentioned you." Wow. It has never occurred to me Christian would talk about me with anyone. "I am glad to meet you in person."

"I am glad to meet you, too."

Kimberley is open and friendly. I remember Christian telling me that her husband, Doug, works for Christian's father. From Kimberley I learn that they have three children. The oldest, Andrew, is in grade one. The little boy in the sandbox is Nicholas, three; the baby, Millicent, is just over six months old. The family alternates between living in the country and the city.

"Mommy." Nicholas is standing in front of us. "I have to pee."

"You just went at the restaurant," Kimberley answers.

"I have to pee now," he insists.

Kimberley apologetically smiles at me. "Sorry, we must go. It was nice meeting you, and I hope to see you again."

"Mommy," the little boy wails, "hurry up."

"All right." Kimberley smiles at him. Turning to me she says, "I hope you get the job." She takes the little guy's hand and they scurry off toward the washroom.

I like Christian's sister. In one day I've met two people I like. Life is good.

The following Friday, we receive our marks. I did well on my finals. Even Mrs. Quinn gave me 87 percent. I decide to thank her. I buy a small box of chocolates and a thank you note.

"You're not here to complain about your mark?" she says, when I stop at the library.

"No," I chuckle. "The opposite. I came to thank you, and to say goodbye. I've learned a lot from you."

"Have you got the job at the museum?" she asks.

"How do you know about it?"

"They phoned me," she answers. "I told them to hire you." Then she asks how my search for Bancloch is coming along.

"Now with school finished I will have more free time and will get serious about it."

The museum phones the same day to let me know I am hired, though I won't start until May. I am so delighted I phone everyone, including Christian.

"Christian, I've got the job," I exclaim.

"I knew you would," he answers.

"And I met your sister, Kimberley at the park."

"How do you know...? How did you meet her?"

"We shared a park bench outside the museum." Then I ask the question I've been putting off for the last few weeks, knowing it would break my heart if he said no. "Would you come to my graduation ceremony?"

"I thought you'd never ask," he answers. "Of course I'll come."

Could this day get any better?

~ ~ ~

The day of the graduation ceremony dawns bright and clear. The celebration starts at ten.

While the speakers ramble on, I think about the graduation parties the Burkes have thrown for their grandchildren—they were like family reunions. Mine will be much simpler because I can't invite both Mom's family and Dad's at the same time; they don't even say hello when they run into each other on the street. I only invited Mom, Dad, Martina, my grandparents from both sides, and, of course, Sarah, and Christian—I wish Nicole were here, too. We plan to have dinner at the Hilton.

The speeches end, and we go up on the stage one by one to shake hands with the faculty and receive our certificates. While we're waiting on the side steps, one of the girls from my study group whispers, "I pray I won't trip in my stupid high heeled sandals or on my gown." I pray too.

The foyer is so crowded, I wonder how I will find anyone. However, by the time I return the gown, Mom and Sarah arrive, followed by Father and Martina.

"Your grandparents are waiting outside at the reception," Mom says.

Father gives me a big hug. "Congratulations."

When he lets go of me, Mom, with a cloying smile, purrs to him, "*We* have such a lovely daughter, don't *we*?"

Father smiles at me with pride and warmth. "Yes, she is a lovely young lady."

"Luckily, she took after her father's family," Martina chirps in.

Mom glares at Martina, then sweetly says, "She managed to finish university, unlike some people, I know."

Martina purses her lips. "Thanks to James's money."

I grab Sarah by the arm. "Okay. Let's find Christian." We march away.

Mom catches up with us. "What do you mean leaving me behind?" she hisses.

"We didn't want to interfere with the fun little game you and Martina were playing. Anyway, I want to find Christian."

"Such an impudent woman," Mom grumbles.

We exit the building. A tea is set up on the lawn outside the auditorium. I notice Grandma Burke and Grandma Cooper sitting by one of the tables, talking. To be more precise, Grandma Burke is talking to Grandma Cooper who is scanning the crowd. When she notices us, she waves. "Over here."

"You've done it." Grandma Burke gives me a hearty hug and a kiss. "You are the first girl in our family to finish university. I'm so proud of you."

"I am proud, too," Mom says. "Though, in my family she comes from a long line of female university graduates."

I roll my eyes. I've never seen Mom behave this rudely. Martina's presence must have addled her brain.

"Where's Grandpa?" I ask.

"He went to bring coffee," Grandma Burke answers, wisely ignoring Mom's nasty remark.

"Okay," I say. "I'm going to find Christian, and we can

head to the restaurant."

Finding Christian in the milling crowd is harder than I expected, especially since there are so many people to say hello or good-bye to. Finally, I notice him.

"Here you are." Christian wraps his arm around my waist. "Congratulations."

"Thanks." I smile. "Now come and meet my loveably dysfunctional family."

By the time we arrive back, the temperature around the table is lower than around the South Pole. Everyone seems incensed, and no one is talking. What other insults were hurled while I was away?

I introduce Christian; he's greeted with forced joviality, then we proceed to the hotel.

Since after dinner everyone wants to go their own merry way, we drive in separate cars.

"What's happened?" I ask Sarah, who's riding with me.

"Mom and Martina kept saying nasty things to each other. Actually, they were ready to pound on each other, until Grandma Burke told them to smarten up."

I laugh. "They are like little kids. Leave them alone for a few minutes and they'll get into trouble."

During dinner Grandpa, Dad, and Christian sit at one end of the table and talk about higher education. Grandpa is proud because—as he says—though he was only a simple mechanic, he put all his sons through college or university. When he finds out that Christian is doing a doctorate in history, his comment is, "You should be studying something useful, business or engineering." Christian's mouth twitches slightly. I guess Grandpa and Christian's father would see eye to eye. "I hope you're not one of those young people who just want to take it easy. They all want to be movie stars, or lawyers, or football players; no one wants to work hard anymore." Not waiting for an answer, he continues his monologue about today's youth, then moves on to his next pet grievance: high taxes. Christian listens with an amused glint in his eyes.

At the other end of the table only Grandma Burke, Sarah and I talk. Mother, Martina, and Grandma Cooper sit in stony, injured silence.

When dinner is over, I receive my presents. Dad, saying he has an important meeting, leaves with Martina, Grandma and Grandpa Burke.

"How could you have invited that woman?" Mom confronts me after the Burkes have left.

"I expected both you and Martina to behave like adults," I say sweetly.

"She's absolutely insufferable," Mom fumes.

"Mom, it takes two to tango."

"I must go now." She stands up. I watch as she leaves with Grandma Cooper. From their body language I can tell they are talking about Martina.

Only three of us are at the table. I lean back and smile, "Christian, please accept my heartfelt apology for any discourtesy my elders inflicted on you."

Christian laughs. "Just wait until you meet my family."

We exit into the bright sunshine and suddenly I feel free. My school years are over. A chapter of my life is closed. For the rest of the day, I just want to wander around aimlessly, enjoying this lovely spring day.

Sarah has a date with Sean. Christian returns to his studies. And I visit the zoo where I happily traipse around until closing time.

Chapter 29

Christian hands in his dissertation on Wednesday, and on Friday we leave for Norbury. It is not a family visit although, at Christian's insistence, I will be staying at Ashton Hall.

"There's enough room to put up an army in that house," he says. "You could probably stay for a year and no one would be the wiser."

When I tell Mom about the trip, she wants to know everything: who I am going with, where we are staying, what places we plan to visit.

Mothers! If only they would grow up with their kids. "Mom, I'm twenty-one," I protest, sounding more ten than twenty-one. "Do I have to give you an account of every minute of my life?"

"What if something happens to you," she says.

"I'll deal with it." I've managed to solve a few problems without Mom's help. I'll manage again.

Friday morning Christian arrives with his beat-up Land Rover. The air is still nippy, the sky is a cerulean blue without a single cloud, and the sun is already warm.

"Are you nervous?" Christian asks while shoving my bag into the back of the car.

"A little." I smile. "Why, do I look nervous?" I hope not.

He scans me from head to toe. "You look great."

So does he. In faded jeans, t-shirt, and a leather jacket, he looks … yummy.

Once in the car I ask Christian if I should follow any special etiquette with his family.

"Yes," he answers with a slight smile. "Under no circumstances mention to my mother anything about the tower, or living in the twelfth century."

"Why not?"

"She is crazy about everything supernatural."

"Maybe she also had some supernatural experience," I say. "Obviously far more people have them than I ever thought possible."

Christian grimaces.

"Christian, why are you so opposed to the supernatural? It's not like you have no experience with it."

He keeps his eyes glued to the road, I place my hand on his arm, and he glances at me. "When I was a kid, I used to visit that castle every day. The only person who believed me and took me seriously was my mother." He pauses for a few seconds. "When I was eleven, she told about my experiences to some stupid tabloid reporter, and he ran away with the story. For a few weeks I was the laughing stock at the school. The kids, and even some adults, teased me mercilessly. Eventually the taunting stopped, but I've learned my lesson. Since that time you're the first person I talked to about my visits."

"That had to be hard. I mean being teased, not talking to me."

"I've survived." He shrugs, then passing into the fast lane, steps on the gas. "My family can be quite snobbish," he says. "Try not to take it personally."

"I won't. Grandma Burke taught me a long time ago not to be offended by what other people do, because it reflects who they are not who I am—I can only be responsible for my actions."

"I like Grandma Burke." He glances at me. "You are more like her than anyone else in your family."

I smile back. "Christian, you couldn't have given me a nicer compliment."

After a short silence I ask, "What about your younger sister, Caroline, anything I should know about her beside that she's married, and has a daughter?"

"I don't think you will meet her this time."

During the trip a companionable silence alternates with friendly chats about different topics; one of them is fencing.

"You know as an alumnus you can join the fencing club at the university," Christian says. "I am staying on as a coach; I am even considering offering a beginner's class."

"The K-girls will be happy," I say. "They sure have a crush on you."

Christian frowns.

Gathering some courage, I ask, "Christian, I know this is a personal question. And you don't have to answer it. Would you tell me how it feels being chased by so many girls?"

He laughs. Did I detect some discomfort in his laugh? "Fun while you're a teen and even in your early twenties; all those girls throwing themselves at you—great for the ego— but eventually it becomes tiresome."

"You seem to enjoy flirting."

"It's self-defense."

"Self-defense?"

"I've found flirting is the easiest way to deal with unwanted attention. I've tried aloof, but girls are attracted to aloof and mysterious far more than a flirt. Even the shy types, who would never flirt, were after me."

I laugh. "When you flirt, we girls think you're interested."

Christian shrugs. "Even if I flirt with everyone?"

"Even then."

Was Dad a flirt for the same reason Christian is? Self-defense. Ha, ha. How about lack of maturity?

The country changes as we travel further north. The traffic becomes lighter, the ugly cement walls and traffic berms give way to green fields, pastures, small towns, and forested hills.

After a five-hour drive and a short stop, we arrive in Norbury. Although it's the largest harbor city in the north, with a population of 150,000, somehow it has managed to stay charming in spite of its size—at least, what I've seen of it has. There's an unhurried feel about the early afternoon traffic, and the people strolling the sidewalks seem purposeful, yet leisurely.

A few miles outside the city a sign reads "Ashton Hall

Next Right." When I ask Christian why there's a sign, he tells me the garden and sometimes even the house are open to guided tours and weddings.

I have my first glimpse of the house from a small rise. Ashton Hall is a large, rambling manor built from yellow stones with gray slate roof. It is surrounded by extensive gardens, and beyond the garden is the blue expanse of the North Sea.

The house seems to have been erected in three stages, with a three-story center part the size of our apartment building, a three-story left wing, and a much longer two-story wing on the right.

"The hall was built in the early eighteenth century," Christian tells me. "The old castle stood where the left wing is; it was demolished except for the foundation. The rest is new. I mean was new three hundred years ago."

The road dips and runs between ancient oak trees. When we emerge, a crenellated wall looms in front of us. Christian turns right.

In spite of the "no cars beyond this point" sign he drives right up to the front door. An older man in green uniform appears by the Rover as we stop. He opens my door rather ceremoniously. "Good afternoon, Ms. Burke."

"Good afternoon." I smile at him.

He nods somberly.

With a few long strides, Christian is by my side. "This is Dickson, the butler."

"Nice meeting you." I smile again.

He nods again.

At the open door stands a brunette woman, impeccably dressed in a pinstriped suit and white blouse. She's no more than thirty, has features too strong to be attractive, and exudes an air of no-nonsense authority. "Good afternoon, Sir," she greets Christian. "Good afternoon Ms. Burke." She nods to me. "I am Ms. McGregor, the head housekeeper. Let me show you to your room. Your bags will be carried upstairs shortly."

"I'll show her the room," Christian says. "Which one is it?"

"The rose suite, in the guest wing."

"You couldn't find anything farther, could you?"

"It was the duchess's request," Ms. McGregor says with elegant calm.

Christian makes a face. "Ms. McGregor, we would like to have lunch in the breakfast room in about half an hour."

We enter the three-story foyer where a curving marble staircase with red carpet and wrought iron railing leads to the second and third floors. The rose suite is the last room on the second floor in the right wing. The plush carpet muffles our footsteps and voices. Family portraits hang on the walls between the doors over mahogany wainscoting.

"When we have only a few visitors, they usually stay in the main building," Christian says. "Mother must have been afraid I'd visit you during the night."

The room lives up to its name. All the upholstery is different shades of dusty rose. The baldachin and bedcover are in a darker shade; the chairs and pillows are lighter. A large mirror in a gilded frame hangs above the fireplace, and a vase of fresh-picked pink and white lilacs sits on the night table.

"Welcome to my family's hovel," Christian says, pulling me to him and giving me a very warm welcome kiss. We are interrupted by a knock on the door; the butler has brought up my bag.

"I'll show you my suite," Christian says. "Then we will have lunch."

On the way to his room he tells me his parents won't be back until the following day, and his grandmother, who lives a ten-minute drive away, has invited us for dinner. Since she believes that it is unhealthy to eat after six o'clock, dinner will be served at five, which means we should be at her house around four thirty; this leaves very little time to do anything in the afternoon.

Christian's rooms face the sea and are decorated mostly in greens and blues. In spite of its cool colors, it's homier than the room given to me.

We descend to the main floor and make our way to the breakfast room, which overlooks the lawn and the sea beyond.

While we eat, I ask Christian what it was like to grow up in such a huge house.

"I wouldn't know," he says. "I hardly spent time here, except for holidays and family celebrations." Then he asks me if I'd like to have a tour of the house.

We start at the main entrance. With the impersonal voice of a tour guide Christian says, "This is the front door. We have many side doors, too. They aren't as impressive as this one." As we enter, he continues with a wide wave of his arm, "And this is the foyer. As you can see, there are stairs. They lead to the second and third floors. The doors lead to different rooms."

"No kidding," I laugh.

Looking at me with mock seriousness, he asks, "Would you like to see the ballroom, or the grand salon, or the state dining room, or the ladies' room—not to be confused with the ladies' washroom, which can be found at the end of the hallway? Or would you rather visit the library, or the billiard room, or the men's smoking room—not to be confused with the men's washroom, which can be found … I guess you don't care about that. Or would you rather see the picture gallery, or the conservatory—"

"I'd like to see them all."

How can I describe the house? It is impressive, elegant, tasteful, luxurious, grand—the only word I would not use is homey.

"Do you feel intimidated enough?" Christian asks at the end of the tour.

"I don't get intimidated by things," I say. I am far more intimidated by the servants. They seem so proper and unflappable.

"That is good," Christian says thoughtfully. "This is not an amiable house. Most houses take on the owners' personality. This house wants you to take on its personality."

Or maybe it reflects its owners' personalities too much.

By the time we finish the tour, it's time to get ready to visit Christian's grandmother.

~ ~ ~

Lady Seymour—Grandam, as Christian calls her—lives in a charming two-story brick house, surrounded by a romantic garden with ancient apple trees and hundreds of red and yellow tulips in full bloom. In front of the house, a gravel driveway circles a fountain with a bronze replica of Andrea del Verrocchio's delightful statue of a cherubim and his fish friend, the *Putto with a Dolphin*.

An older butler ushers us into the parlor. The house is just as charming and inviting on the inside as on the outside. On the right is a comfortable drawing room with windows on three sides, wood paneling, and sand colored carpet. Small tables, books, and cheerful, faded chintz covered chairs are scattered everywhere.

When we enter, the dowager duchess stands up to greet us. She's short, with porcelain skin, well-coiffed silver-white hair, and penetrating blue eyes. She must have been a real beauty in her youth. In a brown suit of heavy silk and a lighter brown silk blouse with a large bow at the neck, a butterfly pendant with sapphires, a gold wedding band, and a gold watch, she's the epitome of understated elegance.

She hugs Christian warmly as he hands her a bouquet of soft butter-yellow roses, then introduces me as his friend.

"So you are the girl who stole Christian's heart," Lady Seymour says.

What?

"Grandam," Christian moans.

"It is about time," she continues, ignoring Christian. "Someone must take charge of that boy." She smiles warmly first at her grandson, then at me. "You seem the kind of girl who can keep him in line."

I can feel my face turning red.

"Grandam, you are embarrassing us," Christian groans.

"That is exactly what I am trying to do," she laughs, her eyes twinkling.

The butler enters the room and asks what aperitif we would like. Lady Seymour and I have Grand Marnier; Christian has cognac.

While sipping the drinks and later during dinner, the duchess questions me about my family, school, and interests. She tells me that she loves reading, gardening, and ballet; she took lessons as a young girl, and is a great patron of the local ballet troupe and school.

She also recounts some of Christian's mischiefs. Once, when Christian was only four or five years old, while his nanny was napping, he smeared lipstick on every bust he could reach. At age three he simply disappeared while on a picnic. Everyone was frantically searching for him all after-noon and night, while he was playing and later sleeping under the caretaker's porch. He returned to the house in the morning, announcing he'd gotten hungry.

She takes out a photo album filled with photos of Christian: Christian as a bright-eyed one-year old, looking like a doll; Christian at his First Communion; Christian as a pirate in a Peter Pan production; Christian as a serious-eyed, unruly-haired teenager.

By the time she finishes the album, I'm in love with the

little guy Christian used to be, and even more in love with the man Christian is. I want to hug him, and kiss him, take him to bed, and make love to him until all my longings for him are satisfied.

"I am sorry," the duchess says later in the evening. "I would love to keep you longer, but I am an old lady; I need twelve hours to get eight hours' sleep."

On the way back to Ashton Hall I think about Lady Seymour's comment of me being the girl who stole Christian's heart. I'd like to ask him about it, but since I have no idea how to bring it up, I keep mum. Especially since Christian is wrapped in an impenetrable silence.

He walks me to my room, gives me an absentminded good night kiss, and leaves. I close the door behind me wondering what is the matter with him.

~ ~ ~

Next morning is bright and sunny again. After breakfast we are off to visit Haukwold.

Professor Rosenthal was right; the ruin is very picturesque. It has a center tower and crumbling outer walls with ivy clambering all over. It doesn't look at all the Haukwold I remember. The forest is gone, replaced by a checkerboard of fresh green and brown fields and hedgerows. The center tower, which might be the original lodge, is intact. In the off-season it's only open between twelve and four. We're not going to wait until twelve. We explore the ruins; there's no déjà vu, no feeling of familiarity.

From Haukwold we drive north to the shore. When we reach the North Sea, I ask Christian to turn right. We enter a valley that reminds me of the valley below Bancloch. There's a small village, called Blenby.

"Christian, can we stop here?"

"Of course."

We park on the main street at the bottom of the hill. "I'd

like to see what's on the top," I say.

We hike a narrow street that winds its way between quaint old houses. Blenby, with charming old stone buildings, is one of the most scenic villages I've ever seen. On top of the ridge, a street runs parallel to the cliff. Some of the houses have been converted to restaurants or bed and breakfasts, but they are still closed. Strolling along the street, we come upon a lookout point from where we can see both the shore and the valley.

As I scan the view, my heart speeds up. "This is it," I gasp. "This is where Bancloch was."

Christian, who's been studying the view with a frown, turns to me. "Are you sure?"

"Yes, I am almost one hundred percent sure. But what happened to the castle?"

He steps closer. "Are you certain there was a castle here?"

"Yes, I am. And I think this lookout point was one of the watchtowers."

"This is too low for a watchtower."

"Maybe this is only the foundation."

"If there was a castle here," he says thoughtfully, "some vestiges must remain." He looks around as if searching for signs of the missing walls. "A stone wall, a legend, an old deed, something. A castle couldn't have disappeared without a trace. If you wish we can stay and explore more, ask questions, visit the museum. I can cancel our lunch at home and the afternoon trip to the folly."

We only have today for exploration.

"I wish we could be in two places at once," I sigh. "I want to see the folly, too. Maybe we can come back here at another time."

I take a few pictures then we return to Ashton Hall. On the way back Christian excitedly talks about the possible sources of more information. Is it the historian Christian

Seymour, or Christian of Bancloch who is so excited?

The day is beautiful—sunny with a pleasant breeze off the sea. We have an alfresco lunch, during which we decide to do our afternoon exploration on horseback. Dickson makes a quick call to the stables, so by the time we finish eating, a stable hand is waiting for us with two saddled horses.

We follow a forest trail that winds its way between ancient oak and beech trees. It reminds me of the forest around the enchanted tower, though it is more open. The sun shines softly through the fresh, still translucent green leaves, illuminating the bluebells that carpet the forest floor. Birds call out to each other, and from time to time sweet scents drift around on the breeze. It's the kind of day when everything seems right in the world.

As we emerge from between the trees, the tower house looms ahead. My heart jumps.

It is the enchanted tower!

Overcome with emotion, I stop the horse and close my eyes. I hear the wizard's words, "If you choose to return to the twenty-first century, you could rebuild this tower, which will be a ruin once you leave."

It takes a minute before my heart stops racing and I can speak. "Christian—" I whisper.

"You don't have to say anything," he interrupts. "You have very expressive body language."

"Christian, how could it happen?" I turn to him. "How did I …? I can't believe this …" I'm not coherent. Christian is silently watching me. Finally, I calm down enough to think and talk lucidly. "This place is about 200 miles from the Mosquito Creek Camp. There's no way I could have hiked here."

"What is Mosquito Creek Camp?" he asks.

"Where I worked last summer."

Christian is regarding me with narrowed eyes, and for the

first time since we met, I don't care whether he believes me or not. "Do you have a chapel on the shore about two miles that way?" I ask pointing to the left.

"Yes," Christian says.

"And do you have a creek delta another three miles beyond it?"

"Yes."

"Is there a stone bench?"

"Yes, but—"

"How about a conservatory with tile floor and French doors in that direction?" I point my arm roughly in the direction of the pavilion.

"Some greenhouses are built into the south side of an old wall." He looks flummoxed. "Ann-Marie, this still does not—"

"Could we ride to the creek delta?" I am in no mood to argue about probabilities.

We follow the dirt road on top of the ridge. I walked this trail almost every day while in the enchanted tower. When we arrive at the chapel, Christian finds the hidden key. The chapel is exactly as I remember it, except now it has pews. "Do you still say Mass here?" I ask.

"Sometimes."

I amble up to the glass wall and look out onto the waves. They seem timeless. As I watch the swelling and retreating water that has been crushing onto these rocks for ages— utterly indifferent to the human dramas around them—I feel intimately connected with all that has been and will come.

Christian slides his arm around my shoulder and I slide mine around his waist. We stand silently watching the waves for a while, then he gently turns me around and pulls me into a warm embrace. The memory of our last embrace in the same spot engulfs me. No words, kiss, or touch can convey the deep love I have for Christian. And I know, without doubt, he has the same love for me.

As if in a trance Christian says in a husky voice, "You know, Ann-Marie, there's something special about you. When I am with you I feel different, I feel ... whole."

"You are very special to me too," I whisper back, and lean my head against his shoulder.

We stand for a long time holding each other, then Christian bends down and we share an impassioned, loving kiss.

"Shall we visit the creek?" Christian asks, when we let go.

Riding side by side in silence, we enjoy the lovely spring day. We dismount at the creek delta, tie the horses, and sit down on the bench.

"How long has this stone bench been here?" I ask.

"Probably forever," Christian laughs and puts his arm around my shoulder. We sit on the bench for a long time, drinking in the familiar view. The last time we were here together and this moment merge in my mind.

"It seems as if I've been here with you before," Christian says.

I don't answer. Why ruin a perfectly good moment.

"Do you want to race back to the tower?" Christian asks after a while.

"Sure."

We descend to the beach and gallop all the way back, just as we did when we lived in the enchanted tower.

"Is it safe to explore the building?" I ask when we arrive.

"There's not much to explore," Christian says. "It's only a shell."

We dismount, tie the horses, and enter through the empty doorframe. The tower seems sad, as all abandoned buildings do. The windows are gone and part of the roof has caved in. We gingerly cross the main hall. The floor is strewn with fallen leaves and other debris, and the stairs are broken in one place. We climb all the way to the top floor.

"Why didn't your family rebuild this after the fire?" I ask while looking at the view.

"One of their sons died here," Christian answers. "Many people believe he is still haunting it. They swear they can sometimes hear music and laughter."

Interesting. Is the place still haunted?

~ ~ ~

We return to Ashton Hall, and Dickson announces, "The Lord and Lady Seymour have arrived and expect you for dinner at six thirty in the family dining room."

That gives us an hour to get ready. I shower, put on make-up, and change into a cocktail dress that I bought a while back because when I tried it on and ventured out from the dressing rooms to show it to Nicole, a guy stared at me with "wow, she looks good" written all over his face.

Christian and I meet at the stairs, and while we descend, I ask, "Christian, how should I address your parents? Am I supposed to call them Lord and Lady Seymour, or your highness, or …?"

"Don't worry about the name calling," Christian says. "Just call them 'hey you.'" I laugh. "Address them as you would anyone else, unless they request otherwise."

It's not even six thirty, but four people are already sitting at the long, elegantly set table. Christian said we would be having dinner with his parents only. I glance at him and see surprise and anger flit across his face, but in the next instant he's back to his usual composed self. Sliding his hand protectively to my back, he leads me toward the table.

"Father, I would like to introduce Miss Ann-Marie Burke. Miss Burke, this is my father, Lord Colin Seymour, the Duke of Norbury."

The man—who, if it is at all possible, is even better looking than Christian—stands up and reaches out a hand. "How do you do?" He is tall and athletic, with Christian's penetrating, notice-everything hazel eyes beneath bushy blond eyebrows; his dark blond hair is mixed with an attractive gray. He's impeccably dressed in a well-tailored three-piece suit, and seems aristocratic, the kind of man who is used to giving orders and making decisions.

I shake his hand. He takes a quick glance at me, and I know he's formed his opinion, though his handsome face does not give away what that opinion is.

Christian leads me to the other end of the table. "Mother, allow me to introduce Miss Ann-Marie Burke. Miss Burke, this is my mother Lady Alicia Seymour."

Lady Seymour is very formal and elegant. She has light brown hair and eyes, and a forced smile. She does not stand up or reach out a hand as she says, "How do you do."

I smile at her and nod slightly. "How do you do."

Christian turns to the woman on the other side of the table. "My sister, Caroline." She's in her mid-twenties and has the same hair color as her mother, with the addition of pink highlights. She's dressed in a style I would call expensive-funky. I remember Christian telling me that she and her baron husband live a rather indolent life.

"Oh," she drawls in a bored voice, "you are the girl who shares Christian's interest in history."

I give her a warm smile. I wish I knew what Christian says about me behind my back.

"Is that all you share?" she drawls.

Christian, ignoring her question, gestures to the woman across from Caroline. "Miss Mercedes Bowden." Turning to me, he says. "Ms. Bowden is Caroline's best friend." The woman, also in her mid-twenties with platinum blond hair and a pretty heart shaped face, gives me a once over with her cold blue eyes. I smile, ignoring her obvious dislike of me.

"I am more than Caroline's friend," she says coldly. "I am Christian's fiancée."

What?

I glance at Christian but his expression is inscrutable.

My heart plummets and my throat constricts. I want to run. I want to be out of here.

I can't.

Not right now.

With all my strength I swallow my shock and smile at Mercedes. "Nice to meet you."

Christian takes the chair across from me. I avoid his eyes.

Lady Seymour nods to the butler who waves to someone else. A young woman in a green uniform with a white apron pushes in an elegant cart. She and Dickson set a plate in front of each one of us, starting with Lady and Lord Seymour, followed by Christian, Caroline, Mercedes, and me.

Lord Seymour says "Bon appétit."

The appetizer is asparagus tips wrapped in smoked salmon with some kind of white sauce.

I am too upset to eat but force the food down my throat. It actually tastes good.

"Alicia, what did you think of the cancer fundraising gala?" Mercedes asks, turning to Christian's mother.

Alicia?

"It was a great financial success," Lady Seymour replies. "They raised far more money than last year."

"Did you see the dress Lady Scottsdale wore?" Caroline pipes in. "It was hideous."

"Lady Scottsdale never had much fashion sense," Mercedes says with a faint smile. "And she should definitely try a different caterer."

The three women talk about the fundraising dinner and the people who attended it. It's hard to join the conversation, since I have no idea who they are talking about, or where and when the event took place.

The discussion turns to another subject, and I pin together

from the snippets of information that Caroline and her husband, along with two other couples, are planning to rent a luxury yacht for three weeks and sail the Mediterranean.

"Caroline, you absolutely must visit that little restaurant on the Amalfi Coast," Mercedes enthuses. "What was the name? …I have it written down; I will give it to you."

"And I will give you the name of the jeweler in Monaco," says Lady Seymour. "The one who made the tiara you so much admire. Do not forget, you will have to make an appointment to visit the store."

They chat on about all the restaurants, stores, nightclubs, and sights Caroline and company "absolutely" must visit. Since I cannot contribute anything to the conversation, I say nothing. Christian and his father also haven't said a word yet.

I would get a kick out of watching the three women— they are so different from the people I know—if not for Christian's betrayal. I try to ignore him, without much success. Every time I glance at him, he is looking at me.

Somewhere in the middle of the main course, Mercedes turns to Christian. "Honey," she says, "you must ensure you are home for the St. Andrew's Regatta. It would be the perfect place and time to announce our engagement."

"We will talk about that engagement," Christian mutters.

"Engagement at St. Andrew's." Caroline clasps her hands. "That's a splendid idea."

This supper has surpassed awful. It will probably go down in history as the worst dinner of my life. How long will I have to linger? I wish I could click my heels and end up at home, or at least in town, anywhere but here. So far no one has spoken a word to me. The women are discussing the regatta. What do I know about the regatta? Only that Christian will announce his engagement there.

My throat tightens every time I think about his engagement, so I try not to; instead, I concentrate on the three women talking about the fall hunt, fashion shows, and some upcoming gala.

What does Christian's father think about me? He must think I am the greatest dolt in the world. Maybe I should say something witty or humorous. No. Christian's family has scored zero with me, why should I try to impress them? Christian warned me about this. Too bad he did not warn me about his engagement.

Finally, after the tea, Lord Seymour rises. "I have some business to attend to; please excuse me." Not waiting for an answer, he leaves.

Here is my chance to escape. I rise, with my best imitation of a smile. "I also have some business to attend to. Please excuse me. Thank you for the lovely dinner. I very much enjoyed the company and the discussion."

"Ann-Marie—" I hear Christian but ignore him. I want to get out of here before I burst into tears.

Outside the room I take a deep breath. Holy mackerel, this was bad. I race to my room, change into jeans and a t-shirt, grab a sweater and head out into the garden.

It's almost full moon. The garden is awash with silver moonlight, and quiet. I can hear the waves breaking on the rocks below. After the stuffiness of the dining room, the cool night air feels cleansing and invigorating. I sit on the low wall separating the lawn from the rocky shore beyond, and watch the indifferent waves. I rise and wander around until I see a bench in the shadow of a large tree. As soon as I sit down, tears well up in my eyes.

I've had enough of Christian. Somewhere deep down I knew he was not free. Why did he date me? Why did he tell me I am special? My tears start to flow. I fish an old, torn tissue from my pocket. Damn. I should have brought more tissues with me.

Time to give up. Christian won't marry me, he won't

believe me, his relationship with his parents is none of my business. His world is so different from mine: fundraisers, regattas, fall hunts, fashion shows. Is this the world he wants to escape?

And ... and within a few months, he will be gone.

I start to sob in earnest and it takes a long time before I calm down enough to think again.

Maybe I've only imagined the wizard and the challenges. Maybe Christian will go on living with those three snooty women.

I hope I'll never see them again.

Actually, if I stay I will have to face them tomorrow morning.

And Christian, too.

No, I won't. I don't want to stay here any longer. And I won't drive home with Christian.

We've failed the quest. The pain of this thought becomes almost physical. For a long time I feel shattered and empty. Finally, the pain eases enough so I can think again.

I will slip out at the first sign of dawn. Ashton Hall is only about three miles from the highway. I can easily walk that distance. I'll hitchhike to Norbury, and take the bus from there. I should leave a thank you note and a note to Christian to tell him not to bother to call me ever again. What makes me think he would call?

Damn these tears.

I was stupid to assume he loved me because he loved me in some alternative universe ... if there is such a place.

I hear a twig snap and a light crunching sound on the gravel. I hope it's an animal. I am not ready to talk to anyone.

The steps are coming closer. I hold my breath. Maybe whoever is coming will not notice me in the shadow of the tree.

"Ann-Marie," Christian says, "I must talk to you."

Chapter 30

The last person I want to talk to is Christian. Still, my heart fills with hope. He sits down next to me, and I slide away from him.

"Christian," I say, wiping my tears with my sleeve, "there's nothing to talk about. I kind of got dreams and reality mixed up. I am … sorry …" Damn. Why am I crying? I don't want to cry. Not in front of him. I try to swallow my tears. "I'm going to leave early tomorrow …" Stupid tears are running down my face. "I—I won't bother you …"

He reaches for my hand, but I pull it away. "I am sorry about what's happened tonight," he says.

"Don't worry, these things happen." I bite my lip. If only I could stop crying. "Christian, I should have known. The best thing to do …" I want to say, "is to part company." Instead of the words a sob comes. Damn. Come on Ann, pull yourself together. "Sorry, I didn't mean to cry," Not in front of him, anyway.

"Ann-Marie, during supper I made my decision." Christian moves even closer, reaches out, and gently brushes my wet cheek. "What I told you this afternoon is true. You make me feel whole. You touch my soul as no one else can. I don't want to live without you. I love you. Would you marry me?"

I close my eyes, barely believing my ears. "Christian," I open my eyes and look at him, "I love you too, and nothing would make me happier than to spend my life with you, but what about Mercedes? You are engaged to her."

"If I hadn't met you," Christian says, "I probably would have married her. God knows she has waited long enough. During supper I realized I could not marry her because I'm in love with you." My heart skips a beat. "From the moment we first fenced in Montfield I could not stop thinking about you. When I saw you again at the dance … don't laugh, this will sound crazy … something inside me said that I should marry you. I tried to fight my attraction … but you were like a magnet … I could not stay away." He pauses. "Mercedes and I have never been officially engaged. Everyone just assumed we would marry one day." Christian takes both my hands again. "Ann, would you marry me?"

Of course I would. "What will your parents say?"

"Father will probably threaten to disown me and never give me another penny as long as he lives and—"

"Christian, you cannot throw your family away."

He slides right up to me. "First, Father cannot disown me. Whether he likes it or not, I will become the next duke unless I die before he does. And if my family decides that marrying you is such an offence they would never want to see me again, it is their loss. Grandam will see me, and maybe Kimberley." Leaning closer he asks, "Will you say yes?"

"Christian, I love you, but I cannot let you ruin your life—"

"Ruin my life." He sits up straighter. "I realized tonight that marrying Mercedes would be a big mistake. On the other hand, marrying the woman I love and doing what I love to do cannot ruin my life." He cups my face with his hands. "Will you marry me?"

"Yes, Christian, I will marry you, but—"

In the next instant his mouth is on mine. And all my arguments disappear.

When we let go, I ask, "When are you going to tell Mercedes you won't marry her?"

"I have told her already," Christian answers.

"You did. You didn't even know if I would say yes."

"I would not marry Mercedes even if you said no." He smiles and pulls his finger along my jawline. "Also, I had a pretty good hunch about what you would say."

I can't repress a smile. "Okay. When should we marry?"

"You said something about me having to marry you within a year or die. We should marry a.s.a.p."

"How soon is a.s.a.p.?"

"Monday, first thing in the morning sounds good."

"It sounds good to me, too." I kiss him.

We stay on the bench for a long time, kissing, and talking about plans. It's well after midnight by the time we return to the building. Not wanting to wake anyone, we use one of the side doors. Christian knows how to open it from the outside without setting off the alarm. Taking off our shoes, we tiptoe through the dark hallway. The door of the reception room is slightly ajar, and we overhear the discussion inside, especially since one of the speakers is not even trying to keep her voice down.

"Ridiculous," Mercedes cries out. "This bitch, this nobody comes along, and Chris wants to marry her. Who is she? A bloody commoner. There's nothing special about her—"

"Don't worry, Mercedes," Caroline interrupts. "Father will never agree to Chris marrying her."

"She has him bewitched," Mercedes wails. "Wrapped around her little finger. How did she do it? I've waited eight years, eight bloody long years and now this nobody will snatch away everything: the man, the title, the money, everything."

"I told you," Caroline says soothingly. "Father will not agree to it."

"Go on, Ann-Marie," Christian whispers, "I want to say a few words to Mercedes. I'll see you in the morning."

~ ~ ~

The next morning, rainclouds hang low and oppressive, echoing my feeling about facing Christian's parents.

When Christian and I arrive in the breakfast room, only Lord and Lady Seymour are present, eating already. Before I can even say "good morning," Lady Seymour says sharply, "Christian, I heard you have broken your engagement with Mercedes. I would like an explanation."

"Good morning, Mother. Good morning, Father," Christian says brightly. I say a "good morning" too, but no one pays any attention to me. "I've decided Mercedes would never make a good wife for me. She was extremely rude last night, and so were you, Mother." The duchess turns red; the duke stops eating and glowers at Christian. "When I visited Ann-Marie's family her folks included me in the conversation, asked for my opinion. The way you treated my guest was appalling."

"Christian—" I begin.

"Christian," growls Lord Seymour at the same time.

Christian ignores us. "I came to announce that I have asked Miss Burke to marry me, and she has said yes."

"You want to marry a commoner?" The duchess is aghast.

"Mother, we are all commoners," Christian answers. "We are all descendants from the same common ancestors. Just because our family kept better track of our lineage, doesn't mean we are any more special." He turns to me. "You must forgive my family. They are very filiopietistic."

What does that mean?

"Stop using big words no one understands," Christian's mother says, irritated.

"It means an excessive reverence of forbearers and traditions," Christian explains.

"Christian," Lord Seymour says, "you can do whatever you want, but if you cast aside your family and social obligations, you will leave me no choice but to disown you. You cannot have your high income and do nothing for it."

"I know, Father," Christian says. "You have been threatening me with this ever since I was a teenager and stopped being slave to your ideals. If you want me to choose, fine. I choose my dreams, and Ann-Marie."

"Your annuity will be cut off," Lord Seymour says coldly.

"I have not used a penny of that money," Christian answers.

Father and son glare at each other, and I realize how much alike they are. Two strong-willed men, neither of them willing to compromise.

Christian's father turns to me. "Miss Burke I need to talk to you in private in my study."

Christian sends me a worried glance. I square my shoulders, suddenly feeling more like Princess Ann-Marie of Ryston than Ann-Marie Burke. I faced the arrows of hundreds of enemies in Bancloch. I can face his father. He does not even have a bow.

~ ~ ~

Lord Seymour ushers me into a well-appointed room with French doors, low bookshelves crammed with books and binders, more portraits of ancestors, and a huge gilded desk that dominates the room. He motions me to sit down, and takes the chair behind the desk.

"Ms. Burke," he begins, playing with a gold pen. "You seem an intelligent and reasonable girl, so I hope you will understand what is at stake."

I nod calmly.

"Christian has been rebellious all his life," the duke says. "He prefers to go his own way and do his own thing. I am certain he only wants to marry you out of rebellion." With narrowed eyes, he studies me. "You seem to have enough influence to reason with him. You must explain to him that he has obligations to his family, his title, society; he cannot just forsake them."

"Please explain what obligations Christian is forsaking."

"He should be working with me, instead of chasing dreams of writing historical novels. He should marry someone who would be an asset, not a burden." I repress a smile. The good old duke thinks I'd be a burden. "He should not turn his back on his position in society—"

"I am afraid I cannot help you, sir," I interrupt with cool formality. "Christian is an adult. He is the master of his life. Neither you nor I can decide how he should live it."

The duke's eyes turn cold as an eagle's. "If you want to marry a penniless social outcast, go ahead, Miss. When the two of you are married I will cut all ties with you."

"Sir," I answer—where is this calm coming from?— "cutting Christian off because he is following his aspirations will be entirely your decision. Do not blame him or me for it."

"You will not give Christian up," he says.

"I cannot give Christian up because I don't own him, Sir."

"You will not try to persuade him."

I shake my head. "I will not."

"Fine, Miss Burke," he answers, disdainful. "We have nothing more to discuss. I ask you to please leave my house."

How can I tell him he is making a mistake? Why can't he see that Christian has the same strong drive he has? I understand him not liking me—I don't think I made a very good impression last night—but he should not let anger dictate his actions. "Fine, Sir," I say. "If you ever find in your heart that your love for Christian is more important than having your way, our door is always open to you. Thank you for your hospitality." I nod and exit the room.

I feel defeated. Damn. Instead of helping Christian and his father to patch up their differences, I've pushed them further apart. Congratulations.

When I return to the breakfast room, Christian is sitting by the table next to his mother with a cup of coffee in his hand and an untouched muffin on the plate in front of him. He asks what's happened.

"Your father and I did not see eye to eye," I answer with

a deep sigh. "He's asked me to leave his house. I better go."

"He did?" Christian says, putting down his cup. "I better come with you." He stands up, then leaning down, kisses his mother on her cheek. "Good bye, Mother, and say good bye to Father for me." Before she can say anything, Christian ushers me out of the breakfast room.

~ ~ ~

"I must talk to Grandam," he says as we climb into his Rover. "Then we will head back home."

I tell Christian about my conversation with his father, and then keep my fingers crossed all the way to Lady Seymour's house for her support. Maybe she can help to heal this rift between father and son.

"I already know what has happened," she says right after the greetings. "And I told Colin he has gone too far."

I feel such relief I want to kiss the old duchess.

"Thank you, Grandam," Christian kisses her on the cheek.

"Please join me for breakfast," she says. "I want to hear about your evening, but I am especially interested to know about your plans."

She ushers us into the dining room where the butler is already adding two table settings. During breakfast Christian narrates the events of last night and this morning, finishing with, "We have decided to elope."

"I knew something was afoot when Christian came home at Christmas and could not stop talking about you." The duchess smiles at me. "When is the wedding?"

Christian brightens. "Grandam, would you like to come to our wedding?"

"I would love to come," the old duchess answers. "However, unless you have the ceremony in my garden, I would not be able to attend."

Christian and I glance at each other. She's our most powerful ally, and she and Christian share such a bond of love. We should include her. It would complicate every-thing, but would be worth it. I nod.

"Grandam," Christian says, "we could have the wedding in Norbury. We have planned to marry as soon as possible in a small ceremony, followed by a dinner in a restaurant, and invite only Kimberley and her family, and Ann-Marie's sister, Sarah."

The butler returns, offers more coffee, and clears the empty plates.

"If you are in such hurry to marry, you could have the wedding at my place next Saturday," she says. "I will take care of the dinner, and ask the bishop to preside. You get the license, and invite whomever you want to; just let me know by Wednesday how many people are coming."

"Thank you Grandam," Christian says. "But we don't want to impose on you. We can have the dinner at a local restaurant."

"You are definitely not eating in a restaurant. We will have the dinner here," she says in an imperious voice. "And you should send an invitation to your father."

"Sorry, Grandam." He shakes his head. "I am not going to."

Lady Seymour sighs, then looks at me. "I might have the perfect wedding gown for you, Ann-Marie."

A wedding gown. I haven't even thought about what I'll wear.

Lady Seymour summons the housekeeper and explains to her which dress she has in mind and where to find it. The housekeeper returns, unzips the bag, and holds up a gorgeous gown. It is bone white, with an empire waist, a heart shaped bodice beaded with small pearls, a thin strap, and a long, layered skirt.

"Do you like it?" the duchess smiles at me.

"It is beautiful," I exhale.

"It was my first ball gown." The old lady caresses the dress with warm, smiling eyes. "You are slender enough to fit into it. Try it on."

The housekeeper leads me to one of the guest rooms upstairs. The dress fits perfectly. How lucky. I don't have to worry about a wedding dress. When I arrive in the drawing room, Christian stares at me with admiration, while the duchess studies me more critically.

"Your heel should not be higher than three inches," she says. "And your hair … I will have my hairdresser do something with it; and I will have a manicure and make-up lined up too."

I've never had a manicure.

Close to noon we part and head back home. On the way we talk about plans for the wedding and our life together.

Chapter 31

"You must wait 48 hours before you can marry," says the middle-aged clerk at the courthouse when we buy our marriage license.

"We've already waited 48 hours," Christian answers. "We met on Friday; today is Monday. That's more than 48 hours."

I giggle. The clerk gives him a disapproving glance. "You must wait 48 hours between the application and the issuance of the license," she says primly.

Christian turns to me. "Do you think you can live for another 48 hours without my forever commitment?"

"After waiting nine hundred years," I purr, "another 48 hours won't matter."

The clerk studies us for a few seconds. I think she's assessing whether we have the mental capacity for marriage. "I need your birth certificate, and another piece of identification, preferably a driver's license," she says starchily.

We meet with Sarah for lunch. We wanted to talk to her the previous night but Mom was home. Since Will has moved, she spends a lot more time at home.

We explain the situation, and our plans. She shakes her head. "I don't think you should elope."

"It's a political decision," I answer. "We don't want to force people in Christian's family to choose between father and son. We cannot invite both Dad's family and Mom's and I don't want to invite only one side. Not to mention letting Mom and Martina loose on such an emotion-filled occasion. No. It's the best for everyone's sanity if we elope."

"When you explain it this way, your decision makes sense." She sighs. "And, yes, I want to be your bridesmaid."

"Okay." I smile. "Here are the plans."

In the afternoon we stop at Christian's apartment. We've decided since Christian owns an apartment and I only own a car, I will move to his place.

He does lives close to the university, but not—as I imagined—in one of the low rent century-old apartments. His apartment is a few blocks further, in one of the most posh neighborhoods. He has three spacious rooms on the second floor facing a lush, bucolic garden. The furnishing is light and modern. The place is clean except for Christian's study-cum-exercise room. It has papers spread everywhere—on the chairs, desk, bookshelves, and the floor. The only furniture free of papers is a weight bench and a treadmill.

"Do you actually use those?" I ask.

"Yes, every day."

Wow. No wonder he has such perfect body.

The exercise equipment is not the only surprise. When we arrive, a plump woman in a black dress, white apron, and frumpy black shoes is reading the paper in the kitchen.

"This is Mrs. Olga, the housekeeper," Christian introduces her. "She comes every day to clean, wash clothes, and do the cooking." Turning to her, he adds, "This is Ann-Marie Burke, my fiancée. We are marrying this Saturday and she is moving here."

Mrs. Olga studies me with squinted eyes. "If she's moving in, you will have to pay me a higher rate."

A higher rate. I am not even sure if we can afford—or need—a full time housekeeper. I would not mind someone once or twice a week. Christian must have the same thoughts because he says, "Mrs. Olga, I know you need this job, but my father is cutting off all financial support, we do not know yet if we will be able to afford—"

"Are you letting me go?" Mrs. Olga asks worriedly.

"Definitely not," Christian says. "We might cut back your hours, though, to one or two days a week."

"I can't keep this place clean in one or two days a week," she protests.

"We have a housekeeper," I interject. "She comes only once a week and keeps a place twice the size of this clean and does laundry for three people."

She glances at me angrily. "What should I cook for dinner today?"

"You don't need to cook today," Christian answers. "We are eating at my sister's house tonight."

At five-thirty we arrive at my future in-laws' place.

Kimberley, Doug, and their three children live close by in a three-story Victorian town house with a large garden in the back.

The butler ushers us to the comfortably furnished family room that overlooks the garden. Toys and picture books are scattered on the floor. Baby Millie is lying on her tummy in a playpen, while her two brothers are building something with oversized Lego pieces.

"Uncle Chris, Uncle Chris," they shout, running to Christian and hugging him in the middle.

"Hi big guys." Christian tousles their hair.

Andrew launches into telling Christian about some event at school, while Nicholas is babbling something entirely different.

"I will listen to you in a sec," Christian says to the boys. "First I must introduce our guest."

Andrew looks up at me. "Who are you?" he asks.

"She talked to mommy in the park," Nicholas says, proud to know something his brother doesn't.

Doug puts his hand on Andrew's shoulder. "A gentleman does not ask 'Who are you?' He properly introduces himself." Turning to me, he reaches out his hand. "I am Douglas Harding." He is tall, good looking with dark hair, brown eyes, and five o'clock shadow.

I feel as if I am role-playing. "Nice to meet you," I say, shaking his hand. "I am Ann-Marie Burke, Christian's fiancée."

"What's a fiancée?" Andrew asks.

"A bride-to-be," Doug answers. "A woman who will soon marry."

Andrew turns toward me. "Will you marry Uncle Chris?"

"Yes," Christian says, taking the word from my mouth. "That's why we are here. We would like to invite all of you to our wedding."

Andrew contemplates this news for a few seconds then asks, "Uncle Chris, do you really have to kiss the bride?"

"Of course." Christian grins.

"Yuck." Andrew wrinkles his nose.

"Sometimes, we men have to make sacrifices," Christian says, deadpan. I repress a laugh.

"Yes." Andrew nods seriously. "The teacher told us we must be nice to the girls."

"Especially if you want them to be nice to you," his father says.

The butler enters the room. "Madam, dinner is ready,"

he announces.

"All right," Kimberley says. "You kids will eat with your nanny tonight. We have some important business to discuss with Uncle Chris."

"We want to eat with you," Andrew protests and takes Christian's hand.

"Me too." Nicholas grabs his mom's leg.

"Not tonight," Kimberley answers, gently pushing him away.

"You don't want to join us." Christian rumples Andrew's hair. "It will be boring adult talk. I would go with you if I could."

"Will you play with us after dinner?" Andrew asks Christian. When Christian promises he will Andrew grabs Nicholas's hand. "Let's finish fast, and we can play with Uncle Chris."

We eat in the dining room. It has dark wood wainscoting, amber colored walls, and elegant antique furnishing. Supper is lasagna, salad, and red wine. Lasagna is one of Christian's favorite foods.

"I have heard Father and Mother's version of the events," Kimberley says as she passes the lasagna dish to me. "Now I want to hear yours."

"Not much to hear," Christian answers, scooping salad onto his plate. "I announced I will marry Ann-Marie, and Father wants nothing to do with me."

"I knew this would happen one day." Kimberley shakes her head. "You both are too headstrong to get along. What are you planning to do?"

"We are planning to have a small wedding at Grandam's place this Saturday." Christian turns to Doug. "Would you be my best man?"

"Who is invited to the wedding?" Kimberley asks.

"Ann-Marie's sister, you, and Grandam."

"I wish we had eloped," Doug interjects, and sends a warm smile to his wife. "It would have saved lots of grief." Turning to me, he explains, "Our wedding was held at the Norbury cathedral, with about 500 guests. No offense Kimberley, it was a two-ring circus."

Kimberley laughs. "It was Mother's dream wedding." She takes a sip of her wine. "Back to you Chris, I don't know about attending … we should visit Grandam, but if Father finds out—"

"Don't tell him." Christian shrugs.

"I don't have to. People talk. Especially the servants, even if they aren't supposed to." She glances at her husband. "What do you think, Doug?"

"Since Christian asked me to be his best man," Doug says, "my answer is yes. What is yours, ma'am?"

"I guess we will come." Kimberley sighs.

~ ~ ~

The week flies by. I transfer to Christian's apartment as many of my belongings as possible without my moving out being too obvious. I will miss my sister, not to mention having access to each other's clothes.

On Friday Sarah, Christian, and I leave for Norbury; we are staying at Grandam's house.

The Hardings have an apartment at Ashton Hall, and since Lord and Lady Seymour are away, Kimberley and her family stay at the manor. (Grandam's house, comfortable as it is, is not suitable for a crowd.) Saturday, when the Hardings arrive, Kimberley announces, "The wedding is not a secret anymore. Father and Mother returned unexpectedly this morning. When Father asked what has brought us here, Andrew answered, 'Uncle Chris is getting married and will have to kiss the bride.' Then, of course, we had to tell them what's happening."

I sigh deeply. I wish Christian had invited them.

Grandam, with the help of her secretary, has organized an elaborate celebration. She's rented a marquee, ordered flower arrangements, hired caterers, a photographer, and even a quartet from the Music Academy of Norbury.

Everyone is hustling and bustling on Saturday morning, except Christian and Doug, who went out for "a drink" last night, and look rather washed out.

In the morning while practicing the procession with Andrew, who is our ring bearer, Nicholas announces that he wants to be "ring bear," too.

"You cannot be," Andrew answers importantly.

"I want to be."

"You cannot be."

Kimberley has to intervene to prevent a fight.

Then, probably feeling the excitement, neither Millie nor Nicholas wants to settle down for their afternoon nap. They keep fussing and whimpering, and whenever Kimberley, who is more and more frustrated, wants to leave them with the nanny, they start to cry. The bishop is antsy too; he has another event to attend.

Doug recommends bringing the kids to the celebration. "Nicholas can sit with you and Grandam," he advises Kimberley, who gives him a withering glance. She wanted the kids asleep, so she can enjoy the wedding without constant interruptions. The nanny quickly changes Nicholas and finally, almost an hour late, the service starts.

Nicholas, overtired and cranky, does not want to sit with his mother and Grandam; he wants to come in with Andrew. Fine. He can come with the procession.

All right, we're ready.

Christian and Doug are waiting by the makeshift altar. Christian looks so attractive I cannot repress a happy smile at the thought that we will belong together. The musicians start. Sarah begins to walk from the entrance of the marquee, and we follow. Nicholas stops. "I want to come with you," he says, looking up at me and slipping his little hand into mine. I smile down at him.

Andrew stops, too. "You come with me." He orders his brother in such a loud whisper it brings smile to everyone's face.

"I want to go with Ann-Marie," Nicholas declares stubbornly.

Andrew protests loudly and refuses to move until Kimberley comes to the rescue. Squatting down beside him, she whispers something into his ears. Andrew pulls himself up, and is willing to march again. We make it to the front without further incident. Christian reaches his hand to me, but Nicholas is hanging onto mine.

"Hey, Nicholas, come and stand with me," Doug beckons to him. Andrew is standing beside his father importantly holding the pillow with the rings. He is so sweet in his suit and with his serious face; I'd love to kiss him. Nicholas looks at them and scuttles over to stand with his dad and brother.

Bishop Grey reads from his book of celebrations, and my high-heeled sandals pinch my feet. We should have had a barefoot wedding. I hope the bishop won't be too verbose. During the speech, first Nicholas then Andrew decides to sit with their mom and Grandam. They scamper over taking all the attention away from the bishop. When time comes for the exchange of vows, Millie starts to wail. The nanny grabs her and, singing a little tune, moves far enough so we can hear each other again.

As soon as the service is over, both Nicholas and Millie fall asleep.

"I've never realized kids can be this entertaining," Christian says at the end of the ceremony. "We should have at least six of them."

"I hope I'll have a say in that." I kick off my shoes and

massage my sore feet.

After dinner, Christian and I say good-bye to everyone, and give Grandam a present, a small gold peacock brooch we picked together.

"Don't worry about Sarah," Kimberley says. "She'll drive home with us."

Kimberley and Sarah have really hit it off. Sarah had planned to explore Norbury on Sunday, and Kimberley has offered to pick her up at Grandam's place and be her guide. The kids are staying with their grandma, Doug wants to visit old school friends, and Grandam says she'll need about a week's rest to recover.

For our wedding night we rented a room in a B&B in Blenby. Since we've already eaten more than enough, we go for a walk. I love this little village with its stone cottages and steep, winding cobbled streets. It feels like home. Could it be because of its connection to Bancloch?

We climb to the lookout point. Christian scans the shore and the sea.

"Does it look familiar?" I ask half-jokingly.

"This view reminds me of the one in my dreams."

I become excited. "That's because the castle in your dream is Bancloch."

He studies the view for a while longer, then looks down at me with a barely noticeable smile. "I have a different explanation. I've seen this bay as a child and incorporated it into my dream."

Damn. "I have a good explanation, too. If you don't want to believe in something you can always find an alternative explanation." I glare at him.

Christian laughs, then holding my gaze, he leans closer. His lips almost touching mine, he whispers in a husky voice, "Do you want to have a fight on our wedding day?"

Maybe it is his closeness, maybe it is his voice, suddenly,

desire flares up in me. "Do you?" I whisper back.

He gently brushes my lip with his finger. "No, I have something lot more fun in mind. Let's return to the B&B."

In our room as soon as the door closes we fall over each other. It is as if a fire is burning in both of us. The outside world ceases to exist. There is only Christian and me enjoying one another until the fire ends in an explosion of pleasure. A pleasure only someone you're madly in love with can give. I'm in heaven as we lie in each other's arms, sweaty and sated; however, soon the fire flares up again.

Next morning we have breakfast in the glassed-in porch that overlooks the bay, then head back home. Unable to keep our hands off each other, we arrive at Christian's apartment in record time, and continue where we left off in Blenby.

Chapter 32

"What are you doing here?" Mrs. Sharman asks me when I show up in her office on Monday morning.

"I thought I was starting today." I feel slightly embarrassed and confused. Maybe I misunderstood some instructions. What a way to begin my work life: being in the wrong place at the wrong time.

"Didn't you get my message?"

"What message?" I ask, alarmed, hoping I still have a job.

"I tried to reach you all day Friday, but couldn't, so I left a message on your home phone. Ms. Bloomberg had to take the week off; you will be starting next Monday."

Damn. We could have stayed in Blenby for a few more days. Oh, heck, at least I still have a job. "I was out of town," I explain, then, unable to resist, add, "I got married on Saturday. I've also moved. I'd better give you my new address and home phone number."

She congratulates me, and writes down my new details.

I return home to find the housekeeper reading the newspaper in the kitchen, and Christian working on his computer in the study. "You're back already?" he asks.

"Short day," I answer, and tell him what happened.

In the evening we visit Mom to tell her about our marriage.

She is studying some kind of papers at her bedroom desk when we arrive. "Mom, I'd like to talk to you."

"Could it wait until tomorrow?" She looks up from her papers. "I have an important proposal to go through."

Of course, it could. Not only could, it should. "Fine, we can talk after your proposal is presented. By the way, I'm staying at Christian's apartment tonight."

"I want his address and phone number," she says absent-mindedly.

I leave it with her.

"I am not sure she even heard me," I tell Christian as we exit.

At home we do what all newlyweds do, head for the bed.

Next evening, Christian and I visit Mom again. Preoccupied, she is sitting at the kitchen table cradling a cup of tea. After saying hello, I pour tea for Christian and me, and we take the seats across from her. "How did your presentation go?" I ask.

"It wasn't my presentation; I am to decide whether to accept a mega-proposal."

"And?"

"It looks great on paper but I have an uncomfortable feeling about it. I'm trying to pinpoint what does not add up."

"Listen to your gut feeling," I recommend.

She laughs. "I have to come up with a better explanation for rejecting a multimillion dollar proposal than my gut feeling." As if noticing us, she asks, "How was your trip?"

"Mom." I place my hand over Christian's so my wedding band is visible. "We have a confession to make. We eloped."

"What?" For a split second anger flashes through her face, in the next, she drops her shoulders, looks at her cup, and begins to whisper, "I wish I could start again. I wish I could live two lives at once."

"Mom—" I say with equal alarm and annoyance.

"I had to choose—like everyone else. I had to choose between career and family. I chose career. I … I took the family for granted. Maybe I should have chosen the family," she says in barely audible voice.

"Mom—"

"I wanted to be the best. I always wanted to be the best in whatever I do. The job at the bank … it was a game, a challenge I had to win at." She's tapping her fingers on the table. "I did not realize the price I had to pay. I did not know how much I would miss in my personal life. I might be a stellar success at the bank, but what good is it, if I end up a lonely old woman."

I roll my eyes. "You're not going to be a lonely old woman. We're not abandoning you. We will visit; you will have grandchildren."

"I let your father go, I let Will go," she continues her monologue. I send an apologetic smile to Christian and shrug my shoulders. "I put all my energy into my job, taking relationships for granted. What's the result? You didn't even want to share your wedding with me—"

"Mom, don't guilt me. Okay?"

"I am not blaming you," she says sadly. "I am blaming myself."

I roll my eyes again. "Don't. Our elopement has nothing to do with you choosing your career. Sarah and I are proud of you and your accomplishments. We eloped for different reasons."

When we explain her why we chose to exclude the families, she agrees with our decision, then asks about our plans, and we invite her to our apartment. After about a half hour chat, she returns to her papers, and we return home.

On the way I tell Christian, "Regardless of how hard I try to be unaffected by her, Mom sure knows how to upset me."

~ ~ ~

Next day we have lunch with my father in a fashionable restaurant close to his office.

"Dad," I say when we have placed our orders, "this may upset you. We have a confession to make. Christian and I have eloped. We married last Saturday in Norbury."

My father laughs. "You did? Welcome to the club."

I look at him confused. "The club? What club? Did you elope with Martina?" As far as I remember, they had a large wedding. Our mother did not let Sarah and me attend it, but we heard enough to know it was huge.

The waiter brings our drink. "I couldn't elope with Martina," Father continues. "She wanted a mega wedding. I eloped with your mother."

"You did?" My eyes grow to twice their normal size. "I can't believe this. Mom gave me this big weepy speech about how she's failed as a mother because we did not invite her to our wedding, and it turns out she'd eloped, too."

Dad laughs again. "Your mother is such a drama queen."

I grin. "Thanks, Dad, you just made my day."

We tell Father the reason for our elopement. He peers at Christian. "Do you mean you are a duke?"

"No, I am not," Christian answers. "If I live long enough I might be the Duke of Norbury one day."

Father looks at me. "And you'll be a duchess."

"If I live long enough." I shrug my shoulders.

Father takes a slow sip of his beer. "Don't mention this to Martina," he says. "She might kill the present duke just so her step-daughter could become a duchess."

"Actually, Dad," I lower my knife and fork, "I've just

realized her in-laws are the Duke and Duchess of Norbury, though they might never talk to her."

"You should not mention that either." Father turns to Christian. "Just tell her you are an orphan if she wants to find out about your family."

I giggle. "Christian likes to tell people his father is a business man. We'll just stick with that story."

Father nods his agreement. "I hope you will iron out your differences with your parents. Family is the most important thing in life." After a short pause he says, "The longer you keep a grudge, the harder it will be to give it up."

Christian makes a face and my father diplomatically changes the subject. For the rest of the lunch we talk about our plans, and Father invites us for Sunday dinner.

~ ~ ~

The following day we receive a letter from Lord Seymour's lawyer. It says in so many words that neither Christian nor I are welcome at Ashton Hall, and Christian will not receive any more annuities, nor inherit anything, except the entailed property.

I guess Lord Seymour means business.

Christian sits at the table staring in front of him, then rereads the letter, then stares some more.

How would I feel if my parents have just told me they want nothing to do with me? Even more important, how will Christian and his parents make peace by October, which is only a few short months away?

Accomplishing the challenges looks more hopeless than ever. If only we had married sooner, we'd have more time to straighten out this mess. I should have been pushier. Pushier? You can't push love and commitment.

A very disturbing thought comes to my mind: what if Christian is sorry he's married me?

Christian interrupts my deliberation. "Father could not

even be bothered to write himself."

What can I say? "I am sorry."

Thumbing the letter, he says, "We will manage. I can teach again, and you have a job for now ... I have some investments, too." He smiles at me. The smile makes him look so attractive, for a few seconds I forget all our troubles. "And we have each other."

"Of course, we'll manage." I smile back. "We managed worse problems before."

On Monday I begin to work at the museum. Two days a week I inventory books and on Saturdays I work in the bookshop, which I prefer. I actually get to talk to people and answer questions. The most common question is "Where's the washroom?"

In my free time, I straighten up Christian's finances. Christian has had a rather a laissez-faire attitude toward expenses. I notice that Mrs. Olga buys enough food for five people, and has it delivered to the apartment. I take over buying groceries. We cut back her hours to two days a week. (I am not proud of this, but we simply cannot afford a fulltime housekeeper who spends most of her days reading the paper.) After two weeks she quits, claiming she cannot do her job in such a short time. I hire mom's housekeeper; she cleans the apartment and does our laundry in five hours a week.

I consolidate Christian's accounts, and some of his investments. I am thankful to Mom for teaching my sister and me (since we were about eleven) how to budget, read bank statements, calculate hidden expenses, judge investments, and other stuff, which at that time I found very boring and useless. And I am grateful to Grandma Burke for insisting we learn basic cooking and housekeeping skills.

Some couples argue about finances, others about how to raise the kids; we argue about an enchanted place. And just like other couples, we cannot convince each other.

"Christian, you still have to pass two challenges," I say one morning during breakfast while smothering my French toast with maple syrup. "You have to make peace with your parents—"

"Ann-Marie," he interrupts, a bad habit he is learning from me, "my father has to make peace with me; he's the one who cut me off."

"Still, you should offer an olive branch to him. Maybe you could write and let him know that you want to make peace and our door is always open to them."

He pours some tea, peers at me, and shakes his head. "No. I won't do it."

"You must make peace with your parents; otherwise, you cannot stay in this time. The wizard—"

"Ann-Marie, please don't start with that enchanted tower stuff, not today."

"You have only until October to pass the challenges, and—"

"Challenges." He sounds haughty. I realized long ago when Christian is upset he acts imperious. "I don't want to talk about this enchanted tower nonsense ever again."

My throat tightens. Damn. How could I make him believe without arguing? "Christian, if we want a good marriage we must talk about everything. As Grandma Burke says, swallowed disagreements, unexpressed feelings, and buried secrets will only create a chasm that will be impossible to cross."

He puts down his knife and fork, leans back in his chair, and gazes at me. "You are right, we should talk about everything. We should also agree to disagree without being disagreeable. I will listen to you, but don't try to force me to believe."

Great. How can I make him believe? "Fine, Christian. Just try to make peace with your parents."

"I have an appointment with my advisor this morning, then I'm meeting Grant for lunch. I'll be back early in the afternoon." He heads to his study, I watch as he collects papers from different parts of his room. He plants a light kiss on my mouth, and leaves.

How can I convince him?

I discuss the problem with Sarah; she has no advice. I talk it over with Kimberley—only the part that concerns Christian's parents—she thinks writing the letter is a good idea, but she does not know how I could persuade her brother to do it.

July is the month of birthdays. First is Grandma Burke's, which is celebrated every year with a family reunion at their country home. Christian has a good time. (So do I.) He readily takes to my father's crazy family, and they readily take to him. When we are leaving, Ian tells me that he approves of my choice for a husband.

Next is Kimberley's birthday, then Grandam's. Since Christian's parents are on a trip in Asia, we are able to attend both events without running into them.

Christian passes his oral exam, and with Doug and Kimberley, we celebrate his doctorate in the same restaurant we visited at Christmas. It turns out Christian's family owns the place.

"All this studying," Christian says, as he hangs up his certificate, "for a piece of paper with which I can impress visitors."

~ ~ ~

Christian and I often have lunch in the park that surrounds the museum. One day in August we happen to get a table next to two heavy, older women.

"I told her," the taller one says in such loud voice it carries over to our table, "that she should have visited her mother, while she was still alive. What good is it to come to the funeral?"

"At least she came to the funeral," the other woman says.

"Marg waited for her until the last minute. She was ready to forgive her daughter, but the wretched woman did not come," the taller woman continues, indignant.

"Did Marg seek out her daughter? Did her daughter refuse to see her?" the shorter woman asks.

"What do you mean?" The taller one glares. "Marg was the injured party, why would she seek forgiveness? No, it was the daughter who broke their relationship, who chose her good-for-nothing husband over her mother; she was supposed to come back and ask for forgiveness."

"When did this happen?"

"In the eighties, I think."

"Such a long time ago!" the shorter woman cries out, horrified. "Why didn't they make peace? Marg should have reached out—"

"Why would Marg reach out? It was the daughter's fault. Anyway, I told Marg's daughter at the funeral that she should be ashamed of herself for not seeking out her mother. And you know what she told me? She told me to buzz off. Right in front of the pastor." The taller woman shakes her head. "I couldn't believe it. She, who should be ashamed of herself, insulted me." She puts her empty paper plates and cups on the tray. "Now that Marg is gone, they are back, wanting their inheritance, I guess. I hope Marg had enough sense not to leave anything for them."

The shorter woman silently shakes her head, wiping crumbs from the table.

The taller one drags herself to her feet. "If we don't go now, we'll be late for the choir practice."

Huffing and puffing the two women take their tray to the garbage, still clucking about Marg and her daughter. Christian and I exchange a glance, and for once I manage not to say a word.

That evening Christian says, "I've decided to write to Father, though I'm still debating what to tell him. What would you write?"

Gladness bursts through me. "I'd tell him what I like about him, and that I still love him, and although I have no intention of changing my life I want to make peace, and they are always welcome."

Next morning Christian reads his letter to me.

Dear Father,

This letter is a peace offering. It is the last thing you will hear from me until you reply.

I am proud you are my father. You are one of those men who left his mark on the world and made it a better place, who cared about others, and never shied away from challenges.

You have taught me to be honest, caring, and reliable; gifts for which I will always be thankful.

I also want to leave my mark on this world, but it has to be my way, using my talents. I am not the executive type; I am a thinker, a teacher, and a dreamer. You are a dreamer, too. We just have different dreams.

I understand you want the best for me, and I realize our idea of the best is not the same. I write this letter hoping we can ignore what separates us, and concentrate on what connects us.

I await your reply.

With everlasting love, your son,

Christian

Although I find the letter somewhat formal, it brings tears to my eyes. "Are you going to write to your mother, too?" I ask.

"No, she goes along with whatever Father decides. I could add a postscript about loving her."

"No, write a separate letter to her."

In the afternoon Christian mails both letters.

Okay, challenge number two's—sort of—complete. One more to go. I have no idea how I can convince him, especially since we've agreed not to force our beliefs on each other.

~ ~ ~

Christian decides to do some shooting on Saturday morning before meeting me for lunch. At lunchtime I hurry to the food court and arrive before him. I wait five minutes, ten, still no Christian. I phone his cell, he does not answer. I feel anxious. Christian is never late. At twelve thirty I buy lunch for myself. I try to phone him a few more times, but still no answer. What's happened?

The afternoon drags on and I don't hear from Christian at all. I am not the worrying type but I cannot shake the feeling something is wrong.

No. He must be okay. Our year isn't up yet.

I can hardly wait to get home. When I arrive, the light is blinking on the phone. Three messages are waiting, the first is a telemarketer, the second is from Sarah, the third is from Kimberley. I can barely make out what she's saying between sobs. "Christian … at St. George Hospital … he had an accident … he is dying."

Chapter 33

"He must live. Our year is not up yet. He must live," I repeat all the way to the hospital.

The Seymours are huddled on one of the two sofas outside the operating room. I greet them, but only Kimberley, choking back her tears, answers.

"What happened?" I ask no one in particular.

"Let's go and talk outside." Kimberley, sniffing, stands up, and we leave the room together.

"Nobody knows exactly what's happened," she says in the corridor. "A semi-trailer swerved into Christian's Rover. There was a ten-car pile-up. Two people are dead. If Christian was in a small car he'd be dead too." She sniffles. "He has some internal and head injuries and a broken leg."

"He will be fine," I say. He can't die yet.

Kimberley bursts into tears. "I hope so."

"What do the doctors say?"

"They don't know anything yet. He was in critical condition when they took him to surgery. He might still die." She starts to sob.

"He won't die," I say with more conviction than I feel.

When she calms down, we return to the waiting room. Christian's parents ignore me. I sit down in a chair across from the family and silently repeat, "Christian must live. He will live. He'll live. He'll live. He'll live."

After an indeterminable time, during which no one says a word, the doctor, a tall man in his forties enters. His mask pushed down to his chin, he is pulling his gloves off. "Lord and Lady Seymour," he says, "we've done the best we could. Whether your son pulls through is in God's hands. He will be in room 323 shortly, and you can each visit for a few minutes."

"Thank you," Lord Seymour says grimly.

Christian's parents rise in silence and exit the room, Kimberley and I follow them. Since we are the only people in the elevator, I ask, "Lord and Lady Seymour, have you received Christian's letters?"

Lady Seymour bursts into tears.

"We received them shortly before the phone call came about the accident," Christian's father answers gruffly.

The duchess sniffles, carefully wiping her eyes, trying not to smudge her mascara.

Usually when you ask for a room location at the nurses'

station, they just point you in the right direction. Not this time. Instead of telling us which way to go, the head nurse escorts us to Christian's room. "I am sorry, sir, only one person at a time is allowed, and only for one minute," she says with excessive politeness. I let Christian's parents and Kimberley visit first.

"We are going home now," Kimberley says. Then, giving me a hug, she whispers, "Call me if you need support."

I enter the room. It looks like a living room with a sofa, armchairs, and a small fridge on one side; a typical hospital bed, on which Christian is lying unconscious, on the other.

He has a bandage around his head and his left leg is in a cast. I sit down on the chair by the bed and take his IV-free hand. "Christian," I whisper, "you must live. We still have a month. You are supposed to believe me, not die." I keep talking to him until my minute is up. No one comes so I stay in the room. Holding his hand, I will him to get better.

Why did this accident happen? Is it one of those misfortunes that will lead to a good outcome? It has brought his parents here. Maybe it will help him to believe, too.

I read somewhere that even unconscious people can hear and understand everything said around them, so when I run out of encouraging things to say, I start to sing happy songs to Christian.

Sometime later, an older doctor, followed by a nurse, comes around. "No visitors are allowed," he says curtly.

"I am Christian's wife. I can't leave. Please let me stay with my husband," I plead. "I will pretend I am invisible. No one will know I am here."

Ignoring me, he takes the chart from the nurse, studies it, examines Christian thoroughly, and shakes his head.

"What are Christian's chances of surviving?" I ask when he finishes the examination.

"He has stabilized a bit, but is still in critical condition," the doctor answers, then studies me for a few seconds. "It is against the rules to have visitors here, but since you are his wife, and this is a private room, you can stay."

Gladness bursts through me. "Thank you." A simple thank you cannot convey how grateful I am.

"Don't hesitate to call the nurse at once if there is any problem," he says.

I promise, wondering if they would let me stay if Christian was not a duke's son.

When they leave, I call Sarah on my cellphone and tell her what happened. She is horrified and wants to rush to the hospital. I assure her there is no need to panic; Christian will live. After talking with her about Christian's challenges, the wizard, and the enchanted tower, I feel calmer and more optimistic.

My stomach grumbles and I realize I haven't eaten since lunch. I check the fridge, and find an assortment of boxed juices and yogurts. I have some orange juice and blueberry yogurt, and return to entertaining Christian.

The nurse comes every hour to check on him, writes something on his chart, says a few encouraging words to me, then leaves.

Around two in the morning I drift off to sleep. I wake up to Christian's loud moans. I call the nurse. She finds everything all right. I am too tense to go back to sleep. I drink another juice, eat another yogurt, and softly sing to Christian again.

In the morning his condition is still the same. "At least he has stabilized," the nurse says. After she leaves, I say more encouraging words to Christian. His eyes flutter, but he stays unconscious.

~ ~ ~

Looking tired and anxious, the Seymour family arrives. Christian's parents seem a bit friendlier than yesterday; they even say hello. Wow.

"You are already here?" Kimberley asks.

"Still here," I answer. "I couldn't sleep, so I've decided to stay."

"You have been here all night," Lady Seymour says, surprised, and glances at her husband, then stepping to the bed places her hand on Christian's head.

"The nurse told us there is no change," Kimberley sighs. "Have you had any breakfast? Or dinner?"

"I had some juice and yogurt."

"Ann-Marie, you must eat something," says Lord Seymour. He's been watching me since they arrived. "Let's go to the cafeteria."

"Thank you, but I'm not hungry."

"We want to talk to you," he says, in a more commanding voice. He's probably used to people jumping whenever he asks them to do something.

"Okay," I say.

"I'll keep Christian company," Kimberley says. She winks at me as her parents turn to exit the room.

I hope we're not going to have another confrontation. I don't have the energy for an argument—not after a sleepless night. Without exchanging a word, we ride the elevator to the main floor where the cafeteria is located. Only a few people, mostly nurses and doctors, are in the large, bright room. We head to the counter.

"What would you like?" Lord Seymour asks as he grabs a tray.

"A latte and a muffin," I say.

Christian's parents only have tea. We take a table close to the window.

Lord Seymour empties a cream packet into his cup, looks up at me, and says stiffly, "I want to thank you."

"Thank me? For what?"

"Kimberley told us that you persuaded Christian to write those letters."

I wish. "He wrote them because of two gossipy old women." I break off a piece from my muffin, and shove it into my mouth. It tastes like sawdust. The latte isn't much better.

"Yes," he says. "Kimberley told us what happened. She also said that you kept urging Christian to make peace with us."

I cannot tell him that Christian had to make peace or die. Instead I say, "In my father's family we can fight and disagree, and make stupid mistakes, but we are always loved and welcomed. I guess I just wanted Christian to have the same." Oops, this was not a diplomatic thing to say. I quickly take a sip of my coffee.

The Seymours glance at each other, then the duke says, "Christian might have made a better choice of wife than I have realized." He—sort of—smiles at me. "I have been keeping an eye on the two of you." I gulp my coffee. He's been spying on us? Great. "You are intelligent, practical—" How can I tell him, without being offensive, that I find spying on us disgusting. "I have noticed from his bank statements and investment portfolio that you are good with finances. You have streamlined his expenses and eliminated a lot of waste."

He keeps track of Christian's accounts and investments. No wonder Christian is trying to escape.

The duke is looking at me with a friendly glint in his eyes, and I feel a bit ashamed. "Thank you for the compliment." I—sort of—smile at him.

"Christian seems to love you," the duchess says, sounding unhappy.

"Thank you, Lady Seymour." This time my smile is genuine.

"Please call me Alicia," she says.

I look from one to the other. They look worried and sad. I want to say something encouraging. "I can tell you both really love and care about Christian."

The duchess sighs. "I wish I could tell him how much he means to us. I do not want him to die without knowing." She's blinking back her tears.

"You will tell him," I say.

She doesn't answer.

What else could I say to make them feel better? Unfortunately, nothing comes to my mind. We sip our drinks in awkward silence.

"We should return to Christian's room," the duchess says after a while.

I don't want to go yet. "Go on ahead, and have some time with him." I cradle my mug. "I'll stay a bit longer."

"Fine." The duke stands up. "We will see you upstairs."

I watch as they leave, and my heart fills with compassion. If Christian dies, it will destroy them.

~ ~ ~

Staring out the cafeteria window, I munch on my tasteless muffin and contemplate my conversation with the Seymours until a familiar male voice interrupts my thoughts. "May I join you for breakfast?"

The wizard is standing by the table with a tray in his hand. He's dressed in everyday clothes, and his beard and hair are trimmed.

"Certainly," I smile up at him.

He sits down, and adds one packet of sugar after another to his coffee. "You have questions," he says. "Fire away. Or whatever the cool new expression is."

"Why is Christian dying?" I ask. "Our year is not up yet. We met at the end of September; we still have more than a month to go."

"You are wrong. The year counts from the time you first met Christian. That was exactly a year ago."

Only a year ago? It seems like three lifetimes.

The implication of what he's said hits me, and for the first time since I heard about the accident my eyes blur. "Will Christian die?"

"Why did you not try harder to make him believe in what happened?"

"Every time I brought up the subject, we disagreed," I answer. "I didn't like our disagreements."

"You would rather let him die?"

"I've also realized that no argument can make anyone believe. Belief comes from the heart. You cannot force it."

"You should have tried harder," he says.

I try to hold back my tears. "Is Christian going to die?"

The wizard's eyes fill with compassion. "You know the agreement. Since Christian has failed his challenges, he cannot stay here."

"Will I ever meet him again?" I lose the battle with my tears.

"Your love connects you for all eternity. Of course, you will meet him again someday."

"I know we blew it, but couldn't we stay together here and now? Is there any way we could make up for our failure?" I wipe my face. "You have insisted that we learn to forgive ... would you ... couldn't you forgive us?"

He peers at me, then begins to smile. "You are right. If I demand forgiveness and love from you, how could I expect anything less from myself?"

"Please forgive us." I put my hands together, pleading.

With a broad smile he says, "Since you have asked for my forgiveness, I grant it."

I can hardly believe my ears. "Do you mean Christian can stay in this century?"

He nods. "I will do even better. He will also remember your previous meetings and will recover perfectly."

"Thank you, thank you, thank you." I jump up, wrap my arms around his shoulders, and kiss him on the cheek.

"You are choking me," he protests, laughing.

I return to my chair. "Why have you forgiven us so easily? No test, no more challenges, no nothing?"

He smiles. "Instead of blaming others or finding excuses, you simply asked for forgiveness."

Oh.

"Besides," he adds, "I love a happy ending."

"Thank you." This time tears of joy are running down my cheeks. "How can we ever repay your kindness?"

"That is easy," he says. "Enjoy your life together, learn to truly love each other; you cannot give me anything more precious in return. Now let me hear your other questions."

I wipe my face. "Why does the Ryston family tree show that Ann-Marie died at age four?"

"Does it?" He laughs. "You know better than anyone else she did not die at age four. I must have forgotten to change the dates."

I laugh, and take a bite of my muffin, which doesn't taste like sawdust anymore. The coffee tastes wonderful, too. "Could you tell me what happened to Bancloch? How did it disappear without a trace?"

"It did not disappear without a trace, but I will let you and Christian discover on your own what happened to it." He drains his coffee.

"Is Christian a duke's son because he refused to marry me in the enchanted tower?"

He nods. "I wanted to see if he has learned his lesson about rejecting love because of a man-made caste system."

I smile. "He passed that one with flying colors."

"He did." The wizard chuckles. "If he had failed that

one, or reaching out to his parents, he definitely could not stay here."

I finish my coffee.

"Do you have any more questions?" he asks.

"That's all for now."

"If you are ready, let's return to Christian's room."

We take the elevator to the third floor.

Only the duchess is in the room. "Hello, Alicia," the wizard greets her.

She looks up. "Hello," she exhales, shocked. Then turning to me, she asks, "How do you know this man?"

"He and Christian have been friends for a long time."

"How … how does Christian know him?"

"It is a long story," the wizard says. "Alicia, please let me step closer to your son."

The duchess rises from the chair and steps away, still gaping at the wizard.

He takes Christian's hand, leans close and whispers into his ear. Christian stirs. The wizard whispers some more then straightens, smiling. "Christian will be fine. It is time for me to go." And he is gone.

Christian moves. "Ann-Marie," he croaks, "I'm still here."

I lean close. "I know. The wizard—"

Christian pulls me closer and whispers in a raspy voice, "Do you think we should restore the tower?"

"Of course."

We seal our agreement with a kiss.

~ # ~

Excerpt from Liz Michaels Novel:

Aaron's Bride

"Look at that gorgeous guy, Sarah," Liv whispers, and I follow my best friend's gaze across the table to the entrance of the restaurant.

She is right. The man is striking. He is in his late twenties or early thirties, in an expensive suit, tall, with shoulder-length raven hair, dark attentive eyes, and chiseled features. But there's something eerie about him. My first thought is that he is not human. Of course he is. What else could he be?

Bewitched, the blond host smiles up at him as she asks for his ticket, then leads him to his table. She's not the only one enthralled.

"OMG," Kaitlin sighs, her eyes glued to the guy.

Brittany does not say anything. We are here to celebrate—belatedly—her recent engagement to Liam, and her twenty-fifth birthday. The dining room is a five-star restaurant on a ship, and the dinner costs about a day's wage of my summer job, lifeguarding. But who would not make a sacrifice for one of her best friends—if an elegant dinner can be considered a sacrifice.

The meal, in which every course has a French name, is sublimely delicious. It's followed by a dance, and the music is—blah.

"This is boring," Kaitlin groans as we watch the dancers. Except for Mr. Gorgeous everyone is much older than we are. "If I knew the crowd would be our parents' age, I would have recommended we go to Eight&Eight. Now we are stuck until the boat returns to the harbor."

"Relax," Liv answers. "You can always adore that eye-candy."

As if on cue, the man gets up and heads to our table. I

know he will ask me for a dance and my stomach tightens. I grab my almost empty wine glass and take a tiny sip.

"May I have this dance, please?" He bows his head to me in a formal manner that belies his age. Liv's face falls, as does Kaitlin's.

I cannot repress a somewhat self-conscious smile. Still, I wish he had asked Liv, who with her auburn hair, green eyes and classic features is much prettier than I am. Or Kaitlin. With her wide-set baby-blue eyes and long legs, she could be a model. They are both waiting to meet their special man, while I have a long-time boyfriend, Sean. We plan to tie the knot as soon as we're both through medical school.

I stand up, and the man reaches a hand toward me. As I look into his eyes I almost stop in my track. They are dark blue, with depth I've never seen in anyone's eyes before.

"My name is Aaron Hunter." He smiles warmly as we reach the dance floor.

"I'm Sarah Burke."

The musicians are playing a waltz. As I put one hand on his muscular shoulder and he puts a strong, warm hand on my lower back, I feel as if I have entered an overpowering force field and, to my dismay, I feel a twinge of desire. He gently takes my other hand and we start to whirl around to the music.

"I'm pleased to make your acquaintance, Miss Sarah Burke. What occasion has brought you here this evening?"

"We're here to celebrate my friend's birthday and engagement," I answer. "What occasion has brought you here?"

"I wanted to meet you." What? "No occasion," he smiles. "I simply wanted to eat out this evening."

Who "simply" eats out at a place like this?

He deftly maneuvers us between the whirling couples. "How did you girls meet?"

"We attend the same medical school. In my first year at

the university I shared chemistry class with Liv, the one with the auburn hair; we met Kaitlin, the blond one, at the entry exam for medical school, and Brittany over a dead body." Why am I telling him all this?

"A dead body," he says with a light smile. The waltz finishes. "May I have the next dance too?" he asks, keeping his hand on my back. "I'd like to hear more about that dead body."

I don't have a chance to tell him, because the next number is a disco, and it is impossible to talk. We only keep eye contact. He has captivatingly beautiful eyes. Aaron spins me, and when I turn back, he has a sword in his hand. He is facing a large, slightly overweight man in his late fifties or early sixties. "Are you ready, Rob?" Aaron asks.

The man nods. Aaron plunges the sword into his chest. My heart skips a beat. In the next instant, the sword is gone. There is no blood, no injury. Everyone is still dancing as if nothing has happened. Aaron turns back to me and Rob turns toward his partner.

No. This is impossible. I must have imagined the sword. "Did you … did you just have a sword in your hand?" I blurt.

Aaron peers at me so strangely, my insides tighten. I should have kept my mouth shut. "You saw the sword?" he asks, surprised.

I nod. Before either of us can say another word, the man whom Aaron struck collapses. Pressing his arm to his chest, he gasps for air.

"Rob," his partner yells, turns pale, and starts to shriek. "My husband! Help! My husband's just collapsed."

I quickly kneel down beside the man, roll him onto his back, tap his shoulder, and shout into his ear, "Rob, can you hear me?" No response. I check for breathing. Nothing. I feel for a pulse. Nothing. I am sure the man is in cardiac arrest, so I quickly pull his shirt open, tilt his head back slightly, and start chest compressions. The man does not respond. I do a couple rescue breaths, then more compressions. Still no response.

Around me is total chaos. The band stopped playing, and everyone is talking at the same time. From the cacophony of voices, I hear a screeching female voice, "Call an ambulance!"

"Yes, and they will drive here on the water," a sarcastic male voice answers.

The man's wife keeps screaming and sobbing. "Help! Please, please!"

Ignoring the mayhem, I keep up the compressing and rescue breathing.

"Let us take over." Two crewmembers with a first aid kit are by my side. One kneels down on the other side of the man. "The rescue boat will be here soon," the younger one says. I sit back on my heels and watch them. They are attaching a defibrillator.

The man is not responding. A long time has passed since he collapsed; it's unlikely he'll revive.

As I look around, I see one crewmember calming the man's wife, while others are shooing the people away, telling everyone that the man will be fine. One of the waiters brings a shot glass full of some golden liquid, probably brandy, and hands it to the wife who is sobbing and shaking uncontrollably.

The rescue boat arrives and the paramedics take over from the crewmembers. They are attaching an oxygen mask and a new defibrillator.

I stand up and look around. Aaron is gone.

The medics lift the man onto the stretcher and wheel him out of the dining room. His wife and another couple, arms wrapped around her shoulders, follow.

The maître d' announces that everything is fine; the people should relax and enjoy the remainder of the evening. No one relaxes. On the way back to our table a guest asks me, if the man will survive.

I'm not going to tell her that he is dead. "He'll be fine," I say.

The rescue boat departs, the music starts again, and everything gradually returns to normal—sort of.

My friends flood me with questions about what happened. Since I have no idea how to tell them about the sword and Aaron's part in the debacle, I keep mum on it. As we talk, I glance at Aaron's table. His place is empty. It stays empty for the rest of the trip.

~ ~ ~

The event on the boat frequently replays in my mind in the next few days. Should I report it to the police? How? I can't say that a man pulled a sword out of thin air. There was no blood, no injury, nothing. They also seem to have known each other. Maybe Aaron Hunter is some kind of hit man. Where did the sword come from? How did it disappear? How did Aaron disappear?

In the end I decide to leave the entire incident behind. There's nothing I can do. I don't even know who the participants where.

I just wish Liv and Kaitlin would stop talking about him.

~ # ~

About the Author

After many years of writing boring letters as an education coordinator, I decided to try my hand at something longer and less boring; this book is the result.

When not by my computer, I enjoy reading, practicing Tai Chi, having coffee with friends, or working in my garden in the sunny Okanagan. But most of all, I love dreaming up new stories.

To connect with me, email lizmichaelsb1@gmail.com.

Thank you for reading this book.

Made in the USA
Charleston, SC
05 November 2013